DAMAGED LOVE

DAMAGED SERIES BOOK 1

Published by Emery & Co. Publishing
www.leeemeryauthor.com

ISBN: [979-8-9933010-0-6]
Printed in the United States of America

First Edition

TABLE OF CONTENTS

DEDICATION

To my loving husband, thank you for always supporting my endeavors. Writing a book was no exception, and I appreciate how you've always kept it real for me, reminding me to laugh along the way. We've shared many laughs about my "ten years in the making" book, but those conversations kept the dream alive. Thank you for believing in me when I needed it most.

And to my mom. My biggest cheerleader and the truest example of strength I know. You lift me up when insecurities and circumstances weigh me down, and you've always been my confidant, partner in crime, and best friend wrapped into one. You are the woman I aspire to be, and without your faith and encouragement, I would have never tried.

This book is for both of you. With love, gratitude, and all my heart.

FROM THE AUTHOR

I want to thank every reader who has chosen to pick up this book. Your support gives me the chance to share my stories with you, and for that, I am truly grateful.

If you've ever doubted yourself or questioned whether you have what it takes, recall the story of the bumblebee. By all logic, it shouldn't be able to fly, its body is too big, and its wings are too small, yet it does. In the same way, you can "bee" anything you want to be if you bee-lieve in yourself. This simple reminder kept me going as I wrote this first book, and I hope it inspires you too.

From the bottom of this debut author's heart, thank you for giving my story a chance and allowing me to share my imagination with you. If you enjoyed the book, please follow me on Facebook and Instagram, and consider leaving a review. Your support not only helps me grow as a writer but also reminds me to keep believing in this dream.

Important Note

This book is a work of fiction. All characters and events are products of the author's imagination.

The book contains mature themes, including depictions of sexual assault and trauma. Reader discretion is strongly advised.

To Parents and friends: Don't judge the smut, it's just part of the story.

Chapter One
QUESTIONS
Emily

Have you ever asked yourself, "What do you want to be when you grow up?" Cute question, until you realize you're pushing thirty and the only answer you've got is a soul-deep sigh.

I'm not some dreamy, impressionable girl anymore. I pay my bills, I own matching towels, and I even floss regularly. Certified adult, right? So, why does my brain keep circling that question, like it's an unsolved mystery?

Letting my mind wander there suggests I'm unhappy, but that's not true. Not at all.

I blame insomnia. And the Hallmark channel, where the baker, the dressmaker, and the hot neighbor all find their happily ever after before the credits roll.

That's not real life. It's definitely not how *my* life's scripted. So, this contemplation is pointless and unproductive. Tonight, if I can't sleep, I'm watching The First 48 or Snapped. To balance it all out.

I sit in my swanky cubicle on the 21st floor of one of downtown Houston's most prestigious office buildings, where I should be focusing on numbers and formulas in a client's accounting spreadsheet. Instead, my mind drifts to the question

I can't shake: I am a grown woman, so why does it feel like that very fact snuck up on me? And why does it feel like something is missing?

As a young girl, I built castles in my head, filling them with vivid fantasies of the life I'd one day have. By now, I was supposed to be married to my prince, with two perfect children racing around. Instead, it's just me, my spreadsheets, and a hollow space where that dream should have been.

My friends, Sarah and Roxy, seem never to ponder this. They are both carefree spirits, happy to party and date as the mood strikes them. I don't recall either of them ever discussing a future that included marriage or children. They're both too free-spirited to settle down, and I doubt either of them believes in fairy tales anyway.

I love both of them and wouldn't change a single thing about either of them. Secretly, I enjoy living vicariously through their wild escapades. I'm the more conservative one among what our college friends often called 'The Hot Three Musketeers.' We met during our sophomore year in an art elective class, and that nickname has stuck with us ever since.

Although I am part of the Hot Three, I know that it is by association only; my own looks and personality are nothing special. Being called hot was so much better than when I was called a Philomath Sociopath in high school, just because of my love for numbers and learning.

Joke's on them: my love of numbers paid off. I received a full-ride scholarship to the University of Houston for a Master of Science in Accounting. As a bonus, it allowed me to pursue my own goals instead of having to let daddy pay and dictate my future. Now I work as a Data Integrity Analyst for one of the largest Risk Management firms in the Houston area. The best part is that I get to embrace and utilize my geekier side.

My full name is Emily Sue Wilson, but I've been called Em since 2nd grade. My birth name was too boring, so the other 6-year-olds started calling me Em.

I'm relatively tall at 5'7" with long, dirty blonde hair and grey eyes. Okay, my eyes are blue, but they're so light that they seem more grey than blue. My hairdresser told me I have a delicately feminine face. I can only assume it was in reference to my softer contours, fuller, bow-shaped lips, and a pert nose, features often found on young children. My looks might not draw a lot of attention, but I can't deny that I have a great body underneath all my clothes. My personal trainer is a strict enforcer who makes sure my body stays in top form.

Just then, my desk phone rings, startling me out of my self-deprecating musings. As I answer, I hear my friend Roxy before the receiver even hits my ear, "YO Biach! Ready for lunch?" I can't help but smile. Roxy is LOUD and proud. She's only 5'5", but her presence is bigger than life. She has dark brown, almost black hair with striking blue eyes. Her blue eyes are the brilliant kind that sparkle when she laughs. *Jealous much?* She is H.O.T. with all the right curves in all the right places; even I have to concede that.

Roxy works on the 15th floor of Wren Tower as a Corporate Trainer; she motivates employees to strive for better. The role suits her personality perfectly. She can make almost anyone do anything. It's a bit scary when you think about her zest for all things fun, and I'm almost always one of her victims. I'm not surprised she's calling to confirm our lunch plans, even though it's unnecessary since we eat lunch together nearly every day.

Ten minutes later, I arrive at the building's courtyard bistro. This small French-inspired restaurant is on the 10th floor. It's unique in that it is an open-air area spanning at least half of the 10th floor. The outdoor seating area features bistro tables set on either artificial turf or cobblestone tile. Some of the tables have two chairs, while others have four. All of them have black-and-white striped umbrellas. The pattern matches the outside awning of the main restaurant. The best part is the views of downtown Houston.

Roxy is already there, talking with rapt interest on her cell. Her blue eyes are bright and almost animated as she motions for me to come to her side of the table to share in listening to her conversation. The other caller was Sarah, our third Musketeer; she was going on excitedly about a new guy she had met the previous week at work.

Sarah is a prominent freelance artist with a large and lucrative client base. She also occasionally moonlights as a bartender at The Rusty Nail. The Rusty Nail is a neighborhood bar we frequent, in my opinion, way too often. Sarah is stunning; she has natural beauty with piercing green eyes and strawberry blonde hair that falls just past her shoulders. When she dolls herself up, she's unstoppable. She earns good tips as a bartender; of course, her double D boobs probably don't hurt either.

"You have to come!" I heard that part over the phone line loud and clear. It was Friday, so of course, Sarah and Roxy would be planning our night out. I heard all I needed to hear, so I took my seat across from Roxy and started browsing the menu. As if something new would appear, we knew this menu by heart.

Since Roxy and I both work at the Wren Tower in downtown Houston and because traffic is such a bitch in this area, we ate lunch at Bistro Monte at least three or four times a week. Sometimes Sarah joined us if she was dropping off artwork or meeting with prospective clients downtown.

I had to smile at this train of thought; besides our lunches, we all lived in the same DalRock Condominiums and often ate dinner together. Yet we were still friends. *Personal space, anyone?*

Roxy hung up just as the waiter arrived to take our lunch orders. We both got the turkey club sandwich combo with water, no surprise there, and Justin, our waiter, just smiled at our predictability. What would he do if we ever ordered something different?

"So, chickie, we're going out to have some fun tonight!" exclaimed Roxy in an overly loud, enthusiastic voice. I cringed, looking around at all the faces turned toward us. I did mention that Roxy is loud and proud, with emphasis on the loud part. You also never knew what would come out of her mouth at ANY time. She has no filter, none whatsoever.

I wasn't exactly ready to *'have fun tonight,'* but I would go. After all, you can't have only two "Hot Three Musketeers" out on the town. Plus, I knew I would lose the argument to stay home with a great book and a large glass of wine. Not to mention, Sarah really wants us to meet her new guy. And, I must admit, I'm curious to check him out since Sarah rarely sounds excited about anything boy-related.

After lunch, my afternoon flew by quickly. At 5:10 pm, I met Roxy in the vestibule. Since we live in the same condos, we often carpool and alternate driving. It works well for us. We both love music, so one of us or the other spends the entire 30+ minute drive home looking for the perfect songs to set the mood for the evening's activity.

The current mood seems to be dancing. I don't mind dance tunes or Hip Hop, but I really dislike the days when Roxy is in the mood for Frank Sinatra. Don't get me wrong, there's a time and place for everything, even the classics, just not when you're trapped in the car with nowhere to run.

I found out over lunch that we were going to The Purple Room Dance Club that night. Sarah's guy will meet us there, and he's bringing friends. Oh yay! I knew what that meant for me. Sarah and Roxy thought I needed help in the man department, and in the past, they've shamelessly tried to set me up with any guy willing. Well, as long as they were cute. The Hot Three Musketeers don't date ugly.

The dance night mood continued as the garage elevator opened into the lobby of the DalRock. Sarah was there, hair in pink spongy rollers, big fuzzy robe, no makeup, and practically vibrating with excitement. She was talking so loudly and so fast. All of this is so out of character for her.

We barely got off the garage service elevator before Sarah was yanking us into the main elevator. She was prattling on about what we were all going to wear and that we needed to get started right away. I looked on with my mouth wide open; all words had escaped me. I mean, seriously, why was she waiting in the lobby, partially dressed, looking like a crazy person? Who does that? Aren't there cameras in our lobby area? I finally found my voice as we reached Sarah's unit, but I had to yell to get her attention: "Calm down and quit yanking us."

At my outburst, Sarah looked contrite but only for a second before she continued, "We need to dress to impress, pull out ALL the stops. Dress as only the Hot Three Musketeers can because we are partying tonight!"

I didn't have to ask what she meant; I knew the drill. I looked to Roxy and saw her smile get wider right before hearing Roxy yell, "Yippee!" I knew then that Roxy would not help rein in Sarah. Not at all.

Taking in Sarah's living room, I was able to tune her out, just from the sheer sight of the explosion of clothes, shoes, and accessories that littered every available surface of this once spacious, tidy living room.

Sarah loves all things about fashion. By the looks of it, almost every stitch of her clothing was in her living room. Sarah turns to me and loudly exclaims, "I have the perfect outfit for you! I can't wait to see you in it." I couldn't stop my grimace if my life depended on it, but sadly, I was unable to utter a single word.

Having Roxy or Sarah play dress up with me was worse than a trip to the dentist. You'd think by now I'd learn how to avoid these situations, but sadly, no.

Belatedly, I notice that Alec and Dex were sitting at Sarah's kitchen table, the margarita blender whirling, huge smiles on both their faces, openly staring at the shit show that was my life.

Alec's smile often did strange things to my insides. Mentally, I shut down that train of thought and moved toward them. I suspected that both guys understood my hesitation and the inevitable pain of being the target of Sarah's enthusiasm and Roxy's joy at tag-teaming up against me.

Tonight was going to be a long night. I suddenly wanted to run away. Just as my feet were about to start moving, Dex yanked me for a second time tonight. I couldn't complain because he was pulling me toward the table for a much-needed margarita. Maybe I'd even think about having a few early shots of tequila for some liquid courage, but that hurts too much the next day to do that to myself.

Dex was another friend and neighbor; he owns a gym that specializes in kickboxing and MMA. He's my trainer, also known as my torturer. At 6'2" with broad shoulders and hard muscles, he is built like a Mack truck and is gorgeous. His amber eyes are known as panty-melting eyes; his thick, unruly, sandy-blond hair beckons anyone to touch it. Sadly, he's a manwhore, and he doesn't deny it.

Dex is considered *'one of the girls'* in that he knows everything about us. Okay, maybe not everything. One evening with copious amounts of alcohol, he admitted to marking each of our times of the month on his calendar. When asked why, he said he wants to be more sympathetic to us when we're being extra bitchy. When in reality, I'm pretty sure he wants to know who to stay away from that week.

Alec, our other friend, is the superintendent of our condos. We girls call him the Latin Hottie. He's tall, dark, and handsome; a former Special Ops military officer, Captain Alec Santos. Even after retiring, he still takes great care of his body. None of us knows why he works at the DalRock now, but we enjoy having him here. His eyes are a deep chocolate brown, complemented by his dark brown hair and olive skin. He's a little taller than Dex and has a much larger build, all solid muscle. His body is nearly perfect, with flawless skin except for a scar above his left temple. His very presence exudes control and focus; he dominates any room he walks into. Some might think he's broody, but I think he's hot. I can easily see him as part of the Black Dagger Brotherhood, a paranormal romance series with super hot alpha males. What he's not is a Manwhore, but he's still off-limits for us girls. I know that because he told us, and I quote, *"I don't play where I get paid,"* and that was that. I won't lie; he's starred in more than a few of my hot and heavy dreams.

I must have been deeper in my happy place than I realized because suddenly, Alec is calling my name and waving his hand in my face. I looked up to see him smiling with an expression that looked a lot like he knew exactly where my mind had gone. God, I hope that one of his immortal powers isn't mind-reading like Edward Cullen. If he were able, then I'm no Bella. Everyone knows Edward couldn't read Bella's thoughts.

Just then, Alec's sexy voice penetrates my mind, and I realize he's talking about going dancing with us tonight. "I'll drive you girls to the club, so feel free to drink up." Alec was fantastic that way; he wanted to make sure we got home safely. I'd feel bad about him being the designated driver, but he rarely drinks alcohol, and an occasional beer here or there was it for him.

Dex was also talking about joining us, but he had to stop somewhere first. It was probably a booty call. So, I ask: "So, Dex, what is your bootie call's name?" He looked confused at first, then a little hurt if I was being honest. That was an interesting reaction. Before I could apologize for my quip, he said he had an errand for work, then walked into the living room. I looked at Alec, then back at Dex, feeling like I was missing something. *Whatever, it could be his time of the month.*

As we were about to serve drinks, we heard Roxy shouting at Dex, "Dude, what in the hell is your problem with me?" Roxy's face was flushed, and she looked seriously pissed off. Dex, for his part, seemed angry as hell.

Sarah spoke quietly, asking, "Guys, what's going on? And what has you both in each other's faces?"

Dex turns around to shoot a few daggers my way before he leaves without another word.

I glance over to see Alec staring at me intently. Strange, but at that moment, he hurt my feelings. What did I do to Dex? So,

I asked, "What just happened? Why does he seem upset with me and angry at Roxy?"

Alec shrugs, and the moment is lost when he gets up and follows the same path Dex just took. *Men.*

Chapter Two
HURT FEELINGS
Emily

With the men gone, Sarah and I walk up to Roxy, but before we can say anything, she raises her hand to ward off our questions. Then, in a volume that was louder than her normal loud, she yells, "I don't understand why he's acting like such an alpha male asshole."

Sarah speaks before I can say a word, "What happened?"

I reiterate, "What did he say to you that pissed you off?"

Roxy didn't reply. Upon closer inspection, I notice that Roxy wasn't just pissed; she had tears welling in her eyes.

"Roxy honey, talk to us," I hear Sarah say in a low voice.

It was then that Roxy must have pulled up her big girl panties because she loudly announces, "Screw him and his opinions. Ladies, we have to get ready to dance our ass off!"

Roxy was over the drama. Sarah and I both understood that the topic was officially finished, at least until later; after some drinks, we might try to get her to spill. I wasn't going to hold my breath; Roxy valued simplicity. Her Type A personality didn't just include her need to keep things organized or neatly on the walls; she didn't do messy. Which meant she didn't do entanglements. She dated, but then moved on when the relationship might have otherwise progressed to the next level.

Roxy once said that she was looking for perfection and felt she would know it when she saw it. Why was I even thinking about her and Dex's exchange? No way was her outburst toward him relationship-related. Right?

Sarah didn't seem to share my relationship train of thought; she was already heading toward the couch with a gleam in her eye. I was worried that gleam meant she was planning to turn me into her life-sized dress-up Barbie doll. *Groan.*

Before she has a chance to yank me toward the chaos of clothes, I turn to the table and finish pouring the much-needed margaritas. We needed to get this party back on track, and the alcohol would definitely help ease the tension.

Unfortunately, as I turn with cups in hand, I realize that nothing is getting easier for me. My tension was about to spike a few hundred knots as I looked at what Sarah was holding up. "I'm not wearing that!" I shout.

"Yes, you are, you'll look gorgeous!" Sarah states, snatching the drinks from my hands and placing them on the coffee table.

Roxy begins circling me like a buzzard on a carcass. She has her index finger firmly over her lips, an intense look on her face, and you can see her brain wheels turning. I'm nervous. Not gonna lie, these two scare the bejesus out of me. I startle when Roxy loudly exclaims, "Okay, Okay, I got it. You need to go braless and nix the granny panties."

"What? No! Are you nuts?" I shout. The dress, if you can call it that, is like a second skin. It's a satin sheath that leaves nothing to the imagination. I mean NOTHING.

Sarah's head is bobbing up and down as she gestures for me to get busy and undress. The idea of taking off my Under Armour makes me feel anxious and combative. "I'm not wearing this dress, and I'm never going out in public without my undergarments, and they are not granny panties!" I snap.

Looking over at Sarah, I notice she isn't going to back down, and Roxy is seconds away from undressing me herself.

As an act of self-preservation, I snatch the dress and walk to Sarah's bedroom. As I strip, I foolishly decide to humor them and proceed to remove everything.

Slipping the dress over my head, the fabric feels like a cool caress. Instantly, I feel pretty and sexy but very much naked underneath. The skin-toned strappy sandals Sarah laid just inside the door are beautiful and fit me perfectly.

Walking back towards the living room, I hear, "Em, you look fucking fabulous, you have to wear that!" Roxy shouts.

Sarah adds, "I've never felt like that dress was a good fit for me, so I never wore it, but it is perfect on you; you look hot as sin, girl!"

I laugh, though a little hysterically. These chicks are nuts if they think I'm wearing this out in public, especially with nothing underneath.

Just then, a knock sounds at the door. Before I can say "Wait a minute," Sarah swings the door wide open. Alec is standing there looking all yummy and just, yeah. He changed into a pair of faded low-slung jeans and a button-down indigo blue shirt, and my mouth waters.

Wait, what? Just because he's the star in my wet dreams and there's just something about him that intrigues me doesn't mean I can drool over my off-limits neighbor. My inner slut and I need to come to an understanding quickly, but she'll probably blame it on the dress.

Before I can completely get my wandering mind under control, I hear Sarah excitedly ask, "Alec, isn't Em's outfit perfect on her?"

Instantly and without my control, I lock eyes with Alec. He's angry. With me? Then, in what seems like a forced reply, I barely hear, "Mother fucker," then in a much louder voice, I hear, "No! That's not an outfit for Em."

I blink slowly before breaking eye contact, feeling a pang of hurt. Does he think I don't look good in this, or that I'm not sexy enough for this dress? The more logical part of me wonders if it's because he knows I'm not the showy, flaunting type. I'm the boring, socially awkward, conservative type that has no business dressing for attention. Either way, it still smarts.

Roxy isn't ready to back down; she's pissed. "Alec, what is your problem? Are you and Dex in some Alpha Asshole Dick Club?"

Sarah, unwilling to let it go, asks, "Alec, don't you think Em looks hot in this dress?" Before I give myself a chance to hear Alec's response, I rush back to Sarah's room and barely avoid slamming the door. I don't want to know what he thinks about the dress or me. What I do know is that my self-esteem can't take the hit.

After removing the scrap of fabric and putting my underthings back on, I pick out an outfit of my choosing. It's not unusual for us girls to share clothes, and it's always a treat to go through Sarah's closet.

The dress I chose is a deep purple chiffon that falls just above the knee. It features an empire waist and a flowing skirt with a lighter, pinkish-purple lining that peeks out with every swish of the fabric. No matter what Alec thinks, I kept the strappy sandals on. They are awesome, and I can probably dance all night in them.

Heading back into the living room, I'm not surprised to see that Alec is gone. Roxy and Sarah are busy finalizing their outfits, but they turn in unison when I enter the room.

Roxy smiles and states, "Girl, you look hot no matter what you wear."

Sarah nods and says, "Yes, but the dress I chose for you was way sexier, I'm just saying." I agreed with Sarah. I had nothing to add to that.

All three of us are now lined up in front of Sarah's large dining room mirror, applying makeup. Not far from our reach are our freshly poured margarita glasses; since we weren't driving, we figured we might as well enjoy the pitcher the guys had spent time mixing.

We've moved on from the earlier dress fiasco. I wish my mind would move on; instead, my conflicted thoughts are centered on irrational feelings of rejection. I'm being stupid. Why do I care what Alec likes or doesn't like? I don't care. Or I don't care anymore.

As I get out of my head, I hear Sarah telling us about this mystery man we're going to meet tonight. She describes how sweet he is and how he's been walking her to her car every night after her shift at The Rusty Nail since the first night they met. The guy sounds like a romantic unicorn, but he's a very sweet one.

Roxy, in her normal no filter voice, asks, "All I want to know is how is the sex?"

To which Sarah replies, "It's to be determined." Really? Wow, before I can ask Sarah why this guy is different, Roxy beats me to the punch.

"What's the delay?" Roxy asks without hesitation.

Sarah, smiling, says, "Other than we just met? I'm holding back. I want to make sure he's in it for more than a quick romp. Plus, I like this one and more than just for the physical."

I couldn't help but notice Roxy's stunned look, just before I saw her roll her eyes as she held back her retort.

My friends shared, they over-shared, and they expected nothing less from me. They genuinely believe I'm too conservative and a bit prudish to share the intimate details with them from my occasional dates. What they do not know, and won't ever know, is that there is no intimacy. I don't sleep with any of them, not since my bad decision during my first year of college.

On the heels of that thought, my mind goes there. *Trace was cute, charming, and persistent. It wasn't a hardship to finally go on a date with him. He took me to a local Italian restaurant that most college kids frequented. We had a nice dinner, a drink, and an easy conversation. Later, when he walked me to the door of my off-campus apartment, he was insistent on coming in for one more drink. I was all caught up on the high of an awesome date, and I complied, willingly letting Trace come in. The one drink turned into two, and I was feeling the effects. I still had some faculties, but barely; my head felt foggy and not wholly my own.*

Before long, Trace was kissing and caressing me. In the beginning, I felt turned on, but when he started removing my clothes, I lost my desire quickly. I soon discovered I had drunk way too much, and I wasn't capable of defending myself against Trace's advances.

Don't go there. Em, do not. Go there. Feeling the fingers of my past grabbing for my sanity, my breathing becoming labored, the panic attack trying to take hold, I will my mind to find something positive from that time in my life. I had to remember the good to push back the bad. Roxy and Sarah, Sarah and Roxy. Struggling, I make my mind focus on their voices, on them.

It was the year after the *'incident'* when I met Sarah and Roxy in an art elective class. They quickly became not just my friends but my unknowing saviors. Their persistence in pursuing a friendship with the shy, withdrawn, and honestly antisocial me promptly became the anchor that tethered me back to the land of the living. They became my lifelines, and we've been inseparable ever since.

I can never let them know that their friendship saved me. Even now, they continue to play a vital role in my daily survival. Before them, I was in my headspace way too much. I was merely a spectator, observing my life, but not truly living it. Freshman year should have been about parties, new freedoms, and learning. But after Trace, my fear and insecurities ruled my world at every turn. Sadly, I had become a paranoid hermit, isolating myself from everything and everyone. I did the bare minimum to keep up appearances as well as my grades.

Looking back now, I see that my paranoia was partnering with my fear. I had become suspicious and mistrustful of people and their actions toward me without any real reason. I was afraid to stay alone in my apartment, but I was also determined not to let *him* take my home from me as well. It was bad enough that my nightly dreams felt plagued by his reappearances. The worst part was that in those first few years, every nightmare seemed to bring to my subconscious flashes of what new and terrifying events I had endured that awful night. He took my will to live in my life and left me as nothing more than a spectator.

I rarely have nightmares anymore, but the memories always linger, hovering at the edge of my thoughts. These memories hold me back; they influence my decisions more than I like to admit. I've come a long way from my self-imposed exile, but I still approach life cautiously.

Roxy and Sarah have always accepted me as the quiet one of our group. I don't share a lot of my past, and they don't push for more than I can give. It's a true testament to their friendship that they don't question me about my life before meeting them. They know I am an only child to wealthy parents who couldn't be bothered, but nothing substantial beyond that.

Suddenly, I hear Roxy yell, "Em! Earth to Em! Get the lead out, sister, our chariot awaits!" Shaking off the residual film of disgust that my inner dark thoughts took me through, I notice both girls are standing by the door, purses in hand, looking at me impatiently.

Blessedly, they must be too engrossed in getting ready to notice I didn't do anything more to my face or hair. Gathering my stuff, I quickly follow. For the first time today, I'm looking forward to the diversion of drinks, loud music, and dancing to erase where my thoughts had taken me.

Chapter Three
GET A CLUE
Emily

In the lobby, we see Alec and Dex sitting on the chairs, deep in conversation. They stand up as we approach. Both of their faces look guilty, like we just caught them with their hands in the cookie jar. I wonder what they were talking about. Usually, I wouldn't hesitate to ask, but I'm still irritated with them both.

Alec's eyes are locked on mine as we reach them. His stare is both intense and caressing at the same time. It's also fleeting; Alec never lets his emotions show for long. He has mastered the stoic disposition.

I smile at Alec and Dex; it's a fake smile, and I know they both know it. Deciding to address the tension, I turn toward Dex, "You over your temper tantrum now?" He doesn't have time to react or say anything before Roxy hooks her arm through mine and pulls me away.

Not before I catch the smug smirk she aims at Dex. Dex shakes his head as he heads for the elevator to the garage. He rarely takes the sassy bait from any of us. Smart man.

As the group nears Alec's Yukon, Roxy lets me go to the other side passenger door. Alec steps back to walk beside me. I look up, way up, to see him staring down at me. "What?" I snap, still annoyed.

Alec briefly looks away before his gaze returns to mine. "You look nice," he says. Then, he rushes ahead to reach his truck before any of us.

It's not a stretch for me to believe Alec has some superpowers. How did he know his comment about the other dress hurt my feelings? He never compliments what we are wearing. Never. That's not Alec.

Why am I even thinking about this? Alec does not influence what I wear or how I feel about it. That dress made me look sexy, but even I know it was a bit risqué for me. Needing to escape this train of thought, I plan to stay out of my head and enjoy a night out with my crazy friends.

We reached The Purple Room Dance Club in under 30 minutes. Impressive considering it was Friday night and we were heading into downtown Houston. As usual, Alec valet parked. He did this every time we went out, whether to a club or a fancy restaurant. It isn't because he's lazy; no matter the reason, my feet in my 3-inch heels always appreciate it.

As we exit the Yukon, Roxy straightens and yells, "Here we go bitches and hoes!" My friend is indeed crazy, and she doesn't mind the attention her outbursts bring. We're getting some dirty looks as we walk right through the double doors like we own the place.

Once inside, the atmosphere assaults us with loud music, strobe lights, and a pervasive purple theme. *Wow, this is a lot of purple. Now, I'm regretting my outfit choice.*

Taking it all in, I barely hear Roxy over the loud pulsing music as she tells Sarah, "Find your man, we need to meet him stat." This place was already packed to what I'm sure is close to capacity.

To no one in particular, I say, "I'm not sure she'll be able to find him or us if she walks away."

Dex must have thought the same when I heard him yell at Sarah, "Meet us back at the right side of the bar near the pool tables."

Alec was already heading that way after Dex said pool tables. After a few steps away, Alec stops to look back, making sure we are following. Or if I wasn't imagining things again, he was looking straight at me. His look seemed protective, or was that possessive? Like I was his.

What's wrong with me tonight? I'm having all kinds of thoughts about Alec, and my lady parts are also trying to get in on the action. I usually can appreciate him without drooling. It's like a piece of cake; you might want it, but you know you can't have it.

I can't explain it, but somehow, I know his reaction in Sarah's apartment wasn't out of meanness. It also wasn't just a typical older brother response; he was feeling something deeper. No matter his reasons, his reaction has confused me and blurred the lines of our friendship.

I don't know how we managed it, but we found a small bar top near the pool table area with a direct path to the dance floor.

Even though the small table was standing room only, it was a perfect spot.

Not a minute passed before Roxy shouted, "Let's get this party started. I'll get the first round!"

To which Alec, as per usual, looks at Roxy, then at me, "I'll be back with your drinks." Turning towards Dex, he asks, "The usual?" Dex lifts his chin, and that is obviously enough communication for Alec. *Men*

I will note that Alec didn't bother to ask us girls what we wanted to drink. It's always tequila shots with a beer chaser for our first round.

While Alec was fetching our drinks, I couldn't help but notice the lingering tension between Roxy and Dex. For her part, Roxy was flat-out ignoring Dex, and Dex was trying and failing to look unaffected.

Leaning over, I touch Roxy's arm to get her attention, and at the same time, I grab Dex by his forearm. Undeterred from their death glares, I ask, "Guys, what gives? Neither of you looks happy, and I can feel the tension between you two."

Both Dex and Roxy looked pissed and a little surprised that I'd call them out. But before they could say anything, which they probably wouldn't have anyway, Alec was back with our drinks that he balanced on a tray he must have borrowed from the bartender.

I decided to let it go for now. I was meeting Dex in the morning for our Saturday run, and he could tell me what was going on then.

Roxy appears unfazed by how the evening began. She was her usual loud self. Having snapped out of her mood, she seemed determined to enjoy herself.

Roxy was singing lyrics loudly while gyrating to the beat as she stood next to our small table. I won't lie, I sang some too, and I was starting to feel the dance vibe. Alcohol was a big help in relaxing my social awkwardness. Plus, the music kicked ass.

People watching is a way to be present and avoid the pressure to speak. Going back to our group, I noticed that as Dex was talking with Alec, his eyes kept flickering back toward Roxy. I decided right then and there that I would get to the bottom of this. Those two were keeping secrets from the rest of us.

My mind was on my upcoming conversation, and my eyes were focused on a couple who needed to get a room, so I was startled when I first felt, then heard, Alec at my ear, "Do you need another drink or want some appetizers?"

I turned my head so quickly he didn't have time to pull back. I swear our lips nearly grazed each other's. As it was, our noses slightly brushed. "Oops!" I mumble.

Alec looks momentarily stunned before he laughs it off, saying, "Sorry, Em, I guess I got a little too close. It's just so loud in here."

Why do I feel disappointment? Is it because he felt the need to apologize for being close to me? His proximity and his gravelly voice, especially when delivered whisper close to my ear, sent shivers to my happy place. I was hoping that he felt something, too. Nope, nada, nothing from the infallible Alec.

I was certifiable; maybe I needed to dust off 'pinky' and get busy. "I do still need orgasmic relief just like the next girl." Dex and Alec both whip their heads around, and I realize to my horror that I'd spoken those words out loud. Typical males can hear anything about sex, even over loud music.

I can't believe I just said that in front of Alec and Dex, holy hell. I'm not right in the head tonight. Sleep deprivation is messing with my sanity.

Avoiding eye contact, I hear Dex ask Alec, "Did you hear what I heard?"

Alec, not missing a beat, responds, "Yep."

Shit. Lifting my chin, I snap, "I could use that other drink now." I hear them both chuckling as I turn fully to face the dance floor. "Whatever," I grumble, feeling the heat of embarrassment crawl up my neck to my face.

Roxy, thanks to my lucky stars, must have missed the whole scene; she turns and loudly requests, "If you're going for beers, get me another tequila shot too. Please."

I couldn't help but notice her first drink was gone within minutes of arrival; I'm surprised she held out this long. Roxy likes her alcohol.

This time, Dex left with the tray to get our drinks. I was about to pull Roxy aside to sort her shit when she lunged at me first, "Why are you drilling me about Dex, in front of Dex?" I'm momentarily surprised by her tone and outburst, then quickly realize this is Roxy's way of deflecting. She's trying to use her infamous diversion tactic to avoid talking to me.

Calmly, I lean in closer so only she can hear, "Something seems different. I want to know what's going on with you two."

She turns to face the dance floor again and then quickly spins back around, whisper-yelling, "You want to know what pisses me off? I'll tell you. Am I the only one who cares that the guys are being Cock Blockers?" I blink, but otherwise, I don't respond.

Roxy continues her rant, "I wouldn't be surprised if they started pissing all around us like we were trees, and they were marking their territory, and I've had enough!"

Roxy seems to realize how loud she was getting and lowers her voice, "Em, get a clue, what the fuck was Alec's problem with your dress, as if he has any say in the matter; you looked fucking fabulous."

She turns to make sure no one is listening and continues, "Think about it, they invite themselves and go out with us every chance they get. They always insist on getting our drinks instead of us going to the bar ourselves. Look around, how many men are coming to ask us to dance? In a dance club, I might add. I mean, Holy Hell, how are any of us supposed to get any action this way?"

When Roxy takes a breath, I hedge, "So is that why you seem pissed at Dex?"

Roxy doesn't make me wait for a response, "Hell, yes! That and he dared to tell me my skirt was too short, and my top showed too much cleavage. Em, you of all people know that was a dick move. I saw how your face fell when Alec dissed your dress."

Since my first reaction had been to feel hurt, I can understand Roxy getting pissed at Dex. He must have hurt her feelings.

Hold on. That's not right; Roxy wouldn't give two shits what Dex or Alec thought of her clothes. There was something else going on here. I was about to ask for more details when Roxy turned completely back toward the dance floor. She was done with this conversation. I'd give her that for now. But later, we needed to talk about all of this. Something else was happening here.

Taking a peek at Alec, I couldn't tell if he heard any of our conversation; judging by his clenched jaw, he heard enough.

Dex returned with our drinks. Other than a few mumbled thanks and chin lifts, none of us said a word. I want to blame it on the loud music, but the tension around us was stifling and oppressive.

People gazing didn't stop my mind from replaying what Roxy said. She has a very valid point. Why hadn't I ever noticed the guy's behavior before? Did Sarah feel the same way as Roxy? Their mere presence alone would block any sane man from approaching us. It doesn't matter if it was intentional or unintentional; the results are the same for us girls.

Reflecting on it, I realize that I'm okay with the blocking, regardless of its intended purpose. I'm not looking for anything other than having a good time with my friends. I don't care who buys my drinks. I enjoy dancing with the girls. Now that I thought about it from their point of view, I could see how both Roxy and Sarah most definitely wouldn't appreciate it.

The problem my mind is struggling to understand is, what's changed? We've all been going out together for a few years now. Why is it suddenly an issue? It's not normal for Roxy or Sarah to hold back their thoughts on anything. Why haven't they complained before? Making a mental note, I plan to ask Sarah whether she noticed how the guys have integrated into our lives. And if so, I want to know what she thinks about it. Although I already expect her to side, at least in part, with Roxy on this one.

Chapter Four
COCK BLOCKERS
Emily

Sarah finally finds us; she approaches with a handsome guy beside her. Behind him are two more guys. As they circle Sarah to meet us, I look up and freeze.

Then I hear a voice from my past, "Emily?" How is this possible? I'm left speechless.

My mouth was surely hanging open, and I still couldn't seem to react in any way. I was frozen. What I had conveniently forgotten, until just now, was that I had tried dating again in college and even tried for more. Enter Josh, better remembered as my attempt at a regular college fling. To my horror, that attempt ended with me fleeing from Josh's dorm room apartment as if my pants were on fire. I'm ashamed to admit that I never spoke to him again after that. Oh, he'd tried countless times, but I'd shut his attempts down, and I wasn't nice about it.

Taking in his handsome face, his kind hazel eyes, that shaggy blonde hair that suits him perfectly, and that 6 ft body with broad shoulders and lean muscle, I'm instantly transported back to another time in my life.

Remorse. I felt deep remorse for how I had treated Josh. I realized that I had used him as a test of my readiness. He was a good guy, a sweet guy, and the time we spent together before the shit storm returned to throw me off course was great. The problem was with me and had nothing to do with him.

As I stare at Josh now, I feel nervous. My heart was beating rapidly as I struggled with the overwhelming urge to flee.

Forcing myself to look into Josh's eyes, I expect to see the anger he has every right to direct at me, but instead, I see warmth and hesitance. Josh isn't mad at me. Seeing his accepting eyes fills me with a not-so-small sense of relief and a hefty dose of guilt.

Before I realize it, Josh pulls me in for a big hug. Surprisingly, I'm not immediately trying to extricate myself from his embrace. Still holding me close, I hear and feel his breath against my ear as he says, "Emily, you look just as beautiful as I remember. How are you doing?"

Josh is a really kind guy, definitely one of the good ones. I don't deserve his kindness. Still, I can't help but blush at his praise, especially since I was expecting a verbal lashing for how I treated him in college. The warmth of his fingers still wrapped around my hand helped me relax enough to utter a lame, squeaky response of "hi."

The other guys and Sarah continued with the introductions, but I was totally in the Josh force field. His smile was radiant and calming, drawing me in. Suddenly, I understood why I had taken a chance with Josh back in college; he was always so easy to be with. I also understood why I shut him out. I knew I wasn't ready for more, and he didn't deserve to be put on hold waiting for me to get my shit together.

Our surroundings, the music, and the chatter of friends all fade into the background. I felt engrossed in everything Josh was saying. We chatted amicably for what felt like hours, but I'm sure it wasn't that long. I openly shared with him the career path I took since college, and he shared his work experience at Toyota as the VP of Marketing. He explained that Toyota has its headquarters in the Dallas area, but he travels to Houston several times a month. He went on to say that, starting next weekend, he would be in Houston for almost a month, overseeing his marketing team at the Houston Rodeo.

"Hey, would you like to go to the Houston Rodeo next weekend?" Josh looked hopeful when he asked this.

I loved the Rodeo, so I didn't hesitate to say, "Yes, I'd love to go."

Josh, flashing his radiant smile, asked, "Give me your phone so I can program my number in it." I had just handed it over when I felt the room shift. That prickling awareness told me we had eyes on us.

Looking up, I see both Dex and Alec standing at their full hulking heights and glaring our way. Josh must have felt the shift as well, which was confirmed when, in a hushed tone close to my ear, he said, "Emily, sorry I didn't think about how this might look to your boyfriend."

"I'm just here with some friends," I answer tersely, as I look away from the guys and return my eyes to Josh. For his part, I noticed Josh tried but failed not to glance back their way.

As I was trying to get our conversation back on track, the sound of Sarah laughing caught my attention. Sarah was in her element, smiling and clearly into her man. "What was his name again?" I ask as Josh hands me back my phone. I quickly called his saved number, so he'd also have my contact information. I was purposely ignoring the testosterone emanating from Dex and Alec.

Josh took his cue from me and kept the conversation going. Successfully blocking out the male posturing from just a few feet away. Smiling, Josh responds, "Michael is the one with your friend Sarah, and the other guy is Eric."

"Thanks, I don't think I heard any of the introductions." I sheepishly admit, looking toward the newcomers. I notice right away that Roxy was getting chummy and chatty with the other guy, Eric. Roxy was talking animatedly about something, and the guy was looking smitten with her. Roxy has a magnetic personality. Her zest for life and living it to the fullest is both attractive and contagious.

Out of the corner of my eye, I notice Dex staring intently at Roxy and Eric. The frown on his face and the twitch in his jaw from grinding his molars tell me he isn't happy about this new friendship.

"Are the guys your bodyguards?" Josh questions with a smirk. To that, I laugh out loud; I couldn't help it. The hilarity of the statement was both funny and surreal. I now couldn't dissuade Roxy's earlier rant. The sad fact is that Josh's statement has a ring of truth to it.

"Nope, they are just friends." I wheeze, still laughing. Roxy's comments were still playing on a loop in my mind. And then there's Alec and Dex confirming right in front of my eyes that what Roxy said is true. For some asinine reason, I'm finding it all very funny. I can't stop laughing. I'm unhinged and maybe a little bit tipsy.

It's like when you're so tired and you can't stop laughing. Even when it takes your breath away and your eyes start watering. You still can't stop. That's how I feel right now. Leaning on the table and partly against Josh, I try to get my laughter under control. He probably thinks I'm crazy. I'm so lost in the moment that I hadn't noticed that Alec had approached us.

Suddenly, a large, hulking arm grabs me around the waist. Then, polite as always, I hear Alec's deep voice say to anyone listening or able to hear, "Excuse us a minute."

As Alec proceeds to drag me into one of the halls, my laughter dies instantly. I'm pissed the hell off.

When we reach the back wall, Alec unmans me and steps away. I spin around and shout, "What is your problem?"

Too late, I realize that Alec looks thunderous. My words hang in the air, his expression shifts from anger to remorse. Then, right before my eyes, he visibly takes a measured breath, instantly returning to his usual stoic self.

Not taking his eyes off mine, he nearly growls, "I don't like him."

Well, nothing for it. I'm so pissed right now that I snap, "So what? I don't care." Alec, for his part, stares at me, unmoving and unreactive. His ever-present control is clearly on display. I want to scream. Then, without warning, I'm engulfed as my anger and confusion start bubbling up inside me. I begin to shake, which pushes me over the edge. I feel my traitorous tears well up in my eyes, not from sadness, but because I'm just so mad. Recalling Roxy's earlier words, I snap, "Roxy was right, you guys are being total Cock Blockers!"

To that statement, Alec steps back. He appears to be rendered speechless and motionless. He wasn't moving a single muscle. Then I saw the expression on his face when the implication of my words registered with him.

Alec was looking pained as he shared, "Sorry, Em, that's not my intention. I only want to protect you." With that parting shot, Alec turns and walks away.

His departure gives me a chance to visit the restroom. First and foremost, I need to get a grip. How the hell is it possible that Alec makes me feel like I was being an ungrateful ass when in fact it's him who's acting like the ass? I never asked him to protect me. Josh is a friend. I don't need or want Alec's unsolicited, overbearing protection.

My mind was trying, unsuccessfully, not to think about the part of me that had hoped he was a little jealous. It's all about safety, nothing more. Still, Roxy was right; it wouldn't matter that they didn't want us for themselves, their presence would make us unapproachable to someone who might.

As I wash my hands, my mind still feels conflicted and confused. I don't understand what the guys are hoping to accomplish with their tactics. Then there's the fact that I don't understand any of my friends' actions today. It must be a full moon or something.

The truth is, the guys protect us more often than not. I can admit that most days, I'm thankful for this very fact. It's a relief knowing I won't have to fend off any unwanted advances. Because of this, I return to our group as if nothing had happened. To avoid testing my resolve, I decide to give both Dex and Alec plenty of space. They might be Cock Blockers, but I won't let them also be killjoys.

Less than an hour later, everyone was settling their tabs and saying their goodbyes. Josh promised to stay in touch about the Rodeo, and I appreciated our conversation as we left the club. Especially considering how none of my closest friends were talking much. It was going to be a very long ride home.

Chapter Five
THE SECRET
Emily

The next morning, I still had to go for my run with Dex. It doesn't matter how late we stayed out the night before; we still try to stick to our Saturday morning routine.

This morning, I woke up just in time to change clothes and brush my teeth. I drank some much-needed water before heading down to the lobby to meet Dex.

Dex was near the lobby doors, stretching when I arrived. He glanced my way but then turned back to his task. I still didn't understand what problem he had with me, but since I was under his mercy for the next hour, I opted to pretend everything was peachy.

We finished our run in companionable silence; neither of us had much to say beyond discussing our run route. That suited me fine. I was dragging ass after last night anyway. It wasn't because of the alcohol, but rather from sleep deprivation. Everything that happened yesterday kept replaying in my mind. I tried and failed to make sense of any of it. I knew instinctively not to bring any of this up with Dex. He wasn't in the mood to talk. Honestly, he seemed like he was on the run by himself, but I wasn't eager to draw attention to myself anyway.

When I arrived at my unit, I found Roxy in my kitchen straightening my glass jar of Splenda packets. I also noticed that she stacked the K-cups by flavor, displayed neatly on the shelf next to the coffee maker. Something was wrong.

We girls jokingly call Roxy *'special'* and ask her if she rode the short bus to school. I know I should be ashamed of myself, but teasing was a big part of our friendship. Plus, we all have our quirks and accept that the short bus is just a fancy limo for girls like us.

Quirk or not, I can relate to Roxy's propensity toward order and structure, where everything in life needs to fit neatly into a box. Roxy could be intense, but when stressed, she took it to a whole new level. It was just who Roxy was. We love her for those quirks, just as she loves us for ours.

I was about to say something witty when she turned to face me. Her face was red and blotchy, and I could tell she had gotten even less sleep than I had. I knew then that something was seriously wrong. "Let me call Sarah, then go grab a quick shower, and I'll be right back," I say quickly.

Roxy nods and heads to my pantry. That should keep her busy for a while. *Is it wrong to hope she works quickly enough to finish it before Sarah arrives?*

It was about 15 minutes later when I heard a knock at my front door, and then I heard Roxy let Sarah in. As I was coming back toward the kitchen, I noticed Sarah handing Roxy a big box of donuts from the corner bakery. I had to smile; we knew how to cheer each other up.

"Good morning, chickies!" Sarah yells as she follows Roxy into the kitchen. "Let's get to cracking that hard head of yours. What is wrong with you, Roxy?"

"Wow, subtle, Sarah," I mumble as I meet up with them in the kitchen entryway. Sarah must have slept just fine last night, or was busy not sleeping from having naked sexy time.

"Let's sit at the table and I'll make you guys some coffee," I sounded much more cheerful than I actually felt. I didn't bother to ask about preferences; we all drank our coffee the same way, with Splenda and creamer: the powdered kind, no sissy milk for us.

As I hand over the coffees, I calmly suggest, "Roxy, you should start by telling Sarah about your theory with the guys." I was taking a chance here, but I had a strong suspicion that Roxy's mood had something to do with Dex and Alec or both.

As we each picked our donut and started drinking our coffees, Roxy blurts out, "The guys are being cock blockers and it's irritating as hell. But that's not the worst of it." I notice then that Roxy has a guilty look on her face.

"Roxy, what's going on? What else has happened?" I ask encouragingly. Sarah nodded her head to signal her to continue since she had a mouthful of donut.

"I've kept a big secret from you guys," Roxy confesses, then, looking remorseful, shares, "It was never supposed to be more than a *'fuck buddy'* arrangement. We both agreed that anything more was totally not what either of us wanted, nor did either of us want anything to jeopardize our friendship," Roxy hurriedly adds.

I knew what she was talking about, but I wanted her to say it herself. Roxy owed us that much for keeping such a huge secret. "I've had a thing with Dex for the last six months," Roxy mumbles, "It started out casually, just bumping uglies, nothing more. We got lazy over time. Sometimes, one of us would fall asleep at the other's place. At first, it was fine; I liked it. Then, the intimacy grew the more time we spent together. That was not part of the arrangement." Roxy's eyes fill with tears and spill over as she admits, "I fell for him."

Wow, it was, and it wasn't, what I expected to hear. I had to understand, "Roxy, what exactly is the issue here? As both of your friends, we would support you guys no matter what. Hell, we'd all be happy for you both. So, what's the problem?"

Roxy looks defeated and sad when she quietly responds, "he doesn't feel the same about me."

"Oh, Roxy, I'm sorry," Sarah says, looking a bit pissed as she reaches over to squeeze Roxy's hand.

Roxy has shared her past with me. Her mom died when she was young, and her dad worked all the time to make ends meet. Roxy was, more often than not, accountable only to herself. She came and went as she pleased and did whatever she wanted. She once confided that she struggled with abandonment issues growing up. I can't help but wonder if this situation brought those feelings to the forefront of her mind. I never asked, and she never mentioned whether Sarah also knew her story. We rarely shared the deep, deep stuff; it was an unspoken rule. One I wholeheartedly supported.

It wasn't a surprise when, only seconds after revealing her secret, Roxy loudly states, "I am now D.O.N.E with this pity party and all the other bullshit!"

We ate our donuts and drank our coffees as if all was well in our world. Roxy didn't dwell. One of her funny sayings was, *"You can't sweat the petty or pet the sweaty."* She was a master at defusing and redirecting most situations. Her carefree demeanor did not fool me; I knew Roxy wasn't as tough or blasé as she pretended to be. I also realized I would think about her, Dex, and their situation for days.

Chapter Six
INCOGNITO
Emily

As predicted, that night I didn't sleep worth a crap again. I woke feeling both disoriented and exhausted. With Roxy on the brain, I sent a text to check on her.

Em: *You okay? What are your plans today?*

Rolling out of bed, I pulled on some yoga pants, an exercise bra, and an oversized shirt that must belong to one of the guys. As I headed to the kitchen, I heard a ping, indicating I had received a text.

Roxy: *Let's go to the beach.*

Since Galveston was only 50 minutes away, that was a great idea. I quickly texted my response.

Em: *Sounds great, I'll let Sarah know, and let's meet at my place in 30.*

Before I can send a message to Sarah, I notice a clapping emoji from Roxy to show her excitement. We're silly that way.

Deciding to combine forces, I sent the text to Sarah via our group text string with Sarah, Roxy, and me.

Em: *Okay, ladies, we are leaving for the beach in 30 minutes. Meet at my place. And, Sarah, it's a cheer-up, Roxy day.*

Sarah: *Awesome.*

I decide to skip making coffee and take a shower instead. It was more essential to shave all my girlie parts; I wouldn't want to scare the fishies. Plus, I was overdue for some self-care. Nothing makes you more aware of that than when you have to put on a bathing suit.

With my bathing suit on under a bright colored summer dress, my hair braided down my back, I was ready for some beach therapy. I couldn't think of anything better than this. I love the ocean air, the water, the waves, and spending quality time with my girls.

I quickly pack a beach bag with all the essentials: suntan lotion, a big floppy hat, and oversized sunglasses. I have a few minutes before the girls arrive, so I pull out a bag of ice and start loading a cooler with water, sodas, and beer.

Roxy will come prepared with drinks too, but she prefers the hard juice. She loves her Sky Vodka with sparkling water and lime.

It was with that thought that my door flew open, and Roxy burst in shouting, "Let's get to the beach, you Beaches!" Our loud and proud Roxy was back! Sarah followed right behind her, carrying her beach bag and a sack of snacks. We all knew the beach routine and what each of us was expected to contribute to ensure we had a good time.

"I have a great idea," Sarah says as she enters the kitchen, "we need to pack some clothes and plan to stay and eat at Fisherman's Wharf for dinner." That sounded like a great idea; I love eating fresh fish while overlooking the Galveston canal.

Before I could say anything, Roxy shouts, "That is the best fucking idea I've heard all week!"

We all agreed to meet in the lobby in 15 minutes after collecting our necessary change of clothes. I knew both my girls, so I knew this also included makeup and cute outfits to impress.

As I passed by the kitchen on my way out, I decided to grab some Solo cups for the hard juice. I thought about sending a quick text to the guys to let them know we would be gone all day. Then I smacked my own forehead, saying, "Don't be an enabler."

As I walked out and locked my door, I felt irritated all over again about the events of Friday night. Alec physically pulling me away from Josh wasn't cool. Why hadn't I realized when exactly the guys stopped being just friends and became our watchdogs? Then I remembered a crucial reason: I wasn't bothered by the lack of male attention, so I wasn't as affected as Roxy and Sarah. However, neither of them seems to have suffered much from the watchdogs. Roxy had been secretly shacking up with Dex, and Sarah was dating a guy she met while bartending.

Thinking about what Roxy had confirmed regarding Dex, I felt there was more to the story. I couldn't forget the angry look Dex shot my way before storming out of Sarah's on Friday. More questions than answers were swirling in my mind. Nothing was adding up.

One of the biggest fears I refused to face, despite failing to push it away since my talk with Roxy, was this: if things between her and Dex blow up, we could lose not only our friendship with him but also Alec too.

That thought had been keeping me awake these last few nights, gnawing at me until I felt twitchy in my own skin. I needed to get out of my head. We needed to get moving. The ocean's calm rhythm, the pull of the waves, was calling my name.

Roxy and Sarah were already at Sarah's powder-blue Volkswagen Beetle, loading their beach chairs and bags. As I reached them, I asked, "Is there room for the cooler, or will it need to go in the backseat?"

Sarah turned, smiling, but said, "It'll have to go in the backseat with Roxy." Since Roxy was the shortest of us three, she always got the back seat when riding in Sarah's Beetle. I wouldn't mind sitting back there to avoid being up close and personal with the windshield and bumper of the car in front of us. But it was too tight a fit for an hour-long trip.

With all the loading complete, we head out of the garage, and I belatedly notice Dex standing by his truck when we exit. He was too far to wave to. At least that's what I decide to convince myself of. "Did you guys see Dex at his truck?" I had to ask.

"Not me," Sarah says, navigating out of the garage.

Roxy responds from the backseat, "Yep, and I don't care what he thinks." Then she quickly adds, "Girls, hand over your phones, we're going incognito today."

I piped up, saying, "I'll need mine back, we're going to want it for some beach tunes since I brought my Bose speaker."

Roxy just whooped and jumped up and down in her seat like a crazy person; her enthusiastic actions shook the entire car. I'm sure any passersby will take a wide berth to steer clear of us. I know I would.

We sang the whole way to Stewart Beach. It's always a treat when Sarah lets her guard down and sings along. She can belt out the tunes. Her voice is the perfect mix of sultry and edgy.

Sarah paid the day pass fee, and we headed to the far left side of the beach. There were still plenty of front row spots available. Pulling into a spot, we climb out and proceed to unload our stuff. We ensured that no one could set up in front of us and block our view of the beach. We learned the hard way to arrive early and secure a front-row spot; otherwise, we might get subjected to seeing things you can never unsee. I'm talking about naked, wrinkly, hairy, scary things.

As we settle in with our drinks and snacks, I hesitate to get my cell phone. We always listen to music while at the beach. I shouldn't be hesitating at all. What's wrong with me? My new awareness of the guys and their actions is making me a paranoid mess. So, what if either of them called or texted? It doesn't mean I have to respond. We aren't doing anything wrong, so why do I feel guilty?

I was so lost in my thoughts that I missed Roxy's comment until she repeated it, "Em, I asked if you wanted to get the music going or just enjoy the waves crashing until the crazies start showing up?"

I knew I was being a chicken shit, but I took the easy way out and said, "Let's wait a bit." Sarah didn't seem to care either way, but Roxy gave me one of her eyebrow lifts that said, I can tell you're in your headspace again.

We fell quiet, listening to the waves and the seagulls calling to one another. It wasn't long before Sarah nudged the conversation back to Dex. "So, Roxy, how was it with Dex? Is he as big as his shoes would indicate?"

I stifle a laugh and say, "Way to get straight to the juicy stuff, Sarah."

Roxy's smile was indulgent. "If I told you, I'd have to kill you."

Sarah giggled. "You wouldn't. Come on, share."

Roxy kept smiling. "Okay, fine. Maybe I wouldn't kill you, but sometimes the less you know about my extracurricular activities, the better."

Joining in on the quest for information, I ask, "Why are you holding out on us? You're usually too forthcoming about your little escapades; it's not like we don't already know you like a little kink."

Sarah followed up with, "And we never judged you for that. I think I speak for both of us when I say we often live vicariously through you."

All I could do was nod; I would be lying if I didn't admit that I had considered the things Roxy was willing to do. I envied her for her strength and her willingness to embrace life's experiences. Her sexual prowess was part of who she was, and she isn't shy about asking for what she wants from her partner.

Her reluctance to talk about Dex says a lot about how she feels about him. I can tell that her time with Dex meant something to her, and she probably thinks that the memories are all she has left.

It was then that I announced, "Okay, girls, let's get some music on and top off our round of drinks. We're here to relax, unwind, and have fun doing it." I look over at Roxy, and she winks at me. She recognized and appreciated my diversion.

Grabbing my phone from the console, I had to admit that I was being a total wuss. The first thing I did was silence my notifications, relieved to see that no unread messages were waiting. It wasn't in my DNA to ignore friends if they reached out, and I knew one of the guys would check in sooner or later. After all, Sunday night football at someone's apartment was our thing, almost every week during the season.

"So," I asked, "did either of you tell Alec and Dex we're not joining them tonight?"

Roxy looked pained and a bit miserable as she shook her head no.

"Not me," Sarah said. "I assumed one of you would have."

Wincing, I sighed, "I think we should at least let them know we're skipping tonight." I felt I had to put that out there; no way was I going to be the only one of us to feel guilty.

I was sure that Roxy was going to say it wasn't their business or something along those lines when she responded, "Yes, they don't deserve to worry about us just because they both have been total caveman assholes." She went on to add, "and dickheads, and cock blockers, suckers and fuckers, and bullies."

"Are you done?" I giggle.

Roxy then mutters, "stupid motherfuckers."

Both Sarah and I burst out laughing. Roxy starts laughing too. I had tears in my eyes before I could get my composure back enough to send them messages. I sent each of them a text letting them know we were at the beach and wouldn't be back in time for football Sunday.

We settled in to enjoy the music and the sun; the beach was one of my happiest places. But today, anxiety kept gnawing at me. I couldn't shake what Roxy had shared: first, how the guys always seemed to shield us from male attention, and second, that she and Dex had been "a thing" for lack of a better word, for nearly six months.

These thoughts unsettled me because it was tied to my deepest fear, losing even one of my friends. I needed all of them to fill the void I felt down to my soul. My parents were alive, but all they freely gave me was money and a bad case of indigestion. Family up North supposedly existed, but they were strangers. Roxy, Sarah, Dex, and Alec were my true family in every sense of the word.

All these thoughts left me melancholy and afraid, my mind spinning with worst-case scenarios I couldn't shake. I knew I had to rein in these emotions before they spiraled into a full-blown panic attack. Something I did not want Roxy and Sarah to witness, ever. Closing my eyes, I drew in a few deep breaths and focused on my surroundings. The rhythmic push and pull of the waves, building and crashing to the shore, slowly quieted the storm within me.

At that moment, I felt lonely even with all these people around me. I don't know why, but I do. I need to refocus my mind on the present and stop letting my past and insecurities control me, my thoughts, or my future. The future will undoubtedly include all of my friends. Although the very fabric of our friendships seems challenged by the falling out of Dex and Roxy, I know I can draw upon unsolicited strength from my two girls. I've known that with absolute certainty since college.

Coming back to the present, with my eyes closed, I slowly divert my focus to their conversation. They're discussing their prospective workloads and Sarah's new guy, and slowly, my anxiety ebbs until once again, their presence is the anchor my battered soul requires to feel grounded and secure.

It was close to 5 o'clock when we decided to get cleaned up and head to dinner. Since it would be an early dinner, we decided to skip the whole dressing-up, makeup, and all the girlie crap. It was a work night, after all, and we still had to drive back to Houston.

I was more than okay with the earlier schedule; I drank a few too many with only a few bites of my snack. I hate chomping on grit from the sand that always seems to make its way into my food. Ironically, I love the beach, listening to the crashing waves, but I'm not fond of the sand. It gets into everything, drinks, food, body crevices, everywhere.

Fisherman's Wharf wasn't busy at all. We were seated promptly in a prime patio location with a clear view of the canal and the various boats that use it.

Since I wasn't up for more alcohol, I offered, "Sarah, I can drive us home if you want to enjoy another drink or two." She quickly digs in her bag and tosses me her keys.

I smile and say to the waiter, "I'll have a Diet Coke, please, and I want a dozen raw oysters for my meal and a salad with balsamic vinegar."

Sarah and Roxy both ordered Cosmos with Skye Vodka. For their meal, Roxy got the fried shrimp platter with a baked potato and a house salad. Sarah got the lobster fondue with a side of steamed broccoli.

"Hey, guys, do either of you know that new chick from the 3rd floor in our condominiums?" queries Roxy.

"Are you talking about the petite redhead who has terrible taste in clothes?" I ask.

Roxy nods and then says with a smirk, "She makes Brittany from Wren Tower look fashion-forward, don't you think?" Brittany has a rested bitch face; she works at the reception counter in our office building, and she dresses like a converted nun who just got out of the convent.

"We should plan an intervention for poor, homely Brittany; she needs help. But, what about her?" I query.

Roxy looks as if she isn't going to answer at first, but then says quietly, "I saw Dex and her talking the other evening in the lobby."

"So, that doesn't mean anything," Sarah protested.

Roxy then adds, "If that's all they were doing, you'd be right, but I saw her lean into Dex, her hand was on his biceps, and she was full on smiling like the Cheshire cat who just got its milk."

"Hold on a second, Roxy," chides Sarah, "He told us the score and I quote, 'I am a self-proclaimed manwhore and I'm proud of it!'"

"I agree with Sarah on this front, he's never hidden his womanizing ways from us," but as I say the words, I realize that wasn't exactly true for all of us.

"Roxy, I'm sorry that was not cool, and I didn't mean to insinuate that what you're feeling isn't real." I sigh then confess, "I'm an ass."

Sarah pipes up, saying, "And I'm a bigger ass."

"No, it's okay, guys, you're right, I'm the dumbass who thought I was special to him and that he'd change for me," Roxy explains shakily. I could tell Roxy was close to tears, so a change of subject was needed.

"Roxy, we're coming back to you. We need more information to formulate an opinion. So, Sarah, tell us about Michael, all about him." I say, batting my eyelashes.

As expected, Roxy got in on the ribbing, asking, "That's right, turnabout is fair play. How's his shoe size measure up?"

Sarah, who doesn't shy away from sharing, says just above a whisper, "He's a great guy and I'm totally into him and I think he feels the same way about me. It's still new, but we've had some meaningful conversations and we've been open and honest about what we both want out of this relationship."

"Wow, Sarah, that's great. You deserve to find a perfect man and be happy." I say with a genuine smile for my friend.

Sarah, with her quick wit, responds, "Yes, and so do both of you."

Neither Roxy nor I had anything to say to that. After a few moments of awkward silence, we shift to easy banter.

We focus on our dinners and discuss work-related topics. I didn't want to think about work, but it was better than the alternative. Happiness was possible, finding a perfect man, not so much.

My mind continued to review the changes in my friend's personal lives. The more I thought about Roxy, the unhappier I got. What was Dex thinking? How could he play Roxy like that? I was hurting for her. And pissed at him.

And for Sarah, I couldn't help but worry because I was protective of her. She was putting her heart out there. I could only hope that Sarah had more skill at reading men than I did.

My biggest hope was that both of my friends would find the 'perfect guy' they were searching for; I wanted them to be happy. And, if fairy tales were real, I wished for them to have their happily ever afters.

Chapter Seven
THE BACK STORY
Alec

Alec recognized that he wasn't thinking rationally. He was going out of his mind with worry. Standing in his kitchen, he was staring at his phone with such intensity that he was surprised it didn't have holes in it. "I just need the damn thing to ring or ping anything but remain silent."

The fact that Em was off the grid, with no communication, was sending his brain into a whirlwind of activity.

His training immediately came to the forefront of his mind, and although unbidden, his thoughts went through the standard investigative process routine, the worst-case scenarios.

He was painfully aware that he wasn't doing a very good job of reasoning out potential scenarios or maintaining his control.

"Fuck!" He knew two of the main rules in his profession that proved to save lives: avoid making assumptions and avoid personal entanglements. He was failing at both of these.

His heart was calling bullshit. When it's personal, no one can help but think the worst. Logically, he knew Em's phone was either destroyed, dead, or her location services were turned off.

As I considered the circumstances and formulated risk assessments, I had to concede that what I was experiencing was gut-wrenching fear.

I *had* to work on the hypothesis in my head, if for no other reason than to keep myself in check.

Fear is not an emotion with which I have much, if any, experience. I know that if anything bad were to happen to Em, I would not be able to live with myself. Even if what happened wasn't my fault. I feel marginally responsible. And this has little to do with the fact that her parents pay me to keep a watchful eye on her. I have an overwhelming need to keep her safe.

I'm painfully aware that my emotions and feelings for Em are surfacing more often than not; it is a daily struggle to keep them at bay. To keep my feelings and my desires to myself.

The alternative, giving in to my wants and desires, would be worse. There is no way I can give only parts of myself. No, Em deserves all or nothing. And I can't risk telling her who I am.

Maybe Em did something to her phone. She was upset with me about my approach to her and Josh on Friday night, and about me manhandling her away from him.

As I had this thought, I immediately knew it wasn't right. Em is not the type of person who would do something vengeful. She doesn't play games.

I had to admit, I *had* let my emotions get the better of me that night. I was twisted up inside watching her smile and laugh with that guy. I didn't like him instantly because he was with

Em. No guy is good enough for her, including me. I reacted without thought to the consequences. Her anger toward me was enough to reset my priorities. A reminder that I was basically on the clock. That I had no right to interfere with who she spends time with. I was out of bounds and at a loss for words to retract my actions.

Now, those thoughts of nobility have gone to shit. Regardless of what I should or shouldn't do, I can't seem to stop myself from sending Em another text. I'm beyond caring what it says about me or how it will be perceived. I feel desperate for a response from her, even if it's to tell me to fuck off.

My emotions are running the gamut, ranging from worry to anger, fear, and resignation. I have to do something, so I also sent Dex a text.

Alec: *Have you seen or heard from the girls?*

Dex: *They left this morning around 9.*

Alec: *To where?*

Dex: *I don't know, they didn't stop to say hi or bye.*

Alec: *Shit!!*

That information did not help me; instead, it gave my overactive brain a crucial part of the investigative process, the *'last seen'* timestamp. I hated feeling powerless. I hate feeling all this shit.

There was a knock at my door. I knew it would be Dex. I always went to great pains to remain neutral and never ask personal questions about the girls or him. I should have anticipated that Dex would pick up on that change right away.

Opening the door, I didn't try to hide my anguish. My trainer taught that an unreadable face could be the difference between life and death, but at this moment, I didn't want to hide my agony.

I saw when my anguish registered with Dex; he just walked by me and headed straight for my refrigerator, asking, "Beer or Soda?"

"Beer," I reply. Returning to stand by my window where I've been doing nothing, seeing nothing, feeling a whole hell of a lot, I take the beer Dex hands me.

Taking a sip of my beer, I have a moment of acceptance. Everyone, in every aspect of life, needs someone to have their back. I knew instinctively that Dex would be that person for me. He was the friend that I'm just now realizing I need.

Taking a seat at the kitchen high top table, Dex cautiously asks, "Are you okay? Are the girls, okay? Give me something, man, you're seriously freaking me out here."

Laughing a humorless laugh, I share, "Em's off the grid and I can't get a hold of her or the girls."

I'm sure I look scary as hell right about then. Just saying those words makes me feel unhinged. But Dex isn't deterred, "Off the grid? What are you talking about?"

Tipping my chin to show I heard him, I take a few moments to gather my thoughts before formulating my reply. We both take a few healthy pulls on our beers as I come to terms with what I'm about to share.

Dex, for his part, seems to get that I need to collect my thoughts. I could tell he was mentally bracing for what I was about to share.

Looking him directly in the eyes, I laid it out for him. "First, what I'm about to tell you does not ever leave this room. You with me?" Dex nods his consent. I reiterate, "Your complete discretion is a must; I need your word, man."

Dex doesn't hesitate to give it, "You got it, I won't tell a soul. Now get on with it. I could cut the tension in this room with a butter knife. And quite frankly, you're scaring me. Did something happen with the girls?"

"Other than neither of us has heard from the girls all day, I don't know anything more," I state.

"I'm sure they are just out doing girl shit. What else is going on?" Dex rightfully questions.

"Okay. Yea. I need to start with the back story, you good with that?" I felt like I had to ask one more time.

Dex, sounding exasperated, says, "I'm good, man, I love story time, so go ahead and hit me. I'll hold my questions until the end, if that will help you get a move on."

I like Dex. He's a straightforward guy, and I never got the feeling that he couldn't be trusted. Now, I just needed to trust my instincts.

Taking a fortifying breath, I begin, "You know I'm a former special ops. What you don't know is that I was the captain of an elite task force team with the CIA. I'm not at liberty to divulge any other information about my former life beyond that."

I hesitate to gauge his comprehension; he appears cool as a cucumber. So, I continue, "I was 26 when I was able to retire from the CIA. I knew I was ready to start living my own life, but I wasn't sure where or what I wanted to do beyond that."

Dex remains focused, so I go on, "My next career fell into my lap. I have a buddy who has this 'famous friend' who was being stalked by a fan. They hired me to be their personal bodyguard and security detail. I was able to resolve the issue with the misguided fan after only a month on assignment."

"Word spread fast within the elite community, and as a result, I had a waiting list that could have kept me busy for the rest of my life. The accolades didn't sway me, and each client was just a paycheck to me." Dex nodded, so I continued, "I picked the assignments based on my gut instincts and the challenges the role would offer."

Dex walked to the fridge for a couple more beers, saying, "I get it, man, you needed to stay sharp."

I nod my agreement, his assumption wasn't far from the mark, so I continued, "A little over two years ago, a good friend of mine gave the Wilsons, Em's parents, my contact information. As a favor to my friend, I agreed to take the meeting."

"First, do you know anything about Em's parents?" I ask.

Dex shrugs, then says, "They're filthy rich and they don't have much of anything to do with Em."

"You're partly right," I inform. "Em's parents are rich, but I wouldn't say that they have little to do with their daughter."

Dex looked puzzled, so I continued, "From the first day that Em left for college until her last day, she had an undercover security detail on her. Her parents couldn't bear the thought of Em being away from home without anyone watching over her. The security firm only had a four-year contract, after which they recommended that no further surveillance was necessary. They pointed out that during those four years, there was no unusual behavior or activity observed."

"Okay, I can, and I can't see what this has to do with you. You just met Em a few years ago," Dex hedged.

"I'm not actually a paid superintendent for the DalRock," I blurt.

Dex doesn't say anything immediately, then, looking chagrined, he says, "Man, it didn't escape my notice that you lack the necessary skills to be a maintenance man, plus you never do any work around here."

I laugh at that; only Dex could find humor in all this. "I do stuff around here, maybe you just haven't noticed." Dex was shaking his head. I realized just then that Dex may seem easy-going, but he was observant. I have to ask, "Do you want me to continue with the details, or do you want me to just get to the point?"

Dex sobers and says, "I appreciate the option, but I want the details, then I'll ask some questions."

"Fair enough." So, I quickly continue, "The Wilsons concluded the contract with the security firm, but they disagreed with the firm's recommendation. I was sought out because of my security detail reputation and my military background."

"They wanted to hire me for two reasons. They wanted me to do reconnaissance work on the prior security team, and they wanted me to be Em's new low-level undercover bodyguard."

Dex was looking intrigued, so I powered on, "I had initially planned to decline the assignment. Based on the Wilsons' introduction, I knew I did not want to be a babysitter to a young 20-something woman. And my surveillance roles aren't taken lightly. It's a matter of life or death. Out of respect for my friend, I listened to what they had to say. The contract they were offering was a 5-year security role with the ability to extend to 10 years," I share.

"Damn, that's a long time," Dex adds.

"That alone was enough to solidify my resolve to decline. That's a long fucking assignment. Plus, it's bad business for one security firm to investigate another. Of course, they offered an obscene amount of money."

Taking a deep breath, I continue, "I was still at the point that I was determined to decline politely. But when I opened Em's dossier, her photos alone told me that something wasn't right. I felt an indescribable draw to Em, and it was at that moment that I knew I was going to take the assignment."

Dex did the universal hand gesture to keep going, so I did. "It was the pictures that cemented my decision after Mrs. Wilson presented her suspicions. She shared that when Em first left for college, she would call home often and visit on some weekends and all holidays. They noticed a substantial change around the end of Em's first year and an even bigger noticeable change during the first semester of her sophomore year. When Mrs. Wilson shared her concerns with the security team, they informed her that, upon reviewing the surveillance data, they found nothing suspicious. The security firm suggested that a behavior change is not uncommon for those just leaving home for the first time in their lives." When I caught Dex raising an eyebrow, I knew then that I had his full attention.

I continue, "When Em's parents tried to get information from Em, to ask her about her change in demeanor, she shut them down. She closed herself off from her family and rarely called or came for visits."

Dex, listening intently, picked up on my own opinion when he conspiratorially shared, "That is *not* normal behavior."

"I agree. Her parents confided to me that they reluctantly accepted the firm's suggestion and gave Em space. They stopped pushing her for visits or for anything more than what Em was willing to give them."

"It was Mrs. Wilson who couldn't or wouldn't accept this change in her daughter as normal. She felt certain that something was wrong. That Em wouldn't change her character and prefer isolation just because she was adjusting to college life. Then, Mrs. Wilson showed me Em's high school yearbooks, and I saw an outgoing, fun-loving, and vivacious young woman. She was featured in her high school yearbook at least a dozen times, showcasing her active, social lifestyle. In every photo, she was smiling."

Reluctantly, I share, "I have to tell you, Dex, the visual before and after transformation was remarkable. The picture I saw was unlike any previous photos. The girl in that photo was only a shell of herself. I left that day from the Wilsons with a 2-year contract, five large boxes of surveillance footage, pictures, activity logs, reports, and daily handwritten notes from the previous security firm."

Smirking, I say, "I had only a week to set up my cover story and now you're telling me I missed the mark?" Dex appeared lost in thought, but then what I said registered, and he laughed.

Dex then hesitantly asks, "I have to know, why are you telling me all of this now? And, before you answer that, it hasn't escaped my notice that you've been living here for about 2 years under a 2-year assignment."

Nodding, I say, "I know I gave you a lot of background, but what I'm about to tell you now is the complicated part." Dex nods for me to continue.

"You aren't wrong about the 2-year assignment deadline; it was up for renewal last month. Despite my best efforts to the contrary, the Wilsons extended the contract. And the reason I'm telling you this now is because the assignment became personal for me."

I let that sink in for a moment and took the other seat next to Dex's. Hell, I was still trying to come to terms with it myself.

Suddenly, Dex spoke as if waiting for the words to formulate in his mind. "You…care…about Em, more than a job and more than a friend." It sounded like a question, but he was making an observed statement.

I nod my consent. I felt a weight lift just by sharing that fact. I've known it, but I wouldn't allow myself to admit it, not to myself and especially not to Em. Yet sharing it with Dex made it feel substantial and surreal.

After a few moments, Dex asks, "What are you going to do about it?"

Already shaking my head no, I share, "Does it matter? No part of this scenario will end with us being together in any capacity. She will never trust me after this. You know her, Dex. She doesn't easily give her trust. She is so guarded. She only allows a handful of people into her inner circle."

Miserably, I force out, "Dex, she holds herself back from everyone and everything outside our group. If I come clean now, after lying to her for two years, it would mean losing her."

"And Dex, you gotta know, I don't just care about Em, I love her. It's one-sided and needs to stay that way." Admitting this to him now, I must also acknowledge it as a truth I had been realizing for myself.

After dropping that bomb, neither of us said a word. The next words I speak feel as though they are being ripped from my soul. "It's because I love her that she can never know the truth," I say, feeling trapped in my circumstances.

"You could just explain that..." Dex's statement trailed off.

Through clenched teeth, I inform, "No. I believe this betrayal has the power to destroy Em."

"Hold up, explain to me what you're planning to do about working for her parents and pretending to work here. How long do you think you can keep this up? And, after the Wilsons stop paying you, are you just leaving?" Dex says all of this with a calmness I know he doesn't feel. There's a bite of betrayal in the air. He's not happy with the situation or me.

"I'll answer all your questions, first let me explain the predicament around why I extended the contract with her parents." I was relieved that Dex was still willing to hear me out, even after learning I had lied and deceived him, too.

"After combing through boxes and digital files, I quickly ascertained that the surveillance logs were not thorough. There were obvious holes in the dates and the timelines. The process logs were not conclusive."

Shaking my head in disgust, I share, "It's crap work considering this agency is an industry leader that makes a shit ton of money for their 24-hour surveillance contracts. If you recall, they hired me to continue with low-level surveillance and to find out if any negligence had occurred from the prior agency."

Dex nods, so I go on, "With the help of my team, we've spent many hours cataloging everything from those five boxes and electronic files. To give you an idea of the volume, consider this. Our starting point was to record all the prior agency's data from Em's four years of college surveillance. We created a chronological list that cross-references the class rosters with any persons who were associated with Em in any capacity over those 4 years. We formulated a list of repeat associations and a list of persons she only associated with once. Every data entry has a time and date stamp."

Dex, looking intrigued, asks, "Sounds painful. What did you find out?"

"It's not complete. There's one aspect of Em's college surveillance that the prior agency ignored. We need that information cataloged so we can compare it to our formulated list. It's not easy either. There are 4 years of 24/7 video footage of the door to Em's off-campus apartment. And the shit part is, the prior security firm did not set up the cameras to record only when motion was activated."

"Oh man, that sounds like a big project," Dex confirms what I know to be true.

"It is. I'm pissed because this should have been discovered and addressed by my team before my 2-year contract was set to expire. In their defense, it wasn't until one of the team members sat down to view the actual video footage that they discovered a pattern. The reason the surveillance logs had holes in the dates and timelines was that they only logged what they physically saw during their drive-bys. He confirmed this by comparing the travel logs with the surveillance logs. They coincided."

"Shouldn't they have been required to sit outside her apartment and not do drive-bys?" Dex asked.

"Yes, that's essentially what 24/7 surveillance means. But from some notes we found, the personnel were instructed not to draw attention to themselves by Em. She was never supposed to find out that she had a security detail following her. That could explain the drive-by versus sitting outside her apartment in their car. After a while, that would be hard to pull off."

Shaking his head, Dex shares. "I can't imagine that Em wouldn't notice people following her or driving by routinely. I feel like she's more observant than that. Anyway, what has your team discovered from the videos?"

I agree about Em being observant now, but was she always? Not something I want to get into at this point. "Last month, I called in a favor. I sent the 35,000+hours of video footage to a Photo Forensics team that has contracted with the CIA before. It will take their expertise and manpower to identify all individuals who came and went from Em's unit. I not only want the time and date information from the video footage, but I also requested criminal background checks on each person. Once the forensic team compiles the information, the plan is to compare the captured photo images list with the chronological list my team created."

Do you think there's something to find? And, I have to ask. Should you even bother digging deeper? It's been what, six years? Em isn't that same girl," hedges Dex.

"I've asked myself these same questions. The simple answer: I'm contractually obligated not to leave a stone unturned. I'm not sure if I'll find anything of interest. I'm not sure if I'm thinking about any of this rationally anymore. That's my problem, I let my emotions get involved, and now I'm not sure I can trust my instincts," I say, hoping to let Dex know where my head was.

"What are your instincts telling you?" Dex questions.

"One of my team's specialties with the CIA was recon work. If my team finds any discrepancies, we will address them. My instincts tell me that not all avenues have been exhausted. Until that time, we are contractually and morally obligated to follow through on what her parents presented as evidence and what we now know to be oversight by the prior agency." I can see that Dex understands the magnitude of the situation.

I continue. "To answer your other questions, I tried to resign with the Wilsons based on my conflict where Em is concerned and because I currently have no concrete evidence to justify the continued cost."

Sighing, I admit, "Man, I went so far as to explain that it was in Em's best interest if I did not continue. That is when the protector becomes emotionally involved with those under their protection, mistakes can happen, lines get blurred, and the protector can no longer be trusted to make rational decisions."

Dex looks at me, his bullshit radar on high alert, saying, "That would never happen."

Nodding because he's right, I continue, "I then informed the Wilsons that although I would not extend the assignment, my team had one last avenue we were pursuing. I promised to provide them with the details when they became available."

Feeling defensive and needing a break, I get up and walk away, saying, "I'm still here and not just because of the assignment." I left the rest unsaid. Dex can interpret it how he wants because I still don't know what it all means.

Remembering that day, Mr. Wilson proved to me that I wasn't thinking clearly. He pointed out that he could not accept my resignation because he felt certain I would find something. The legal contract would be necessary to justify and support the investigative searches. He was correct; how did I miss that?

Suddenly, I felt exhausted and suggested we hit the couch, order some pizza, and watch the game. On the way out of the kitchen, I grab a couple more beers and the pizza delivery menu. The Cowboys were playing the Eagles, and both teams had five wins and two losses this season. It should be an exciting game.

As messed up as it all was, I knew where my head was at with all that I just shared. What I had no clue about was what Dex was thinking.

As I hand Dex his beer, he lays it out for me, "I want to be pissed at you, but I get it. I understand why you didn't share who you were or what you were doing. The inner turmoil must be a bitch. However, I want to go on record as saying that you need to trust Em with all of this. It's true she doesn't give her trust easily, but she did give it to you. Because of that, I know Em will forgive you. She might get upset, but she won't want to lose you forever. You have to give her that chance."

I don't say anything back to Dex. What can I say to make him understand all my fears when it comes to Em? Dipping my chin to let Dex know I heard him, I focus on the game. Focus isn't the right word. I'm looking in that direction, but I'm not seeing it.

On some level, I get what Dex is saying about Em. I know it's not fair for me to take that choice from her, but the risk is too high. I'm not willing to take a chance on losing her. I'd rather have her friendship and unrequited love than not have her in my life at all.

"Who do you predict is going to the Super Bowl this year?" This question from Dex brings me out of my head and back to the here and now.

"The Kansas City Chiefs are the favorites to win, followed by the San Francisco 49ers. I'd like to see the Cowboys make it. They are having a great season," I share.

"It would be nice to see the Cowboys win the whole thing. They are due. Maybe this year they won't choke." Dex says hopefully.

We talk stats and drink more beer. The Pizza delivery came, and we devoured it.

The text came in at 3:30 pm stating that the girls were at the beach and that we should plan on dinner without them. I was relieved. Dex, on the other hand, was pissed. His angry comment surprises me, "What the hell are they playing at? That is not cool."

"Guess they wanted some girl time, so they took it." I'm trying to hide the fact that I'm annoyed, too.

Dex tersely snaps back with, "They might have all agreed to head to the beach for girl time, but I guarantee Roxy was the ringleader on icing us out."

That's the opening I need to broach the subject that has been on my mind, "So you and Roxy, huh?"

I could see the denial was on the tip of his tongue, but a lot was shared between us today. So, I was relieved when his following words confirmed what I already knew to be true.

Taking a deep breath, Dex says, "Yep, I'm into her, but it's complicated. We started as *fuck buddies,* her words, not mine, and she's not willing to go beyond that. She can't see past my reputation, nor will she let me in there. She refuses to admit that we could have a relationship. Instead, for the first time in my life, I'm someone's dirty little secret."

"Do you have a plan?" I ask.

To which Dex replies, "I'll keep being whatever she'll allow me to be in her life, and hopefully one day she'll want more from me. Oh, and I gotta say, please don't share this with Em or Sarah. Roxy will crush my nuts like a squirrel on crack if she finds out I even told you."

"That's your story to share. Not mine." I concede. Damn, poor Dex. I had nothing else to add to that, and since he delivered his message in a straight-to-the-point manner, I knew he didn't want to talk about the Roxy situation anymore.

Plus, I'm the last person who should offer up relationship advice. I had no prior experience with women beyond the mutually agreed-upon hookup.

It was close to 5:00 pm when Dex decided to go home. As I walk him to the door, he turns to face me, saying, "To the grave, man," as he gives his heart a fist bump. Then, from down the hall, he yells, "You gotta tell her, man!"

Chapter Eight
GUILT
Emily

Monday morning came early for me. I was totally dragging ass because, although I was beat, I simply could not sleep last night. Those fucking text messages consumed my mind.

There were several other reasons sleep eluded me. I was worried about Roxy and Dex, worried that Dex would hurt Roxy, and then I was concerned about Sarah and Michael's relationship. They were moving fast, considering they had just recently met each other. But what did I know about that?

What really had my mind overactive were the barrage of text messages on my phone when I finally enabled my notifications last night. As I was getting in the shower, I could hear my phone pinging like warning bells as the messages filtered in.

My shower was quick, and I hurried through my nightly routine of brushing, flossing, and moisturizing. I knew without a doubt that I wouldn't like the messages. I had waited until I climbed into bed before I started reading from the top of my unread messages.

Alec: Hey, what are you girls up to today? 10:00 am

Alec: Is everything okay? 11:36 am

Alec: Where are you guys? Roxy and Sarah haven't responded either. 12:05 pm

Dex: Hey, 12:10 pm

Dex: Where'd you girls go? 12:30 pm

Alec: Please let me know you're okay. 1:10 pm

Alec: I'm sorry about Friday night. 1:30 pm

Dex: You girls shouldn't shut us out. 1:32 pm

Em: At the beach for the day, will not make football tonight, see you tomorrow. 3:30 pm

Alec: At least I know you're okay and not in a ditch somewhere. 3:31 pm

Dex: Thanks for taking the time to inform your friends of your whereabouts. Hope that consideration didn't hurt too much. 3:33 pm

Alec: Are you home yet? 6:15 pm

Alec: Please text me when you get this — doesn't matter what time. 7:10 pm

I had deliberated on what message to text back for several moments. I knew nothing I could type in an IM would convey my sincere regret for how we treated them. I thought I'd send a quick message now and follow through with verbal groveling in the morning.

Em: To Dex- *We're home, went to Fisherman's for dinner, sorry.* *9:12 pm*

Em: To Alec- *We're home, went to Fisherman's for dinner. 9:12 pm*

Em: To Alec- *Hey, I'm so sorry to make you worry unnecessarily. We needed some girl time, but no excuse, I should have let you know sooner. 9:13 pm*

Alec: *I'm glad you're home safe. Thanks for letting me know. Sleep well. 9:14 pm*

Dex: *Good. 9:22 pm*

I wanted to respond with something, anything, to make myself feel less like a total ungrateful friend. But there was nothing else to say, at least not via text.

The guilt was the main reason I couldn't sleep. After reading the messages, guilt had reared up and slapped the snot out of me. I felt like a total heel; even worse, I felt sick to my stomach.

Dex and Alec were my friends and my chosen family. I treated both of them as if they meant nothing to me. I owed them both a huge apology and a chocolate cake for each. I wasn't naive enough to think my chocolate cake had the power of forgiveness, but I hoped my begging and pleading would make up for where my cake failed.

As I lay down, exhausted from a day in the sun with drinks and seafood, I was sure I'd pass right out. But no such luck. My brain decided to throw a party in my head and invite all of my life's sucky moments. And, even though I was only 25 years old, I had plenty of them.

Feeling both physically and emotionally exhausted, I had no fight left in me to block out my brain's recriminations.

Nothing for it, I had to let my brain sift through my failings and shortcomings with as much solemnity as I could muster. My anxiety issues proved that my brain loved to play the guilt card and the what-ifs game. Unfortunately, I was rarely the winner.

Now I'm facing Monday, sleep-deprived, with eyes gritty and hair a tangled mess, and my brain is already busy conjuring up those feelings of guilt again.

Making a much-needed cup of coffee, I notice a piece of paper under my front door. Everyone knows nothing good comes from a note delivered under the door.

Retrieving the folded sheet of paper, I read, "Need to talk, let me know when it is a good time, Alec."

Chapter Nine
THE DILEMMA
Emily

That note was taunting me. If Alec was mad about Sunday and wanted to yell at me, why not just call or text me? The formality of leaving a note is confusing and prolongs my discomfort. The sooner I can let him know when we can talk, the better. It's the right and responsible thing to do. But I was being a chicken shit.

What did I think Alec was going to tell me? He would probably share his displeasure with me for not responding to his test messages. Or it had nothing to do with yesterday.

Fat chance. Alec has never asked to see me outside of group events. I was acting like a petulant child, hearing her mom say, *"Just wait till your dad gets home."* The anticipation of the impending punishment was causing heightened fear.

Not knowing what to expect from the meeting with Alec intensified my anxiety. It doesn't matter what his intentions are or what he wants to discuss; I have to meet with him to find out. Tonight was as good a night as any.

Roxy, Sarah, and I met at our building's bistro for lunch. I wanted to ask if either of them received a cryptic, under-the-door request to meet with Alec or Dex, but I was too much of a chicken to ask outright. Instead, I asked about their evening plans, making sure nothing had changed with Roxy.

Roxy confirmed she was still going to her Pilates class and then grabbing a drink or two with some of the other girls from there that she also works with.

"You're welcome to join us, Em," Roxy adds as she takes a big bite of her sandwich.

"No thanks," I respond. The girls know I enjoy curling up with a good book and a glass of wine, so they don't always push me to join them during the week. Since I didn't want to lie about my potential plans with Alec, I'm relieved neither of them asked me about my plans.

If tonight didn't work for Alec, I'd happily stay home and read some Half Moon Hollow. I loved the shenanigans Dick and Jane's posse got into.

Sarah shared that she has a shift tonight at The Rusty Nail. With a smirk, she adds, "And I will be getting a personal escort to my car after my shift."

She seems excited about this guy, Michael. I was happy for her, so I told her, "You guys seem good together." Sarah just smiled almost shyly, but I knew better.

"Hey, Sarah, ask Michael if Eric asked about me. If Eric wants my number, tell Michael it's okay to pass it on," states Roxy in a matter-of-fact tone.

Interesting. Both Sarah and I look at each other. Sarah mumbles, "Sure, Roxy."

The next time Sarah and I had a chance to talk, I wanted to find out what she thought of Roxy's request. For my part, I believed Roxy had only flirted with Eric to make Dex jealous.

After lunch, when we all went back to work, I had one more personal task to finish. I needed to do it before I lost my nerve and chickened out. I sent Alec a message about possibly meeting this evening.

Em: I'm available after work today. 1:15 pm

Alec: Great, I'll get Chinese, your place or mine. 1:17 pm

Okay, the butterflies in my stomach were having a party. I was nervous. What did it say about me if I told him to come to my place? I didn't want to send the wrong message inadvertently. Was his place any better? I mentally chided myself for being silly and making a bigger deal of this than was necessary.

Em: Your place works. 1:32 pm

Alec: See you around 6:30 pm. 1:35 pm

Em: Okay. 1:35 pm

I did it. I'm having dinner with Alec tonight. Just him and me. "OMG!" I immediately felt sick from the butterflies in my stomach and the whirlwind of thoughts racing through my mind.

My mind took off and started planning my evening. I made a mental checklist of what I needed to make the chocolate cake. I had to make a quick run to the grocery store for some eggs, but I had everything else on hand. The cake would still be too warm to frost, but I could do that after we ate. Should I go in my work clothes? Did I shave this morning? Should I bring wine? "Stop!" I shout, before realizing I'd said that out loud.

Joey, the little guy who sat closest to me, leaned back in his chair and waved with a big smile on his face. Joey tended to handle me like I was one buckle away from a straitjacket. He probably thinks I escaped from a mental hospital or an asylum.

It's not my fault that he can hear me talking to myself or overhear my phone calls. Most of the time, he only catches a one-sided conversation, but when Roxy calls, he gets an earful.

Hurrying through my tasks for the day, and since I had driven myself to work, I decided leaving early was a great idea. I had to get to the store, then get home to start the cake right away. I'd bake the *'I'm a little shit,'* apology cake for Dex another night when I had more time.

Traffic wasn't too bad yet. My racing mind was my biggest complaint. It had been hard for me to stay focused on my work after Alec confirmed our dinner plans. I couldn't help but think about tonight. I was acting like a giddy teenage girl going to her boyfriend's first hangout and watch TV date. I couldn't hold back the part of me that secretly wished this dinner with Alec meant something more. As I thought it, I chided myself for letting those thoughts into my mind. This evening was just two friends having dinner, with a side of guilt for not telling him about our Sunday plans. I was overthinking the whole thing.

Corralling my thoughts toward more legitimate imaginings, I resign myself to the talk. I knew I deserved a tongue lashing from Alec, and not the fun kind. I could tell from his text messages that he had been legitimately worried. Dex, on the other hand, seemed annoyed.

Then I wondered if Dex would schedule a meeting with me as well. It's no secret that I'm supposed to be the voice of reason among the three of us girls, the rational one of the trio. I knew then, as I know now, that I didn't handle the beach trip or Roxy's approach to going incognito the way I should have.

That's what this dinner is about. I don't need to make it into more than it is. I had let Roxy's issues and comments sway my better judgment.

I made it home; the cake would take close to 40 minutes, and I barely had enough time. Usually, I strip the moment I arrive home to get more comfortable. But, since I was in a rush to get the guilt cake in the oven, I threw on an apron in hopes of saving my blush-colored blouse and brown slacks. Now what should I do? It's 6:20 pm, should I go as I am? Feeling overdressed and like I'm trying too hard. No, I should go casual. It's not a date. Plus, he won't care. I showed up at his place in footie pajamas for brunch last Christmas.

Mentally, I slap myself for getting hung up on this. I grab my yoga pants, exercise bra, and the large shirt I wore yesterday before changing into the beach outfit. Slipping my feet into my Old Navy flip-flops, I grab the still-warm cake wrapped in a towel and the can of frosting. Heading for the door, I snag my keys from the small entry table and practically jog to the elevators.

Alec's unit is two floors above mine. Taking the elevator up, I don't hesitate to knock. I was proud of my heroics until Alec opened his door. Holy hell, I hoped I wasn't visibly drooling.

His large body was definitely hot, but also imposing and almost predatory. He wore a tight black t-shirt that stretched across broad shoulders and tapered just above his narrow hips. His faded jeans hugged the thick muscles of his thighs perfectly. He was barefoot. That alone made my mind wonder what he'd look like naked. Yep, my mind went there.

He was living up to his nickname of the Latin Hottie. Taking it all in, I knew my mind would replay this image multiple times and probably for multiple orgasms.

Coming here alone, seeing him in this relaxed state, looking both approachable and perfect, I knew I was in trouble. And the problem I was referring to had nothing to do with the potential scolding from ignoring his text message.

Chapter Ten
REALIZATION
Emily

"Hi," I say, hoping he can't tell where my thoughts had gone. No one likes to be objectified.

Alec steps aside for me to enter, but before I can pass him, he loosely tags me around the neck with his arm. The momentum brings my body against his side as he says, "You're safe," then kisses the top of my head. Just as quickly as it happens, he releases me, saying, "Let's eat before the food gets cold."

I was momentarily stunned. I could count on one hand the number of times Alec showed any physical affection to any of us in the group. Then what he said registered, and I found the two-word comment, *"you're safe,"* odd.

Did it mean something more than the obvious? Was the comment meant to reassure Alec that I was indeed safe, or was it meant to reassure me that I was safe with him? And was that a brotherly kiss on the head?

Before I could get too wrapped up in my thoughts, Alec was back in front of me, taking the cake and frosting while directing me to the couch. Looking right at me with a playful smile on his face, he says, "I was wondering where that shirt went."

Alec then headed for the kitchen, asking, "Do you want a plate and fork, or do you prefer to eat your Chinese out of the box?"

"I'll eat out of the box, but I'll take the fork," I retort. "Also, this is my shirt from my closet. I don't know what you're talking about," I say with a giggle.

I giggled. *WTF?* Why do I feel nervous and off kilter? I had more game as a teenager. I don't know what's wrong with me right now.

Alec was smiling when he popped his head out of the kitchen to ask what I wanted to drink: "Do you want soda, beer, or wine?"

"I'll have a glass of wine, thank you." I probably needed some liquid courage to calm my anxiety and my apprehension.

Waiting for him to return with our drinks, I realize that Alec was being all smiley and approachable, considering he was upset with me yesterday. I don't think upset is the right emotion. His text messages showed he was worried, if not marginally annoyed.

He could have rung my neck as I entered; instead, he kissed the top of my head. I never quite knew what to think or feel about Alec. He made me feel off balance and lately pissy during our one-on-one conversations, but I felt relaxed with him in our group setting.

I knew I lusted after him, but I bet Roxy and Sarah both have done the same. It's a normal reaction to someone as handsome and mysterious as Alec. At least, that's the story I'm telling myself, and I'm sticking to it.

As Alec hands me my glass of wine, his gaze is intense, both exciting and confusing me. Taking the seat beside me on his couch, he was studying me before saying, "You had me worried yesterday."

His probing, accusatory stare was making me twitchy, and was it hot in here?

I was still trying to get past the image of him as he opened his front door. So, absently, I respond with, "I know."

Alec's brow quirked.

I knew I needed to take responsibility for my part in his worry. As I stared right back at him, he seemed to be trying to read me. I did not want him to be able to read all the feelings or thoughts his nearness made surface within me.

I took a rather large sip of wine before admitting, "What I meant to say was sorry."

Alec didn't respond as he kept looking at me. For some reason I couldn't explain, Alec's stare made me feel exposed, vulnerable, and a little squirmy. It was like he was seeing and revealing the parts of me that I would otherwise hide.

Before I could look away, I saw several emotions fleeting across Alec's features. As I had that thought, I had the realization that Alec wasn't masking his feelings from me. His usual stoic expression was absent; his ever-present shield was gone.

For the first time with Alec, I felt fear. I wasn't afraid he'd harm me; I was fearful of how seeing his emotions made me feel.

In his eyes, I saw that he cared; he had been concerned and was now relieved. My parents cared about me, but in his probing stare, it seemed to mean more.

I'm startled when Alec bends his head towards mine and asks, "Em, what are you thinking right now? I felt your body go tense."

Shaking my head, I stay silent. What could I say anyway? You scare me, which isn't completely true. Or, your eyes make me want things I had long ago buried and forgotten.

For just a moment, I surrendered to happy thoughts and fantasized about how Alec might kiss. Would his touch be tender or forceful? Would he be demanding? In bed, would he be considerate or selfish? My inner carnal desire for him made my outer body shiver.

"Don't," I hear Alec warn in a low guttural tone. That snapped me back in the moment. Looking at him closely, I see a look of pain and discomfort.

Oh, no! Did I say something out loud again?

"Alec?" I rasp as I continue to look directly in his eyes. Not breaking eye contact, Alec takes my food container with his and sets both on the coffee table.

Turning back to face me fully, he warns, "Em, you cannot look at me like that. I'm not strong enough to resist you."

Oh God, he knew what I was thinking. Alec really did have superpowers. Now I felt mortified. Turning bright red, I got up to escape, though I wasn't sure where to go, but I knew I couldn't sit under his scrutiny any longer.

At first, Alec let me get up and walk away. But it didn't last long. Before I knew what was happening, Alec had me up against the wall of his living room with our bodies aligned in all the right places.

I wasn't scared, although suddenly I was breathing heavily. The connection was carnal and exciting, and the dormant parts of my body came alive. I've never experienced this level of want for any man. My body was responding to his nearness, and my desire for him flared to life.

Although my body had needs, my experience wasn't enough to know what I needed from him in that moment. I felt frustrated with myself and the situation. If only I could channel some Roxy or Sarah, but nothing they ever shared felt right for this moment with Alec.

What felt right, what felt natural, was to lean into Alec more deeply to align our bodies more intimately. I could feel that he was not immune to me, as evidenced by his hard length that was nestled expertly against my core. Was he going to kiss me? Did I want him to kiss me?

Reaching a hand up, I remove my wayward hair from his whiskers and unconsciously whimper his name, "Alec." I could hear the pleading in my voice, but felt powerless to control it.

Then, just as abruptly as he had me against the wall, Alec let me go, and instantly we lost the connection we had.

I stood there unmoving; I was so confused. Feelings of hurt and humiliation reared their ugly heads. The sting of rejection was a slow burn I felt down to my toes. Alec started this; he's the one who grabbed me. I only reacted to what he initiated.

Oh shit, was it me that started it? He said Don't. What have I done? Alec is my friend, and I've put him in an awkward spot. It was I who took it further. I can't believe I practically begged him to do something, anything, to douse the burn of desire I was feeling.

His response was visceral, as any man faced with a clingy woman would experience. I knew better than to let my feelings cloud my perception of him. Of course, he would not feel the same for me. I was an inexperienced child in comparison to him.

"I'm sorry, Alec, that was my fault," I admit in a whisper.

"Em, don't talk," Alec demands, and in a softer voice says, "I need to think for a minute." *Alex was thinking, all right; he was thinking that this was all Dex's fault. Dex had convinced him that coming out to Em was the right thing to do. But now, he was filled with doubt and panic.* Just then, Alec saw that Em was experiencing some panic of her own.

"Alec, no. It's okay, let's pretend that didn't happen. I'll heat our food, and we can finish our dinner and have another drink," I quickly stammer out.

"Shut up, Em!" Alec barks as he heads to the kitchen. "Em, sorry, just give me a damn minute, please."

I blinked; the comment came from the kitchen, where Alec had practically run. He was now keeping the opening of the kitchen bar between us. His telling me to shut up annoyed me, but I felt a lot was riding on us having the talk he initially asked me over for. So, I stayed quiet. Well, for about a minute, as I opened my mouth to say something, not sure what, Alec held up a hand in protest. I couldn't help but glare at him; he was dragging out my humiliation.

I saw the moment Alec had his thoughts in order. He visibly straightened his shoulders, and his full attention was on me. My jaw went slack. His eyes were not only a chocolate brown; they were blazing with beautiful flecks of gold. He was staring at me with such an intensity, I was afraid any minute I'd turn into a big puddle of goo.

Then I hear him in a calm, controlled voice say, "Em, this was not supposed to happen, but it did, and I honestly can't hide my feelings any longer. I have a personal interest in you. You have become important to me. I don't only want to protect you, I *need* to keep you safe, and I need you to trust me."

Looking at him, I see the sincerity in his eyes. I'm unsure how to feel, and I'm equally unsure what to say. It must show on my face because Alec quickly goes on, "Em, I know this is not right, and it's a lot to throw at you at once, but I had to let you know."

"Alec, I don't know what to do or say," I whisper back. Honestly, I need him to lay it out for me. In that moment, I was scared, not of him, but I feared losing him if I reacted the wrong way.

I've always felt drawn to Alec; I thought we had a different level of closeness than I had with Dex. It wasn't just that he held the starring role in my dreams. It was more. I already felt safe with him around me, like he would take a bullet for me or even kill for me.

But thinking it meant more was just childish imaginings, a fantasy world of my creation. I was twisting the bond of our friendship into more than it was. Deep down, I knew I was not capable of more than being a friend to him. So, why was I allowing my mind to wander? I was giving my dreams headspace to think about the fantasies that can never come true.

"Sweetheart, you don't have to do or say anything. I'm not trying to pressure you; actually, that's what I hope to avoid." I watch Alec take a deep breath before continuing, "Em, I'm putting myself out there, I'm letting you know how I feel upfront, and what you decide to do with this information is entirely your decision."

I was stunned. Stunned, speechless, and unable to form a coherent thought for what I should say back to Alec. There was a part of me that felt hurt. Why was he doing this? His declaration could ruin our friendship, just as it did with Dex and Roxy, and now Alec has instigated this.

Alec had moved closer to me, and I hadn't even realized it. He was looking at me with a hint of sadness I couldn't comprehend, "You don't have to make any decisions now. And Em, our continued friendship is not contingent on your decision. I would rather have you in my life as my friend than not have you at all."

He *can* read my mind.

Chapter Eleven
REGRETS – PRESENT DAY
Alec

It was shortly after I told Em she didn't need to make any decisions right now that she made the decision to leave. Neither of us ate much of the Chinese food, and our drinks were still half full. It was a visual confirmation that this evening didn't go well.

Sitting down heavily on the couch, I grab my now lukewarm beer. I felt empty and raw inside. My conversations with Dex the day before and with Em today were both haunting me. My brain replayed the conversations over and over.

Too little too late, but I can now see a hundred ways I could have handled or communicated the situation with Em better. Unfortunately, I can't go back and change what I did or how I did it.

For a man who specialized in reconnaissance work, I dropped the ball with Em. I failed to conduct proper intelligence collection and instead entered the mission only marginally prepared.

As a result, I failed to communicate what was essential to the goal or share what she needed to know. Instead, I made assumptions and presented everything recklessly. Just because I felt confident about my feelings for her didn't mean she thought the same about me.

I fucked up. And now, I was disgruntled with myself for allowing Dex to influence my better judgment. I knew better than most that life was not about rainbows and unicorns, and I knew that better than most. What we seek is rarely what we get.

The truth is, I wanted to believe Dex when he said that Em wouldn't let anything come between our friendship. I took that to heart. His words helped convince me that she would value our group's unity enough to forgive any indiscretion.

But Dex was wrong. No one will need to tell me I hurt Em with my admission about my feelings for her; the fact that she ran says it all.

My admission challenged the very fabric of her small, highly selective family unit. I saw the hesitation, the disappointment, and the betrayal in her beautiful eyes. She was terrified by what I shared, and the look she gave me will fucking haunt me forever.

Instinctually, I knew then that telling her how I felt would be the only truth I could share. She would not be able to handle knowing who I really was and why I was initially there. Em can never learn of my role in her life nor of her parents' involvement.

All I can hope for now is that Em doesn't shut me out of her life. My life was beginning to be mine to live, and it was because of Em that, for the first time in my adult life, post-CIA Special Ops, I wanted more out of it.

Now that I am a civilian, I have the freedom to settle down and live for myself. I served my country well; now it's time to do something for my own happiness and future.

Once I allowed myself to acknowledge that my feelings for Em ran much deeper than the surface, I was reluctant to act on them, and that was for good reason. Based on Em's quick departure, I should have followed my instincts. Dex meant well, but I knew better. I had foolishly and desperately wanted him to be right.

It had been several months since I began taking the necessary steps to settle down in one place. I bought my own unit and started a new security analysis venture. It felt good to make some permanent plans. My work with the CIA required me to travel worldwide, and the missions could last months or even years. In my role as a bodyguard, I traveled wherever my assignment took me, often being away for months at a time.

My new security company, Ace Checkpoint Security, was local to Houston. Some of my operatives from my Special Ops team have joined me in my business venture. These measures allow me the freedom to establish permanent residence and hopefully one day have a wife and family. Unconsciously and naively, Em has been at the forefront of my mind throughout all these plans to settle down.

However, I'm unable to think about the future right now. I couldn't see anything beyond the fear and pain in Em's eyes. The thought of hurting her made my chest ache. The thought of losing her left me feeling hopeless. The small amount of Chinese food I did consume wasn't sitting well with me.

Em has a way of lighting up any room she enters. Her personality and her kindness make her a treasured friend. She is loyal to a fault. Her beauty is not just on the outside, but also within. And her friendship means the world to me.

Admittedly, the churning in my stomach and the ache in my chest are from the overwhelming need for her to trust me. To want me.

I told her that whatever she decided would not affect our friendship. Keeping my word only works if she trusts that I will never ask for more than she is willing to give. I'd accept whatever she gave me, but what I couldn't handle was not having her in my life at all.

Remaining friends should be my main focus. Of course, I want her to feel safe with me. And I hope she trusts me enough to share if anything happened to her during her college years.

All these thoughts sounded so noble, but the truth is, I want all of her. I want a future with her. But at this point, I knew it was a pipe dream at best.

If Em ever learns the truth about who I am, how will she trust me again with anything? How will she feel knowing that her friendship with me started as a lie? Although we became true friends, I continued to deceive her for over 2 years.

I know firsthand that trust is the necessary component required for genuine friendships and relationships. In Special Ops, trust could be the difference between life and death. And I'd recklessly thrown caution to the wind and challenged it all in one single night.

On top of all that, I knew that Em felt responsible for how we both responded to our body's closeness. It wasn't her fault. I feel like an ass for letting her leave, thinking she was the one who crossed the line.

The fault lay solely with me. I had this delusional plan to lay it all out for Em. To come clean about who I was and why I was in her life. To let her know how I felt about her and what she meant to me. But then I opened my door to her, and everything in my mind scrambled.

She was looking at me as if she were mentally undressing me. I could interpret her hungry gaze. It shattered my resolve to come clean. My big head was losing the battle over my little head, and I couldn't think straight.

Pulling her against my body was the dumbest thing I've done in a long time. I told myself I did it to comfort myself because I was so relieved she was safe. Yeah, that was total bullshit. I wanted her. Seeing my shirt on her messed with my inner possessive caveman. Kissing her hair filled my senses with her sweet, honeyed scent, a mix of her shampoo and Em's unique smell. I knew right then I was fucked, so why didn't I abort the mission?

I knew instantly that my split-second lapse in judgment with Em had compromised my control and my noble plans. Maintaining her trust wasn't the priority at that moment because my jeans had suddenly become a lot tighter. My mind could only think about how much I craved to have *all* of Em.

Recognizing my mistake and showing weakness, I fought to bring us back on even footing. I used our dinner as a catalyst to move past the temptation and take back control.

On the couch, Em had given me a look that I struggled to ignore. It was *the* look. She was only responding to the heat she saw in my eyes. That's when I tried to warn her that I wasn't strong enough. I tried to get the evening's agenda back on track and to tell her everything. I had good intentions.

But as I was looking at Em, her beauty, her unintentional sexual pull, and the desire I could see mirrored in her eyes, it was my undoing. I lost the hold I had on the situation, and my body reacted before I could think better of it.

Pinning her up against the wall, with our bodies intimately pressed together, I lost the battle against my better judgment. Em felt amazing against me; her more petite body fit perfectly against my much larger frame. It was such a heady feeling that momentarily, I was knocked off balance.

Then Em reacted with her body, looking at me with both longing and uncertainty. It was the latter that was equal to a large glass of ice water poured on my nether regions.

I jumped back to put space between us and regain my composure. But it was too late; I saw the flash of hurt and rejection that Em tried to hide before she gave in to the embarrassment.

I should have told her that she didn't do anything wrong and that she wasn't at fault. But instead, I snapped at her.

The truth is, I didn't want her to discount her body's uncensored response to me. It gave me hope that Em might, or one day might, feel the same way about me as I did for her.

Tonight is going to be a long night: Em and the what ifs are already consuming my thoughts.

My mind kept replaying everything that transpired between Em and me from every angle. My brain was searching for any sliver of hope. Instead of finding hope, I saw several ways I fucked this whole thing up. Regret was never a friend you wanted sleeping with you, but I didn't know how to get rid of it or move past it.

One of the biggest regrets is that I lost my chance to tell her the whole truth. I saw fear in her eyes. Because of that fear, I no longer believed Dex's theory that Em would forgive me. My instincts were yelling at me to take all the rest to the grave.

Seeing Em gather her keys and walk out my door had been symbolic of closing the door on my hopes and dreams

Chapter Twelve
THREE DAYS LATER
– DAMAGED
Emily

It had been three long days since I walked out of Alec's unit. The memories of how good he made me feel in our brief moment of intimacy still challenged my resolve to leave. But it was Alec who pulled away from our heated embrace. Adding to the confusion was that his actions and his words were at odds with each other.

Of course, my gifted brain knew exactly what to think to demolish my own self-esteem and sense of worth. Why was it so difficult to accept that Alec had a personal interest in me and needed to protect me? He said those things, yet I still walked away from him.

Adding the physical element was likely the trigger for both of us. For me, I knew deep down I couldn't trust my feelings, and that was why I had to leave. Alec made me feel things I hadn't allowed myself to feel in years, to want things that I can't allow myself to want.

It was those moments of disbelief, like hearing him say that he *needed* to keep me safe; although a balm to my soul, I couldn't allow myself to accept it.

Running was my only option. All I could think was that I needed to try and keep him safe from the true me, who's damaged and unworthy. I couldn't let myself admit how much I wanted Alec. How much I needed him. Or how deep, how genuine, my feelings were surfacing for him. I needed to keep him as a friend; that has to be the most important thing for me.

Alec shared his feelings with me, and I panicked. I can't change the past, and I would if I could. If I could change it, I'd go back to my first year at college. Now, that's a thought I can't afford to linger on.

Three days is a long time to feel regret and the void that Alec's absence has caused. Have we ever gone so many days without talking, texting, or running into each other? The answer was no, and I only had myself to blame.

Rubbing my eyes, I felt exhausted. The magnitude of the situation weighed heavily on me. These past few nights, I lay in bed for hours before sleep finally decided to grace me with its presence. My mind would not shut off. I kept revisiting every detail from the evening with Alec.

In the end, I realized I didn't understand that evening at all. What actually happened? What part did I play, and what part did he play? Nothing about that night made any sense to me. The more I thought about it, the less I understood what had happened.

Alec said he had feelings for me; he was giving me the choice to accept it as truth, rather than pressuring me. More than anything, it seemed he was asking me to trust him. To believe what he was telling me, and ultimately, the decision to take it further was mine. But he didn't know that what he was asking was something I was incapable of giving him.

No one knew that I was an imposter; I rode the shirttails of Roxy and Sarah to hide behind the fact that I was too conservative, boring, and damaged. Their philosophy on dating was to try as many as possible until the *perfect* man came along. I was incapable of even contemplating that approach.

The fact was, I wanted so much more than I allowed myself to believe was possible for me.

My fairytale, if I could plan it, would be to meet a man who loved me despite my flaws, a man who could heal the parts of me that are broken. The man of my fantasy would want a friend first and a lover second. Our goal would be to have a true partner to share life with.

The sad truth is that I never even looked for my fantasy man. I didn't even try because I had no trust in my decisions. I knew firsthand that making bad decisions and trusting the wrong person was the easy part. It's living with the consequences of a poor choice that will destroy you.

I won't let myself try for the fantasy because, for me, the fantasy is out of my self-inflicted reach. I'd accepted a long time ago that I was okay without the *perfect* man. I was happy with the two great guy friends in my life and my girls.

There's Dex. I consider him one of my closest confidants. We spend a lot of one-on-one time together because he's my trainer. Actually, instead of trainer and trainee, it's more that we now work out together. Even on weekends, we run at least five miles on either Saturday or Sunday.

Dex challenges me to push outside my comfort zone. What makes our friendship work is that we don't pry. If we have something on our minds, we can feel safe sharing it, but we don't cross the line into soliciting information.

Then there's Alec. He's been a close friend, but at a distance. His stoic and mysterious facade doesn't intimidate me anymore. His presence alone causes me to feel safe. He exudes control. Never giving too much away.

On occasion, he is a silent ally when it comes to our group's shenanigans. Outwardly, he maintains a neutral stance within the group; we are all aware of this, and we have mutually accepted that this is just the way it is. He will not, despite our multiple attempts, wade into any discussions or debates. It is so annoying. And he never chooses sides.

Alec is also my wet dream man. I tried and failed to think of any other guy, but nope, my brain keeps conjuring up Alec. It's irritating as hell, and it pisses me off.

To make matters worse, I now have firsthand knowledge to add to my fun time fantasies. When I close my eyes, I can still see Alec standing in his open door, looking ruggedly perfect and tempting. His beautiful face expressed so many unguarded emotions. Lowering his shield made him even more attractive and approachable. His eyes had shone brightly with longing. At least, that was my brain's interpretation.

Add to the knowledge that my body molded perfectly with his, as he pressed me into the wall, and how it felt with his hard length wedged between my thighs, and now, my fantasies have become my daymares. With his arms wrapped around me like a cocoon, I had quickly realized that having him in my arms was so much better than having him only in my dreams.

What haunts me the most about that night is the knowledge that he had verbally put himself out there, and I gave him nothing of myself in return. He looked me straight in the eyes, willing to risk his heart, and I ran. I wanted to tell him how I felt about him; I truly did. I just didn't know how. I didn't even know what to say. I'd suppressed my interest in Alec for so long that it felt strange to acknowledge it, let alone say it out loud.

Unprovoked, I realize that feeling safe with any one person has seemed so out of reach for me, but now it's something I deeply desire. Not with just any person. Nope. My thoughts centered around Alec.

The sad part is, I'm not capable of giving more of myself beyond friendship. The risk of trying and failing is just too high. I don't need more than Alec's friendship, and I'm not looking for love. In fact, I'm not looking for anything at all because life hasn't been fair.

Everything a young woman could dream of, the idea of love, her hopes, and happily ever afters, was ripped away from me in a single night.

Unbidden, my thoughts start to get all tangled up like a giant rubber band ball made up of layer after layer of misconceptions and fears. The tightening in my chest is the only warning of an impending panic attack.

Bouncing from thought to thought, my mind challenges the theory that I'm incapable of more. I still have feelings. I still have dreams and desires. I care deeply for Alec, and I feel drawn to him, not just in the emotional sense, but also in the physical. The issue is trust, in him and in myself. The collateral damage for a wrong decision is the potential loss of my friend. That price is too high to pay.

The happenings of that day at Alec's apartment have bounced in and out of my thoughts. In the quiet, the scene plays over and over in my head like a bad sitcom rerun. The more I think about it, the less I understand what Alec was asking of me.

I remember Alec saying that it wasn't supposed to happen and that it wasn't right. What wasn't right? What exactly happened? We didn't even kiss.

He said he didn't want to pressure me into anything, that I was important to him. He wanted to protect me and keep me safe. What he didn't say was what he wanted *from* me.

So consumed with my thoughts, I startle when my desk phone rings. It was Roxy. Just hearing her voice gives me a much-needed reprieve from my mangled thoughts, enabling me to repress what was beginning to be close to a full-on panic attack.

As per usual, Roxy is talking before I can get the receiver up to my ear, "Hey chickie, Sarah called, she wants us to come to

The Rusty Nail for Happy hour. Michael is also planning to be there. I figured we could also grab dinner while we're at it."

"You don't have to ask me twice. You know I love the burgers."

The Rusty Nail doesn't look like it would serve the best burgers in the world, but it does. The thick hamburger patty is juicy to the point of dripping, and the bun has a generous spread of butter on top. When the wait staff delivers the burgers to your table, they also bring a container of wet ones with the ketchup and mustard condiments.

It is a delicious mess. And, if that wasn't enough, the waitstaff also brings a massive mountain of fries or onion rings. The single order covers an entire tray. *Nirvana.*

"I'll have to run an additional five miles this weekend to combat the fat consumption. You could join me on my run, you know?" I say, already knowing Roxy wouldn't join me, she rarely chose running as her means of exercise.

Roxy snorts, "Will the guy from Texas Chainsaw Massacre be chasing me? If not, then no, I won't be running."

Thinking of running, I knew I needed to stop running from Alec and talk to him about all that he'd told me and what had happened.

Making a mental promise to get my thoughts in order soon, just not right then, I proceed to finish up my work while thinking about a big, juicy burger instead.

Chapter Thirteen
YOU'RE THE TREE
Emily

When we finished work, Roxy and I hurried home to change before heading to The Rusty Nail. Sarah would already be there because her evening shift started at 5 o'clock.

Roxy and I both had the same idea on what to wear tonight. We each had on tight jeans, boots, and nice tops. My top was a pale pink, pagan-style. Roxy's was a bright pink, skintight top that showed a whole lot of cleavage. It was amusing to realize that her bright pink top and style perfectly suited her personality, while my muted pink, flowing top was more in line with my more subdued nature.

Instinctually, I wanted to call or text the guys to join us. The hesitation alone had me feeling sad and torn.

Alec had told me in no uncertain words that this, whatever all this was, wouldn't influence our friendship. But he was wrong. I already felt the division. His admission and then my reaction were like a deep cut that would not easily heal.

If the guys were invited to join us, it wouldn't be because I extended the invite. This mental acknowledgment was disheartening. It made me take a closer look at my motivations. If I didn't call, I was hiding. If I did call, was it because I wanted more? Since I didn't have any answers, I was unsuccessfully trying to ignore the whole thing.

Of course, my head wasn't having any part of that exoneration attempt. I've already been regretting the outcome of the nothing we did together, and for that, I'm blaming Alec.

We arrive at The Rusty Nail around 7 o'clock, just in time to enjoy the half-price drinks during happy hour. Finally, something was going my way.

We commandeered an area at The Rusty Nail as our spot a few years ago, even before Sarah started working here.

As we head that way, I spot Michael, Eric, and Josh sitting at the large table, waving us over as soon as they spot us.

I should have realized that Josh would be here with Michael, but I hadn't even thought of him once since the night at The Purple Room. That's a terrible realization.

As I make eye contact, he gives me a warm smile and invites me to sit next to him. Without hesitation, I sit in the chair he pulls out. He reaches over and gives me a small, affectionate hug. He's such a nice guy. His smile is bright and inviting; his arm around my back is both warm and comforting. Still, I can't help but notice that my body doesn't react to him. It dawns on me then that I feel comfortable and relaxed with Josh because I have no attraction to him. Huh?

With Alec, my body comes alive with an energy I can't explain. My mind starts imagining more than my physical body will allow for itself.

Sitting next to Josh was not the right time for my memories of the night with Alec to come flooding back or for me to recall how my body responded to his. I needed to stop thinking about Alec, at least for tonight.

Pasting on a big smile, I turn my full attention to Josh. Tonight, I'd enjoy my evening, and then tomorrow I'd put my big girl panties on and stop running from Alec. Anything less was cowardly of me, and the price of indecision was that I'd lost my easy connection with Alec. It now felt awkward to reach out to him via text or conversation, and that was on me.

I had to fix this; tomorrow, I'd face Alec and face the facts of what he'd presented to me. Part of my mind's obsession was undoubtedly a result of the need to have him provide some clarification. So, tomorrow, I'll call Alec and see if he has time to meet with me.

With a decision made, I order my usual bacon burger. Josh agreed to share both the burger and the onion rings with me. With drinks in our hands, we fell into an easy conversation that was both enjoyable and entertaining.

Josh was one of the good guys. I hoped that he would find his happy one day. I had a strong suspicion that the woman who captured his heart would get her fairytale.

As the food arrived, so did Dex and Alec. Alec snagged a chair from a nearby table and wedged himself next to me, opposite Josh. I was surprised to see burgers placed in front of Alec and Dex. They must have called in their orders. Did that mean they knew we were coming here all along?

Around the table, brief hellos were exchanged; everyone was acting as if this were a planned outing. Perhaps it was, and I wasn't privy to it.

Just then, Alec leans closer to me until his lips graze my ear, asking, "How are you?" How am I? What kind of bullshit is this? Was he not there Friday night? I wanna throw attitude. Instead, I'm barely able to control my body's visceral response to his nearness and to hearing his sexy voice so up close and personal. His presence is challenging my earlier decision to stop thinking about Alec tonight.

Instinctually, I turn toward his voice. His mouth is painfully close to mine. The temptation to throw my arms around his neck, kiss him, and tell him I accept, I accept, whatever he was proposing is nearly impossible.

From my other side, Josh interrupts that train wreck of thoughts, "Emily, here's your half of our burger."

Turning toward Josh, I felt Alec's body go tense. I also felt the mood around the table shift. Looking up, I notice all eyes are looking at Alec, then me, then Josh.

"What?" I snap at nobody in particular.

Roxy cheekily returns with, "You're the tree tonight."

I shoot Roxy with what I hope is a scathing look until her comment registers. Then, I remember. I remember her theory about Dex and Alec pissing to mark their territory.

Returning a sarcastic look her way, I say, "Hilarious," but I can't deny what she was implying. The possessive vibe in the air was obvious.

I decide to ignore the table at large. Otherwise, my head would be turning left then right like a toddler's "no–no" response. Sitting between Alec and Josh was a special kind of hell for me right now.

Ignoring the testosterone bookends, I turn my focus on my burger and start eating. Between the burger, the onion rings, and my second drink, I should have been able to relax. Nope, I'm wound tighter now than when we arrived.

I was trying to look anywhere but at Alec. Josh, too, because Alec seems to puff up every time Josh and I interact. My eyes land on Dex. He was sitting next to Roxy, who was sitting next to Eric. Roxy was basically ignoring Dex as she chatted away with Eric. Dex, for his part, did not look happy.

Roxy and Dex were keeping secrets. I wasn't sure what was going on there, but I knew I wouldn't be the one either of them would go to for advice.

There was so much tension around the table that it could be cut with a butter knife. For my part, I was trying my best to ignore it.

I wouldn't think it was possible, but just then, Alec scoots his chair even closer to me. His nearness caused my brain to short-circuit for a moment or two before slowly coming back online.

Alec's closeness thoroughly demolished the hope of getting out of my head and enjoying my evening. His warm, firm thigh pressed against my leg. His cologne, or was that just his own unique scent, was intoxicating. His gravelly voice as he conversed with the others was both soothing and enticing.

As we sat with our bodies close and touching, I sensed that we both were experiencing the same internal battle. My reason and resolve to run again crumbled in the face of my desire for him.

"Alec?" I whisper, unsure that he would even hear me over the noise.

Alec tilts his face towards mine, responding, "Yes?" For just a second, I forgot what I'd wanted to say. My internal naughty girl fantasies flashed in my mind.

Searching my eyes, Alec leans in closer and asks, "Em, you said my name?"

"Yes," I answer breathlessly, unable to tear my eyes from his long enough to compartmentalize my thoughts properly.

A corner of his mouth twitches as if he knows where my thoughts have gone. Or can he tell like the men from the Black Dagger Brotherhood with their ability to smell a woman's desire?

I'll admit, I've experienced some envious moments while reading about the hot Alpha males in the BDB series, but right now, I felt sorry for the women they seduced. I was hoping Alec wasn't immortal, couldn't read my mind, or had any other special powers.

Before I can get it together enough to respond, he rasps, "Em, sweetheart, I really want us to talk. I hate how we left things."

Looking in his eyes and seeing the sincerity there, I almost forgot we weren't alone and let myself get lost in his eyes. I didn't trust my ability to respond verbally; instead, I just nodded. It is, after all, what I, too, had decided to request from him.

The next hour was entertaining. Eric was sharing a funny story about Chicken Shit Bingo. Apparently, it's a real bingo game where people toss corn into a cage of chickens, and whatever number the chickens' poop on is the bingo number they use.

Eric had to provide proof; none of us believed him until he showed us all a YouTube video. Of course, this game originated in Texas. Go figure.

We had a few more drinks. The conversations seemed casual with friendly banter. If we remove the tension between the groups, we could have fun together. Josh, for his part, seemed to accept that I was being marked as Alec's territory, at least for tonight.

Eric and Roxy both became more inclusive with the rest of us in the conversation department, and Dex seemed to relax a bit.

Josh and Eric were the first to leave. They both had early starts tomorrow. Michael had planned to stay and walk Sarah to her car after her shift. That statement must hold more than one meaning.

Just as I was about to tell Roxy, Let's go, Alec beats me to the punch, stating, "Roxy, is it okay if Em rides home with me and Dex rides with you?"

My eyes shoot to first Alec and then to Roxy before landing on Dex. I was sure that a personal line was crossed at that moment, and I was sure Roxy would protest.

Instead, I hear her say, "Sure, Alec, no problem."

What the hell just happened? Just as I was about to ask that very question, Alec tags me by my shoulders, grabs my purse for me, and nudges me toward the exit door.

I felt a strange excitement as Alec opened his Yukon passenger door for me. I let out a squeal; instead of waiting for me to climb in, Alec had scooped me up by my hips and sat me down in the seat. Shutting my door, he instructed me to fasten my seatbelt.

If I wasn't mistaken, he had a mischievous smile on his face as he got in on the driver's side. I opened my mouth to say something, but snapped it shut and swallowed what probably would have been a humiliating admission anyway.

We rode in companionable silence for the first ten minutes of the trip. My mind was going a mile a minute, thinking of so much and unable to focus on any one thing.

Alec broke the awkward silence a few moments later to ask, "Can I ask you something?"

"Sure", I answer, hoping he wasn't going to ask me something I wasn't mentally prepared to share.

"You and Josh. Is there a story there?" His tone was casual, but I knew better. His demeanor around Josh had been possessive and guarded.

I sat there quietly for several minutes before answering, "We had a brief thing in college, but it ended there." I didn't want to lie to Alec, but I also didn't want to get into the details with him.

Alec looked at me briefly before continuing his questions, "Why do I get the feeling you're fighting this? Do you not want more to happen between us?"

I had no idea how to answer his question. I still felt like there were several pieces of the puzzle I was missing. So, I asked a question of my own. "Alec, you shared how you felt, but you didn't say what exactly you wanted from me?"

It seemed like he wasn't going to respond; we were only blocks from our condos when I finally heard his reply. "Em, I want all of you."

It's dangerous to want more than a person can give, and Alec was in grave danger.

After parking his Yukon, he came around to once again lift me out of his truck. I felt compelled to say something. I didn't know what or how to tell him how I felt. Or how to explain why I couldn't give him what he wanted.

My internal debate was waging a war between what he said he wanted and what I knew I couldn't give him. Momentarily, the fight left me when he leaned in and gave me a brief, reassuring kiss on the forehead. Without warning, the battle commenced, and all thoughts slammed back into place when Alec looked me directly in my eyes and said, "Em, come home with me."

Chapter Fourteen
CONFRONTATION
Emily

I couldn't sleep. Hearing Alec say, "Em, come home with me," triggered my flight mentality. The sad part is that I can't think clearly enough to pinpoint what I'm running from anymore.

Should I run into his arms and accept what Alec was offering, or should I run away to protect Alec from the part of me that could never give him what he wanted? And what does all this mean for our friendship?

I'm not sure if my brain shut down at any point last night. So many thoughts swirled and tumbled in my mind. At 2:00 am, I relented and grabbed a new book I was reading. I love mysteries and humor, with a touch of romance. The Miss Fortune Series from Jana DeLeon was quickly becoming a favorite of mine. Especially when I didn't want anything too serious or heavy, it was slapstick comedy with totally unbelievable shit going on. It was escapism at its finest. And I needed to escape.

Escape again. Last night, Alec said he wanted all of me, and I ran. Again.

Suppose Jesus himself came and asked me why, I wouldn't be able to put the reason into words. I didn't understand my reaction. I was certain that Alec didn't understand either. But he let me walk away, so something must have been clear to him.

Instead of sleeping, my mind replayed all my actions and his reactions several times throughout the night. Reading is a good distraction. It should help me redirect my thoughts before I do something stupid, like call him and beg him to take *all of me* that he wanted.

Around 5:00 am, I realized that even though I was on Chapter 12, I couldn't remember the mystery Fortune and her crew were trying to solve. It seemed this time that reading a book didn't help calm my jumbled thoughts.

With my exercise clothes on, I head to the small gym we have at the condos. It isn't large and doesn't have much equipment, but it does have a treadmill.

Plan B was to clear my thoughts from my head. I put in my earbuds and played some pop tunes. After stretching, I hopped on the treadmill. My goal was to become so exhausted that I reach a state of numbness.

Starting slowly, I developed a rhythm until I was running at full speed. Unlike most people, I enjoy running. The rhythmic footfalls allow me to unwind in a way that nothing else can. Well, except for several shots of tequila, but who wouldn't unwind after that?

Setting my pace, I focus on maintaining steady breathing and syncing my stride with the beat of my music. It wasn't long before I was blissfully running without a care in the world. That was until the treadmill's speed suddenly decreased, and it started to shut down. The abrupt change in speed caused my feet to stumble and my momentum to falter. Popping my eyes open, I see Dex smirking at me.

"What the hell, Dex? I could have hurt myself," I snap.

He looked unfazed as usual, and stated, "I would have helped you back up."

"Gee, thanks, very gentlemanly of you," I retort. "What's up? Why are you crashing my party?"

"I've been worried about you," Dex says with a serious expression on his chiseled face, then an unfamiliar expression flashes across his features.

"I'm good, nothing to worry about," I respond, hoping to nix this conversation right from the start.

"You haven't been to the gym this week, and I noticed some other changes," he says hesitantly.

I jump on this diversion opportunity right away, saying, "I've noticed some changes, too. I've been meaning to ask you, why would you make Roxy one of your conquests?"

Instantly, Dex's expression turns thunderous. His features are dialed right into pissed off. He responds through gritted teeth, "Em, you of all people know the kind of schedule I keep, and how long has it been since you've seen or heard me talk about a woman?"

He didn't wait for my reply and added, "It's been over 11 months since I've even been out on a fucking date."

I had to concede his point, now that I thought about it. "So, why would you start something with Roxy, knowing the impact the relationship could have if it didn't work out, which I might add is what we're all facing now?"

"It's true. The original arrangement was crap; I should never have agreed to that with Roxy. It's been hell. I regret the decision to keep it casual every day," Dex confides, looking miserable.

"So, what happened? Roxy told us girls that you don't feel the same way about her as she does about you," I confess.

Dex was looking hurt and defeated at my comment.

"Dex? What?" It might have started as a diversion tactic, but at this moment, seeing the defeat in his eyes, I want to help him.

"Em, I care a lot about Roxy, and it hurts me that she can't see past my prior reputation. None of you can. I've never felt like someone's dirty little secret in my life until now. I've tried talking her into letting us join the group as a couple, but she won't hear of it. The more I push, the more she pulls away. Because I can't live without her in my life, I'm stuck being her booty call." He tries to smile at that, but I saw the hurt there.

"I'm sorry, Dex. That can't be easy for you. Roxy just told Sarah and me on Sunday. We were a little hurt, too, that you guys kept such a big secret from us. But I have to tell you, she tells the story differently," I admit.

Dex jumps at that and asks, "What did she say?"

"I'll tell you this, she thinks you don't feel the same way she does. So, I recommend you sit her down and tell her how you feel. All of it and don't hold back."

Something occurs to me just then. "Dex, I'm sorry about the booty call comment last week. It makes sense now why you gave me a go to hell look," I say with a small smile.

"You caught that, huh? I felt pissed because that was the second time that day that someone had accused me of being an insensitive dick," Dex says, smiling too.

Looking determined, he states, "You've been grumpy this week, and you haven't worked out at all."

"I'm on my period," I say, knowing I'll get a reaction from him.

Dex grimaces and says, "So, that hasn't been an issue before."

"Well, this period has been super heavy with loads of cramps," I shoot back cheekily.

Dex pales a bit. He hates when we girls overshare about our monthly visitor. But still, he brought it on himself when he confessed to marking our time of the month on his calendar. I don't feel sorry for him at all.

He then says with newfound strength, "I call bullshit, but I'll let you have this win. But please stop talking about it."

I laugh at that. Dex is funny; he can talk about some of the grossest things, but when we talk about our periods, he can't bolt fast enough.

We are both sober. I look up to see Dex staring at me. He then asks, "Want to talk about it?" taking me by surprise.

"My period?" I say with a mischievous smile.

"No! You know what I'm talking about," he says back.

Did I really know? His question surprised me, but I somehow felt confident that Dex knew. Knowing what he was referring to didn't change the fact that I still didn't know what to say, think, or even how much he knew.

Then Dex, being the awesome guy he is, says, "I'm here if you want to talk about anything. Wait, maybe not everything." He says with a twinkle in his eye.

"Thanks, Dex, but there's nothing to talk about."

I try for levity, but I must have failed because he follows up with, "Alec and I talked."

"I don't know what he told you, but there's nothing to tell. He wants something that I'm incapable of giving."

Just saying the words caused an ache in my heart, but I knew they were true. The realization hit me. It didn't matter what Alec wanted from me or felt for me. None of that would change the facts; I was incapable, regardless of what my body's reaction was or what my heart wanted. All of the restlessness and anxiety came from my mind's attempt to change the facts and the outcome. That was the issue I had with all that Alec had shared.

Dex, knowing a little something about what Alec must have asked, says, "Em, you're the most loving, giving, kind person I know. Any man would be lucky to have you."

I felt visibly shaken by Dex's high praise of me; it made me feel like the fraudulent imposter I knew I was. All I could say in reply was, "You're wrong."

Dex looked like he wanted to say something more, but with my eyes, I implored him to let it go. I couldn't reconcile all the feelings that this recent development with Alec made me question, so there was no way I could explain them to Dex.

He must have noticed my moment of panic because he changed the subject. "When are you signing up for my kickboxing class?"

He knew that would diffuse the situation because it wasn't the first time he had asked me to sign up. "Dex, I told you it would be a waste of your skills to train me; I don't see myself getting into a ring with an Amazon woman who'll hand me my ass on a platter."

"You've been in my gyms enough to know that our matches are with individuals who are similar in weight and skill level. You're just being a chicken," Dex retorts.

"Bok, Bok," I say with a smile, but then add, "Dex, thanks, and I'm sorry that I didn't notice that you've changed."

"It's not like we have heart-to-heart talks all the time. Don't worry about it," Dex says as he heads for the exit.

I stop him and say, "Dex, talk to Roxy."

He gives me an over-the-head wave and then is gone.

Wow, I really have a lot of nerve insisting he resolve his issues with Roxy while I was still running from my problems with Alec.

Chapter Fifteen
THE OLIVE BRANCH
Emily

"This is the longest day ever," I say into my phone. Roxy called to say she was getting a ride home with Sarah. They want to hit the mall before going home.

It goes without saying that mall shopping was not my favorite thing to do. Give me Amazon any day. Once I found a brand and style I liked, I ordered it online. In multiple colors, if that was an option. My idea of going shopping was to head straight to the store I knew had what I needed, buy it, and leave.

Since I was a shopping buzzkill, Roxy's words, not mine, they seldom invited me to join them anymore.

Roxy kept jabbering in an effort to persuade me to go out tonight to a New Age bar. She was trying everything she could to guilt me into saying yes. Her biggest complaint was that no single woman should stay home on a Friday night.

Since this was the second time today she was trying to convince me to go, I wasn't very nice when I responded, "Roxy, I'm not going shopping, and I'm not going out tonight. Give it a rest."

"Fine, your loss," she snaps.

Then, in a nicer tone, she asks me, "What are you going to do then?"

"I'll probably go to bed early. I didn't sleep worth a damn last night, and I got up early this morning to work out." That's all I'd tell Roxy; she didn't need to know that I only went to the gym in a last-ditch effort to stop thinking so much.

As if on cue, Roxy asks, "What's up?" She always wants the details, and of course, she picked up on my inadvertent clue; I just gave her the equivalent of a treasure hunt.

Realizing my error too late, in response, I decide to turn the tables on Roxy and say, "Dex showed up at the gym this morning."

"Oh, really?" Roxy tries and fails to sound unconcerned.

"Yep, and we had a little chat about you guys, too." I disclose.

She didn't say anything at first, and then she asked, "What did you guys talk about?"

"His version of your relationship is different from yours," I state. I wanted to see if Roxy would open up and talk about it.

"There is no relationship." Roxy quips.

"I think there could be," I reply.

"Em, can I have a rain check on this conversation?" Roxy's request was closer to a plea.

"Of course, and I'm always here if you need me, okay?" I reply.

"Roxy, I will tell you this: you need to have a sit-down with Dex. Both of you need to be honest with each other. I told him the same thing." I hope my insistence registers with her.

"Yeah, okay, I hear you. If you change your mind about going out tonight, just let me know." Roxy's quick response was her way of shutting down this conversation.

Since I knew that if the shoe were on the other foot, I would want the same thing. I let it go, saying, "Don't spend too much money at the mall, be safe tonight, and have fun."

"Fun is my middle name," Roxy replies just as the line goes dead.

After we hang up, I realize that I really wanted to stay home tonight, and going to bed early sounds wonderful.

I felt a little guilty; here I was, telling my friends how important it is to talk openly with one another, yet I didn't even practice what I preached.

On my way home, I stop at the grocery store. I decide to make myself a healthy meal of fish, asparagus, and sweet potatoes. With all the inner turmoil I've been experiencing lately, I forgot to bake an apology chocolate cake for Dex. I also decide to pick up the ingredients I need for that. Then, as a treat to myself, I add a nice bottle of wine and some butter pecan ice cream.

Pulling into the garage, I see Alec getting out of his Yukon. Exiting my car, I grab my grocery bags and laptop bag, then meet him at the elevators.

Without asking, Alec takes my bags at the same time he asks, "How are you doing?" He was smiling, and I instantly felt at ease. I wasn't sure what I thought he'd do or say, but I knew by running *again*, I didn't deserve the warm smile he was giving me.

"I'm good, how are you doing?" That was my automatic response.

With a chuckle, he asks, "Are we going to talk about the weather too now?"

I laugh; I knew he was referring to the formality of our conversation. The joint confirmation of our awkward behavior was what we needed to get us back to a more relaxed rapport.

It was a spur-of-the-moment decision, but I felt deep down that it was the right thing to do and that the time had come.

Turning to Alec, I ask, "I'm making fish for dinner, would you like to join me?"

The radiant smile Alec aims my way is beautiful, even if he said no; that smile made it worth the potential rejection.

"That sounds great. What time should I come over?" Alec responds as he holds the elevator doors open for me to step in.

I was still smiling when I proposed, "Is 6:30 too early for you?"

"No, that's perfect. I'll bring wine," Alec says with another panty-melting smile. I considered telling him I'd already bought wine, but I'm no dummy. Alec has excellent taste in wine.

We arrive at my floor first, and Alec, carrying my groceries, walks me to my door to bring the bags in for me. As he steps back, he turns and, still smiling, says, "I'll be back." Then he closes my door and is gone.

Staring at the door he just left, I felt a moment of sheer panic, "What have I done?" I say this aloud before I realize I'm acting crazy. Not just for talking to myself, but because I was panicking over having a friend over for dinner.

But it was more than that. All day, I thought about my conversation with Dex. I didn't lie to him; there wasn't anything going on between Alec and me.

What I didn't admit to Dex was that a big part of me was hoping for something to happen. For the first time since college, I wanted to feel and behave like any other single woman approaching 30.

Being *damaged* might keep me from ever giving myself emotionally and completely to Alec, but physically, my body wants to experience all that being intimate with Alec would surely bring.

It's disheartening to realize that Dex and Roxy, who are both emotionally capable of forming a genuine relationship, are only focused on the physical aspects. I, on the other hand, would love to give myself emotionally, but I know that I am incapable of it.

Seeing Alec and his smile earlier made me realize I wanted to accept all that I could from Alec's offer. But just admitting it to myself wasn't enough; I had to act on it and not run this time.

I needed to accept him, and hopefully, in return, he'd accept having *part of me* instead of *all of me*.

Alec wouldn't hurt me. I trusted him more than I trusted anyone else in my life. As I had that thought, I knew it to be the truth.

Making myself take some deep breaths, I head to my room to change into something more comfortable before starting dinner.

Of course, I didn't want to overdress, so I threw on a blue chambray button-down shirt over a braless tank top and black leggings. I stayed barefoot, which was always my preference.

My mind was still plaguing me with doubts; it's never been easy for me to get out of my head and just do it. Nike gives false hope.

Would Alec give me another chance to tell him that I wanted him, too? Or had I shut him down and pushed him beyond the point of no return? Would he think I wasn't worth the effort? Too messed up to pursue. Would having a *part of me* be enough for him?

I had to trust myself too, and I had to stop fighting my body's physical response to Alec. I trusted Alec. Giving that trust was something I swore I'd never do again. To give a man that much power over me and then let what I was feeling to give credence to my wants and desires.

With so many thoughts and worries swirling in my mind, I had to focus on the most pertinent facts. I trusted Alec to make the right decision for both of us, and I trusted the strength of our friendship.

Even if this didn't last, even if this turned out to be a huge mistake, I'd rather live with the fallout than spend the rest of my life asking myself what it would have been like to give myself to Alec.

For tonight, I had to put the brakes on my thoughts and doubts. I had to trust in Alec and believe in myself; we would get through this uncertainty.

With my many thoughts, doubts, and fears correctly compartmentalized, I pour my energy into what I know I can do well. I proceed to make one kick ass meal.

Alec arrives precisely on time. As I open the door, something comes over me. Standing on my tiptoes, I gently brush my lips against his and say, "I'm glad you came." Then I quickly stepped back because that was the extent of my courage.

Taking in Alec's expression, I see a flash of surprise, then something else I can't quite decipher crosses his features.

As Alec steps all the way in and closes my door, he says, "I don't want to be anywhere else." Then he offers me a warm smile as he moves to set the wine down on the entry table. Before I knew what was about to happen, he closed the gap between us, wrapping his warm, muscular arms around me.

My cheeks warmed, and my body tensed. I couldn't tell if it was from embarrassment or arousal. Alec, steady as ever, doesn't appear to be affected. He just held me until the rigidity in my back and arms slowly melted away. It should have been awkward, but it wasn't. It felt nice. Really nice.

Tilting his head closer, Alec never takes his eyes off me. Then, unhurriedly, he rests his forehead against mine. There is no way I could look away. Studying him up close leaves me motionless. That sexy hint of scruff along his jaw is lighter than the hair on his head, dark chocolate rather than black. His thick brows and long lashes shadow his eyes, giving him a serious, stoic expression that somehow intrigues me more than it unnerves me.

Then all thought is gone when Alec leans his face down and presses his lips against mine in a sweet kiss. The arms already wrapped around me tighten slightly, but not so much as to be uncomfortable. The kiss is both gentle and commanding, with just the right amount of pressure. Warmth radiates from his body to mine; it is both comforting and overwhelming.

My mind began to notice all the subtle details of the moment, and it was his constant control that started to chill me. Alec was holding back; he was holding me so gently, as if I were made of porcelain. His demeanor was nothing like the passionate, full-body connection against his wall like before. Doubt was creeping back in. Was he holding himself back because I was a flight risk? Or was his kiss just a natural reaction to the one I gave him?

Those insecurities had me pushing back from him. Consciously, I knew there was no need to rush into any level of intimacy. My brief brush of lips might have started it, but he was the one who extended the olive branch by kissing me. To me, his response signified he hadn't given up on me. Yet, I couldn't stop myself from pushing against his chest again.

I push a little harder, but Alec, being *the all-in control Alec,* continues to hold me close, sensing my need to retreat or run. I feel his determination; he's not letting me go. His eyes are expressive; I can see his intent not to let me push him away. Belatedly, I also see his unshielded wants and desires.

That realization freaked me the hell out; Alec wasn't shielding his emotions. Curiosity alone meant I wasn't going to run, but I did need some space. Anyway, running wasn't an option since this was my apartment, and the food I prepared smelled delicious.

Faking a calm I didn't actually feel, I stopped pushing and tried a distraction instead, "Why don't you open the bottle of wine and let's get ready to eat the dinner I stood over the stove to prepare?"

Reluctantly, Alec let me go, saying, "I'm starving, and the food smells amazing."

His stepping away to do my bidding will give me the space and time I need to regain my equilibrium. Feeling out of sorts with Alec was normal for me, but feeling more and acting on those feelings was a whole new experience.

Chapter Sixteen
GOLDEN OPPORTUNITY
Alec

Nothing could have prepared me for the tailspin Em sent me in with that one brief kiss. The fact that she initiated it was both sweet and bold.

Kissing her back was meant to be brief and reassuring, but the taste of her, the feel of her against me, was snapping the leash I had on my control. I had unconsciously tightened my hold and deepened the kiss.

Not surprisingly, it was Em who pulled back first. It should have been me, but nothing goes as it should where Em is concerned. She is my personal form of kryptonite.

Not wanting to fuck up this golden opportunity to become more for Em, I forced myself to let her go and get started on the wine. I needed to take a few minutes to get my shit together anyway.

As I walk into her kitchen to retrieve the wine opener, one thought settles firmly in my mind: I need to tread more carefully with Em. My wants and desires press hard against the edges of my control, threatening to take over, and if I let them, I risk pushing her too far, too fast. Instinct tells me she will resist and run. Her body might stay in the moment, but her mind often drifts somewhere safer, away from what requires her to let her guard down.

Moments ago, she was pliant in my arms, moving with me as if we were one. Then, suddenly, Em seemed to realize the closeness, and a need for space took over. I felt it just as sharply as if she'd physically jumped away. That change told me everything. I hadn't just come on too strong; I had also taken more than she was ready to give, driven by my own need.

The dinner she made was excellent; as we ate, the conversation was easy and casual. It felt good to be back on solid friends' ground. No way would I admit this to anyone, but having Em treat me as her friend again, without weariness, was precisely what I needed at that moment. It was a reminder of what kind of man Em needed me to be in her life.

Em values our friendship above everything else. It's my duty to show her that regardless of what happens between us, I will always be there for her. Despite her pushing and pulling away, she should see that I keep coming back. I'll keep returning again and again. Of course, I want more, but with friendship comes opportunity. With opportunity comes hope. So, there's a chance for more.

As we settle on the couch with another glass of wine each, it is Em who addresses the elephant in the room, "Alec, I'm sorry. I know I've been pushing you away and shutting you out. Or running. You even mentioned that you felt I was fighting against us. I can't help it. I feel powerless to stop my reaction because I know it won't work."

Squeezing Em's hand in encouragement, I wait to see if she has anything else to say. "Babe, what do you mean by it won't work?"

Watching Em struggle to compose her thoughts, I immediately try to soothe her. To fix it, but anything I say to the contrary will only make her shut down. The last thing I want to do is give her a reason to doubt herself or run. Or, to doubt me.

The unsatisfied man in me wants to push for her to say more, to hear her tell me she wants me as much as I want her. To know I'm not the only one feeling the pull we have for each other. But I won't.

Uninvited, my mind reminds me that Em's acknowledgement about running and pushing me away, along with her apology, are in no way a declaration of love. And it's not an indication of her desire to be with me beyond friendship, even if she didn't feel that it would work.

Her apology wasn't clear either. Was it because she hadn't reciprocated my spoken desires, or was it for pulling away from me and our friendship during those few days? *What does she mean by feeling powerless?*

For long, excruciating moments, I wait on Em as she clearly fights an internal battle. It's frustrating to watch, but I'm really hoping she collects her thoughts enough to clarify what she means.

I've seen her barely hidden desire for me, and I felt the warmth of attraction that had radiated between our melded bodies. Neither of those base reactions can be fabricated. They are a body's natural response to mutual desire. I don't understand what she is trying to convey.

Coming out of my musings, I hear her voice just above a whisper confess, "I want to be able to give you all of me. But I can't."

"You do?" I wasn't expecting that response. It felt essential to get confirmation. Could she want me as much as I want her?

With her eyes directly on mine, Em continues, "Yes, that is what I want, but can you accept having only the parts of me I'm capable of giving?"

After hearing her say yes, the rest of her statement is suppressed by my need to be closer to her. Unable to stop my body's reaction to what she just said, I reach for her and pull her across my lap.

Em squeaks in startled surprise before settling on my lap with her back resting against the armrest of the couch. Her body feels perfect against mine.

She was studying me, staring intently at me. Her trusting eyes serve as a reminder that I must maintain control and let her set the pace. To let her determine our next steps and how far we should take them. *Easier said than done.*

Using the arm still at her back, I pull her firmly to my chest. Slowly, I lean my head toward hers and gently brush my lips over hers. A trembling sigh escapes from her lips as she melts against my body. And before I can rein in my need for more, I'm kissing Em. I'm kissing her like my life depends on it. Best of all, she is right there with me as she lifts and twists to straddle my lap. As her lips part, I greedily devour her mouth, sucking on her tongue as it reaches out to taste mine. All thoughts to proceed with caution are long gone.

What started gently quickly became more frenzied as the kiss deepened. Within the cocoon of my arms, Em arches against me. I dig my hands into her hair and give myself over to the pleasure of having her, the way my body has burned to have her for so long. Our sexual chemistry is like nothing I'd ever experienced before.

With a strength I didn't even know I still possessed; I pulled back from the kiss. I need to take a breather while I still have the fortitude to keep my hands from exploring every inch of Em's body or from scooping her up to carry her to bed.

I'm not used to feeling out of control, but if Em asked me for more in that moment, I would've been powerless to deny her. I had to remind myself that being with her isn't about the sex. I love Em, and what I want goes far deeper than that. I want a future, a family, a life built together. More than anything, I need her trust. I know I can't rush the steps to getting her trust; it has to grow with time. And for her, I'd wait. However long it takes, in whatever way she's willing to let me in, I'll take it.

Taking a deep, steadying breath, I lean in closer until my lips are just above hers and boldly say, "If you still have any doubts about what I want from you or how I feel about you, I'll gladly spend the whole night showing you. I'll stay as long as needed to convince you of how much I want all of you."

We stare at each other for long moments. As if in slow motion, I see a flash of desire in her eyes, then time speeds up as she jumps off my lap and says, "I bought dessert, turtle cheesecake, we have to eat it."

As we get up to head toward her kitchen, I can't help but smile. I know when I whispered what I wanted to do to her, that if Em was still planning to be done with us, she would have slapped the shit out of me for talking to her that way and asked me to leave. She didn't do either, and for the first time in days, I felt a spark of hope.

My smile slipped when I saw Em bending over the refrigerator to get the cheesecake. I couldn't stop myself; I wanted Em. The need to kiss her and to hold her in my arms was strong. Dessert could wait. As she rose, I spun her around to face me, grabbing her hips to once again devour her lips.

Em, for her part, responded with a need of her own. She tilted her head to give me better access to her mouth as she arched against me. With surprising strength, Em pushed me toward the opposite counter.

My thoughts were consumed by her nearness, awed by how responsive and almost assertive she had become. My hands, as if acting on their own, caressed Em's breast through her shirt, my lips traced the line of her neck, and I nibbled at her earlobe. I burned for her, eager to explore the desires her closeness has ignited within me.

Warning bells hammered at my thoughts, clanging in alarm that we were moving way too fast. Nothing broke through. I was losing the fight to deny the longing I'd hidden for her.

Looking at the passion in Em's eyes, my mind fills with several X-rated possibilities. I can't help it. Em isn't helping my internal turmoil; her fingers are in my hair, pulling slightly as if wanting so much more than she is capable of taking or asking for.

Reluctantly, I pull away from our entanglement. I want to see Em's expression. I know that Em's eyes say so much more than her words ever could. I notice desire building in her, but I also see apprehension, and it doesn't sit right with me, a discomfort I need to understand.

"Alec, I need you," Em boldly states. Instinctually, I know she's never been this bold with a man before me. The magnitude of that realization is almost crippling. I need to remember that Em is special and that she needs me to handle her with care.

My expression must convey that I'm hesitant and concerned. Before Em can read anything into it, I ask, "Em, are you sure? I feel like there's still so much we need to discuss. So, I need you to be certain, I won't be able to live with the regret if you hate both of us in the morning."

Em smiles and says without hesitation, "Yes, Alec, I want you."

Time seemed to stop for me as I automatically pulled her tighter against me. Her soft curves, the sweetness of her breath against my ear, and her silky hair caressing my arms as they hold her tightly are everything to me.

Nothing on earth could have stopped me from giving Em what we both wanted. Not even my own reluctance to tell her the whole truth, or from her look that seemed to say she was looking for an escape. From what? I had no clue.

My voice came out rough, weighted with an emotion I couldn't identify. Pulling Em closer, I whispered, "Em, I'll give you whatever you need." I wrapped my arms around her, holding tight for a beat before loosening my embrace, my hand moving slowly over her back as if she were something precious meant to be cherished.

Em pushed back just enough to look up at me, her voice soft, almost shy. "Um, Alec? I like hugs, and maybe I can even admit I've needed a hug lately, but that was not the need I was referring to."

Her honesty caught me off guard, and I couldn't help it; I burst out laughing. That was Em, bold in one breath and reserved in the next. But I got the message. Pulling her firmly against my chest, I kissed her like she already belonged to me. Like her kiss was the very thing I needed to keep breathing. It carried raw need, aching desire, and the unshakable conviction that I had to show her how right we could be together.

Giving us both a moment to catch our breaths, I pressed a kiss to her nose, then rested my forehead against hers. Her eyes met mine, brilliant blue and impossible to look away from, holding me captive. Her blue eyes, which I love so much, were saying more than her words ever did.

Chapter Seventeen
EM'S CHOICE
Alec

Looking into Em's expressive, lust-hazed eyes, I surrender my control. I permit myself to let go of the residual caution that I've carried since I allowed myself to infiltrate Em's life.

After a moment or two, Em didn't show regret or run away. I tighten my hold. Then slowly I let my eyes drop to rest on her lips. Those sweet kissable lips. Returning my gaze to her eyes, I see glimpses of affection and want. No regrets. No hesitation. In that moment, I vowed never to take those expressions for granted. I realize the gift they are.

My determination to seize this opportunity and fulfill my desires, along with her wishes, is strengthened because it was Em's decision to take things further.

I kiss her until neither of us can breathe. There's an undeniable hunger beneath the surface, vibrating with need. Em's legs move restlessly, trying to achieve purchase as she attempts to rub her most sensitive parts against my painfully hard erection.

I don't know who made the first move tonight. Or who can I blame later for my total loss of control? But feeling Em's need, which mirrors my own, is the green light I've been hoping for.

With her body writhing against my own, our kiss ignites an instant fire. A savage spark of desire that fuels me with an all-consuming hunger. It brings forth every ounce of desperation I've felt since that first kiss against my wall with Em.

We stumble down the hall toward her bedroom. I take as much from her as she takes from me. Our movements are hurried, our hands clumsily exploring every reachable inch, our kisses lacking finesse. It's all tongue and teeth, but incredibly hot.

My subconscious, along with my more intuitive instincts, is warning me to slow down. To proceed with caution. But this is my Em, and all the signals she's sending are telling me she wants me just as much as I want her.

Reaching her bedroom door, I easily lift Em, allowing her to wrap her legs around my waist. The solid feel of Em in my arms and beneath my fingers, as her body molds to mine, anchors me to this moment. We're in this together. Thank fuck.

Hesitating just a second longer, I take Em straight to her bed. There's a moan of protest as I momentarily extricate myself from her arms and legs. Her pink, slightly swollen lips are pouting, and damn, if that's not the cutest thing I've ever seen.

Not hesitating a minute longer, I remove my socks and shoes. Leaving everything else on. I join Em where she's settled in the middle of her bed. Her eyes aimed at me blaze with an intensity that rivals my own. Her open, reaching arms welcome me.

There's a magnetic pull urging me forward. I'm not sure if I'm the one succumbing or if Em is pulling me, but I lower myself partly onto her outstretched body. Our lips meet as the magnetism guides us.

The warning bells still ring faintly in the back of my mind. My attempt to stay in control leaves me uncertain and hesitant. I've never lost my grip on reason like this. Hell, I'm acting more like an untried horny teenager than a grown man. It's Em. She's my weakness. I'm a healthy male responding to the woman I love and desire more than anything.

What's holding me in check and honestly scares me is that this *is* Em. My Em. Not a woman to use just for mutual pleasure, but someone so much more. Em should know the truth about me. She should have the option to deepen our relationship only after she's fully informed. There are so many things we need to talk about before we get to this point. I want more than a one-night stand with Em. And I need her complete trust to understand her perceived limitations better.

"Sweetheart, I want you, but I also want you to be comfortable with us, with this. We should talk."

"Alec, I want to want you. I'm comfortable with that." Em says, wrapping her arms back around my neck.

Kissing her again, the taste of her, the feel of her lips parting under my own, scrambles all rational thought. She feels too perfect to be wrong. I forget all about my hesitations and my reasons to slow down; instead, I let myself get lost in our mutual desire.

Deepening the kiss, I slip my hand under her top. With each teasing caress, I feel her need more insistent. My little Em is proving that patience is not one of her virtues as she writhes beneath me.

Kissing was never an integral part of my sex life in the past. With Em, I feel like I can't get enough. The experience of kissing the one you love is almost overwhelming.

Em struggles to pull my shirt over my head, dislodging our lips. Without missing a beat, she makes quick work of unbuttoning my jeans. It's not hard to understand that she wants to undress me.

I take over the task; if her hand even slightly touches my junk, the untried teenager thought from earlier will become my reality.

I'm not opposed to getting naked before her. Junk touching aside, I know that I need to go slow with Em, let her set the pace.

Admittedly, at this moment, her pace seems more frantic than mine. If she needs to feel in control, I'm willing to give her that power.

At her urging, I stand to remove my pants and boxer briefs. Her gaze is both seducing and heady. She wants me, at least I thought so, until her eyes stop their perusal of my body to focus solely on my manhood. I know my stature is immense. I'm a big guy, and she's not petite, but she is small. I see the apprehension flash in her eyes as she bites her lower lip.

I can't help it; I chuckle at the look on her face. Her reaction is more visceral than genuine concern. I have to say something, "It'll fit, I promise."

That comment breaks through. Em laughs a humorless laugh, reaching for me to come back onto the bed.

Before I join her, I say, "It's your turn, get naked!" I almost laugh at her expression. I can practically read everything she's thinking from her beautifully expressive blue eyes.

Em was laughing now as she asked, "What am I going to do with you?" I had some ideas, many of them. But I'd rather show than tell.

Chapter Eighteen
PERFECTION
Alec

All humor is put on hold as I lean in from the side of the bed and capture Em's lips in another warm, wet kiss. Trailing kisses along her throat to just below her ear, I whisper a few suggestions that leave her breathless and blushing.

My fingers, on a delectable path, reach the hem of her shirt. With quick efficiency, I tug Em's top up and over her head. Wow. The stark white bra against Em's milky pale skin is sheer unassuming perfection.

I decide to leave her bra on for now for self-preservation purposes only. I'm still trying to keep my inner teenage boy in check. Boobs. I love boobs. And I'm trying really hard not to embarrass myself.

Working together, we remove the rest of her clothing. Her thong went with the leggings. But not that illicit bra. That stays. I've had many, many dreams about Em and her breasts. Good dreams. The best.

The sight before me now, even with her breast covered, tells me my dreams were way off base. Her body is beautiful art. Her toned runner's form is firm and smooth. Not hard. But flawless softness.

She's bare. Shit. Stats. I need stats. Baseball. Will the Rangers go all the way?

Em, who usually is more reserved, doesn't seem embarrassed, shy, or scared in this moment. Em is right here with me, being courageous and sexy. Unaware of the teenage boy in me fighting against pre-ejaculation.

As Em lies vulnerable on her bed, her lingering perusal of my body has my dick standing at attention and bobbing. My body's blood supply is all heading in that direction. Stats. Baseball stats. Now.

Before I can protest, Em removes her bra, tossing it to the floor. Holy hell. She's perfect. They're perfect. Her rosy nipples have exquisite buds centered on the mounds of perfection.

My mind can't seem to think of another worthy description other than she is gorgeously perfect, she is mine, and I want her.

Joining her on the bed, my hungry gaze takes it all in. Landing on her beautifully trusting eyes. It's the green light I wanted and needed.

My hands, no longer patiently waiting, eagerly touch and explore of their own accord. My kisses seem to light a blaze inside Em as I glide my lips and tongue down her neck to her breast. Em's body is already writhing with need. She's so responsive to every nuance and every touch as I continue the pleasurable task of worshipping every inch of her body.

"Em, you are so beautiful and you're perfect," I whisper against her skin. Loving the vanilla fragrance from her body wash and the soft feel of her skin under my rougher hands, loving her through my touch and words.

No sooner than the words leave my mouth, I feel Em's mood shift. Her once pliable body is now rigid. Pulling back, I'm immediately on high alert. The look she's giving me, I've seen before; she's trying to get control of some overwhelming emotions. Then I see the first of several tears leak from her eyes. I'm gutted.

The change in Em's manner is immediate. I'm confused and worried. It's as if someone had flipped a switch. Sweeping a few tears from her cheeks, I ask, "Em, Sweetheart, what's wrong? Did I do something?"

For the briefest of moments, something flickers through her eyes. Before I can decipher it, the emotion becomes veiled behind a curtain of resolve. It reminds me of what I'd see in the eyes of my team when an assignment is doomed to fail.

As I cautiously move off her and to the side, Em hurriedly sits up, grabbing the comforter to pull over herself. She's gripping the comforter desperately tight; she's not just using it to cover her naked body, she's using it as a barrier.

Em still hasn't answered my questions. She won't even meet my eyes, only shakes her head no.

"What just happened, babe?" I need to know, though I hate asking.

Every part of me aches to hold her, but I force myself to stay still. To give her space. The memory of her warm, naked body burns through me, while my heart reels from the sharp whiplash of her pulling away.

Finally, Em looks at me, really sees me. My heart cracks at the sight. The tears on her cheeks, the defeated look in her eyes, I know I pushed her too far, too fast, and I hate myself for it.

That faraway look tells me the truth. Em's retreating, fighting the urge to run, and all I want is to keep Em safe here with me.

The guilt is instant, sharp. I should've slowed us down, should've protected Em instead of letting things spiral.

I grab my clothes and pull them on fast, then snag a robe from the back of the closet door and hand it to her.

Once she's covered, I can't deny myself the need to hold her. To comfort not only her, but myself. I fucked up, and I feel bad. Pulling her in for a reassuring hug, I share, "I'm so sorry, Em."

Because I'm holding her, I feel the rigidity in her back ease. Relief. In that moment, I felt an undeniable sense of relief. I don't know if I was expecting her to push me away, scream at me to leave, or hug me back.

I rest my cheek against the crown of her head, feeling her body melt deeper into my embrace. I don't deserve this kind of trust, not from her, but I can't let go. I need this moment, need her, even as guilt shouts, I've already taken too much.

Once her emotions settle, at least a little, I take her hand and lead us out of her room. There's no way I can have this conversation with her sitting on that bed, the same bed where I just held her naked body in my arms.

As we move into the living room, resignation settles over me. I need to know where Em's head is at. Until we discuss what's causing her to throw up walls, there's no moving forward, no next level for us.

Em needs to stop running from her fears and allow herself the freedom to want me. To confide in me. To accept that I want her. All of her, regardless of what she views as a barrier between us.

As we reach the couch, I see fresh tears spill down her cheeks, and helplessness crashes over me. The anguish etched on Em's face is unbearable, and every bit of it feels like my fault. My chest burns with anger, but it's not at her. It's at me.

By allowing my dick to rob my brain of coherent thought, I allowed us to move faster than what was right for us. I knew jumping into bed after only moments before admitting what we both wanted from each other was a mistake. I knew better.

My voice raspy and choked, I say, "Em, I'm so sorry. I hate that I didn't show more control."

Watching her intently, Em struggles to swallow a sob. I see the effort it takes to bite back the lump in her throat. Visibly, Em takes a deep breath before stating, "You're wrong. But Alec, it's not you, it's me." When what she says registers, she gives me a small, broken smile at having used that tired old phrase.

Cupping her face in my hands, I state, "Sweetheart, it's okay, we can wait. There's no need to rush this, I'm not going anywhere." Taking her lips in a gentle, sweet kiss to seal my promise, I feel even more of her resistance start to melt.

Pulling back from the kiss, Em calmly states, "It's me, Alec. And there are so many reasons why this is true and why you have to believe me when I tell you it isn't you."

Understanding this is her attempt to take total blame or try to scare me off, I say, "Em, I hear what you're saying, but you need to confide in me. We need to talk about what is troubling you. I won't hurt you, I promise that, but I need to understand what just happened." Wiping more of her tears with my thumbs, I continue, "There's nothing you can do or say that will ever make me run from you, please believe that, Em."

Chapter Nineteen
BAD CHOICES
Emily

It was easy for Alec to say I could confide in him, to trust him, to believe in his words. And I did hear them, every single one. I understood the promises they carried, saw the sincerity etched into his handsome face, and felt the warmth radiating from his chocolate brown eyes.

But believing isn't something I can force. No pep talk will erase my fears or magically give me the ability to trust. Doubt and hesitance are woven too deeply into me.

Part of me aches to tell Alec about my past, to explain why I pulled away, why it really is me and not him. But where would I even begin? And how much is too much? I don't know.

The truth terrifies me. If Alec knew everything, he wouldn't see perfection; he'd only see the fragmented pieces left of me. He wouldn't look at me with appreciation, but with disgust. His promise to stay would break under the weight of my reality. How could it not?

Deep down, I know I'm not someone who deserves to be cherished or worshipped. I'm damaged, and Alec deserves better. He deserves someone whole, someone normal.

Wrapped in his arms and ignited by his kisses, I momentarily forgot. But the fairytale, 'girl meets boy, boy falls in love, they get married' type of relationship isn't for me. Not anymore.

My brain is quick to remind me I don't deserve such a beautiful life with a beautiful man.

The fact is, I don't feel perfect; my self-image and self-worth feel fractured beyond repair, broken, and shattered.

A recurring memory makes me feel dirty, how I let Trace, a depraved monster, put his hands on me and use me.

How can I let Alec touch me now with such reverence, knowing he doesn't know the truth?

Looking into Alec's eyes, I only see sincerity. He believes every word he's telling me. But what he's offering is an impossibility.

Accepting my fate, I know it has to be me who sets him free. Once he learns the truth about who I really am, he won't be able to keep his promises, and it isn't fair to expect that from him.

Alec needs to understand I'm not the one for him. So, I'll give him at least a partial truth, enough to protect him from getting entangled with my fractured heart. Enough to shield him from the broken pieces left of me.

The thought twists me up inside, my stomach does a pitch and roll as though I'm on a rollercoaster without brakes. Conflicting emotions batter my mind: desire, fear, the echo of old dreams, the shadow of demons. All colliding, all grasping for control.

But no words come. Nothing forms in my mind. What could I say that would make Alec understand?

I'll have to dig deep, past my wants and fears, past the emotions clawing at me, and find the courage to share just enough for Alec to see the truth: that the problem is me, not him. I can't reveal too much; the truth would drive him away forever. And I can't lose him completely. If nothing else, I need him in my life as a friend.

My thoughts crash together like fragmented shards pulled toward a magnet, and suddenly, I spring from the couch to my oversized chair, putting distance between us.

Every cell in my body protests, my body humming with the urge to stay close, to curl back into his arms. But I force the space, needing it to gather my words, to try and explain why my heart insists we could never work, and to do it in a way Alec might accept. It won't be easy to explain my rioting thoughts and emotions to him, because I don't understand them myself.

Alec gratefully lets me have my space. He stays on the couch, watchful, silent, present, and protective. The kind of steadiness I admire in him. Allowing me the time I need to get a grip.

After a few more quiet moments, his exhale suddenly fills the room, sharp against the thudding staccato of my heartbeat. I can sense his patience wearing thin.

Before I can form words, Alec cuts in, "Em, I'm not wrong about how I see you. You're courageous; you have a natural strength about you. I think you're perfect. I think you're perfect for me."

His words make my heart lurch, each one replaying slowly in my mind before sinking straight into my chest. I hadn't realized how badly I needed to hear his impression of me until that moment. Those beautiful words were like superglue to my shattered heart.

So caught up in the revelation, I don't notice Alec move until he's scooping me up from my chair and settling me onto his lap. He presses a sweet kiss to my nose, then rests his forehead against mine.

His voice soft, almost pleading, requests, "Talk to me. Let me help you work through this. I'm not going anywhere. I want to understand so I can help. Please, don't push me away."

My heart swells with gratitude for everything Alec is offering. He truly believes what he is saying, and that makes me want to share everything with him. At the same time, I am aware that sharing my thoughts, feelings, and fears with him is also a perilous endeavor. The truth has the power to change how he sees me.

"You're wrong, I'm not perfect. You deserve to know the real me, but it's not easy for me to share that with you. I'm damaged, Alec. I'm not right for you. You deserve more than I can give." The admission comes out in a whisper; I feel oddly shy to reveal so much.

He takes my hands in his. Looking at me with genuine warmth, he responds without hesitation: "Tell me. Tell me everything you can. I want to know it all. And Em, I don't think you're damaged; you're everything good in this world. These aren't just words to me. I mean every word. Please, sweetheart, let me in. Let me be here for you."

I nod, "Okay, Alec. I'll try." I take a deep, steadying breath and begin where it all started. "In college, I made some poor choices. As a result, I had a bad experience with a guy." *Understatement of the fucking year.*

Alec threads our fingers together. He looks calmer than his body would indicate, and asks, quietly, "What happened?"

Surely, Alec notices how nervous I am. I can't stop picking at a snag on my robe until my fingers nearly make a hole. He says nothing, watches, letting me find the words. His steady presence is its own kind of support. His ever-present control remains firmly in place.

We lock eyes. There's tenderness there, but a shadow of trepidation too. Alec can sense this will change things. It will change everything.

I swallow and downplay it, cowardly and resigned. "It was just that, a bad experience. But I allowed it to happen. Now I can't trust myself to make good choices."

Alec squeezes me. "I hear you, sweetheart. We all did stupid shit in college. It's like a rite of passage. Whatever you did was then, not now."

Alec cradles me as if I'm fragile, and for a moment, it's exactly what I need. His warmth holds me reverently, but he's wrong; it's not that simple. Tears start again despite myself.

Back to picking at the snag on my robe, I sniffle out, "What I did was bad."

He tries to lighten it. "Did you kill someone?" Alec asks. *No, but I really wanted to.*

"No. I didn't break any laws. I just made some dumb decisions."

"That's part of the college experience," Alec says. "We learn best from our mistakes. If you didn't break any laws, no one should hold the foolish things we did in college against us."

He means well; he makes it sound so simple. Like I had a choice in how I accept my mistakes. Do I? Can I file the darkness away and focus solely on the lesson? Chalk it up to youthful stupidity and move on?

I want to move on more than anything. I've never wanted anything for myself more than I want that.

Sharing my burden with Alec, acknowledging to myself that I would want more if I could. That I am more than my mistakes. Feels oddly freeing. It opens a door I've only ever dreamed about, the possibility of more with Alec, the man who cares for me and calls me brave.

Telling him a sliver of the truth lifts a weight I've carried alone. I've never revealed this to anyone before. Could it be that simple? A stupid thing in college that people survive and learn from.

Permitting myself to accept that possibility, I feel relieved, a little revived, almost whole.

What I shared was only a small part of the story, a partial truth. But Alec's acceptance, without judgment, is the balm my fragmented heart desperately needed.

Chapter Twenty
EVER PRESENT CONTROL
Emily

Before my mind can sabotage me, I force the words out. "Yeah, we do tend to learn best from our mistakes, but learning and moving on are two totally different hurdles. I'm not sure if I can fully move on from my past. What I do know is that I want to try. I want what you're offering. Most of all, I want you. I want to be with you, and I want to give you everything you want from me."

Alec doesn't move, not an inch. His facial expressions range from surprise to disbelief and apprehension. Then he says quietly, "Em, I'd feel like I'd be taking advantage of you right now. There's no reason to rush this."

I look into his eyes, searching for the rest of what he's not saying. He reaches up, gently tucks a stray hair behind my ear, and shakes his head. His touch is incredibly tender and completely unexpected; my chest feels like it might break under the weight of his acceptance. He's not holding back because he doesn't want me; he's holding back because he is concerned for me.

"Alec, please," I whisper.

I observe his beautifully sculpted face and see the battle inside him fade as his resolve breaks, realizing he can't deny me.

It's a heady feeling to know I can rattle him; that he heard my plea. He wants this as much as I do, and that knowledge hums through me. There's power behind learning that Alec is not so strong as to deny me. Oh, the possibilities.

"The bedroom?" he asks, lifting us effortlessly from the chair. His warm palms grip my ass cheeks under the robe; I only manage a nod. I wrap my legs around his waist, hoping the movement says what my unspoken words can't.

This time already feels different, steadier, surer. An eager willingness settles in me.

He eases his grip and allows my feet to touch the carpet. But I don't step away. Instead, I rise onto my tiptoes and press a soft, lingering kiss to his mouth. When I pull back slightly, I'm mesmerized by his chocolate brown eyes that hold mine as if he's looking all the way to my soul.

With sincere emotion, I whisper, "Alec, I fought hard against this, against the idea of us. I felt I didn't deserve you, thinking I'm too broken. My past choices have made me distrustful of myself and others. Tonight, I see that your steady strength and belief in me have helped me overcome my fears. I want you. And I want this."

Alec crushed me to his chest, and together we tumbled onto the bed, not very gracefully, but I loved every second of it.

"You're precious, Em," he vowed, his voice rough with conviction as he framed my face with his large hands. "If it takes me the rest of my life, I'll prove that to you."

My eyes fluttered shut in anticipation and longing, only to startle open when his low rumble brushed across my lips. "Open your eyes, Em. I love everything about you. You're so beautiful, inside and out."

Then his mouth claimed mine, hot and insistent. The kiss was wet, consuming, and full of intent and promise. Heat coursed through me, igniting a fire that we've been stoking for what felt like weeks.

Alec was saying all the right things. Everything I want and need to hear. And I believe, he believes them to be true. These are not empty platitudes he's spewing to get in my pants.

I wished his words were enough to erase my past, to cleanse the tainted memories that still haunted me, to make me believe I was everything Alec saw when he looked at me. But nothing could change the fact that I was damaged. A part of me was lost long ago, the part that could have been everything he deserved.

As always, Alec sensed the doubts in my mind. His next words snapped me back to the present. "I'm going to make love to you, Em. I'm going to savor you, enjoy every inch of you."

It was more than a promise; the pressure of his impressive bulge indicated he fully intended to keep it.

In moments, Alec had me beneath him, shedding his own clothes just as quickly. He supported most of his weight, yet the warmth of his skin pressed against mine seeped into every part of me, like a personal weighted blanket, steadying, grounding, comforting.

Alec was already showing signs that he would make good on his promises. Starting with my lips, Alec trailed kisses across my face, behind my ear, down the curve of my throat, until he reached my breasts. The way he lingered there left no doubt, Alec was very much a breast man.

He gave my girls special, methodical attention, and the warmth of his mouth on each sensitive nipple aroused me far more than I ever imagined possible. I was beyond turned on. I'd never experienced this kind of pleasure before.

When Alec finally leaves my breasts to trail kisses down my ribcage toward my navel, a small cry of protest escapes me, one I know I'll blush over tomorrow. But all thought vanishes as quickly as it arrived. Alec's broad shoulders nudged my thighs apart, and all I can feel is the heat of his mouth as his sensual kisses travel all the way down to my sweet spot.

I can't stop the gasp as Alec places a soft kiss on my mound, followed by a languid lick over my clit, before blowing his warm breath over my now-wet core. That shouldn't be so hot, but it was. I was writhing with intense need that shattered my inhibitions and woke dormant parts of me.

My body trembled with anticipation. I felt truly alive. My fingers grasped Alec's hair, gripping and tugging in an effort to draw him closer. To force him to finish what he started. "Alec, please," I shamelessly beg, not recognizing this version of myself.

"Em, honey, I'll take you there. I want you to cum for me, I need you relaxed," Alec says, forcing his shoulders more firmly between my thighs while lifting one of my legs to rest over his shoulder. Alec was determined to keep his promises. "You taste so fucking good. No way would I stop after having that teasing taste."

I was about to combust. Boom. My first experience with such a carnal act felt mind-blowing. I should feel embarrassed or exposed, but I knew from the girls that this was a mutually pleasurable experience. Plus, this was Alec. He wouldn't do something he didn't want to do.

All thoughts fade as Alec maintains a relentless pace. The triple assault of licking, sucking, and nipping has a coil tightening in my gut, causing me to squirm and pull harder on his hair. When he adds a finger, then two, I lose the ability to breathe. Or maybe I was holding my breath?

Tighter and tighter the coil built, causing my hips to buck and tilt of their own accord, writhing with a desperation I couldn't vocalize. No words came to mind, at least not any I felt comfortable saying.

Blessedly, Alec doesn't slow his assault when his focus zeroed in on my needy clit, burning pressure intensified until the coil snapped in a glorious release.

I screamed his name. Of course, I did. I never knew a sexual experience could be like this. I thoroughly enjoyed every second of what he just did to me.

Before I can fully recover, Alec is kissing his way back up my body. His fingers, still wet from my juices, trail around each of my nipples. His warm lips follow the sensual path.

I knew it! Alec likes breasts. He stalls to give each of my girls extra attention as his fingers then his mouth continue their caressing path down my body. The almost light touches tickle as they glide over my ribs, past my navel, before returning to my still pulsing core. The erotic, sensual contact causes a feverish need to coil and tighten anew.

Alec must be in a mood to tease, as he only places a few kisses on my pubic bone before starting the path back up my body. I can't really complain as he lavishes my body with warm, wet kisses that add fuel to the fire already building within me. His fingers, his large, long fingers, circle my clit. Then alternately dip in and out of my core. It's not enough, though.

He's relentless in his quest to taste all the other parts of me. My body is so attuned to his every touch. Squirming and writhing from the persistent assault from his mouth and his touches. "Alec, please. I need more," I beg.

"Baby, I got you. I'm taking it slow to explore every inch of your body and give your body time to adjust. You tell me if I need to stop at any point." Alec offers.

"No! Stop teasing me!" I snap, not recognizing this desperate side of myself. Too turned on to give a damn.

Alec slides his fingers from my core. I want to protest until I feel it. With his body hovering over mine, I felt the slow, shallow nudges at my entrance by the warm velvet head of his rock-hard cock.

With him over me, I clearly see Alec grinding his teeth to keep his control. He was not rushing this. Instead, he entered me slowly with reverence. Only the tip, pausing, then retreating. A rocking rhythm, giving my body time to adjust and accept.

"Sweets, you are so fucking tight," Alec clinches out, right before slamming home. Alec's intense stare was watching me closely, looking for any signs of distress or regret. Ascertaining that I was good, his hold on me tightens as he starts to move. Unhurried and sure. Reaching parts of me that I never knew were there. It was exquisite torture.

As my body adjusts to his bulk, a delicious moan escapes my lips before I can stop it. His name is a plea for more, "Alec."

Alec keeps me enveloped in his arms, taking me with a slow and steady rhythm that both frustrates me and ignites me.

Managing to keep my eyes open, I watch the intensity and strain on Alec's face. I realize he is struggling, just barely holding on to his control. But he *was* managing.

The ache and the craving for more were foremost on my mind. I hated his ever-present control even more now than ever before. Arching against him, I push myself back into the mattress to urge him to take me deeper. "More," I beg, if not demand.

Alec was searching my face for signs of reluctance or permission, I'm not sure which. The words to express what I need and my dislike of his self-control escape me. Wrapping my hands around his upper arms, those beautifully infuriating arms that are holding him above me, I clutch him to me while also tightening my pelvic muscles.

I can tell Alec isn't immune to my feeble attempts at forcing him to take me as a normal, non-damaged partner. He's fighting against his own instincts to take what he wants. Is it because he can tell I'm not experienced, or is it because he thinks I'm fragile?

Digging my nails into his arms, I wrap my heels tight around his ass and squeeze my inner muscles again. I'm determined to break his control.

"Alec. Please," I whimper, feeling on the verge of frustrated tears.

It was at that moment that I could feel Alec's control snap. His answering groan sounded like he was pulling it from deep within him. He was unable to stop his primal reaction to my plea. His body began to take over, ignoring his mind's need to proceed with controlled caution.

This version of Alec is new and exciting. He was pushing faster, harder, deeper into my body. He was gripping my hips, driving into me without pause as he took us both on a desperate, brutal ride to pleasure.

All I could do was hold on, gasping as he filled every part of me, even the parts I swore I had lost forever.

The man here with me now is my Alec, who didn't give up on me. He was showing me that I am who he wants and needs.

Having Alec lose control is a heady feeling. I love that he wants me as desperately as I want him. As he pounds in me, he reaches the very deepest parts of my damaged soul. I am completely his for the taking.

My body responds to his primal dominance over me. The wonderful coil of desire has me pulsating with the need for another equally intense release.

The glorious pressure builds and tightens. As it snaps, I cry out Alec's name. My body is clutching and milking all of him as Alec groans through his own release.

Wow. I'm still trying to catch my breath and absorb what just happened when Alec rolls us both, putting me on top. Our bodies remain connected as he buries his face in the crook of my neck, rasping. "You're mine."

Since I liked the sound of that, I didn't say anything. What I did was tighten my inner muscles again, a show of my new superpower. Strong enough to fracture Alec's control. His groan confirms it. His following words prove it. "You so own me."

I laugh. "You sound pitiful. If it makes you feel better knowing, you own me too." I don't hesitate to tell him what I know to be true. Of course, I'm not naïve enough to think it will be smooth sailing from here on out. But for the first time in a very long time, I have hope.

I'm not sure where Alec's thoughts were, but mine were that I had greatly underestimated Alec's prowess. Sex with the real Alec was way better than my dream version, and much more satisfying.

I'll keep this new discovery to myself. Alec never needs to know that he's been my wet dream man for about 2 years. That is skirting the edge of creepy.

With a satisfied sigh, I slide off his now softening dick to lie at his side. Neither of us seems inclined to get up or say anything.

Contentment. That's what this is. I feel peaceful lying half-on, half-off of Alec, eyes closed, completely relaxed. With his free hand, he traces slow, lazy circles over my shoulder and arm before threading his fingers through my tangled hair. His touch feels even more intimate than what came before, gentle, grounding, and impossibly tender.

With my right knee bent across his thighs, my right foot tucked between his spread legs, and our fingers intertwined over his stomach, I've never felt happier than I do right now.

Imagine my surprise when I hear Alec's hoarsely whispered questions. "You, okay? Did I hurt you? Was I too rough?"

Lifting myself onto my elbow, I look him straight in the eyes as I share my truth, "Alec, no. That was wonderful. It was perfect."

Framing his face with both of my hands, I kiss him tenderly and share, "Thank you for waiting on me, for believing in me."

"Oh, sweetheart, you don't have to thank me. That was all you. You're stronger than you give yourself credit for, and it wasn't a hardship, not when the reward was so spectacular." Alec says, his voice muffled as he showers kisses on my face and down my neck before placing a sweet kiss on my nose.

Just then, Alec's expression sobers, and with a contrite look, he confesses, "I didn't use a condom, and I didn't ask if you were on any birth control. I'm clean. I get checked every year, and anyway, it's been a long time since I've been intimate with anyone. None of that matters because I've *always* used a condom. Well before you." He says the last part with embarrassment all over his face.

Placing a finger over his mouth, I can tell he's worried I might flip out or get mad at him. Even though I've never made love before, I know that contraception is the responsibility of both partners.

"Relax, Alec, I've been on birth control since high school for heavy periods. And I've only ever been with one other person, and that was in college." Instantly, my face flames with embarrassment after revealing so much and confirming my lack of experience. He probably already figured that out.

If I weren't still lying half on him, I might have missed how his body grew tense. He was looking at me with an expression I couldn't interpret. "Alec?" I whisper, as he continues to look at me. Was he angry? At me?

"Em, you should have told me. I should have been gentler with you. I shouldn't have taken you so hard." He was directing his anger at himself.

"Alec, don't. What we shared was perfect. I enjoyed it thoroughly," I say, offering what I hope is a sincere smile.

Before Alec can say anything else, I ask, "Stay with me tonight? I want you here with me." I don't care if my request makes me sound a little desperate and needy. I'm not ready for Alec to leave. I don't want this night to end, or for this bubble of happiness to burst once we face the real world again.

Chapter Twenty-One
STAY WITH ME
Emily

Selfishly, I knew asking Alec to stay with me was a sure thing. Alec would never deny me anything he could easily do. Plus, we hadn't discussed whether we wanted our friends to know or even if we plan to continue whatever this is. All I knew for sure was that I didn't want this night to end.

Alec was staying. Leaning over, he presses a kiss to my forehead before getting up to turn off the living room lights and secure my apartment. He returns with a couple of bottles of water and our cell phones.

Heading to the bathroom to get cleaned up and ready for bed, I notice Alec is staring at his phone intently.

"Everything okay?"

Alec, still looking down at his phone, responds, "Yeah, babe, I missed a couple of texts and a voicemail. It's okay. Go get ready for bed."

A few minutes later, I came out feeling refreshed and a little giddy. I was wearing my hair down around my shoulders, and I had on the shirt I unknowingly took from Alec. "I set an extra toothbrush on the sink for you with some toothpaste," I say, pulling the covers back to get into bed.

The way Alec looked at me sent chills running down my spine. As he headed to the bathroom, he paused, looked back, and said, "Em, love seeing my shirt on you, but I want you naked." Then the door closed behind him.

I'm not going to lie; several responses run through my mind. I could've told him no, that I always sleep in a T-shirt or a sleep set. Or maybe I could have said, *You don't always get what you want.* A dozen rebuttals hovered on my tongue, but I swallowed every one of them.

Obediently, I remove the shirt, but I pull the covers all the way up to my neck.

As Alec emerges from the bathroom, he rasps, "Such exquisite beauty."

"You say the sweetest things, but I'm all covered up. You can't even see me," I say, laughing.

"Humm. Well, I'm about to remedy that." Alec says as he comes over to me, but before joining, he pulls all the covers off the bed and tosses them to the floor.

"Hey! That's not very nice, and I might get cold," I snap.

"I'll keep you warm," Alec says as he presses his body against mine. "I need to see and touch all of you. To worship this hot as fuck body of yours."

With just his words, I am already starting to feel the slow burn of desire, and he hasn't even done anything yet.

This time, Alec made sweet, gentle love to me. A part of me wanted him to lose control again, to dominate my body. I knew I had enjoyed it when he took me hard, but his gentle approach was spectacular. It allowed me to savor the pleasure as my orgasm seemed pulled from deep within my soul.

We lay tangled in post-coital bliss until Alec slipped away and returned with a warm cloth to gently clean me. It was thoughtful, and I was grateful, too sated and too boneless to move.

Alec climbed back into bed, pulled the discarded covers over us, and drew me against him, my back snug against his chest. In his arms, I felt safe, secure, and loved. A smile curved my lips as I drifted into a deep, dreamless sleep.

I woke up with a warm, hard body pressed protectively against mine. Alec's left hand cupped my right breast; he held me so close that there was no part of me not touching a part of him. I wasn't sure if he was intentionally or unconsciously aware that he was poking my ass with his very impressive erection.

To check if he was awake or not, I pressed back into his rock-hard dick. Squirming a little when I didn't get an immediate response.

In a sexy, raspy voice, Alec mutters, "You keep that up, we won't be leaving this bed anytime soon."

"Promises, promises," I say in a low, hopefully sultry voice.

Alec demands, still in a gravelly voice that sounds more awake now, "Throw your leg back over mine," His voice and his demands have me doing what he asks.

Alec slowly caresses my breast, circling my already puckered nipples before finally moving to the junction between my thighs. I feel like I can't get enough of him. After just one night, my body has become greedy for his touch and his unique brand of control.

"Em, you're so fucking wet for me already," Alec says, rubbing my clit with his thumb while dipping one, then two fingers into my core.

"Alec, I need you," I moan, pushing back to add pressure to his hard cock.

Before I can ask again, Alec enters me from behind with a sure thrust. "Oh, Alec." I whimper. Not expecting the quick invasion, but at the same time relieved to have it right where I need it most.

Alec fucks me from behind while we're lying on our sides, and he plays with my clit in time to each thrust. I'm pretty sure he can feel my climax building; the tightening of my inner muscles is a strong indicator. He doesn't slow his assault against my clit as he pounds a steady rhythm into me. "Your greedy pussy is trying to test my control." Alec grits out.

When I scream his name after a powerful orgasm, Alec is done playing nice. "Get on all fours," he demands.

I do as Alec instructed. And I'm rewarded when Alec reenters me all the way to the hilt. Gripping my hips, he moves in and out of me a few times before demanding, "Put your face to the mattress, tilt your ass in the air, and play with yourself while I fuck you."

I had a moment's hesitation, but then quickly did what Alec demanded. This was a new side of Alec. I suspected it was his true nature. I wasn't scared. Not at all. I was trembling not from fear, but from the need pulsating within me again.

Alec did fuck me well and good. When I exploded this time, my screams joined Alec's guttural groans.

I felt the sudden loss when Alec pulled free from within my body. Before I can move, Alec kisses my back and says, "Good morning, sunshine."

"Hmmm, it is a good morning," I mumble with my ass still in the air and my face planted in the mattress.

"Let's get you up before I can't control my urges not to take you again," Alec helps me right myself on the bed.

Instead of looking at Alec's handsome face, my eyes focused on his impressive cock. I'm surprised to see it's already semi-hard again.

"Um, I thought men needed some recovery time," I hedge.

Alec tilts my reluctant face up to meet his eyes. Smiling, he shares, "I'm insatiable when it comes to you. I feel like I can't get enough of that perfect pussy, and I know I can't get enough of you."

I laugh. What else can I do? Then I sober, wondering if a pussy can break.

"What were you just thinking?" Alec asks, looking concerned.

My cheeks flush pink from my naivety and childish wonderings. I was embarrassed but told the bossy man anyway, "I was just wondering if my pussy could break."

Alec laughs, a beautiful, rich sound, before he sobers enough to share, "I would never break it; I'm very fond of her. She's mine now."

"Umm, Alec? Why now? After all this time?" I hedge, not realizing until the words had already escaped that I truly wanted to know this.

Looking at Alec, I notice hesitation and apprehension on his face. I'm about to demand answers when my cell phone rings. Reaching over Alec to my nightstand, I see the caller ID before I answer, "Hey, Josh, what's up?"

Because our bodies are close, I felt Alec's body stiffen with tension as if on high alert.

Not taking my eyes off Alec's assessing ones, I tell Josh, "Let me confirm how many of us want to go, and I'll call you back in about 10 minutes."

Ignoring Alec's posturing, I send texts to the girls before returning my gaze to Alec's waiting chocolate brown eyes. "Josh wants to know how many tickets for the Rodeo to put at will call. Do you want to go?"

Alec shook his head no, but didn't say anything. I wish he would say something. I know he has reservations about Josh. He's not sharing any of his thoughts or concerns about it, but I can tell he really wants to. Surely, he knows that if I were into Josh, I wouldn't have let us get to this point.

So, I ask again, "Are you sure you don't want to go? I can extend the invite to Dex as well?"

Looking more resigned, he answers, "No, I have some work to do today. You girls go and have fun."

While talking with Josh about Rodeo events we should visit and then confirming the details with the girls, I noticed Alec listening to voicemails and sending messages alternately. Since I was watching him closely, I clearly saw the change in his demeanor. Right before my eyes, his features morphed into his more stoic, controlled mask.

"Everything okay?" I hesitantly ask.

"Yeah, Babe, just work stuff," Alec shares, setting his phone face down.

Returning my phone to the nightstand, I say, "I'm meeting the girls in an hour downstairs. What about you?" Purposefully letting the sheet slip, giving him a glimpse of the top mounds of my breasts.

Growling softly in his throat, Alec responds with a question of his own, "I have some time, what's on your mind?" As he runs his finger along the edge of the sheet, he teasingly grazes my breasts.

I surprise myself when I boldly say. "I have *you* in mind." Raising to my knees, I let the sheet fall away while I move to straddle Alec's lap.

This time it was faster but no less satisfying. It was all about the connection, the intimate closeness. Being on top did not mean I had any control. Alec made it clear with words and actions that he was fucking me. Not the other way around. Fine. Twist my arm.

We agreed to shower separately because we both knew we would be late for our appointments if we didn't put some space between us during our naked shower time.

Alec made coffee while I took a shower first. With hot water cascading down my body, memories from last night and this morning swirled in my mind, all vying for attention.

Alec had broken down my walls. I couldn't decide which time we made love was my favorite. And a part of me couldn't believe we were at this place, that I was at this place. Together with Alec. Finally.

Part of me wanted to cancel my plans for the day, so we could stay here in our bubble of bliss a little longer. I was already eager to see him again. Although my body was sore from using muscles that had been dormant, I felt needy around Alec.

Walking into the kitchen after rushing through my morning routine, I blurted, "Are you doing anything tonight?"

"You," Alec answers with a wicked, flirty gleam in his eye. No hesitation.

I laugh at Alec's quick and eager response. It was the answer I was hoping for. "I'm not sure when we'll get home. I know there are a couple of bands playing this evening that the girls might want to catch."

Alec hooks me around the neck to give me a lingering kiss before saying, "You text me when you get home, no matter what time. If you're tired, we'll meet up sometime tomorrow. Just let me know. And Em, have fun, but stay safe."

Alec says this casually, but the underlying message is that he'd worry until he knew I was safely home.

As he reaches my door, he turns, winks, and then he's gone.

Chapter Twenty-Two
BLURRED LINES
Alec

Leaving Em this morning was harder than it should have been. We both had plans that didn't include staying in bed all day. My thoughts keep replaying our time together, and I'm amazed by how responsive Em was, how her inexperience wasn't obvious. On the contrary, sex with Em as my partner was the most memorable sexual experience of my life.

Sex is an act I've always enjoyed immensely, and I've had my fair share of partners. But it wasn't until Em that I felt truly consumed by it as my body connected intimately with hers. Not just once, but every time I took her. It was like two halves becoming whole.

The realization of how perfectly we fit together filled me with a fear I couldn't fully understand. I must admit that part of it comes from the fact that Em has more control over me than I have over myself. She holds the leash to my self-control.

Of course, I'd go to the grave before admitting that to anyone. As the Captain of the CIA's Special Operations Task Force Team, with over thirty men and women under my command, maintaining control meant saving lives.

After Em fell asleep last night in my arms, I lay awake for a while. I couldn't shake the feeling of impending doom. Here I was, with everything I've ever wanted, literally in my hands, and

I felt like it was slipping away. No doubt, the reason was that I was a deceiving coward who hadn't used this night as an opportunity to be completely honest with her.

I love Em, and I have no doubts about that. What I was really uncertain about was telling Em the whole truth, everything. Who I was. Why I entered her life. All of it. I wasn't just a coward; no, I was a deceitful, gambling coward, clinging to hope that I'd never have to reveal those truths.

When Em confided that she had a bad college experience, I chose not to pressure her to share more. I wasn't surprised that Em didn't trust me with much; I understand it will probably take her some time. Telling me she made poor choices and had bad experiences doesn't mean she's letting me in.

Ironically, just that small admission into her past was enough for her walls to start crumbling, enough to let me connect with the woman beneath. The one that had physical needs, even if she wasn't ready to share her whole story.

If I wanted Em to trust me with her heart, I had to trust her with mine. Her story. Her past. It would be shared freely when I had all of her. I was sure of it. That was my last thought before drifting off to sleep beside her.

After a much-needed hot shower, I made myself another cup of coffee. Em's coffee was weak, and I could see a Nespresso machine in her future.

On my voicemail, Frank and his photo forensics team said they'd uncovered something I had to see in person. I couldn't fully explain the weight in that request or why I felt a sense of foreboding, but I did.

Then a wave of fear hits me in the chest, gut-wrenching fear. Fear of what Frank's team found. Fear of how it relates to Em. Mostly, I fear my time with Em might already be running out. Because whatever they discovered would inevitably mean my truths would have to be revealed, whether Em was ready or not.

Part of me wished the appointment with Frank was earlier than noon. But the other, more rational part knows I need these two hours to get my collective shit together.

The noon meeting sucked ass. I didn't have my act together; I wasn't adequately prepared for all that I learned and all that I didn't. I left with no definitive answers, only more broken pieces to carry. More regrets. More failures.

I've not only let Em down, but I've also let myself down. I got too close and too involved, and as a result, I wasn't thinking strategically. The professional warnings about not blurring the lines between client and operative are there for a reason. Being smart and a good leader means knowing all the facts before pursuing or proceeding. I would never enter any situation without completing my reconnaissance first. But this time, I did.

Now, I'm backed into a corner with no options left. The only way forward will cause severe pain for Em. It will ruin her forward progress and destroy the fragile bond we shared as an *'us.'* My goal to keep her safe has failed, especially since the one thing I should have protected her from was actually me.

I need a plan of action. It's time to step back and reassess, to get my head out of my ass. I'm making a personal vow to focus on what's most essential and to compartmentalize the rest. Time to return to the basics: focus only on concrete facts. Do damage control.

I'd sell my soul to go back in time. If this were a mission, my whole team would be dead. That's how badly I've mishandled my personal involvement with Em.

Not only me. Em's parents, although well-meaning, will also play a part in what, on some level, I know will destroy the progress Em has made toward moving on with her life. Whatever Em has hidden behind her barricaded walls might now be exposed.

It's wild how, just a few hours ago, I had everything I never knew I wanted within my reach. Now, I'm left with regrets and remorse.

Staying focused in the face of what this could all mean for the woman I love will prove to be my most challenging mission yet. But I must stay on course.

What I need right now is to talk it out with someone who knows the real challenges I'm facing, having learned so much today. Someone who knows me and knows Em. A friend. And hopefully, an ally.

Chapter Twenty-Three
PRELIMINARY RESULTS
Alec

Knocking on Dex's unit, I really hope he's home and has no plans. There's absolutely no one else I can talk to who will understand the cluster fuck I created better than Dex.

I'm already speaking when Dex answers his door, "The preliminary results are in." I immediately notice when what I say registers, and Dex steps back without a word to let me in.

"Do you have plans tonight?" I ask as I walk inside.

Dex shuts his door, saying, "None that can't wait. What did you learn, man? You look a little green around the gills."

"It's fucked. I'm fucked. I knew there was something to find. My gut was telling me that something was missing, and we found it!"

Plopping unceremoniously onto Dex's sofa, with my head in my hands, elbows resting on my knees, and eyes cast downward, I can't bring myself to meet Dex's gaze. I'm sure his expression will be one of pity. Shit. I pity myself, sitting here with a posture like a broken, beaten man, because the foolish part of me knows what's at stake, knows that loss is imminent.

Dex retrieves a couple of beers before sitting in the chair adjacent to me, "Let me hear it, man. Don't hold back."

"Thanks, man. And thanks for letting me dump this on you. I feel selfish for roping you into my shit. Especially now that it's become more complex." I say, looking up to see Dex watching me.

"Dude, seriously. I told you I had your back. I'll keep having it no matter how fucked up it gets. We're friends. So, lay it on me." Dex says without hesitation. Dex means what he says, or he wouldn't have said it.

"There's a lot to share. Before I go into it, I need you to know that I don't have proof of shit. It's fucking maddening. I'm so frustrated with what we learned versus what we don't know." I share, running my fingers angrily through my hair. Deciding I'd like to keep my hair on my head, I attack my beer instead and take a deep pull.

"You already know that I like story time, so hit me." Dex says as he goes to retrieve a couple more beers, "Looks like the first round isn't going to last long."

Taking a deep breath, I start, "You remember I told you about the video surveillance footage that needed to be vetted out and cataloged?"

Dex nods, so I keep going. "There was this guy who appeared on the surveillance footage with two prior sexual assault charges. Both cases were dropped before any legal action happened. The guy never even went to court. That's not even the worst part. My team got the original police reports on both charges. It's bad, man, and I can't even imagine that this bastard might have gotten to Em!"

"Why did the charges get dropped? Was there no proof or something? Was he definitely connected with Em?" Dex inquires, leaning forward in his chair. I understand the need to be on the edge of one's seat. If his body language was any indication, he did not like this possibility either.

"The case details may be difficult to hear. It isn't good. The first case against the perpetrator involved a girl who said he took her to a nice restaurant. When he took her home, he wanted to come inside for a drink, and she agreed. She reported that shortly after he was there, his demeanor changed. He was no longer charming and attentive. She says she regretted agreeing to the drink because she was getting weird vibes from him."

Looking at Dex, I inform, "I was planning to give you only the gist of it. But honestly, I really need to get all this off my chest, which makes me an even bigger selfish prick."

"Man, don't worry about it. I can handle it." Dex confirms.

"Appreciate it," I say, continuing the story. "The girl says she told him that after the one drink, he should go, that she had an early morning class. As they had the drink, he asked her nonsensical questions and didn't really pay attention to her answers. These were her words."

"It gets pretty graphic from here, you good?" I ask again, he's not dumb, he knows where this story is headed, at least in part. The truth of the matter is that I need to share what I learned with a friend, especially since there was video evidence that Em spent time with this guy.

"I'm good, quit stalling," Dex says, looking me straight in the eyes.

Nodding, I continue, "The girl said she pretty much gulped down the drink and got up to show him to her door for him to leave. She reports feeling wrong, woozy, and disoriented. At that point, she still had the mindset to get him out of her apartment. She said in her panic, she remembers urgently and loudly telling him to leave while she stood on shaky legs at her open front door." I was stalling. Shit.

"Here's the kicker, she said the guy boxed her on the side of her head. She claimed that she must have blacked out. The next thing she remembered was him undressing her, and that he was already naked. She said her brain only came online in snippets and flashes of consciousness. What she did recall was not good. She said he brutally raped her repeatedly. During moments of lucidity, she said the pain was severe. Her exact statement was that he was ramming into her viciously while squeezing both her breasts with brute force. She said she had no concept of how much time had passed as she went in and out of consciousness."

"That guy is a sick motherfucker. I assume he drugged her. But that must have been some strong shit," Dex says, looking disgusted.

Nodding my head, I hedge, "He is sick, and it gets worse. Man, I don't want to give you these images. They will fucking haunt you for life."

"Alec, don't worry about me. It's not my first exposure to shit like this. If you need to share it, share it." Dex states. With a look in his expression that backs up his statement.

"What do you..." I start, but Dex cuts me off.

"Not now, maybe someday soon I can reciprocate with the storytelling. That time is not now. What else did the case reveal?" Dex invites, without wavering.

Nodding, I continue, "In the report, the girl says at one point she woke on her stomach; he was yanking her head back by her hair to kiss her, she thought. She remembered him shoving something underneath her before he forced himself as he sodomized her. She was grateful to blackout at that point."

"Yep, one sick motherfucker," Dex repeats darkly, visibly grinding his molars.

"I can't argue that point. That level of depravity is most definitely a sickness," I say before continuing, "The girl's next memory was waking up alone, feeling nauseous and in unmeasurable pain. When she finally managed to get up, she realized she was and had been bleeding. There was a good amount of blood on her and the sheets." Taking a few more pulls of my beer, I give both of us a moment. It's a lot of twisted fucked up information I'm sharing.

"That poor girl. It sounds like he's pretty fucking guilty to me. How in the hell did he not get charged?" Dex seethes.

"The girl showered before she called a friend to come take her to the police station to report the assault. Here's the issue:

because the girl showered, the judge ruled the rape kit inconclusive. And her friend, thinking she was being helpful, had stripped her bedding and trashed them all."

"Regardless, I'm sure one look at her would prove a crime had been committed," Dex states.

"It was her word against his, and this guy is the son of a wealthy businessman. An influential businessman who also serves as a criminal judge. Shortly after the girl's family filed a report, the case was dropped before seeing any court time."

"Oh man, that's just wrong," Dex tersely responds, heading to the kitchen for more beers.

"You and I both know he's guilty. Those police officers who took her statement knew he was guilty. No girl would make up a story like that." I respond, knocking back beer number two.

"The next case isn't any easier to hear, but fuck Dex, I can't stop thinking about what if this guy got to Em," I tell him before I get too caught up in my murderous imaginings.

"You can't know if he did get to Em for sure. Don't go down that path, man. Finish telling me what you do know." Dex suggests.

"The next assault charge was only about a year ago. The girl filed a police report. Same MO. Took her out, brought her home, and stayed for drinks. At some point while at her place, he drugged her. Same sick ass shit, he repeatedly raped her and sodomized her. What was different from the first case was that he left bite marks on her breast and back. And get this, there was a witness who placed him in the apartment."

"And this case was dropped, too?" Dex asks, looking dismayed and pissed.

"Yep, it got dropped. Talk about abuse of power. We haven't uncovered how dear old dad was able to manipulate the justice system just yet. My team is on that task as we speak," I share.

"The 2nd victim reported that in her apartment, she had kissed and fooled around with this guy. Some heavy petting was involved. But after her second drink, she said she must have passed out. At 10:40 pm, her roommate unexpectedly came home. The roommate claims that the guy stuck his head out of the girl's room, only half-dressed, and told the roommate that they must have fallen asleep. He allegedly told the roommate that her friend was still asleep and that he needed to head out. The roommate says about 15 minutes later, the guy hollered through her closed bedroom door to come lock up because you never knew who was lurking around, then he was gone."

"Seriously? What a fucked-up parting shot!" Dex was shaking his head in frustration.

"The roommate reported that she got up and locked the front door. She said she peeked in on her friend. She couldn't see much because of the darkness. She could make out her friend on the bed. She thought she was on her stomach and was all covered up."

"She didn't notice anything out of the ordinary?" Dex queries.

"Apparently not," I state before continuing, "The roommate reported that she returned to her own room, did homework until around 3:30 am, and then went to sleep. She says she was woken up around 5:00 am by her friend's sounds of vomiting and crying. When she went to check on her friend, she couldn't believe what she saw. Her friend was naked and leaning over the side of the bed, vomiting. The victim had splatters of blood on her back, and the bed sheets had blood all over them. She helped her friend sit up and noticed then that her friend had a busted lip and bite marks across her breasts. She also had bruised fingerprints around her neck."

"Even with daddy's help, I gotta hear how this fucker managed to get out of this one." Dex was just as disgusted with this bastard as I was.

Taking a deep breath, I continue. "This assault was more violent in its severity. Because the first case got dropped, the prosecutors couldn't present it as more evidence against him. Even with the roommate confirming his placement in the apartment, he still got off on a technicality. Stating that he left the apartment around 10:50 pm. That she could have met up with someone else that night. And, after he left, her roommate hadn't reported anything out of the ordinary until the next day. He basically used the roommate's own testimony to create doubt. It didn't help that the roommate had admitted to checking on her friend before retiring to her own room for the night. The charges were dropped."

Dex was up pacing the floor now; he was agitated, "But wait, couldn't they subpoena his dental records to compare with the bite marks?"

"The Attorney General took the subpoena request in front of a judge, but the request was denied. No doubt that was his dad's doing," I relay, feeling my own frustration mounting.

"This motherfucker and his dad must have some friends in high places." Dex snarls before sitting back down.

"He does," I say, "Trace Junior alone is nothing. His dad, however, has money, power, and influence. Edward Trace Roberts Senior has actually held two roles in the justice system, as an international government official and as a judge in criminal cases in the United States. His true reach and influence are yet to be determined."

"I still don't understand how anyone could have enough power to sweep those reported crimes under the rug, and you're saying they didn't even show up on the guy's record? That shit is messed up," Dex says, looking as frustrated as I felt.

"It's beyond messed up. My team is currently gathering details. I want to learn everything about who we're dealing with and what secrets might be hidden in their pasts. I also need to understand why, if both girls reported a crime, they didn't press formal charges. It would then be up to the state to pursue criminal charges. Instead, there are no records of sexual assault or aggravated sexual assault charges being filed in court. This suggests there's a real chance the cover-up extends beyond Trace Roberts Senior's reach. I'm convinced of it."

Sharing this fear with Dex doesn't do justice to the potential magnitude of the issue. No matter how powerful Trace Roberts Senior is, the legal system isn't that easily manipulated. Regardless of how many pockets Daddy padded.

"I gotta know, what did you find on this guy in relation to Em?" Dex's expression looks like he really doesn't want to know the answer, but needs to hear it. I know the feeling.

"The not-so-short answer is that they are just acquaintances. All morning, I reviewed what my team had discovered. I watched the video footage of the guy myself several times. I understand why the previous firm didn't flag anything as unusual. But my instincts are telling me that something isn't right. At 9:15 pm, you can see Em and Trace Roberts Junior arriving at her apartment, smiling and showing friendly camaraderie. Then, at 11:28 pm, he leaves. The next day at 10:12 am, the video shows Em leaving her apartment. She was wearing a ball cap, pink sweatpants, and a long-sleeved black T-shirt, which wasn't typical school attire based on earlier surveillance. As she leaves, she never turns her face toward the cameras. Her head makes a few quick side-to-side glances as she walks to her car parked right in front of the walkway. She returns to her apartment 36 minutes after leaving, carrying two grocery bags. Still, she doesn't show her face to the cameras. After entering her apartment, she doesn't reappear for over 78 hours."

"Okay, so…I'm thinking this is good. Right?" Dex shares.

"Possibly. But right before I left to come home, the team received additional, more incriminating information, which they want to dig deeper into." I share, taking a few more swigs of my now room-temperature beer.

Dex was on the edge of his seat, hanging on every word I said. "A few of my team members are still contractors for the CIA. They took the initiative and uncovered some underground files that included the two dropped cases. The files contain some extra information that we believe they would prefer to stay buried."

"Does it tell how the cases were concealed? Any names?" Dex queries.

"Not that I've been informed of yet. Our focus right now is to take all this information and try to connect some dots. When the photo forensic team identified Trace, they started the deep dive. After they unearthed the concealed criminal background reports, they went back to examine the video footage more closely. When they enhanced the visual effects of the video feed, they could zoom in on Trace in great detail," I share, watching Dex closely.

"In summary, they observed these potential red flags. When he exited Em's apartment, he cautiously glanced both ways before departing. They identified three deep scratch marks on the left side of his face. And they noticed his shirt collar was stretched beyond its normal limits. They can't confirm whether the marks were new or old. Nor can they confirm if his clothes are normally sloppy." I continued.

After sharing these dismal findings, my throat gets tight. My breaths come in short bursts, and I feel my hands get sweaty. I felt consumed by the knowledge that Em was alone with this guy. The thoughts only get more prominent when my mind registers what Dex just asked.

"Do you and your team think this guy also raped Em?" Dex whispers, looking just as ill as I felt.

Lowering my head for a beat to rein in my control, I answer the only way I can. "I don't know, man. My team pulled Em's phone records a few days before and after that day. She made no phone calls out. Two calls went unanswered. One call was from her mother, and one call was from a classmate. Em also didn't send any text messages out. One text was received from the same classmate, wondering why Em skipped class. Taking it a step further, we obtained a copy of her grocery receipt. The two bags contained Aleve, Neosporin, feminine napkins, a gallon of chocolate ice cream, a loaf of bread, and a pound each of smoked turkey breast and Vermont cheddar cheese. With my CIA connections, I had Em's medical records pulled. In the four years she was away at college, Em only visited her primary care doctor once and her OBGYN doctor twice. And none of those appointments were around that time. I've spoken with both doctors personally today and learned that Em hadn't sought medical treatment for anything outside of the norm."

Dex was openly gaping at me now. Then what I just revealed hits me.

"I know what you might be thinking, all the HIPAA laws I broke. Well, I'm still with the CIA; they didn't need to know that I'm retired." I respond sheepishly.

Dex barks out a laugh while mumbling, "I need to remember never to piss you off." He sobers before asking, "What does this all mean?"

"Dex, I'm trusting you to keep everything I've shared with you to yourself. I'm struggling with the idea of doing the same," I admit.

"You can't not report this!" Dex booms.

Sounding exasperated, I retort. "Report what exactly?"

Then, more calmly, I confess, "Think about what I'm facing with all this. Do I submit my findings to the Wilsons, knowing that although a crime appears obvious, I have no proof of anything? Even the dropped charges my crew obtained illegally can't be used as proof. The guy was never convicted of any wrongdoing. The charges were dropped! We also can't forget his father is still an active criminal court judge with prominent business dealings in the Houston area. I can't smear Trace Junior's name without concrete evidence. That would be professional suicide. After learning these details, the Wilsons will want to fight for justice, but I know they don't have a case. They won't win anything but a powerful enemy. I would be giving them information that will only hurt them and none that they can benefit in any way from knowing."

Taking a deep breath, I admit what is really eating at me. "Dex, fuck, but we don't know that Em was one of his victims. Em never reported that a crime was committed. She didn't call anyone for help. She never visited a campus counselor or any doctor around that time. She got up the next day and went to

197

the fucking grocery store!" I shout this last part; my frustration mounting with every fact I was retelling to Dex.

Holding it all in my head was one thing, but sharing my thoughts and fears was a whole other ball game.

Dex, for his part, looked deep in thought. "You need to talk to Em."

"It's not that simple, man. I'm contractually obligated to report my findings, whether confirmed or not, to her parents since I agreed to extend my assignment. Do I hand over the findings and let them figure out what happened, question Em, themselves? Or do I talk to Em first, before reporting anything to her parents, and ask her to confide in me, trust me, which means I have to tell her every... fucking... thing. She's not going to admit anything to me after that." I say, reiterating my position.

"You have to tell her," Dex confirms. No hesitation.

"Shit! I have really fucked all of this up." I can feel the bite of betrayal as these words are ripped from my throat.

"Tell me. Do you want me to pull out the whiskey?" Dex was being supportive, probably because he was beginning to understand the magnitude of the situation.

Ignoring his question, I confess, "I slept with Em, and I told her how I felt about her. What I didn't tell her, but should have, was the truth about who I was and why I was there in her life. And it gets worse; she told me that she had a bad experience in college, but that was it. She didn't say anything else about it. Fuck Man! I wasn't gentle."

Unable to sit any longer, I get up and walk away from Dex to hit the john. I wasn't ready to see the disgust on his face. Not when I could look in the mirror and get my fill.

After I use the facilities, I wash my hands and splash some cold water on my face. I felt off balance and defeated, unsure of what to do or how I could fix the mess I had made. None of these thoughts or feelings have I received training for.

When I return, Dex has two glasses of whiskey poured for us, and without preamble, he declares, "I know you, man, there is no fucking way you'd do anything to Em that she didn't want you to do. So, get that shit out of your head right fucking now!"

I love this guy. I needed the mental clarity his words delivered.

"You're right, I was precariously close to feeling sorry for myself. Thanks for the mental slap," I retort, both loving and hating how well Dex could read me.

"Nothing changes the fact that this is a no-win situation for me. Em will never trust me again. For me to tell Em everything I've found out, I first need to let her know I have been lying to and deceiving her for over 2 years. Then if that's not bad enough, I'm going to question her about something tragic that may or may not have happened to her years ago."

Pacing now, I ask a rhetorical question, "And, do I really think she'd be honest enough to tell me anything other than to get the hell out of her life? Especially after I explain that I'm contractually obligated to report anything I learn about her to her parents. The same parents who have been basically spying on her, her whole life."

Sitting back down with a groan, I confess, "This is so fucked up, and for the first time in my life, I feel defeated and powerless. And okay, maybe I also feel sorry for myself. Em will never forgive me for keeping the truth from her."

We were both quiet for a few minutes, neither of us commenting on what was shared. I was grateful for this time. All that I laid out to Dex pales in comparison to the knowledge that no matter how I respond to this situation, Em will not want anything to do with me after this. And I don't blame her. I'm a selfish asshole for not coming clean with her before now and for laying all this shit at Dex's doorstep.

Watching Dex drink his whiskey, I can tell he's deep in thought. It is confirmed when he shares, "You have to be the one to talk with Em. It has to come from you. She's closer to you than she is to her parents. If there are any painful details to share, Em is more likely to share them with you. Not me, not Roxy, not Sarah, and especially not her parents. Man, it has to be you."

Although Dex was adamant about this, and I had to admit that his logic held merit, he doesn't understand what this will mean. "I'll lose her," I whisper.

Dex retorts, "I disagree. For the sake of argument, let's say she never wants to see you again, but she confirms the abuse.

You're then able to lock that motherfucker away, and Em can find healing in knowing that she helped prevent this from happening to another girl. We both know if this guy did rape Em, then there have to be other girls out there. And I'm sure Em will feel safer knowing he's locked up. Then I think she'll come around." Dex sounds so sure, but he still doesn't get it.

"It's not that easy, man. I'm contractually bound not to disclose my cover to Em, and I'm contractually required to report any findings to the Wilsons. That means I need their permission to speak with Em and disclose my position. But first, I have to tell them I've found something suspicious, even though I have no proof. Then I must convince them to give me time to talk with Em before I share any of those details with them." I admit, dreading all of it.

"Semantics," Dex says, not giving me an inch.

Shaking my head, I inform, "They would be within their rights to ask for my findings and even my suspicions without agreeing to my requests. There would be nothing I could do other than break the contract. Which would not allow me to help them with a potential case."

"I don't envy you; you're in a tough spot. Still, you have to try to get them to agree with your plan. Em will need this to come from you," Dex warns, looking forlorn, which doesn't help me at all.

"What if I'm wrong? What if I've let my emotions and feelings for Em cause me to dig deeper when there were no prior findings? Em herself never reported anything. Never confirmed that anything happened." I feel miserable acknowledging this scenario.

"You have to follow your instincts." Dex firmly reminds me.

"If I'm wrong, this will all have been for nothing. I was a few months away from being clear of my contractual obligations. Free to live my life on my own terms. Now, I'm going to lose the only thing I've ever truly wanted for myself. I love her and I can't bear the thought of being wrong about the investigation and losing her or being right and learning that my sweet Em has been violated."

Dex is quick with his response, "You have to be strong for her, and you gotta have a plan. Collect your thoughts. Focus on the facts. Determine what has to be shared first and foremost. She'll forgive you, man. You have to keep believing in that."

Dex wasn't about to back down from his belief that Em would forgive me. I really wanted Dex to be right. From his lips to God's ears.

"I hear you, and you're right about the fact that I need to have a strategic plan." With everything on the line, getting organized has to be my next priority. Which means I have to put my emotions and fears on the back burner. My focus needs to be on what I have to relay to Em.

Settling on a plan of action, I inform Dex that I need to head out. Reaching his door, I turn back, "Thanks, man. You can't begin to know how much your friendship means to me."

Before I can leave, I hear Dex say, "I'm here if you need me. Even if you call me to help you hide the cold, dead body of that fucker. I got your back, no questions asked." He was smirking, but I think he meant it.

Giving him a thumbs up, I say, "I'll keep that in mind." As I leave.

Chapter Twenty-Four
THE LIST
Alec

I felt more in control and focused after my talk with Dex. I only wish I had his confidence when it comes to Em. I may not share his assurance that everything will work out in the end, but I do have a plan of action. First and foremost, I need to set aside all my emotions and doubts. My focus must be on Em and what I need to do for her.

Sitting at my kitchen table with a pen and notebook, I realize that Dex was absolutely right about one thing. It has to be me who talks to Em. If for no other reason, I'm the only one who knows just how much I've deceived her. I should never have let us become more than friends. At least not until she knew everything about me, and not until the contract with her parents was either over or void. With Em knowing everything, it should have been her decision to take our relationship further. Instead, I took that decision away from her.

I started my list with a chronological approach. If I ever want to regain Em's trust, she needs to know where and when it all began. The list will need to include *all* details, regardless of how damaging they may appear. This task may be my only chance to lay it all out for her. To try to explain my position.

The more I write, the more daunting the task becomes. Nothing I list puts me in a favorable position. I messed up badly. I jumped the gun and made this situation personal. I'm no longer just the security detail or the neighbor friend. I'm the man who lied by omission, deceived her, and, knowing it was wrong, began a sexual relationship based on false pretenses.

Recounting the details to share with Em, I can no longer hide from the fact that this mission is a complete snafu. At no other time in my career have I been part of an assignment that got off target this badly. The only thing left to do at this point is damage control. Well, and begging might help.

After my call with the Wilsons, my apprehension increased. They agreed to let me speak with Em first before they contact her. They also reluctantly agreed to wait until Monday to hear the findings, which was the deadline they set for me to discuss my suspicions with Em. The timing might be tight, but it's still generous. They didn't have to give me any extra time at all.

With the time constraints in place, I suddenly feel both mentally and emotionally drained. Leaving my notes and my phone on my now cluttered table, I lie down on my couch to give my brain and eyes a break. As far as missions go, this one blows chunks.

Of course, my mind wasn't cooperating to give me any rest. Swirling in my head were numerous unfamiliar feelings accompanied by a sense of urgency that unsettled me. I felt overwhelmed with remorse and guilt, and there was also a heavy dose of fear. I had no experience with any of these emotions, and I didn't know how to process them.

Ironically, I can't apply any of my Special Forces training to my current predicament. At least not after ignoring the most crucial rule that says you should avoid all personal entanglements. *You think?*

There is no special training for this kind of situation. On a mission, if you ignore your protocols, you die. Period. Knowing what I need to do and being able to do it are two entirely different hurdles.

I'm struggling to focus solely on the facts. I want to plead my case and tell Em that I know I wasn't thinking clearly. I believed my contract was ending. There are so many things I want to say to explain away what I know will undoubtedly hurt Em. Unfortunately, I lost that chance when I didn't reveal who I truly was before sharing her bed. My actions have added to the deception to a point where Em won't be able to forgive easily. If at all.

Lying here, I can't stop thinking about the inevitable loss that's coming for me. There's no way Em will trust me after this, and I don't deserve forgiveness, even if it's vital for my future. The future I pictured was with Em when I think about my long-term civilian life plans.

Since Em is out with the girls at the Rodeo, I make mental plans to tell her tomorrow. Tomorrow, being Sunday, will give me the whole day with her to answer any questions and to find the time to grovel and beg for forgiveness. Whatever it takes to keep Em in my life.

The memory of Friday night and this morning with Em, when I was happy and had everything I wanted, already feels like a dream.

What I won't forget is the moment I saw her in the kitchen, truly happy. The happiest I've ever seen her. That look will stay with me for the rest of my life, knowing that in just a few hours, I'll be the one to take it all away.

Closing my eyes, I try to will the inevitable pain away and brace myself. The hardest part to accept in all of this is knowing that I was about to hurt the one and only woman I've ever loved. That was my last thought as I finally drifted off to sleep.

The ping from my phone woke me from a restless nap. I wasn't sure how long I had been asleep or what time it was, but I was confident that the message was from Em.

And thank God I wasn't wrong. Her text said, "Home now. Want to come over; we could watch a movie or something."

My mind immediately fixates on the *'or something'* part of her message, and my body, having a mind of its own, is already reacting. If I was already getting hard just from her unintentional pun, how was I planning to get through this evening without losing control?

The girls arrived home much earlier than anticipated. Which means I have no reason to put off the inevitable. The talk will happen tonight.

I send a quick text, telling her I'll be over soon but that I have something I need to discuss with her. Em didn't reply.

Ripping my scribbled notes from the notebook, I fold the pages and tuck them into my pocket. As a final thought, I grab a bottle of wine and some popcorn. I am being overly optimistic that this talk will end well, but I can't let myself lose hope just yet.

When Em opens her door wearing only a cami and short sleep shorts, I almost turn around to leave. I am a red-blooded male, after all. Seeing her, her outfit, and her happy-to-see-me expression, I know my resolve to talk to her and do the right thing is about to be tested.

"Come in," Em says as she pulls my arm to get me to cross the threshold. "What's wrong? Why the hesitation?" she asks, not realizing I must have paused my reactions.

"Hey, did you see my last text? There's something I need to talk to you about," I ask instead of answering her.

"Yep, I saw it, but no talking tonight. We can talk in the morning. Can you stay? I missed you," Em says, bravely putting these feelings out there. Her boldness shows me how much she has started to trust me.

"I missed you too," I respond. It's the truth. And even though I know I don't deserve it, I can't deny Em anything, including tonight. It doesn't change the fact that I'm being even more of a selfish jerk for not insisting we talk. But in case this is our last night together, I want this time with her. I want her as she is right now. Fully aware that I'm a greedy bastard for taking it.

"You want me to open the wine?" I ask, rather than insisting, that we talk.

"Yes, please," Em replies as we both head to her kitchen for the opener and wine glasses.

"How was the rodeo? Did you girls have fun?" I ask, opening the wine.

"We had a blast; the tickets were VIP full-access passes, which meant all the drinks and food we wanted were included. Toyota sponsored several companies, and we also had access to their tents. All three of us brought home a sack full of vendor giveaway merch. It was fun. It would have been more fun if you were there," Em says, taking a sip of the wine, I just poured.

Taking a sip from my own glass, I say, "It sounds like Josh really hooked you girls up."

"It was nice of him, but now I want to talk about you. What did you do today?" Em asks, with happy confidence.

"I had a work meeting around lunchtime, and I spent some time with Dex," I reply, hoping Em doesn't pick up on my vague answers.

"Did Dex say anything about him and Roxy?" Em asks with genuine curiosity.

"No, guys don't kiss and tell," I say, smirking.

Then a thought crossed my mind, and I couldn't help but wonder whether Em had talked and whether the girls knew about us. "I have to ask; do you kiss and tell?"

The little minx giggles as she walks toward the living room, asking, "Want to watch a movie? We can rent The Greatest Showman from Amazon."

"Sure, whatever you want, but next time I get to pick the movie," I say, smiling at the look of mock horror on Em's face. But I caught sight of her smile too as she took our glasses to place them on the coffee table.

"Babe, I want to point out that you haven't given me a hello kiss yet," I say, tagging Em around the waist to pull her down on the couch with me. Em takes this opportunity to turn and straddle my lap before raining gentle kisses along my jaw, down, then back up my neck, before finally landing on my lips.

"Are you better now?" she asks, well aware of the answer. Her grinding against my hardening dick is a good indication. The added pressure, combined with her tender kisses, stirs a growing desire in me. The real chance that this could be our last night together like this ignites a fire that's been simmering just below the surface of my need for her.

Gone is the need to be gentle with her. Putting my hand in her hair, I pull Em close as I deepen the kiss. She's right there with me. The kiss grows hungrier and more frenzied as our intertwined desires ignite.

I not only want, but I need, to be skin-to-skin with her beautiful, perfect body. "Em, take this off," I rasp, reaching behind my neck to pull off my own T-shirt.

Em surprises me by removing not just her top but also her bottoms. Not to be outdone, I maneuver her weight to take off my own jeans. "Commando?" Em asks with a hungry look, staring directly at my dick that is now standing at attention.

Smiling, I pull Em back to me as she straddles my lap again. "You were commando, too," I say, smiling.

"True. Now, where were we?" Em asks with a naughty little smile, a smile I've only ever seen her share with me. I absolutely love this assertive side of her. It pleases me greatly that she's as turned on by me as I am by her. With Em on her knees, her perfectly perky breasts are directly in my face. I capture one pink bud in my mouth, sucking lightly as I pinch the other taut nipple. Her response is immediate and captivating.

Eyes sliding closed, I bite back a moan when Em begins to rub and grind, applying exquisite pressure with her warm, wet core against my rock-hard dick. Opening my eyes, I see Em enjoying her newfound power as she seeks to pleasure herself. As her need intensifies, she moans, "Alec, I need ..."

Reaching down between our bodies, Em's not just wet, but drenched. "I got you, baby," I say, applying pressure to her clit in pace with her movements.

"Come on, baby, take what you need." I rasp, barely able to maintain control over my own need to flip her and take over.

Watching Em ride my finger, taking herself to orgasm, is an exquisite torture I'd be happy to sign up to endure for the rest of my life. Feeling her body shudder above mine, I can't wait another second longer. Guiding my dick to her core, I take advantage of the slickness and readiness of her pussy to slide in. She's still so tight that it challenges my self-control.

It was Em's gasp that had me hesitating to move. Searching her eyes for any signs of discomfort, I only see contentment. "You okay, babe?" I ask to confirm.

"Yeah, I'm even better now," Em shares, not taking her eyes from mine.

Lifting her by her hips, I control her movements. Sliding her up and down my shaft, I keep a slow, steady pace. Our kisses start soft and sweet, then turn hungry and needy. Em ignites as she once again takes control and begins to move faster, taking all of me in with long downward strokes. "Oh Em, you feel fucking fantastic," I moan, hoping I don't blow my load now that Em is chasing another release.

I let Em set the pace for only a few more strokes before my control snaps, and I can no longer handle it. Grabbing Em's ass with both hands, I lift up before slamming back down. Setting a punishing rhythm that Em is all about.

The noises she's making urge me on. Flipping us, I take us both on a wild ride. I'm not gentle, yet Em's verbal responses encourage me not to hold back. "Harder, Alec," she whispers as she lifts her knees higher at my sides, allowing me to go even deeper.

Em is on fire. This time is different. Better. More intense. I keep up a punishing pace until I feel Em's channel tighten on my dick and her nails score my back.

"Em, come on, baby, I'm close," I say in a hoarse voice, fighting against my own needs to hold out for her. Shifting my weight, I make sure each downward stroke hits her most sensitive spot.

"Alec, Oh God Alec!" Em screams as her body clenches around my dick, taking me over the edge with her.

"Wow. Did I scream? I think I just screamed," Em whispers, lowering her legs from the sides of my ribs.

"Yeah." I respond wholeheartedly, agreeing with the 'wow' assessment and confirming that she was loud. I fucking loved it.

Shifting my weight off her, I gently kiss her, asking, "So do you still want to watch the movie?"

Em is adorable when she asks, "Well...can you stay here tonight? If so, I think we should turn in early." My little minx says, knowing there's no way I could leave her now.

Chapter Twenty-Five
THE TALK
Alec

Slowly, I wake up, realizing I'm once again spooning Em. My right hand cups her left breast, and my erection is nudging for any point of entry.

I've decided that sleeping over with Em is my all-time favorite thing to do. The only problem this time is that Em is trying to extricate herself from my hold. I involuntarily stop her when my arms reflexively tighten around her.

Em pauses her struggle before quietly asking, "You awake?"

"No," is my rough reply.

"I gotta get up, I have to meet Dex in 20 minutes for our run," she whispers, still trying to wiggle free from my hold.

"No, it's too early," I rasp, squeezing her closer.

"You stay in bed; I'll be back in an hour or so. Then we can shower together," Em says, offering me a tempting proposition.

Reluctantly, I loosen my grip. Before Em leaves the bed, I pull her back for a passionate, lingering kiss. Morning breath be damned.

"I'll be back," Em says, grabbing a stack of clothes from her dresser before heading to her bathroom.

"You could skip the run and stay here with me." I feebly suggest, laying the guilt on.

I must have made her feel bad because she shares, "Next time I'll reschedule with Dex, but it's too late now. I only have a few minutes to get downstairs and be ready for my run. If I cancel, he'll get his knickers in a twist and make me run twice as long the next time."

Next time. Please let there be a next time. "Hurry back, sweetheart. We still need to talk," I say, yawning widely before drifting back to sleep.

The next time I woke, it was to the sound of the shower. I must have really needed the sleep to fall back so quickly and deeply.

Today is the day. The day I have to talk with Em, I need to convince her that she can still trust me. That it goes beyond just wanting her, I also need her in my life. For just a second, I considered waiting for her to finish her shower. But the selfish, greedy side of me couldn't resist being with her again.

"Good morning," I say. Delighted to see that, although I startled Em, she is completely on board with me joining her. Taking the hand she extends toward me, I step into the shower before giving her a gentle kiss on her smiling lips. "Pass me the soap, baby, let me wash you," I offer, grabbing the terry cloth loofah hanging on a shower hook.

Creating a lather between my hands with the bar of sweet-smelling soap, I begin the enjoyable task of washing Em. My hands are eager to explore every inch of her irresistible body, paying special attention to my favorite areas. "Em, you're so beautiful and your body is perfect; I can't keep my hands off of you."

"Then don't," the little minx states, also touching my body with her soapy, exploring hands.

"Give me your foot," I say, as I lather a loofah with more soap. "I plan to wash every inch, by delicious inch, of your gorgeous body." Starting with one foot, I methodically glide the loofah and my soapy hand up her leg, to her stomach, then proceed to her other leg, before returning to the other foot.

Em's body is a masterpiece. Her skin is smooth and flawless. Her runner's figure is firm and well-defined.

Sliding my hands back up, I drop the loofah and spin Em around, placing her back to my front so I can wash the junction between her thighs. Caressing and exploring, I take my time leisurely. Em spreads her legs further, giving me easier access. My left hand continues up to wash her breasts, making sure each one is clean.

Em's soft mewling and moans have me fighting my instincts to take her right then and there. When her small, eager hands start to roam my body, stroking the parts she can reach, I'm momentarily distracted.

Em, taking advantage, turns her body back around to continue her exploration. As her eyes intently follow her every touch, my dick stiffens. When she reaches for me, my thoughts falter. Her soapy hand strokes up and down as she strokes me, while her other hand makes a teasing trail over my pecs, stopping to pinch a nipple.

"Em, I'm going to fuck you right here if you keep that up," I groan, grinding my teeth. My control is slipping.

In response, Em bites her lip and looks up with her most beautiful, mischievous smile as she pinches my other nipple.

"That did it!" I groan before loudly demanding, "Em, turn around and put your hands against the wall. Spread your legs and tilt your ass for me."

Without hesitation, Em turns and follows my instructions. I stand there for a minute or two, watching but not touching her. Watching her squirm is all the proof I need that she wants me as much as I want her. I was worried she might be too sore, but her responsiveness erased all concern.

"Alec?" I hear, barely above a whisper. Lathering my hands again with the soap, I begin rewashing her. This time, I start from the back of her legs to her ass, then to her shoulders. Gliding down her spine, I return to her ass before lightly touching between her thighs.

"Alec, please," Em moans. The waiting, not knowing my next move, along with the intimate caressing, is making Em impatient.

"Bend forward more, keep your legs spread wide," I command in my low, gravelly voice. Em's legs are now trembling slightly, anticipating what I'm about to do to her. My little minx enjoys being told what to do and trusts me to take care of her.

This discovery is good news, especially since I like to be in control, not just in my life but also in the bedroom.

"Tell me what you want. I need to hear you say it," I demand, continuing my soapy glide over her body and between her thighs while nudging my rock-hard shaft against the crack of her ass.

"Alec, I want you inside me," Em bites out with a hint of exasperation.

Hearing Em say those words strips the last of my ability to take it slow. Putting one of my large hands between Em's shoulder blades, I push her down further. At the same time, I enter her balls deep.

Em cries out, which for one moment scares me at least until Em starts rocking back and forth against me, urging me to move.

Gripping her hips, I'm lifting her ass to accommodate my height as I take us both on a magnificently rough ride.

To my relief, Em is right there with me. She doesn't mind me going deep and hard; with her hands against the tile, she's pushing back thrust for thrust.

"Alec! I'm going to come," I hear, right before Em screams my name as she shatters. My own release is sucked from me by the tightening and spasms of her inner muscles.

"Okay, I'm serious, I think you broke me," Em says with a smile in her voice.

Turning her to face me, I give her a long, hot kiss before smacking her ass and saying, "Actually, if either of us breaks, I think it would be me." Looking down at my now sated manhood.

Em busts out laughing before saying, "Oh, poor baby, you were so mistreated."

"I wouldn't say that, but I can admit that you totally won that round," I say, as I spin us around to give my body a quick rinse. Dread was already starting to creep in from knowing I was about to rock the very foundation of Em's world, and not in a good way.

"I'll make some coffee for us while you finish your shower," I say, climbing out to do just that.

"Okay, I'll be out in a minute," Em replies, shuffling under the spray of water.

Chapter Twenty-Six
DECEPTION
Alec

Stepping out of Em's shower, the heaviness of what I was about to share pressed heavily against my chest like a boulder, threatening to crush the air from my lungs. *Death by stupidity* might as well be etched on my tombstone.

My instincts told me this conversation was a pivotal moment in our relationship, but I had no illusions about how it might end.

Being with Em last night and this morning, knowing what my team suspects, only strengthened my resolve to tell her everything. The truth is, no matter what the forensics uncovered, I owed Em the truth about who I am and what I've done.

But my approach is riddled with flaws. The first is simple: I am a selfish asshole. I had no right to take comfort in her arms, to seek pleasure with her, not after what I know. Even the unconfirmed parts are enough to damn me.

The second flaw is more serious; I'm not entirely sure how much pain our conversation will cause the person I claim to love.

Sharing my backstory with Em is just one part; understanding her background and experiences is the other. The pain from sharing and learning is unavoidable, yet oddly comforting.

Because there is some comfort in coming clean, carrying guilt can weigh heavily on a person. Harboring physical and emotional baggage can be destructive. The old saying, *'The truth can set you free,'* comes to mind. I really hope there is some truth to that old statement.

Em might decide to cut me loose after learning her parents hired me. That's not even considering all my other deceptions. I just hope that Dex is right, and Em will forgive me.

I can't delay any longer. I must face the pounding fear in my gut about what is about to happen, what I have to share, what Em needs to learn from me and only me.

Throwing on my clothes from last night, I head to the kitchen. I have coffee, eggs, and toast made by the time Em meets me.

I hope this isn't synonymous with the last meal.

"Ooh, you made breakfast," Em says, grabbing a cup of coffee.

"It's only toast and scrambled eggs, nothing fancy," I say, grabbing my own cup of weak ass coffee.

I'm fucking nervous as hell watching Em add Splenda and creamer to her cup. I'm not used to feeling unstable and rattled. I really hope Em won't pick up on my inner turmoil. Not until I can formulate the words.

What I do know is that I need to be strong and stay in control of the situation, if not for me, for her.

Em surprises me by saying, "Okay, Alec, what's going on?"

"You picked up on that, huh?" I say, feeling the dread take root in my stomach.

"You're acting different. Kinda weird, to be honest. What's wrong?" Em looks so concerned for me. It makes me feel like an ass.

Here she is worried about me, even though I've been a selfish bastard for taking what Em so freely gave last night and this morning, knowing that afterward I would shake the very foundation that allowed Em to give herself to me in the first place, her trust.

"I need to talk with you, and I have something I'd like to ask. But sweetheart, please hear me out. Listen to everything I have to say before you respond," I plead, hoping she gives me the chance to explain. Surely, if she hears me out, she will see that I didn't intentionally try to deceive or hurt her.

"Alec, you're scaring me. What's going on?" Em whispers, her face looking a bit ashen.

"Em, for what it's worth, I don't like that I have to tell you any of this. It's something I should have discussed with you before now. Long before we expanded on our relationship," I say with a calmness I don't actually feel.

"Is something wrong? Are you sick or something?" Em asks, concern clear on her face.

"It's nothing like that," I reply, taking a deep breath to gather some much-needed composure.

"Before I get into it, I want you to know that I care for you very much. I never expected to fall for you, Em," I share, hoping she hears the sincerity in my voice and sees the truth in my eyes.

Taking a moment longer, I try to mentally prepare myself to tell Em everything. "You remember I told you I was with the CIA Special Ops division right out of college?" Seeing Em nod, I continue. "Well, I was able to retire from there at age 26. Too young not to do something else with my skills."

Em, looking dismayed, asks, "So you decided to be a maintenance man?"

I wanted to laugh at the look on Em's face, but managed to keep that shit contained. "Umm, I'm getting to that. Okay?"

I can tell Em has a million questions on the tip of her tongue, but she stays quiet. "Long story short, I became a personal bodyguard and security detail for a few high-profile clients. A couple of years ago, a new client hired me for a job that brought me here to the DalRock. I'm working undercover as the building's superintendent."

Em, trying to hide a smirk, says, "I always wondered why I never actually saw you doing any work around here."

"Dex said the very same thing," I share, realizing what that comment just revealed. Now Em will know that Dex knew before her.

Before I can address that snafu, Em asks, "Who are you working for? Why here?" Em's face turns a little pale and pensive as she hesitantly asks me these questions. Her reaction seems strange. Does she know more than she's letting on?

Feeling sick to my stomach at the thought that she already knows, I blurt out the truth. "The way your parents explained it to me was that because of their financial situation and your father's line of work, they wanted eyes on you for your protection."

"My parents hired you?" Em asks, barely above a whisper. That dreaded question. It packed the punch I had hoped to avoid.

Tears shimmer in her eyes as she struggles to swallow the lump of deception lodged in her throat. Her voice faltering, she croaks, "But why?" I reach out to wrap an arm around her shoulders, but Em jerks away. The rejection guts me.

"Why? I don't understand what you mean!" Her voice spikes, raw and close to breaking, sounding on the verge of hysterics, her gaze darting everywhere but at me.

"Em, sweetheart, please, look at me. Just let me finish explaining." The words tumble out quickly, desperate to prevent her from kicking me out. "Your parents hired me as your low-level bodyguard. My job was to stay in the shadows, to watch over you, not to invade your privacy. They've had eyes on you since you left for college, always for your protection." Even as I say this, I realize too late just how fucked up this must sound to her.

"You've been watching me since I was 18 years old?!" Em screeches. Not handling any of this well. Instead, Em appears seconds away from totally losing her shit.

"NO! No, I've only been working for your parents for the 2 years I've lived here," I urgently supply.

Em was nodding, as if she were accepting it and calming down, but she wasn't. This fact was evident in her next question, delivered with so much hurt, "You've been observing me the whole time?"

Staring me straight in my eyes, Em challenges, "And now? Do you work for my parents? Are my parents still paying you? Are you still on their payroll, Alec?" I can see her barely concealed anger. Mixed with betrayal and hurt. There's hope there, too. But my answer isn't going to be the one she's looking for.

"Yes. But it's because your parents have me looking into some surveillance files that…." I don't get to finish what I was trying to say. In that second, Em is screaming at me.

"Get out! GET OUT!" Then, in a calmer voice that frankly scares the shit out of me, Em says, "I need you to leave. Now."

"Em let me tell you the reasons," I plead. Ready to get down on my knees and beg her to give me a chance to explain.

"Alec, you need to leave NOW! Get the hell out of my apartment! You and I, we're done having our little talk!" Em screams, looking totally pissed and utterly devastated.

Speaking softly, I try, "Em, I need you to understand why I didn't tell you sooner. You need to understand that upsetting you was never my intention. You promised to let me explain."

Em, showing a bravery that I've never witnessed before, looks me straight in my eyes and delivers a blow of her own, "and you promised me that I could trust you."

Em was trying to be brave and barely able to hold back her tears when, in a small, defeated voice, she said, "You need to leave. I'm asking you to go. Now, please, go."

I had to go. But fuck if it wasn't killing me. Em agreed to hear me out, and did for the most part, but Em never agreed to understand it or accept it.

"Okay, sweetheart, I'll go, but please know, you are more than the job to me. You are precious to me, and I care deeply for you." I wanted to tell her that I loved her and that I tried to quit working for her parents. That she was the one and only woman for me, but instinctually, I knew she wasn't ready to hear any of it. And no way could I broach the topic of Trace or ask her if she was a rape victim.

Seeing her face stricken with pain and betrayal, I hate to leave her. Hearing the barely audible "Go," from her breaks my heart.

Before exiting her apartment, I turn back to see that Em has lost the battle to contain her tears. Seeing one tear after the other fall, my heart squeezes. What the fuck do I do now? Nothing productive can come from insisting she let me stay to talk, let alone ask her questions.

It is killing me inside knowing I did this, and now I have no choice but to walk away from her at this moment. But I vowed that I wasn't walking away from us. Not now and not ever. I will fight for her.

Chapter Twenty-Seven
THE JOB
Emily

After Alec left, my knees gave up the fight to hold me up, and I crumbled to the floor. Aside from the sharp pain radiating from heart breaking, I felt numb and in shock. I can't understand why both my parents and Alec would deceive me like this. I'm confused, hurt, and furious.

Screaming at the top of my lungs, the only word that escapes the jumbled mess in my head is, "WHY?!" That outburst is just the beginning of this fucked upness.

As I start to shake, I notice a pressure building in my chest. A tightness that grabs and squeezes like a vice grip. These are clear signs of an oncoming panic attack; it's been a while, but I recognize the signs.

As the gravity of the situation begins to overwhelm me, I struggle to take a deep enough breath to regain some control over my chaotic thoughts and to compartmentalize the hurt and deception.

Rolling onto my side, I struggle to find my center on the floor, trying to fight off the shortness of breath. I will myself to relax, to try and prevent the attack by grounding myself both physically and emotionally.

My brain is well-acquainted with grounding techniques, but I struggle to follow the steps. It's a battle of wills. The need to focus on what I can see, touch, smell, or taste. *Inhale. Exhale, one, two, three. Repeat.*

I don't know how long I lay on the floor before moving to the couch. It must have been a hot minute or two if the almost-bruising pain in my shoulder and hip is any indication.

Soon, the numbness and the urge to scream subside. I'm left feeling conflicted, wondering why my parents thought I needed to be watched all this time, and conflicted about why Alec would keep all of this from me.

It's upsetting and hurtful. They had no right to invade my privacy without providing a reason, a reason that should have been given to me long before now. I'm so angry at my parents and so mad at him.

Replaying what Alec told me; a renewed sense of hysteria begins to bubble beneath the surface. The feeling of being violated all over again threatens to consume me.

Tears well up in my eyes as breathing becomes difficult again. This time feels even worse. Tiny dots dance before my vision. My mind is consumed by the burning need for oxygen and relief from the ache in my rapidly rising chest. I can't think clearly or stop the full-blown panic attack that hits me so quickly, too fast to recall my calming thoughts. I couldn't fight it off or keep it at bay. The intense, overwhelming fear, dread, and hopelessness take control of me.

Clutching my chest, I felt like I might die from a heart attack or a broken heart. My body trembles intensely. Tears stream uncontrollably from my eyes. My chest burns with the need for a steady supply of oxygen.

My broken, battered heart is struggling to keep going, fighting to regain control over its choppy, irregular heartbeats. Am I going to die right here on my couch, curled in the fetal position, if I can't fight off this attack?

Then, by some miracle, reason slips back in. My breathing evens out, the shaking stops, and awareness returns. *I'm okay. I'm going to be okay.* The steps of my mental health checklist slide back into focus.

Curled up on my side, my head tucked under my knees, I focus on breathing. *Inhale, hold, one, two, three. Exhale, one, two, three. Repeat.* It's a fucked-up ritual, but it's all I've got.

Moments ago my breaths were too short, too shallow, starving me of oxygen. Now dizziness fogs my head while the fear of dying hovers just beneath the rhythm I'm forcing, *one, two, three, pause. Repeat.*

The key is simple: inhale deeply, hold for the count of three, and release slowly. I know this. Doing it, that's the battle. My body is still lacking the necessary life-giving oxygen it needs for a full recovery. Desperate for the calm it hasn't yet found.

Blocking out the dreadful, debilitating thoughts from moments ago, the grip on my chest releases. Air rushes back into my starving lungs, causing tears of relief to cascade down my cheeks.

I don't know how long I've been lying here, essentially fighting for my life, trying to make sense of everything I'm feeling. The intense urge to run and escape everything I learned today, along with the sting of betrayal and feeling violated all over again, was the pull of the trigger I wasn't able to dodge.

It's been a long time since I last experienced a full-blown, debilitating panic attack. During this episode, the memories I've kept locked away in the dark recesses of my mind resurfaced. It wasn't easy, but I had built walls around them, brick by painstaking brick, to contain the emotions that had nearly taken me down six years ago.

I survived the only way I could: treading water in a relentless sea, lungs aching, barely keeping my head above the surface of what was left of my life. I forced the horrors of that night into the deepest depths of my mind, because burying them was the only way to stay afloat and keep moving forward.

Now, the pain of Alec's revelation mingles with the pain I've spent years suppressing. I know comparing sexual violation to having my privacy violated isn't fair, but for me, both mean the same thing: someone taking from me without my consent.

My therapist, whom I eventually saw for my panic attacks, once said that every minute I don't face my past, is another brick added to my wall. A wall I'll have to climb if I ever want to stop the panic that stalks me each time I let myself remember.

She would also tell me to stop giving those thoughts and memories power over me. Not that I ever shared those thoughts or memories with her.

I didn't face anything then or now; instead, the wall I built was even bigger. It barricaded not just my mind, but my fractured heart too.

These new memories. What my parents and Alec did is just as horrific and destructive. And sad. I had long given up on the happily-ever-after and thought that Alec had somehow broken through my barrier. For a brief moment, Alec made that fantasy real. He made me believe again, and he gave me hope once more.

Then, he tore it all apart. He never truly cared. I was just a job to him, for my father... for my mother.

It was simply an exchange of goods for services. And I willingly gave up my goods, and Alec serviced me.

Heading to the shower, I felt the need to wash away the stigma of my stupidity, along with all the other labels that could apply, pathetic, weak, gullible, used, and a job.

Chapter Twenty-Eight
THE AFTERMATH
Emily

Waking up to the sound of my alarm, I immediately knew I couldn't go to work. I felt terrible. My head was pounding, and my eyes felt like I'd used sandpaper instead of the pile of Kleenex I saw tossed on the floor.

Still lying down, I can barely manage to send a couple of texts. I told my boss I need a few days off and would call him later. Scott will be okay with it. He's a great boss and knows I rarely take time off. The next message was to Roxy; I don't want to hold up her commute to the office any longer than necessary. Leaving even 10 minutes late can make a huge difference in Houston traffic.

Em: Hey, girl. I'm feeling under the weather and plan to stay home.

Roxy: You okay? Need anything?

Em: Nope, I plan to rest.

Roxy: Good for you. Call me if you need me.

I manage to sit up, and everything from the night before floods my mind, each thought fighting to be the loudest. The weight of it all feels like a boulder crushing my chest. Memories surge into me, ruthless and unyielding, crowding out every other thought.

My breathing turns erratic and uneven. I'm one wrong thought away from another panic attack. *Focus on something good*, I tell myself. *Find something positive.*

But the truth is, I don't know what to think or do. I can't see any good coming out of this betrayal. The pain I'm feeling is personal, touching everything I hold dear, my friends, my home, my future, even my already-strained relationship with my parents. The deception seeps into everything.

How the hell can I build a wall around my entire existence? There aren't enough bricks in the world to protect me from the disaster this chain of events has caused.

I understand that everyone expects me to be the rational one, the glue for my friends and family. To fix problems, to smooth things over. Forgive and forget.

But all I feel is loss, heavy and suffocating, clouding everything else. I can't stop thinking about how broken and hurt I am.

This betrayal cuts deeper than anything from my past because it came from people who know me and claim to care about me.

My parents planned this violation of my life for six years. That alone is disturbing and wrong. But Alec's involvement? That's what destroys me the most.

They have no idea of the destruction their deceit has caused, the hole it's torn in my chest. How can they think doing this *"for my protection"* wouldn't also devastate me?

Snippets of last night swirl and echo in my mind, stirring a new wave of anxiety that threatens to trap me in place. I can't move my body. My focus narrows to the pain, nothing else.

Anxiety has been my shadow for years, but right now it's on steroids, my mind racing, stomach churning, muscles locked tight. Dots swim and dance before my eyes, sweat slicks my palms. The panic is coming.

The urge to run and escape is overwhelming. But run where? To what end? There is no scenario in my brain that doesn't end with me losing all that I hold dear.

Come on, Em. Breathe. *Inhale deeply, hold, one, two, three. Exhale, one, two, three. Repeat.* It took me four tries to regain control.

The dancing dots fade. My breathing steadies. I've fought off the panic, at least this time. My reward is the ability to focus on the present, to break things down into what I can do and what I can't, thereby regaining some modicum of control.

Even that small victory, plus a quick trip to the bathroom, leaves me drained. Lying back down, my mind races to understand why this happened to me again.

My therapists advised, *"With understanding comes acceptance."* I'm not sure if I believe that, but I'll try. Eyes closed, I allow myself to remember, to compartmentalize, to break each act of betrayal down to its bare bones. To try to understand.

My parents have a lot to answer for soon. A lot to confess to. Namely, the why. Regardless of their reasons, nothing they say will erase the overwhelming feeling of being deceived and betrayed. Played and lied to. And Alec, who said he cared for me, wanted to protect me, and even loved me, is the leading man in the shit show of my life.

I'm not blameless. I let Alec cross the line from friends to lovers. And I can't ignore how hypocritical I am. If I'm honest with myself, I am responsible for my own broken heart. Just this past week, I accused Dex of ruining our group's dynamic by hooking up with Roxy. Then I was a hypocrite and let Alec pursue me.

Hell, I was a willing conquest. I admit that I let it happen because, hello! This is Alec, my wet dream man. He fit perfectly into my fantasy along with all my unfulfilled wants and desires. What girl wouldn't want to feel normal and believe in fairytales?

Just thinking about Alec. The man, not the deceiving asshole, makes me feel sad. Not just sad but devastated. It is painful to realize that he isn't the man I believed him to be, and this past week wasn't the happy breakthrough I thought I had achieved. That hurts a lot.

Instead of feeling happy because I finally allowed myself to need and want someone, I'm left with debilitating pain, uncertainty, anger, and frustration.

Here I am, trapped in this situation of my own making that has once again left me vulnerable and emotionally unstable. I opened myself up to getting hurt. Again.

The worst part is, I no longer know where I fit into my own life. How will this disaster affect my group of friends? What will it do to the stability of my little family? And what about my real family? What motives could my parents possibly have that would justify this level of deception?

Once again, I gave in to desire and made a choice that could cost me everything. My self-worth, the life I've created, and even my successes now feel threatened by my failures and weaknesses.

The worst part is knowing this mistake will have a trickle-down effect on how I view others. My forward progression will now have to go to the end of the line. My trust will no longer be freely given but will need to be earned. Well, except for Roxy and Sarah, I have complete trust in them.

I risked everything when I gave my heart to Alec. In return, I lost my happiness and the fragile belief in fairy tales I still held. My parents betrayed their only daughter, but Alec's betrayal overshadows theirs.

I have a thousand questions I want answered, but I don't want to talk to those who actually have the answers. Because in what universe is it okay to pursue a woman while deceiving her, and also getting paid to do it?

For more than two years, Alec was undercover. He convinced me we were friends, and even worse, he made me want to believe there was a future between us.

I once felt like I was incapable of giving my heart, body, and trust to anyone, but Alec made me believe I could with him. I vividly remember what Alec told me, *"You can confide in me. I won't hurt you, Em, I promise that."* Well, he broke those promises spectacularly.

How could Alec ever think that any of this was okay? I can't even stomach the thought that he's on my parents' payroll, that they basically paid him to sleep with me, to play the role of boyfriend while he *"guarded"* me. The idea makes me sick. I was so blind.

I had thought he was a friend turned lover, the one I trusted with the pieces of myself I'd never given to anyone. But now, I can't help but wonder if it's because he's trained to infiltrate and deceive. If so, he's mastered it. He fooled me completely.

Never in a million years would I have thought I'd need protection from Alec, that he was the wolf in sheep's clothing. The good guy turned villain.

Spending all day wallowing in my misery isn't going to help me. My mind won't shut up long enough for me to find any semblance of peace. Finally, I give up the fight and take two Xanax. I hate taking it, but I have the prescription for a reason.

Blessedly, I slept most of the day, only occasionally waking to use the bathroom and drink water. Food did not interest me at all. During brief moments of clarity, my mind fought against a flood of thoughts crashing back in. Not being fully conscious, I have little strength left to ward off another monster panic attack. During my last pee break, I decided to take another Xanax in the hope that it would help me get through the night without an attack.

Chapter Twenty-Nine
THE SHIT – SHOW UP
Emily

Startled, I wake from a restless, drug-induced sleep when I hear pounding at my door. Rolling over, I decide not to answer it. Let those peace intruders pound away. Just as I have that thought, I hear keys jingle right before someone unlocks my unit door.

Instantly, I knew it had to be Roxy. Only she had a spare key to my place. Oh, wait; it could also be the building's "superintendent." Ha-ha.

"Go take a shower, I could smell you before I even opened the door," Roxy yells as she unapologetically walks right into my bedroom.

"Don't listen to her, Em, but if you want to shower, we'll order some pizza and get the drinks started," Sarah offers, following right behind Roxy. Sarah is a diplomatic and tactful friend, something Roxy doesn't care to be.

"Come on in, why don't you?" I say, with a bit of snarky tude. Making eye contact, I can only imagine what they see. I'm sure my eyes are red and swollen. The T-shirt I put on yesterday, or was it the day before, was a wrinkled mess. And was that a piece of my hair stuck to the side of my face? I'm sure I look how I feel. Like shit.

Struggling to stand, a wave of emotion hits me. I can't speak past the lump in my throat because all my bravado has disappeared. My two best friends came here for me. From their facial expressions, they already know something happened, and they're here to support me.

It was Sarah, with an understanding smile, who gave me the reprieve I needed to choke down my tears and get a grip. Linking her arm through Roxy's, she says, "We'll just give you a few minutes and meet you in the kitchen."

Belatedly, I notice that around Sarah's other arm, she's holding a Randall's grocery bag with what seems to be ice cream, my favorite flavor, if the color of the tub is any indication, and some pastry. Behind them, near my doorway, I see a bag that Roxy must have set down; it contains several bottles of alcohol, from the looks of it. She was probably planning to make my favorite drink, Rum Punch, based on the variety of liquors.

Still choked up with gratitude, I can only nod as I head to the bathroom.

Not ten minutes later, I step out in clean clothes, with my teeth brushed and body misted. Now I feel ready to face my friends.

Before I can say a word, they envelop me in warm hugs. First Roxy, then Sarah, who hangs on a little longer. Fighting back tears, I can barely whisper a soft "thanks, guys." They can't know what having their support means to me.

Roxy, looking concerned, asks, "You okay, girl? Alec came and talked to us. He told us about himself and why he was here at the DalRock. No other details, though. Dex was with him."

"He also told us that he cares deeply for you," Sarah offers.

"Yeah? Well, he has a funny way of showing it," I retort, getting angry at hearing how casually he told the story of his monumental deception. "Did he also share that he waxed poetic about how he felt about me? That he loved me. That I could trust him. Then, after he slept with me, he told me who he really is. That my parents hired him to be in my life. So basically, I got fucked literally and figuratively by my parents' money," I snap, right before a wave of nausea hits, forcing me to sit down.

"Wow. No. That's all kinds of whacked." Roxy seethes, showing several emotions fleeting behind her eyes.

Sarah responds, saying, "No, he did not. Not cool."

"You want a shot? It sounds like you could use one," Roxy offers, reaching for the tequila bottle.

"Umm. I don't think that's a good idea. What time is it anyway?" I ask, while shaking my head no. I'm not sure how much time has passed since I took my last Xanax; I assume it was sometime in the middle of the night. But it could have been just a few hours or even a few days ago. Plus, I can't remember when I last ate anything.

"It's 3:40 pm. We both left work a bit early to check on you because you haven't responded to any of our texts or calls. We decided to give you some space. Alec told us Sunday night," Roxy explains with sympathy.

"Sorry, it wasn't intentional not to answer either of your calls. I turned my ringer off. I'm struggling with what to think, let alone what to say to anyone about it. I don't have any answers. I'm having trouble reconciling the reasons behind my parents' actions. Also, I need to eat something before I drink anything," I admit, feeling remorse on all accounts.

"No need to apologize. We both figured you needed a little time to yourself. We got you, babe," Sarah shares.

"Pizza should be here in about 10 more minutes," Roxy remarks, taking a seat at my small table.

"So, you don't know why your parents hired Alec?" Sarah questions.

"I don't. My parents never told me anything or gave me any indication that I was in danger, let alone that I needed a bodyguard. I'm still trying to process it all myself, and my family owes me several answers." I hedge, needing them both to understand that I literally know next to nothing about what happened.

"No matter what you want to talk about, we're here for you," Sarah states, with a look of complete understanding and sincerity.

"I know. Thank you, guys," I whisper, not trusting myself to say much more. It's too fresh. Too raw.

"Okay, but I gotta say something. I can't believe the lengths your parents go to keep tabs on you. That's worse than fucked up," Roxy states, looking totally disgusted.

"They've always been a bit controlling. My mom had enough hours to qualify for her pilot's license from all the time she spent as a helicopter mom when I was younger. But I'm an adult now. Why would they want to keep tabs on me now? It doesn't make any sense to me. They set up this shit show on their own, without giving me any precautions to live by." I state.

"It's creepy, actually," Sarah says, then grimaces.

"It is totally creepy and plain wrong," Roxy remarks, then she gets up to grab the pitcher to make some rum punch.

In their own messed-up way, Roxy and Sarah are trying to make light of my situation, to find the funny in it. Because let's face it, our sense of humor is twisted at best.

To give them some shit back, I add, "I'm pretty sure they were also watching everyone that is associated with me, which means there's probably a file out there on both of you."

"What? Seriously? No way? No telling what they've learned about me or *all* that they've seen of me. You both know how I like to show my ass. Figuratively and literally." Roxy says, with a mischievous laugh.

"Ew! I don't want to know," Sarah says, with a look of mock horror on her face.

Genuinely smiling for the first time in days, I say, "It serves them right if they see something disturbing. Have either of you considered that Alec probably got to see and hear it all, too?" Right after the words leave my lips, my stomach dips and rolls, and my eyes sting with unwelcome tears.

"No. Actually, I hadn't considered that, so thank you for bringing it to my attention. I need that rum punch just as much as you," Roxy says, measuring out the ingredients.

"I second that," Sarah states.

Needing a minute, I head to the refrigerator to grab three bottles of water. Staying hydrated before drinking is a must, especially since I haven't eaten since, oh yeah, since the plate of eggs Alec made me before *"our talk"* Sunday morning. Our talk, right? I take a deep breath in, then out, focusing on my breathing: *Inhale, hold, one, two, three. Exhale, one, two, three.*

Sarah startles me when she snatches one of the water bottles, "Go monitor Roxy, you know how heavy-handed she can be." That was the reprieve I needed; I didn't want to cry in front of the girls.

True to their word, neither Roxy nor Sarah questioned me about anything that evening. We simply enjoyed each other's company, and I was pleasantly surprised by how much I needed this time with my closest friends. They help keep me balanced. Ground me.

We ate the whole pizza, had warm brownies with ice cream, and polished off two large pitchers of rum punch by the time the girls decided to crawl home.

As I tidy up to get ready for bed, I realize two important things. One, I actually had a good time tonight. And two, I don't need more than Roxy and Sarah in my life to be happy.

I was glad my girls broke in. I needed the laugh, the distraction, and the perspective. The validation. I will be okay. I will survive this. The girls have my back.

Blessedly, the copious amount of alcohol combined with the residual amount of Xanax helped me fall into a deep, dreamless sleep that night.

Chapter Thirty
THE DECEPTIVELY FRUITY DRINK
Emily

Waking up naturally, I'm relieved to feel rested and strangely clear-headed for the first time in days.

Leaning over, I grab my cell to check the time and notice several unread text messages. I snicker as I read the start of Roxy's group text string.

Roxy: Please tell me I had fun last night because the way I feel this morning is overshadowing my memories. 9:15 am

Roxy: P.S. Your mom has called me twice; she is insisting I let her in your apartment because she hasn't heard from you and is worried. 9:18 am

Roxy: I'm awake. You both need to wake up, too! 9:19 am

Roxy: Hellllllloooo – wake your lazy asses up!! 9:21 am

Roxy: Misery needs her company......hellooo 9:22 am

Roxy: Seriously, did we have fun? Hey!!! 9:25 am

Em: OMG! Yes, we all had fun last night. 9:45 am

Sarah: I hate you both, 9:47 am

Em: DO NOT *let my mom anywhere near me. If she calls you again, tell her you told me, and that I said I'd go to them when I was ready. You love us, Sarah, 9:48 am*

Sarah: Who knew a deceptively fruity drink carried such a punch? No pun intended 9:50 am

Roxy: You got it, sister – no mom 10:02 am

Em: You guys working today? 10:03 am

Roxy: Unfortunately, 10:03 am

Sarah: Yes, and I hate working with hangovers 10:04 am

Roxy: Sarah, suck it up! 10:04 am

Em: Thanks, guys – love and hugs 10:05 am

Sarah: No thanks needed - Love and hugs, girlie 10:07 am

Roxy: Ditto – what she said. Gotta hit the shower 10:07 am

I'm comforted knowing that both Sarah and Roxy have my back and will be there for me if I need them. Although I had a good time last night, apparently not as much as they did, I need some time to myself. Time to think. Time to process. Time to accept. And then, time to heal.

Over the past few days, I received several text messages and a few voicemails. The ones from Dex were short and sweet. He's showing his support. He asked when we would be working out next and if I needed anything, but not anything too heavy or uncomfortable. I love Dex. He is always there, but rarely in my face about anything.

There were a few text messages from my mom and one from my dad. The five voicemails were all from mom, and I didn't bother listening to any of them. Of course, Roxy and Sarah both sent several texts. Those are the only ones I've responded to so far.

The only message I got from Alec was, *"I'm sorry."* Which pissed me off, made me cry, and made my anxiety spike.

I wanted to delete Alec's text messages from the very beginning and block his number, but it turned out unnecessary. That was the only message I received from him after I demanded he leave my apartment.

Thinking about Alec, which I can't seem to avoid. I keep wondering exactly what he's sorry for. His simple *"I'm sorry"* doesn't seem enough to cover all the ways he's hurt me.

The hardest thing to face isn't the end itself, but the doubt that comes with it. Was what happened between us real? Or were his words and the way he held me just a façade? A part of his job requirement.

I know the words of affection and love he spoke could just be words. And the connection I felt with him could be a physical response to the lust I've harbored for him. For my part, I wanted to believe Alec truly had feelings for me, that he wanted me just as much as I wanted him.

Thinking about it now, I realize I was an easy target for him. Not unlike the classic example of a young, inexperienced girl who falls for the first guy to give her the attention she craves.

Sadly, this wasn't the first time I did this, but I vowed it would be my last.

Loneliness isn't a new experience for me. I had isolated myself emotionally long ago and tried as much as possible, physically too.

What cuts deepest is realizing I never questioned Alec's sincerity. Never asked *why me?* I wanted it to be real. I've been drawn to him since the start, convinced he felt the same, the heat in his touch, the passion in his eyes, the reverence in his voice when he said my name. The kisses. The caresses.

Then the memories hit, vivid and merciless, leaving me gutted with an intense sense of loss. I barely make it to the bathroom before I'm puking up what little I ate yesterday, that deceptively fruity drink Sarah swore packed a punch, burning on the way back up.

Slumping back, I close my eyes. *Deep inhale, hold, one, two, three. Long exhale, one, two, three. Repeat.* I force the rhythm until my body begins to obey.

Through the breathing technique and splashing cool water on my face, I manage to prevent another anxiety-driven panic attack. I really hope these breathing exercises continue to work, if only because I don't want to become dependent on Xanax.

Clearly, the few days I took off won't be enough. I decided to extend it for the entire week. Maybe longer if I still can't manage to think about everything without crying, feeling sick, or having to dodge sneaky panic attacks.

After talking with my boss, I realized that the best way to spend this time off is to find my happy place. It's there. I might have to dig deep down inside my battered and bruised soul, but I will find my happy. True happiness, not just the surface happy.

I realize something else. Although this recent betrayal is hard to accept, especially since the deception originated from my own parents, who roped Alec in on their scheme, I'm still a survivor.

Even though Alec had his own scheming agenda, I'm still standing. Although my past left permanent scars and this new attack has left me feeling raw, I need to remember that others can't see that. I don't have to be defined by those events.

Being with Alec as a boyfriend, although only briefly, has revealed to me everything I am missing from not living my life to the fullest. Additionally, following that deceptive outcome, I realize nothing is stopping me from rewriting my own fairytale ending.

Society and Disney movies often portray fairy tales around Princes and Princesses. But when I think about what will make me happy, once I remove the prince from the picture, I remember that I've always wanted a dog.

Dogs love you unconditionally, and they will never lie or deceive you. They bring happiness like no other. Dogs are loyal and protective. If you think about it, a dog is an excellent alternative to having a man.

Chapter Thirty-One
THE DEEP DIVE
Alec

Leaving Em to think that everything between us was a lie is killing me. I haven't slept well over the past few nights, and my appetite has been nonexistent. I feel horrible, and I know I deserve it. I was incredibly selfish. If I never get another chance with Em, I only have myself to blame.

The only thing stopping me from losing my ever-lovin' mind is the chance to review the results from the Photo Forensics results against all the data we've gathered ourselves. I've been digging for anything that could incriminate Trace Roberts. I hope what they found is significant enough to put him away for life.

I'm not doing myself any favors, especially if I ever get a chance to go to trial. The methods my team uses to search for information about him aren't all legal or permitted. It's a risk I feel I have to take.

A few months ago, I recruited several of my former retired special ops teammates, each with their own unique specialty, to join my new security analysis venture. That decision is already paying off. It's all hands-on deck now, digging into everything we can find on this bastard, his family, and any links to Em and hers.

We uncovered that Trace's father, Edward Trace Roberts Senior III, isn't just a wealthy businessman; he's also an International Criminal Court Judge within the Office of the Prosecutor, with influential ties to dangerous terrorist organizations.

The ICC's role is to investigate and prosecute individuals accused of genocide, crimes against humanity, war crimes, and crimes of aggression. Judge Roberts's division determines whether there's enough basis to initiate such investigations.

Our digging revealed he's currently suspended, with pay, pending an inquiry into his suspected involvement with a notorious terrorist organization.

My sources suggest the investigation centers on Judge Roberts accepting bribes in exchange for leniency in prosecutions. With the case still pending, there are no conclusive documents we can hack into yet.

So when a call came in scheduling a 0900 meeting with my former Task Force CO, Commander Nelson, who is still with the CIA, I wasn't surprised. Digging this deep into the Roberts men was bound to raise flags.

Nelson and I go way back; our friendship was forged over years of service and has been strengthened since I moved into the private sector. He's no longer my superior, not one of his reports, just a trusted ally. When I pitched the idea of launching my own security venture, he was my biggest supporter. Gave me a solid by verbally agreeing to let me tap certain resources with limited clearance. Background checks are okay. Opening sealed court records, not so much.

What surprised me about the meeting was how much I learned about my case that I didn't already know, all of it *"off the record"* and wrapped in a harsh warning. Professional courtesy, my ass. I'd stepped over the line and put a potential target on both our backs.

Even so, Nelson had his current team dig. What they uncovered suggests Trace Roberts Junior didn't pick his victims at random.

There are also online murmurs that Trace Junior created his own *"insurance policy"* by photographing his victims after the assaults. So far, there is no solid evidence to support that.

Right now, Nelson's team is combing through possible additional victims. As of today, no official cases have been linked to Trace Junior. Only the two expunged records where he was never convicted.

The warning Commander Nelson issued was twofold. Straight up, I'm too close to this case. Then he reminded me that without probable cause and a warrant, anything we dig up is inadmissible under the Fourth Amendment's exclusionary rule.

What stopped me cold was his next point: my weak ass bodyguard contract won't pass as reasonable cause for a valid search. He warned, we don't have enough solid intel. We need proof that a crime was committed. Without witnesses or open cases, all we've got is a hunch. And that hunch could cost us our careers and leave us financially ruined.

To emphasize how severe his warnings are, he let me know he's already received a few calls about the matter. He didn't elaborate.

Message received. My team should back off or at least do a better job of covering our tracks before any of us gets personally sued for illegal searches. He didn't need to say it; the CIA connection needs to be downplayed for both our sakes.

What Nelson never said was how he knew so much about my investigation, or that we should stop. On the contrary, he offered help, albeit limited.

Cryptically, he advised me to look at the connection between the fathers, not just their children. Before I could press him for more, he shook my hand and walked out.

That was two days, copious amounts of coffee, and little to no sleep later, and I still don't see the connection.

Reflecting on Nelson's warnings, I know he must've realized I'd ignore them to some degree. I don't have another choice but to keep digging. If there's a connection between the Roberts family and Em, I have to find it.

I briefed my team about Nelson's warnings. They're skilled at research, adept at covering their tracks, and they understand the risks; there's no guarantee our deeper searches won't get flagged.

The missing link has to be the connection Nelson hinted at. To find it, we'll have to go deeper, not just into Roberts Senior, but also into Em's parents and the parents of the other two victims from the expunged cases.

Thinking of Em, I still don't know if she was actually one of his victims. The thought threatens to crush me every time I imagine the possibilities.

Right now, my mind needs to focus on gathering reliable information that shows probable cause, rather than dwelling on the what-ifs. I need to gather warrant-worthy facts.

First, I need to establish the connection between the Wilsons and the Roberts, and I have to understand the whole story about Trace Junior's relationship with Em, directly from Em herself.

Getting Em to talk to me again will be challenging enough. Getting Em to share whether she was raped or victimized in any way with me, well, that's going to take a miracle. But I have to try.

Chapter Thirty-Two
DESTINY
Emily

Allowing the idea of getting a dog to take hold in my mind, I felt something shift in my heart just from thinking about it. There was a buzz of excitement for the possibility.

Could I get a dog? My mind is challenging the idea, reminding me that I work full-time and have never cared for another living being. But isn't that the same situation for most pet owners?

Deciding it wouldn't hurt to do some research, I grab my laptop and look up the local pet shelter. The website had a wealth of information to help me make an informed decision. I learned about the adoption criteria, which helped me understand the time constraints and recommended space requirements. There were several articles featuring what others had to say about owning a pet. What breeds are best suited for apartment living versus those that require a lot of room to run?

The more I read, the more excited I began to feel for the first time since learning about the callous disregard for my privacy and the subsequent betrayal.

"I'm going to get a dog," I say out loud, feeling the rightness of that decision settle deep within me. Getting up, I put my hair in a messy bun. The yoga pants and oversized sweatshirt I slept in will have to do. My current energy level can only do so much.

Grabbing my purse and keys, I notice a folded note just inside my door.

The note was probably from Alec. As I pick it up, I don't bother reading it. Instead, I toss it onto the side entry table as I leave and lock my door. Whatever is on that note isn't going to make me happy, and today I'm on a mission to find my happy place.

I reached my car without anyone stopping me. I see that as a win. Arriving at the shelter, I don't hesitate to go in and tell the counter worker what I was hoping to accomplish.

The worker was pleased. I can only imagine that most visitors coming here are looking to add to their burden, not to lessen it.

As we walk down a long corridor with dogs in cages on both sides, I start to grasp the weight of my decision. Taking it all in, I feel overwhelmed by the sheer number of pets in need of homes.

There are so many dogs; some are big, some are small, some are old, and some are puppies. The shelter worker talked about the shelter and its pets as we walked. She'd stop to give a little background on a few she noticed I looked at.

With everything she said and even what she didn't say, I understood this was a big decision and that I needed to think rationally about it. I knew without a doubt that I couldn't handle a puppy; they require more time than I could give. A big dog should really have a backyard.

As we near the end of the corridor, I take a deep, calming breath. Starting my return toward the front, I move at a slower pace.

Walking back the way we came, I notice a small dog that wasn't barking or jumping around like the others. This dog leaned toward the back of the cage, trying to get as far away from us as the confines would allow. The dog looked weary and untrusting.

"What is the story behind this dog?" I ask.

With a small smile, the worker responds, "She's only recently been moved to the adoption side. When she was brought in, she wasn't in great shape. She probably had been living on the streets for a while and hadn't had an easy time of it. She had several abrasions and was suffering from malnutrition."

You could see that the worker was visibly sad about the condition this dog was in. It's clear the worker loves what she does here for the pets. "She's been friendly with the staff. She needs to get to know you before she can develop trust. We think she is two or maybe three years old. She's a Maltese mix, but we're not sure what she's mixed with. She has a clean bill of health now," the worker says with no small amount of pride.

Seeing the dedication and pride these workers have for their jobs was humbling. It must not be easy for them to work with unwanted or mistreated pets every day.

"Can I pet her?" I ask, already feeling that taking her home is the right choice. Her white and tan fur looks soft, with a slight curl at the ends. Her brown eyes, filled with hope rather than guardedness, seem to reach her soul. She's beautiful. I notice a connection; we've both had tough times but survived, and we both struggle with trust.

"Sure, let me bring her out, and we can have you two get acquainted with each other in one of our visiting rooms." The worker looks pleased to be setting up a visitation for this dog. I can only imagine how attached the workers become to the pets they help care for.

When I was led to the visiting room where the dog was waiting, I initially felt nervous. But when I saw the dog sitting there, looking apprehensive, I knew I wanted to soothe the pet's worries.

Sitting on the floor next to her, I wait a moment before reaching out slowly to pet her, and the dog doesn't flinch or move away.

The worker gave me a big smile as she left the room. I found myself smiling back. I felt like I must have passed some test.

Instantly, I knew this dog and I were kindred spirits. This adoption would be mutually beneficial for both of us.

I sat with her, slowly stroking her fur, for several minutes before the worker returned to check on us. By that time, "Destiny" was sitting on my lap, eating up the attention I was giving her.

"I want her. Can I take her home today?" I ask, not taking my eyes off this furry little bundle of joy.

Let's see if we can make that happen. I can tell the pup likes you too. Let's head up front and complete the paperwork. From our donations, we have some supplies you'll need to start your life with your new fur baby. You'll want to plan a trip to a pet center within the next day or so. We include a list with our adoption packet with our new pet recommendations," she shares, giving me a thankful smile.

The worker genuinely appears happy and confident, which reassures me that this is the right choice. Driving home with Destiny in the passenger seat, I felt happy for the first time in several days. Deciding to adopt Destiny made me feel like I'd found at least the front porch to my happy place.

Chapter Thirty-Three
THE AMBUSH
Emily

Before taking Destiny to her new home, I decided to bring her to the park down the street from the DalRock. The worker told me Destiny seems fully potty-trained. She recommended I take her out on a consistent schedule, explaining that pets do best with a routine.

At the park, Destiny did great on the leash. She looked excited to be outside. She stopped and sniffed what seemed like every blade of grass until she finally did her business.

Apparently, as the owner, I had to pick up said business in a small plastic poop bag and toss it into the designated trash bins. So far, that was the hardest part of my decision to adopt her.

After Destiny finished all her business, we sat on a grass embankment and watched the ducks swim in the pond. At first, I thought she would want to chase them, but Destiny simply sat down happily beside me, looking content and relaxed. It seems we both made a good choice today. It was our *Destiny*.

You can't help but relax at our neighborhood park. The area features nice walking trails around the lake and through the nearby woods. Gorgeous panoramic views of the water and trees. It's like a diamond in the rough, nestled inside our busy city.

Today was a good day, the first day of Survival 2.0, when my primary focus was taking care of myself and Destiny. And Destiny will look after me in her own way, too. Her demeanor has already relaxed me, and my gloomy mood has improved. The views, fresh air, and sunshine are the reinforcements.

Just then, a large shadow of a man appears over us, eclipsing the sun's rays. Destiny emits a low growl of warning before she stops to sniff the proffered hand of none other than Alec.

How in the hell did he know to find me here? Is he stalking me? Did he put a tracker under my skin somehow, like what I learned was injected in Destiny by a vet?

It's good to know early on that I can't depend on Destiny as a guard dog or a good judge of character.

Sitting here, I don't give him any reaction. I don't say anything. I don't even look at him. Part of me feels tempted to ask Alec if he's been following me, but I doubt he'd tell me the truth. I wouldn't trust his answer anyway.

Out of the corner of my eye, I see Alec lower himself to the ground next to us, as if I had invited him. He isn't saying anything either. We sit here, both of us, lost in our own thoughts.

The silence is preferred. I'm not ready to talk to him. There's nothing Alec can say that I want to hear.

There's a small part of me, if I'm honest, that admits it feels good to have him nearby. My traitorous body has no idea what my mind has learned; it only remembers how Alec made it burn with desire and passion. The pleasure he gave was like nothing I'd ever experienced before in my life. But that was then. This is now.

Before I can let my mind and thoughts pull me back into my dark, anxiety-filled place, I decide it's time for Destiny and me to go home. As I start to stand up, Alec quietly pleads, "Em, please."

Making the mistake of looking at him, I see that his unreadable mask is gone. In his eyes, I notice so much pain, remorse, and is that fear? Before I'm aware of what I'm doing, I sit back down. It's probably close to another three minutes before I hear Alec say, "I'm sorry, Em. I never meant to hurt you."

"How did you see this playing out? How could I not get hurt? Were you planning never to tell me?" I snap, surprised by my outburst. Feeling more anger than sadness, which is a welcome change.

"Em, I won't lie. When I first realized that my feelings ran deeper for you, I naively thought it was best if you never knew the details. I purchased my unit in the DalRock, and I had planned to finish my contract with your parents and not extend," Alec says with no small amount of regret in his voice.

Seriously? That's messed up. Before I can reply, he continues, "Em, before I knew you, I met with your parents, who wanted me to do reconnaissance work on data from the prior security team."

"None of this makes any sense to me," I say, sounding bitchy to my own ears.

Taking an audible breath, Alec continues, "Your parents hired me based on a concern. Your mom felt certain that something had happened to you while you were away at college. She showed me high school pictures of you, compared to some taken during your college years as evidence. She told me how you had changed after you left home, that you rarely called them or visited."

"Look at me, Em," Alec confides, watching me closely. "Em, when I saw your pictures and the visual transformation, I agreed with her assessment. I didn't hesitate to take the assignment."

It took every ounce of strength I had not to flinch or show any outward reaction. Internally, my mind was at war with my body's urge to run from Alec. From everything he was saying.

Maintaining a neutral, even tone, Alec proceeds as if he understands I'm a flight risk. "At the end of my 2-year assignment, I went to your parents to tell them I didn't want to extend my contract. I told them it was because of my personal interest in you."

"You told me you were still on their payroll," I accuse.

"That's true," Alec says. "I had mentioned to your father that my team has identified items of interest that we are still reviewing. As a result, I had to extend the contract. It was necessary to give my team legal authorization to continue the research." Alec was staring at me intently, trying to gauge my reaction and using his CIA skills to read me. But I've become a master at hiding my thoughts and feelings, holding in the pain and fear.

With his eyes still fixed on me, I sit immobile and unresponsive. My mind tries to absorb this information and understand its meaning. Clearly, I need to hear what Alec has to say. That doesn't mean I have to accept it. What I truly want to know is the reason behind his and my parents' actions.

Alec briefly looks away before returning his gaze and says, "Saturday, while you were finishing your shower, I listened to a voicemail from my team lead. They found something they wanted me to see. It was at that meeting that they gave me a criminal background check on Trace Roberts."

Don't react, Em. Breathe in, breathe out. I can feel Alec's stare locking onto me, like a physical blanket draping over my entire body. His eyes are searching for even the slightest twitch, a reaction. But I can't respond or show any sign of what I feel. I don't want him to see the anguish that just hearing that name stirs inside me.

"Em, the report said he was a known contact of yours, and that he was bad news. The report detailed just how bad he was. So, I need to ask you: when you told me you had a bad experience in college, were you referring to Trace?" Alec reaches over, grabbing my hand as he drops that verbal bomb.

After brief moments of resignation and hearing his genuine concern, along with feeling the warmth of Alec's hand holding mine, I had no fight left. Squeezing Alec's hand tightly, I realize I'm tired, worn down, and exposed.

With surprising clarity, I realize I no longer want to hide who I am by keeping everything that happened to me a secret. The memories still attack me freely, and my life choices are driven by the need to hide my mistakes. I carry the shameful truth that I allowed it, and it's my bad judgment that I can't trust. What happened to me is the main reason I keep myself separate from others.

Sharing the details of my past with Alec will be a crucial step in regaining control of my life and future. I've barricaded that shit long enough. From the tender look Alec is giving me, he either suspects or hopes I'll share the details. The damage is done; the lock is broken, and the box holding the memories of my living hell is ready to be opened.

Alec already knows something happened. He's a wise man. No doubt he's already guessed that it was something sexual in nature. All that remains for his report are the sordid details.

Although the idea of reopening those old wounds is frightening, I'll share my story with Alec. Then, when we part ways, there will be no more secrets linking us. There's no other reason for me to be a burden to him. Nothing will remain between us, not even friendship. His betrayal has sealed our fate.

"I'll tell you what you want to know. What I'm able to verbalize. Then you'll understand the real me, the damaged and unworthy one," I whisper, feeling oddly shy to reveal and expose so much.

Alec squeezes my hand and, still looking into my eyes, encourages, "Tell me. Tell me everything you can remember. Take all the time you need. I'm here for it. Here for you. And Em, you're wrong, you have great worth, and you aren't damaged to me."

Shaking my head no because he can't understand what he doesn't know. Only I know the truth. Taking a deep, strengthening breath, I began to tell my story. God be with me as I share my pain.

I was a freshman in college when I caught the eye of a popular senior. All the girls in our group wanted his attention. I thought I was special, believing that out of all the options practically thrown at his feet, he was interested in me. He was charming and handsome. He asked me a few times to go out with him, and I turned him down each time. I wasn't stupid; I was just a freshman, new to the campus, and he was a popular, wealthy senior. Still, he kept trying to persuade me to go out with him. Eventually, I gave in because he was taking me to a local Italian restaurant that was a common hangout for students," I reluctantly share.

Suddenly, the words stopped flowing. I pause for a moment, filled with hesitation and uncertainty. Can I share these terrible details with Alec? Is what I'm about to reveal something he genuinely needs to know? "Alec, are you sure you want me to tell you everything? I've never told anyone about any of this. Just the thought of sharing it with you makes me feel uneasy."

Alec, lacing our fingers together, pulls me closer and says what I know he believes is true, "You need to share this with me; otherwise, we'll have no foundation to build a more sustainable relationship on. You can do this. Take your time."

Realizing how calm I feel is unsettling, to say the least. These details have been barricaded in the back of my mind for years. Sharing them aloud now feels strange. But being here with Alec, even when I'm very upset with him, has a way of calming my uncertainty.

Releasing my hand from Alec's grip, I shift away slightly. I feel the need to do this on my own, without relying on Alec's comforting touch. Stroking Destiny's fur is the only comfort I allow myself. Sitting up straighter, I summon my courage.

Before retelling the gruesome details of my foolish mistake, I want to address one important fact. "I'll share this with you for your work and your reports, but only because I want to move past this. You need to understand. There will be no 'us' after I explain what happened."

Taking a deep breath for strength to keep going, I continue with my story before Alec can challenge my statement, "The dinner went better than I had expected. We had a lot in common and shared several of the same interests. With dinner, we both had a glass of wine. The restaurant was a popular spot because the owner didn't quibble over age. If we were in college and had the money, we were allowed to drink."

With Alec watching me closely, I'm sure he notices how nervous I am. When he reaches out to steady my hand, I realize I've been unknowingly pulling on a thread of my shirt. A small hole is already visible where I've pulled.

Casting my eyes toward him, I see a tense yet somehow knowing shadow cross his face. I decide to pick my battles and let Alec hold my hand. My focus needs to be on telling the story before the emotional baggage weighs me down and makes it harder to speak. "After dinner, Trace drove me back to my off-campus apartment. He wanted to come in and have another drink before calling it a night. I was caught up in the moment and willingly agreed to let him come in."

Pausing to get my bearings and align my thoughts, I continue succinctly, aiming to share only the facts in a neat, compartmentalized, and detached way. "The one drink turned into two. That second drink was my third of the night. It tipped the scale for me. I was feeling the effects of the alcohol, but still aware enough to know what was happening. He started kissing me. Touching me. I participated at first, that was until he started trying to remove my clothes."

Noticing Alec was now clenching the hand not holding mine, I hesitated to continue. He doesn't look right.

When Alec starts squeezing my hand with a thunderous look on his face, I wince, not just from his expression but because he's hurting me.

"Alec, you're hurting my hand," I say cautiously.

Immediately, Alec releases the pressure just before bringing it to his lips for a gentle kiss, "I'm sorry, Em. Continue."

Destiny, sensing my unease, snuggles against my leg and hip. Leaving the string of my shirt to run my fingers through her fur has a calming effect.

There is no doubt in my mind that I need to finish telling my story now. Not later. "As Trace continued to remove my clothing, I tried to fight him off. I remember pleading with him to stop. I know I said no. That was what we were told in our self-defense class: 'No means no.' I was so drunk that I couldn't stay conscious. I couldn't defend myself against his much larger frame."

To my mortification, my eyes fill with tears that spill down my cheeks uncontrollably. Sharing that part of the story, expressing how stupid I'd been, brings back many of the painful details.

How scared and alone I felt. The pain from what Trace did to me is still unbearable, even if it's only a memory now.

Before I can protest, Alec grabs me and pulls me onto his lap, cradling me like a baby. It's precisely what I didn't know I needed. His warm body was holding mine protectively, as if I were something precious. That thought brings fresh tears to my eyes.

My tears were falling uncontrollably now, leaving wet spots on both of our shirts.

I'm not sure how long Alec holds me before I manage to regain my composure. Or enough composure to at least tell him the ending, the end of so much for me.

Barely above a whisper, I tell Alec my biggest, darkest, most painful secret, "He raped me. It was my fault. My stupidity allowed him to do it."

After sharing that last bit, I get off Alec's lap to sit back down on the grass next to Destiny. Instantly, I feel the ache from leaving his warmth and comfort. But it's something I have to get used to. Telling him my secret changed nothing for us.

"Em, there's something you need to know. Trace is the only one at fault. He is also connected to two other assault cases where there's evidence that a date rape drug was used. From what you've just shared, he has a pattern. He'd take them to dinner, then bring them home. Once at their place, he'd ask to come in for a drink. That's when he must slip his victims the drug. Then he would assault them. It's not that you drank too much, and you didn't give permission. He stole your ability to defend yourself," Alec shares.

"So, is he in prison?" I ask.

"No. The other cases happened one before and one after yours. The most recent was last year. Unfortunately, both of those cases were dropped," Alec says, anger still evident in his voice.

"Dropped? What do you mean? How?" I don't understand what Alec is telling me. If they reported the crime, he should have been charged.

"The theory we're exploring is that his dad has some influence or may have paid off the accusers or prosecutors somehow. And it doesn't help that there hasn't been any solid evidence that a crime was committed. It was their word against his." Alec again reaches for my hand, giving it a gentle squeeze.

"I'm sorry that happened to those girls," I say, withdrawing my hand from his. "Alec, is there anything else you feel you need to tell me?" I notice that my voice sounds completely emotionless. My emotional walls are fully rebuilt.

Alec, looking taken aback and a bit unsure, hedges, "You can pursue a case against him. We have surveillance footage, along with your testimony, that could be enough to indict him. We could reach out to the other two girls to get their statements, and we're investigating more potential victims."

I laugh in disbelief, hurt, and anger. Scoffing, I ask, "And what about what I want? Or doesn't that matter?"

"Em," Alec begins to say something.

"No, Alec! No. I've been assigned to you for 2 years, so you've been watching me. You know me. Now you know what happened to me and how I've handled it. So, no." Fresh tears pool and threaten to spill down my cheeks again. But I'm done crying with an audience over this. Squeezing my eyes tight, I try to block the traitorous tears as I shake my head back and forth.

"I'll help you; you won't have to face this alone," Alec counters.

"I hate that you know what happened to me," I say harshly. "I hate..." I pause, trying to find my voice again. I take a deep breath. The words I manage to squeak out sound like they're scraping over shards of glass. "I hate that you know just how damaged I am and how, on some level, I let it happen."

I can tell Alec wants to argue the point, but revisiting that dark time in my life is not something I want to discuss anymore with him. With anyone.

"Alec, don't. Please just... don't," I quickly blurt, trying to end this excruciating conversation.

Alec reaches for me again. I quickly stand up and step back out of his reach, saying, "I can't help you. And Alec, this little talk changes nothing. The foundation you referred to between us doesn't exist."

Turning away, I walk off with Destiny by my side. Not once did either of us look back. Such a loyal dog.

Chapter Thirty-Four
THE VILLAIN
Emily

By the time I get home with Destiny in tow, I feel exposed and vulnerable. My thoughts are ping ponging all over the place, scrambled and uncertain.

But I did it. I gave Alec the explanation and answers he wanted, regardless of the cost to myself. The price for revisiting the painful memories I've long locked away and never shared until now will probably be more than I'm mentally prepared to pay. But it's done. It's out there.

Bringing those thoughts to the forefront of my mind required a tremendous mental effort. Those memories I had managed to lock away for so long in the darkest recesses of my mind, a place where I painstakingly built walls around, brick by brick, barricading the past and never intending to revisit or relive.

After more than six frigging years, I never expected that talking about what happened to me would reopen old wounds and bring back my humiliation. The younger me was so dumb, stupid, and naive. Now, Alec knows, and so will my parents. Then everyone else they decide to share it with will know.

As the protective walls around my past collapse, old wounds reopen and fester. Raw and painful. It shatters the illusion that

I'd ever truly moved on from the physical and emotional scars of that tragic night.

The truth is, I hadn't fully healed. I only managed to suppress the most tragic experience of my life. Those devastating memories were just waiting for the right moment to break free from the walls I had built to protect myself.

The timing of my grand reveal is taunting me. Seems cruel that just a few days ago, I started to believe I could have the fairytale of my dreams, living the life of a modern-day princess rescued by her handsome prince.

But I forgot something. There's a villain in every fairy tale story, lurking and conniving for the first chance to take and destroy, to trick you. My downfall was lust; lust for Alec pulled me in, made me lower my guard, and exposed me to this twisted, deceitful reality I'm now living in.

I was an easy target. Getting my happily-ever-after was always something I yearned for, something I wanted to believe in, remembered from the hopeful imaginings of my youth. But that was then, before Trace. Before my parents and Alec orchestrated their own brand of deception.

Moments ago, Alec held me in his arms. I selfishly depended on his strength and support to get through telling it, knowing it would be the last time I allowed myself to have his protective support.

Alec told me things that could be true or not. It might explain the reasons behind his actions and lies. I listened, but in the end, I dismissed what he said and him.

Alec might have temporarily breached my carefully crafted walls of self-protection, but I will survive. I've done it before, on my own. I'll do it again, starting by removing myself from the situation. Alec and my parents didn't need my input when they made their little plan of deception. They can all keep doing whatever in the hell they want without me getting involved.

Because of the callous disregard for my feelings, I feel forced to operate in survival mode again. I wish *the talk* on Sunday morning had never happened. I wish Alec hadn't told me anything. That was his original plan: to keep his involvement with my parents and his purpose for being at the DalRock a secret from me.

Wishing can be a double-edged sword. Without hope, is anyone really living? But to wish is to give way to disappointment. Both can gut you.

If I were ever granted one wish, I would wish I had never met Trace Roberts. The course of that introduction, and later the date I initially declined, changed my future and affected my ability to live my best life.

But for a few blissful days, I managed to leave my past behind. Alec showed me a glimpse of a life that will never be mine. My past assault will continue to haunt me, hovering just beyond sanity and never granting me freedom from the nightmares of my earlier mistakes.

Retelling the horrible details of that night was painful. Sharing it with Alec was humiliating. But words are just words; they can't truly capture the experience or convey the fear and pain I went through. I need to remember I will always be "damaged." What's done can't be undone, and what I learned from that mistake can't be erased.

The trip down memory lane sparked me to reject what my heart desired and what Alec tried to offer. Instead, I told him to stay away, even though my body desperately wanted him to stay, despite his lies and betrayal. My heart can be a masochistic little bitch.

Slumping back against the couch in defeat, with Destiny right there with me, my chest tightens. By verbalizing the attacks that had once paralyzed me in the days and weeks after the assault, I fear I've reawakened buried vulnerabilities, allowing those memories to flood back into my already turbulent dreams.

I'm scared of the nightmares. Those bastards are brutal. For months, they replayed the attack over and over, adding more details. More demented scenarios. They felt horribly realistic each time. It was like Groundhog Day set in a horror flick.

The nightmares had kept everything at the front of my mind, starting each new day with paralyzing fear and pain. The aftereffects would last all day, only to be repeated at night, each more sinister than the last.

They've surfaced in fragments all week, piggyback riding along with the all-consuming panic attacks. If I analyze myself, the nightmares make sense; they stem from having my choices stolen, my power stripped, my life violated without my consent.

And here I am again, thrust into another situation I never agreed to, past tragedy colliding with the present. Every memory, every emotion, is a fresh trigger, a battle in the mind.

I lower my head to my knees, forcing air into my lungs. The realization hits hard, just how powerless I feel in my own life.

When will the assaults end?

My breathing turns ragged, the edges of a panic attack closing in. I force myself to focus, take a *deep inhale, hold,* and count *one, two, three. Exhale, one, two, three. Repeat.* Just keep breathing, Em.

I run through the mental checklist I've heavily relied on over the past few days, breathe slowly, clear my mind, and relax each muscle one by one. Sometimes the checklist works, sometimes it doesn't. This time, stroking Destiny's fur calms me down, her quiet presence soothing enough to tip the scales. Crisis averted.

It probably doesn't hurt that I'm still mad as hell at my parents, and at Alec.

Chapter Thirty-Five
WE KNOW
Emily

I'm startled out of my vegging-out state when my doorbell sounds. Destiny lets out two sharp barks but is looking to me for further instructions.

Is it Alec? Should I answer? My hesitation must have lasted longer than I thought because I hear keys jingle just before Roxy and Sarah walk in.

"Hey," was all I could manage, not really caring that they walked in unannounced and uninvited.

"Hey, babe, are you okay?" Sarah asks.

I could only manage a nod in response. Blinking rapidly, I try to hold back the tears that are threatening to fall again, traitorous little assholes.

The girls circle the coffee table and surround me, each on one side. Before I can react, they both wrap their arms around me, effectively trapping me. Their warm embrace provides all the comfort and support I didn't realize I needed. Just having them nearby means the world to me. Surrounded by their support, I can't hold back my tears.

Roxy pulls back first. When she speaks, her tone is gentle and cautious, like she's walking through a minefield, worried I might blow up at any moment. And I just might.

"Em, you know we are here for you, and we always will be. Please let us know what's going on with you. Alec sent us a text saying that we should check on you," Roxy shares.

Sarah follows up, "We're worried about you, and who is this little bundle of joy?" referring to Destiny, who, not wanting to be left out, has crawled onto my lap.

"Her name is Destiny, she's my new fur baby," I say with a slight smile that is genuine but feels forced.

Without further prompting, I respond, "There's nothing to tell you guys. I ran into Alec today at the park, and I'm feeling sorry for myself, I guess. It still hurts seeing him, and I can't get past what he's done."

Roxy and Sarah lock eyes for a long moment. Time seems to stand still as they make a silent decision. Then, Roxy stands up to face me, hands on her hips, her body language showing she's about to let me have it.

"You're such a moron; you can't sit there and spout that bullshit to me anymore. I've been to that particular pity party with you before, and it wasn't any fun for either one of us."

Reaching toward Roxy to stop her rant, she steps back and snaps, "No, you had your chance to share with us, and even after all these years, you still shut us out. Now, you're going to listen. It's time for some tough love."

Looking at Roxy, I hedge, "there's nothing to…." Roxy cuts me off again to share, "Sarah and I both have talked about you, yeah, behind your back, since college. Not to make fun of you or to talk shit, but because we care. We know. We know something tragic happened to you."

I curl my fingers around Sarah's hand and lick my suddenly dry lips, which always happens when my anxiety kicks in. Still, I don't say a word.

Roxy continues, "We know...we've known Em since we first met you. That fact has never defined who you are. What happened to you isn't who you are to us. You once told me, after having a few drinks, that you're damaged. Don't use that as an excuse or a crutch in life. If you're damaged, then allow yourself to get fixed. That can only happen if you let down the walls you've barricaded yourself behind. You've handicapped us and others from being able to help you. Keeping us at arm's length only strengthens the walls you have up, instead of getting the help you need to demolish them."

As Roxy gently encourages me to sit back, she kneels in front of me and explains, "I'm not trying to say what happened to you wasn't tragic or bad, but don't let that define your future. Don't let that event control your actions. You need to choose to want better for yourself. You need to choose to live life."

After delivering those unexpected words of wisdom, something I never saw coming, I'm momentarily thrown off balance. Before I can respond, she stands and walks toward the kitchen, and that's when I notice it, the faint sheen of tears in her eyes.

Roxy and Sarah are the best. My love for them runs deep and genuine. Roxy is right. I need them. I need to talk about what happened to me. Talk with people who care about me and love me.

Sarah hands me a box of Kleenex. I wasn't even aware I was crying. "You okay, you know Roxy gets carried away sometimes, but she loves you."

"Yeah, no, she's right. I was wrong to shut you both out. I'm sorry," I whisper, realizing Roxy needs to hear my apology too. "I'm sorry! I never realized how much you both picked up on and how my unwillingness to confide in either of you hurt you both."

Roxy steps out of my kitchen with a tray of drinks; I give her a grateful smile. I'll need the liquid courage to share what I should have trusted with them years ago.

"It's... complicated and not pretty," I admit, my throat tightening. Squeezing my eyes shut, I try to gather myself and my thoughts. Ironically, having just shared them with Alec makes this huge task less intimidating. I haven't had the mental energy to push them back into the farthest corners of my mind yet. After taking a deep, calming breath, I add, "I want. No, I need you both to know the whole story."

Chapter Thirty-Six
COME TO JESUS MEETING
Emily

I've procrastinated long enough, but it's got to happen now, the sooner the better. I just haven't had the mental strength to handle my parents and their bullshit.

The family meeting they've requested through voicemails, texts, and Roxy is unavoidable. If I didn't attend, they'd follow through on their threat to break in and force me to sit down with them.

Surely, they can understand why I don't want to talk to them, let alone sit down with them. I'm pissed and I'm hurt, and I have a right to feel both emotions about them.

What kind of parents spy on their kids almost their entire adult life and even pay for them to have a man in their lives? For what reason?

Only one way to find out. I grab my phone and dial my mother's number. A shameful part of me hopes she doesn't answer, thinking I could leave a voicemail. I'm not calling to hash everything out; I want to know when I can meet with her and Dad together. I only want to say what I have to say once.

Mom answered and confirmed I should come around 3:00 pm. I hated how formal and strained the phone call felt. But I wasn't really inviting conversation. I was direct and to the point.

Mom followed my lead but asked if I needed anything. Yes! An undo button would be nice. That request was just in my mind, though.

Deciding I needed to prepare for combat, I took a nice hot shower, shaving areas that hadn't seen a razor in days. No ponytail for me today. Taking my time, I blow-dried and styled my hair with a large roller brush. The result was my hair hanging in loose, bouncy waves, shimmering with a healthy glow. It's beautiful, if I do say so myself. My makeup isn't dramatic, but it's a bit edgy. I will need my warrior's paint.

With my outside appearance ready for battle, my inner strength still didn't feel right. I couldn't shake the feeling of being off kilter, unsure and lacking the confidence to face this meeting head-on. It was hard telling Alec. It was sad telling the girls. Telling my parents is going to kill me.

Getting dressed, I notice that my form-fitting jeans are now loose. I hate the physical implications of once again letting someone else's actions control my life. I wasn't taking care of myself. I hadn't had the desire to do much of anything. Even my love of reading wasn't enough to hold my interest. Well, that was until I got Destiny. She calms me, so I made myself take her on a walk three times a day. Exercise is necessary for both of us.

Today's meeting with my parents is another step toward getting my life back on track. Roxy and Sarah helped me face the harsh reality that running wasn't the answer.

To begin, I had to stand up for myself and confront my parents. I wanted answers. Alec shared his reasons; now I needed to hear my parents' reasons.

First, I needed to feed and walk Destiny.

Destiny proved to be a good companion and an excellent cuddler. I quickly learned that she wasn't the least bit interested in the doggie bed. From the very first night, she hopped right onto my bed. I had no problem with that; I loved feeling her warmth as she slept against me. I was also happy to discover that Destiny slept all night.

Thinking about Destiny was the highlight of my life. I'm not sure how it happened, but I already love her, and I can tell Destiny is happy to be with me, too.

Two hours later, I stood on the doorstep of my childhood home, a fortress nestled in an established, older neighborhood. Homes here offer privacy because they aren't built right against each other but instead sit on large acre lots. Trees lining both sides of the estate create the illusion that it's the only home for miles. It's beautiful, but I find it hard to focus on that.

Standing here, I try to shake off my frustration and keep my anger in check. It's tough, because just being here brings up all my deep-seated resentments. The spying is just one of many things I resented my parents for. I'm here for answers, and I won't leave until I get them.

Deciding to be a petty pest, I ring the doorbell instead of walking in. I don't know why I did it, but that small act gives me some sense of control.

Mr. Whitaker responds, as pleasant as always, and tells me that my parents are in the back sitting room. The sitting room, with an entire wall of floor-to-ceiling windows, is my favorite room in the house. Opposite the windows are several bookcases, a writing desk, and a gas-lit fireplace in the corner. In the center of the room, two loveseat-sized leather couches face each other. There are two oversized accent chairs in beige and burnt orange that swivel to face either the couches or the fireplace. This room feels warm and inviting. It's a stark contrast to the other common areas, which seem more like a model home than my childhood home.

Entering the room, I see my mom right there. With a big, familiar smile, she wraps me in her arms and gives me a warm hug. Pulling back slightly, her smile fades as a look of worry replaces it. Looking into her eyes, I see they are full of unshed tears.

"Mom," I say quietly, before we're both wrapped up in my dad's strong arms. I was mad at my parents. But they love me, and I love them. That doesn't mean they have the right to invade my privacy or try to orchestrate parts of my life. But I'm here to try and understand their motives.

"Sit down, sweetheart," Dad encourages. Instantly, the endearment sends a stabbing pain to my chest. Alec called me sweetheart, and thinking of him and his betrayal still feels painfully fresh.

Taking a deep breath, I decide to start the conversation. I need to say what I came to say before my parents can spew their version.

"Mom, Dad, I recently found out you've been spying on me since I left for college, and you're still doing it now. I want it to stop immediately, and I don't want either of you to violate my privacy again. Do you understand?" I was breathing heavily just from the effort it took to say that to my parents. My tone is borderline disrespectful, but it's necessary to get my message across.

My mom and dad exchange looks before my dad responds, "I hear what you're saying, but let me explain. Okay?"

Seeing my nod, Dad continues, "When you were three years old, I had an attempt on my life. Leading up to that, I had received several unidentified notes that threatened retaliation against my family."

Dad was speaking in a calm, composed manner, but I could tell that sharing this information had shaken him.

Feeling shocked, I hedge. "Why would someone do that?" Asking that question, I realize I truly wanted to know. It scared me to hear this, but I needed to understand.

Dad continues, "Long story short, I was key to the prosecution of a known terrorist army leader who was sentenced to death. I was one of two military officers in criminal court who ruled in favor of his prosecution. He had powerful followers, and they were not nice people."

Searching my face for something, Dad continues. "The other tribunal officer, my counterpart, was shot but not killed while getting his newspaper. It was a drive-by, no way to confirm the source."

I nod again. So, Dad continues, "Then, I started receiving threatening notes in the mail. A week later, my car exploded when I used the auto start button on my car's key remote. Thank God it was cold that day, and I wanted the car to be warm when I left to go home."

Admittedly, I experienced a moment of pure panic when I asked, "Did they ever find out who did it? Are you still getting threats?"

They found out who put the bomb under the car, but were unable to link him to the person we knew was the source. The other prosecutors and I were advised to maintain a high level of security from that day forward.

"You've had an undercover security detail following you since preschool. You were never supposed to know they existed, and they were never allowed to interfere in your life. They were only there to observe and protect. They were to report anything they suspected was suspicious. It was for our peace of mind. I'm sorry, but I won't apologize for protecting my family." Dad shares with conviction, raising his chin with defiance.

Hearing all of this and the reasons behind it, it felt like someone let the wind out of my sails. I can't be mad at the reason behind their decisions, but I also don't understand why they didn't tell me. "Why have you kept it from me? I'm an adult now, shouldn't I have known that I was in potential danger?"

"We never wanted to burden you with this information or make you worry unnecessarily. It's not easy looking over your shoulder all the time. I didn't want that for you." Dad grabbed my hand and squeezed as he shared this.

I understand his thinking. I get it on some level, but it still smarts. Does he really think I'm that weak?

"So, what changed? Why was it okay for the undercover person to get involved in my life this time?" I ask, not sure I really want the answer. I can totally hear my mom saying in my head, *'It's because we want you to get married and give us grandchildren.'*

When my mom opens her mouth to respond, I almost laugh. Then I snap out of it when my mom shares, "That was not planned."

"I don't understand. You said security shouldn't interfere in my life?"

"What don't you understand? It's clear to us that he fell for you," Mom replies.

Wait, what? I was beginning to feel even more confused. I don't know which part upsets me the most anymore.

Then Dad shares something that surprises me. "Alec met with us three months ago at the end of his two-year contract. He told us he didn't want to extend it. Said the job had become personal, and we shouldn't trust him to make rational decisions because of his emotional involvement."

That comment makes me pause. Alec had said nearly the same thing to me yesterday, but I didn't believe him. Could he be in cahoots with my parents?

My mom's next words snap me out of my thoughts. Smiling, she says, "I think he wanted the freedom to pursue you."

You have no idea. If Mom only knew, but telling her would be over-sharing, a TMI moment, for sure.

"Emily, sweetheart, did Alec talk to you about the research he did for us?" Dad asks, his hopeful look almost tears down my resolve to stay strong.

"Yes, but I'm going to stop you right there. I'd rather not discuss it. Not with Alec and not with either of you," I reply, hoping my statement will make them drop the subject.

"I understand, honey. Really, I do. But you need to know that I can't let this go. It doesn't have to be today. When you're ready, we need to talk about some recent developments that have come to my attention. It's about Trace Roberts and his father."

"Dad?" I ask, unsure if I want him to keep talking or stop entirely.

"It can wait, sweetheart; I'm having a team look into this, and Alec's team found something he wants to discuss with me tomorrow. I'd rather have the details before we talk more in-depth anyway," Dad responds, right before he kisses my cheek.

A wave of relief washes over me; it's comforting to know I don't have to share the details of my attack with my parents right now. I can talk to them about it later. For now, I need time to process what he shared about his reasoning for my safety.

Anyway, I can't even put into words the many mistakes I made regarding Trace. And dad will want to know everything.

My brief moment of relief is suddenly clouded by fear and uncertainty. Discovering that our lives have been at risk for years is a shock I wasn't prepared for. My mind struggles to process the overwhelming emotions while also trying to figure out what information I need to ask about.

There are so many questions running through my mind. I'm curious about Dad's meeting with Alec, but I won't ask him about it. Instead, I ask, "Have there been any more threats?"

"No, not specifically related to the previous issue. We received some hate mail a few times, but none of the letters were connected. Threats aren't uncommon in my position."

"So, there's no reason I need further security?" I ask, lifting my chin in a defiant gesture. They need to see that I am serious about this, stopping right now, right here.

"No, we don't believe so. But I'd love it if you'd let us continue with your protective services detail," Dad pleads.

"Dad, I don't want it. Understanding why you did it doesn't change how I feel about it. I'm disappointed that you didn't share with me when I was old enough to understand. I can't help but feel violated." I want to add again, but I don't want to open up that potential side note for discussion.

"Will you think about it?" Dad pleads.

"I'll think about it," I respond, knowing I mean it. I understand the why now. I don't like it, but I get it.

"I'm sorry, sweetheart. We never meant to hurt you or use it to spy on you or keep tabs on you. We only wanted the reassurance that someone was looking out for you when we couldn't. I hope you know how much I love you. I regret not spending more time with you when you were growing up." Dad is now visibly shaken by his admission.

Mom quickly adds, "I love you very much, too, and the only thing I want for you is happiness. I'm here for you if you need me or want me for anything; we both are." Tears welled up and ran down her face as she shared this.

Walking over to them, I wrap my arms around both of them, "I love you too. And I will make a better effort to come visit you both."

"Good, we'd like that very much," my dad says, looking so relieved that I feel guilty for having shut them out of my life for so long.

"Why don't you bring that nice young man and join us for Sunday brunch?" Mom is being shamelessly pushy. I'll let that comment slide; otherwise, my snarky retort will ask if she's referring to the guy they paid to be in my life.

I'll be bringing someone; her name is Destiny. She's a sweet dog I adopted, and I already love her.

The genuine smile that stretches my cheeks just thinking of Destiny makes me happy. "I gotta run. I need to stop by the store before heading home. I love you both," I say, getting up to leave my parents' house.

"I can't wait to meet our grand dog," Mom says with a genuine smile.

"Yep, can't wait," Dad adds indulgently.

"We'll see you both Sunday," I add, grabbing my purse. Just as I reach the door, I hear it.

"You could still bring Alec," my ever-persistent mother calls out. I just wave a hand over my head and escape.

Driving back home, I was looking but not really seeing. The landscape flashed past, and the thought of going to the grocery store was almost forgotten. My mind was fully focused on what my dad shared. I never would have thought that having my parents invade my privacy could actually be construed as an act of love. It's a little twisted and fucked up, but I can see it came from a place of concern for me.

My parents love me. Sometimes they show it in unconventional ways, but it's still there.

Instinctively, my heart knows that what they shared was the truth. Understanding that they did all of this to protect me helps ease the sting of betrayal.

Hearing my dad support the story Alec told me has also made it easier to bear his deception.

Since Sunday, I've felt hurt, betrayed, deceived, and blindsided by Alec and my parents.

Over the past 24 hours, I've realized that my parents and Alec believed they had valid reasons for their actions. So, I faced a choice: I could accept their reasoning and forgive them, or I could stay miserable and keep having my pity party for one.

My heart wants to forgive them. I'll get there, but the offenses are still fresh in my mind, so I can't completely follow what my heart desires.

Even if I tell them right now that I forgive them, I am not yet at a point where I can forget it. I still focus on how betrayed they made me feel. Until I can move past that, it's not true forgiveness. It's just lip service, as my accounting professor used to say when we gave an answer to a math problem in words but not in actions. Still, admitting that I want to forgive is a big first step.

Chapter Thirty-Seven
DECISIONS
Emily

Waking up with a gasp, my heart pounding, I realize I dreamt of Alec. Having him invade my dreams is preferable to the nightmares. But seriously, why can't my dreams be about kittens, unicorns, or aliens like normal people?

Yesterday, after coming back from my parents' house and taking Destiny out, exhaustion hit me hard. My thoughts ricocheted like ping-pong balls, one after another, never settling. Conflicted. Unsettled.

Sleep didn't come easily. Neither a book nor Netflix could quiet my restless mind. I tossed and turned until finally drifting off near midnight.

Dreaming of Alec wasn't a surprise; I can't stop thinking about him. His betrayal feels different, heavier. He's the one person who knew all the answers, every missing piece to this fucked up puzzle of my life. His deception can't be cloaked under the disguise of an assignment. It was deliberate. Calculated. Personal. Wrong.

In my dream, Alec held me, pleading his case, but my refusal was swift, harsh, and absolute.

Then the dream shifted; he was still holding me, but urgency pulsed through it, like a ticking time bomb ready to explode. My answer teetered on the edge of something monumental. Panic surged as I watched him turn and walk away.

Wide awake now, the longing to believe him, to ask him to come back, still lingers. Fear of being too late claws at me, sharp with loss. I can't undo what's been done. The real possibility of losing Alec, as both a lover and friend, guts me.

But was I too late? Our last conversation didn't come with any ultimatums. He never said, *"Accept me now or never."*

I'm unsure whether to trust my head or my heart. My mind insists he wronged me, even as he admits to taking a calculated risk, knowing I might discover the truth about his involvement at any moment. He even confessed he never intended to tell me everything. That doesn't feel right. Yet, my heart whispers what I can't deny: Alec genuinely cares for me.

I also can't deny that the dream made me pause. The biggest question is... can I forgive them? I honestly don't know. But I hope so. Living in a constant state of anger and mistrust would be a lonely existence.

Over the past few days, I've settled into a routine with Destiny. I've turned down invitations from friends and family, choosing solitude instead, to have time to think and reflect on what the dream revealed. Destiny has been the perfect companion, curling up with me while I did a lot of soul-searching and deep thinking.

It's been nearly a week since I walked away from Alec in the park, and days since that strange dream. The dream reminded me that a decision about Alec looms over me. Yet I haven't heard a word from him. No one's mentioned him. He's vanished from my life, just as I asked him to do, and that realization stings.

A cruel little voice whispers that I'm not worth the trouble. Not even enough to be his friend.

Alec now knows my past: the ugly, sordid details. Maybe Alec finally believes what I tried to warn him about, that I'm damaged. Just a shell of the woman I could have been.

Still, part of me knows I'll see him again. We have unfinished business with the case. Sunday can't be the last time; we can't end like that. I won't allow it. But now that he knows everything, the best I can hope for is a casual friendship with him. And that will have to be enough.

If what my dad said is true, then maybe Alec really did try to do right by me.

Setting my anger aside, I know Alec is honorable, and what he told me was his truth.

Reflecting on our conversations and everything I learned from him and my parents, he has never actually lied to me. Yes, he left out a big detail, but he was legally obligated to do so by my parents.

How would I have handled things if the roles were reversed? I don't know. But I do know that, deep down, I was probably looking for reasons to fight against *'us'*, the us I don't really feel I deserve.

Setting the Alec debacle aside, what my dad revealed frightened me: the threats, the fear that pushed him to protect his family at any cost. That's the *'why'* behind everything.

Dad's words also helped me regain pieces I thought I'd lost: my progress, my strength, and the control I found after the assault. Those survival skills are still with me. I hadn't become a victim again. Not really. Jumping to that conclusion seems foolish given what I've learned. Sexual assault is not the same as having my privacy violated, especially when my parents' actions, though misguided, came from love rather than hate like Trace's.

With that understanding, I can finally see the root cause of their choices. I still don't understand why they kept me in the dark for so long, but I can't blame them for trying to keep me safe.

Do they realize, though, that despite everything, their protection couldn't save me from my own reckless choices or keep me from getting hurt? That conversation is coming, and I'm not looking forward to it.

Now that my thoughts aren't a jumbled mess, I see more clearly. I understand their actions, my reactions, and even Alec's role in everything. And it's fucked up to realize that even the best intentions, for the right reasons, can still cause so much pain.

I have decisions to make about my future. Like Roxy so eloquently pointed out, it's time to end the pity party and get on with my life.

I'm not naive; I know reclaiming my life will take effort. There's a lot to face and move beyond. But this time, I don't have to do it alone. My friends and family are here for me. All I have to do is ask.

Alec asked me for help, and I refused. That's not the person I want to be. When someone asks for help, you should give it.

When Alec told me about the other victims, I shut it out, ignored it. Same with the mention of the date rape drug. I couldn't process any of it through the haze of betrayal and anger. But since then, I can't stop thinking about it, the victims, the implications.

In my case, the drug explains why I couldn't fight back. It wasn't stupidity or naivety that night. I was targeted. The truth doesn't erase my guilt, but it reshapes it. And it fuels something else, determination.

I can't live with myself if I stay silent and let someone else go through what I endured. As much as I want to bury those memories and avoid exposing the dirty details, I can't. Justice demands otherwise.

Chapter Thirty-Eight
HELP
Emily

Learning about the date rape drug was like applying a Band-Aid to a deep, open wound. It might cover the worst part, but it can't stop the bleeding entirely. I really wanted it to.

And even knowing what Trace used doesn't fully lift the guilt I carry. It doesn't erase the feeling that I also share in the blame, that somehow my own actions might have invited the assault.

When I shared a bad experience I had in college with Alec, he offered his support and compassion. He was ready to give me all the time I needed. With him by my side, I felt strong enough to face my demons, bold, courageous, and free. For a little while, he erased the shame and turmoil of my past. Our time was brief but meaningful. And if he's still willing to stand by me, I believe together we could finally lock Trace away.

But first, I need to get myself in check. Put aside my emotions and prejudices. Be prepared to help in whatever way Alec or my father needs, knowing that every detail of my assault will come to light, no longer hidden in the dark corners of my mind. And no longer my dirty secret.

Uncertain about when or if I'll see Alec again, I choose to wait until my dad brings up the topic. Then I'll hope like hell I'm mentally ready to do what's right.

Alec would have made sure I was prepared, both mentally and physically, and he would have stayed by my side. Facing my demons without him feels terrifying. And knowing I was the one who pushed him away makes the loss even more cruel. With him gone, I've misplaced the strength I'd only just found.

But I can't forget, I am a survivor. My strength, my resolve, and my determination are my own.

And who says I have to face these challenges alone? Nothing is stopping me from taking the initiative, from being the woman who fights for her man and gives second chances.

The clock on my dresser startles me; I've lost hours sifting through my thoughts, replaying past choices, and sketching out plans. Plans that, inevitably, have Alec at the center.

That thought makes me remember the note Alec slipped under my door, the one I carelessly tossed on the entry table, now buried under mail and magazines. I'll find it later. For now, I've promised my parents Sunday brunch, and I have less than an hour to get ready.

As I shower, I feel lighter, comforted by my decisions and grounded in my progress. My plans to help with the case still need shaping, but at least I'm no longer running.

On that thought, I decide to reach out first. I'll text Alec after brunch to ask if he wants to come over for pizza and football. It's a small step. It might not signify that I'm putting on my boxing gloves for the fight of my life, for the battle for justice, but it's a start.

At the very least, I owed him a small apology. More than that, he needs to know I don't want to lose his friendship. That, on some level, I understand his position. That I've changed my mind. I want to help.

Chapter Thirty-Nine
CAPTAIN GRUMPY
Alec

"Hey, Captain, I got something you're gonna want to see," Stewart says as he walks into my office without knocking.

"What is it?" I ask, giving him an annoyed stare for barging in so loudly when I was feeling like shit.

"It's the mother of all finds, the granddaddy of details, it's the missing piece! Man, it's the connection between the Wilsons and the Roberts we've been looking for," Stewart shares, plopping into the chair that faces my desk.

Belatedly, I notice how exhausted he appears; his clothes are wrinkled and disheveled, and he probably hasn't shaved in two days. If he had a one-night stand, it wasn't the fun kind.

The team I assembled for my business venture has each been a valuable addition. Even though we already had clients, they willingly contributed to researching everything we could find on Trace Roberts and his family. We all believed we'd find evidence of the crimes we knew had happened and others we could only assume had occurred.

"Let's see it, and I thought I told you to stop calling me Captain. I'm not your Captain, and we're not CIA Special Ops anymore," I say, to bust his chops a bit.

Stewart, not one to hold back, retorts, "Trust me, it's better than what we all want to call you; you've been a real grump ass lately."

"Fine, then it's Captain Grumpy Ass to you," I say, laughing at our easy camaraderie and probably from a bit of embarrassment. I have been in a shit mood ever since I learned about Fuckwad Roberts.

While reviewing the document, I look back to see Stewart sitting back, almost melting into the office chair, silent as he watches me read the report. He's right; this is a significant missing piece. It's also highly sensitive information that wouldn't be found in a typical database. Still, how something this important, this monumental, was buried and not simply erased from existence remains a mystery.

"Who discovered this and how?" I ask, still reviewing the details.

"Janet, our resident hacker, did her magic and peeled back many layers to uncover it," Stewart says, appearing deep in thought.

"What? What aren't you saying?" I ask, noticing his hesitation to speak further.

Janet had to dig deep into the weeds on this one. She feels certain the searches will trigger red flags as security breaches. She wants your approval before moving forward. She believes she can find all the missing components. She thinks we will uncover details of a terrorist connection." Stewart says this without blinking, looking straight at me and gauging my reaction.

Stewart knows that Commander Nelson already warned me about doing system searches without legal authorization. That warning doesn't even account for the various databases and sealed documents Janet must have accessed to obtain this information.

Stewart understands this could negatively affect me and, by extension, the team. There are not only legal consequences but also a real risk of threats to harm those involved. They must have a broad reach to hide this information and maintain their position of power.

"If Janet's intuition is right, then we're already in trouble," I say.

"My thoughts exactly," Stewart says, before adding, "I got your back no matter what, and I know Janet is in. As a matter of fact, that's why she isn't here now; she hasn't stopped, and you know how she gets when she's on the hunt."

I ask, "I thought she was waiting on my approval?"

"Nah. Man, she told me to say that. She knows you wouldn't want her taking all the risks. She said this would give you the illusion that you actually had a say in it." With a chuckle, Stewart adds, "She's committed to the cause now, you know her moral compass is her guiding force."

"Thanks, man, but I think I should schedule a meeting with the others, too. Also, I believe it's time for me to talk with Em's father again. He owes me some details," I say, turning toward the computer to send a meeting request to the team.

Just then, three heads peeked into my doorway, and in unison, I heard, "We're all in Captain Grumpy!"

I laugh despite how serious the situation is. "Have you guys been eavesdropping the whole time?"

"Nope, just testing some new long-range surveillance equipment. Works great too," says Rudy with a cocky grin.

Rudy was the Sapper on my team. Our missions were successful because of him. He ensured our routes were safe and our communications were secure. He was responsible for coordinating our movements, allowing us to enter and exit undetected. To ensure our success, he mastered disrupting the enemy's communications. He's a technology genius. We used to call him Casanova until he met Amber; she has been his girlfriend for nearly three years now.

As they enter, one by one, Juan, who was my second-in-command on my Special Ops team, smirks and says, "I already spoke to Felix and Mike; they're all in too."

"Hey, boss man, if Stewart didn't tell you yet, I'm in too. I gotta run, though, I'm uploading files as we speak," Janet says, popping back out the door.

Janet is a master at hacking into systems. At 5ft 3in, you'd think she might be intimidated by all of us men over 6ft tall and over 100 lbs. heavier, but not Janet. I once saw her take down a 6ft 3in rookie during floor mat exercises. She might be small, but she's mighty. I'm just glad she's one of the good guys. She has the skills to cause significant harm.

Juan, who has as many years of service as I do, was next in line to take over my Special Ops team captain position when I retired. Imagine my surprise when he called to ask if he could join my company. That was an easy yes for me. My trust in him and his abilities runs deep. Good for me, but not so good for the Commander; he lost a good man.

Mike and Felix were the primary combatants during our missions. We all trained to handle direct armed conflicts, but Mike and Felix often took the front line, letting the rest of the team focus on their assigned tasks. Their job was to keep us alive, and they were damn good at it. We are all here today as testament to that fact.

Not ready to show how moved I am by their support, I partially turn back toward my computer and ask, "Should I cancel the meeting invite I just sent, or should we use that time to review what information we have on hand?"

I'm not ashamed to show my gratitude or appear vulnerable. We've been through hell and back together on more than one operation. Stress and emotions run high, especially during our search-and-rescue missions or long days and nights of reconnaissance work. This mission is different; we don't have the government behind us, only each other now.

The fact that all six team members are willing to put their necks on the line for me, even though we are now civilians, means a hell of a lot to me.

"Keep the meet, maybe Janet will have deciphered her last data dump by then," Rudy suggests.

"Thanks, guys, I don't know what to say," I manage, trying to show my appreciation without losing my man card for being overly sappy.

"What's the plan, Captain?" Rudy asks, taking the other empty chair next to Stewart.

Shaking my head, I decide to ignore him for calling me Captain, old habits, and all that.

"Have Janet report any findings directly to the team through our Comtech data link. Tell her, and honestly, any of us, to use the secure tactical encrypted data storage link. Hopefully, this will prevent any reverse hacking efforts. Especially since we've already triggered red flags," I say, glancing over the group.

"You got it," Rudy says.

"I've been reaching out to several loosely connected organizations. I'll upload my call log, including each contact's name and affiliation. Maybe we can find a few more common details," Juan offers.

"I guess I don't have to say it, but please remind everyone to cover their tracks when possible." A little chagrined to feel the need to say it.

"We know what's at stake. None of us is going into this blind to the risks and blowback possibilities," Juan shares, knowing precisely what I need to hear.

"Okay. Yeah, okay. Thanks," I say, accepting that they want to do this. They want to help. They want justice.

Clearing my thoughts of the emotion that threatened my composure, I quickly discussed my next plans. "I'm going to be meeting with Mr. Wilson as soon as I hear back from him. Juan, can you join me to get a read on him? I want to know if you expect him to be telling the truth or not. None of us has a bullshit radar like you do."

"Sure," Juan says, as Rudy chuckles.

Each of my team members has a unique skill set. Juan has many, but the fact that he's like a human lie detector has come in handy on several missions. He hasn't been wrong yet.

"After we meet with the Wilsons, I'll schedule a meeting to discuss an action plan and get our marching orders. Are the other clients all covered?" I ask.

"Yes, we're good on that front. No worries, man," Stewart assures. Getting up with a cheeky grin, he says, "I need a shower and some food. I'll see you guys at 0800." Then he's gone.

Ten minutes later, I confirmed a meeting with Mr. Wilson for tomorrow at 9:00 am.

Mr. Wilson agreed to come here and meet with both Juan and me. That gives me the next seventeen hours to come to terms with what Janet found out and to formulate my questions.

The meeting with Em's father probably won't help my new title, Captain Grumpy. If anything, it might get me a nickname upgrade to Captain Grumpier Asshole.

310

Learning that Em's father had previously been a high-ranking military officer with the United States Military Tribunals was something he should have shared with me long before now.

I'm even more annoyed to learn that Mr. Wilson played a key role in the prosecution and eventual execution of Hassam Bahram, who was the leader of the Terrorist Army and suspected of making numerous threats against the United States.

Military files revealed Bahram financed the entire operation, from his headquarters in Sudan to the U.S. mainland. His vast weapons network fueled the bloodiest year of fighting in the Middle East, a war driven by land, oil, and power.

Wilson's role as lead prosecutor in securing Bahram's death sentence put a target on his back. Bahram's death didn't stop his mission; it ensured loyal supporters would carry on his agenda. There's always another terrorist ready to take up the cause.

Another shock came when it was revealed that Roberts Senior is an International Criminal Court Judge in the Netherlands. He was recently accused of accepting bribes from a well-known Bahram affiliate but remained active until his recent suspension. The case involves more than just bribery; a guilty verdict is expected for treason.

Janet is committed to uncovering more details about those charges while also looking into any links to Trace Roberts Senior and Trace Junior. If the evidence is there, she'll find it.

Chapter Forty
THE MEETING
Alec

Janet's hacking skills revealed that the death threats and retaliation threats the Wilsons received years ago came from followers of Army Leader Bahram. The murder attempts against Mr. Wilson's associates are also directly linked to Bahram's followers.

It was the United States Military that was responsible for hiding the link between Em's father and Bahram as part of a witness-protection program. The failed effort to keep Mr. Wilson and the other Tribune members secret only shows how deep Bahram's ties are within the U.S.

Sharing what we learned with Mr. Wilson was an interesting exercise in itself. He initially wanted to deny the correlation. My team and I assume that witness protection told Mr. Wilson never to speak of his involvement with Bahram. Once we laid out the facts, there was no denying his involvement then.

Mr. Wilson then filled in several missing pieces. He connected dots and helped paint the picture of what happened and why. With my team's hacking skills and Mr. Wilson's detailed background explanations, we uncovered the link to Edward Trace Roberts Senior.

Trace Roberts Senior's role with the ICC was connected to Bahram, who was connected to the Wilsons.

Janet found emails and other correspondence belonging to Trace Junior. He had a misguided, twisted belief that it was his duty as the only son to seek justice for anyone who had wronged his father. Some of the correspondence used to support our findings was between him and his father directly.

As suspected, Trace Junior did not randomly choose his victims; instead, four targets are mentioned. We knew about three of them, including Em, and there is a fourth one.

Trace Roberts Senior not only used his power to prevent the prosecution of terrorist acts, but he also manipulated his influence to shield his son from prison and avoid accountability for his heinous crimes. How far his reach extended remains a mystery.

Em's father listened closely when Juan gave a broad overview of what those crimes involved.

I neither confirmed nor denied that Em was among the victims. Oh, her father asked, but that's Em's story to tell, not mine.

Neither Juan nor I intentionally shared the gory details of the cases involving Trace Junior. Em's father has his own resources to get that information; I didn't feel it was my place to share those details with him.

Looking into his eyes, I knew he understood it was bad. That is something no father willingly wants to accept could happen to their daughter.

Em, her father, and her mother will need a lot of healing. Her father will need to let go of the guilt he will undoubtedly feel and be there for Em.

It was late when we finished the main part of our meeting. I felt relieved to finally have the answers to the questions that had been bothering me for a while. Still, I hated the answers all the same.

I was grateful Mr. Wilson agreed to let me out of my contract extension. Hearing that Em emphatically declined further security detail had me fighting a smile.

She thought she was weak, but I believe she is one of the strongest women I have ever met. She overcame everything that happened to her without assistance, and she went on to build a successful life for herself.

She's independent, beautiful inside and out, and perfect for me. If it takes the rest of my life to convince her of that, I'll gladly sacrifice my desire for instant gratification because I know she's worth the wait.

As Mr. Wilson was packing to leave, he mentioned that his wife wanted him to invite me to Sunday brunch. The sparkle in his eye told me all I needed to know; Em's mom was playing matchmaker.

I politely thanked him for the invite but responded noncommittally. I'll accept any help I can get, but I need to consider the best way to get Em to give me another chance willingly. I have to think more about whether I feel brave enough to show up and surprise her on Sunday.

Em's parents loved her, and I felt guilty that they were mostly misunderstood by others in our group.

Their willingness and almost eagerness to let me out of my contract was just another sign of their love for her.

Shaking Mr. Wilson's hand, I thanked him for coming and for filling in the gaps. I understood his position and approach much better after this meeting. There was a purpose to his actions. A method behind his madness. A reason for being over the top. Protective.

Mrs. Wilson's invitation was her way of helping her daughter find happiness. I knew it. Mr. Wilson knew it. Honestly, I'm tempted to let both of them step in on my and Em's behalf. Let her dad tell Em my side of the story, to paint a better picture of how I handled everything with her. But this has to stay just between Em and me. She's already heard my side. Now it's totally up to her how she moves forward.

Chapter Forty-One
SUNDAY BRUNCH
Emily

Destiny and I arrive at my parents' house with 10 minutes to spare. I decide to use those extra minutes to let Destiny sniff around the front yard before bringing her inside. My mom loved her Persian rugs. I'd hate for Destiny's first accident to happen here.

After Destiny tinkled a few times, we let ourselves into the house. I didn't want to push my luck by ringing the doorbell again.

Mr. Whitaker was there to greet us. He probably noticed my car arriving on the security monitors.

"Good morning, Miss Emily. Who do we have here?" Mr. Whitaker's warm smile wasn't aimed at me. Nope. He was smiling at Destiny.

"Good morning. Her name is Destiny. She's my new roommate," I share.

"She's a pretty little pup," he says while letting her sniff his closed hand before gently petting her on the head. With a quick glance my way, he adds, "Your parents are in the sitting room already entertaining a guest."

I wanted to ask who was here, but Mr. Whitaker was already heading toward the kitchen.

Not knowing how Destiny will respond to meeting new people in an unfamiliar environment, I decide to keep her leashed until she becomes acquainted with my parents and her new surroundings.

Entering the room, I freeze, momentarily immobile. Not Destiny, though. Her little body trembles with excitement, and her tail wags so enthusiastically it could be mistaken for a fan as she pulls me further inside on her leash. She's on a mission to see a familiar face. Alec was here, at my parents' house for Sunday brunch.

Destiny remembered him and was apparently determined to reach him. She was being a little traitor, but I understood the allure that only Alec has.

Seeing Alec here felt surreal. It should feel wrong. He shouldn't be here. This is my family home. My family time. But seeing Alec sitting in the adjacent armchair next to my dad, talking, also felt right. Natural. Predestined.

Then my brain thawed enough to realize that Alec and my parents set me up. Alec orchestrated this entire thing. Or was it my mom? Or my dad? Does it matter?

Looking down, Alec had stepped away from the chair and was now kneeling in front of Destiny, petting her. Of course, the little hussy had rolled over, giving him access to her belly.

"Hey, sweetheart," Dad says, as he wraps me in a big hug. Mom follows with a warm embrace of her own.

Over my mom's shoulder, I see Alec watching me. He smiles one of his panty-melting smiles and says in a gravelly voice, "Hi, Em."

Before I realize my traitorous body, I smile back at Alec but respond dryly, "Hey."

Then the full weight of the situation hits me, and a wave of confusion and uncertainty rushes over me. My flight mentality rears its ugly head, and I struggle to suppress it.

Mom and Dad both love up on Destiny, who is in doggy heaven. They seem unaware of the difficulty that having Alec here has caused me.

Alec, for his part, hasn't taken his eyes off me even once. Where his first smile had a punch, he now offers a smile meant to reassure.

Managing to nod at him, I walk away. I need a moment. Just a second to process the shock of seeing him in my childhood home, talking with my parents, loving on my dog, smiling at me. I'm not sure how to feel about it.

It hits me then. I realize that the image before me resembles the life I've only dreamed of, a glimpse of the life I want. If only my hopes and dreams hadn't been stolen from me by poor choices and my tendency to pick the wrong men.

The heart wants what it wants. Seeing Alec here, knowing that my heart desires him, wants to give myself to him, and hopes he can heal and put back together all my broken, scattered pieces, has shaken me deeply. It threw me off balance. Teetering on the edge of what I want versus what my mind is telling me I can have. Having Alec here, I wish this could be my life. My fairytale. My reality.

I want Alec to be a permanent part of my life, lasting forever. My heart desires him and this connection. However, my damaged soul has doubts. Still, my heart knows I love him, and if what he said is true, he loves me too.

This realization brings an almost paralyzing fear. What if Alec no longer wants those things with me? Or what if I can't allow myself to have the happily-ever-after life? What if he's only here in a professional capacity? Can I handle potential failure or rejection?

The cowardly part of me wants to keep walking out the back door and run away from here. To avoid the unknown. To avoid facing Alec or seeing the pitying looks my parents will give me. What if Alec already told them what happened to me? What if having Alec here means they planned an ambush? Is Alec on the clock?

I hate being blindsided. Without warning, my emotions spike from panic to anxiousness to paralyzing fear. The uncertainty about having Alec here and not knowing what they've discussed is the main cause. Taking several deep breaths, I focus on the voices coming from the other room while trying not to cry.

As a distraction, I focus on the stunning view of my parents' perfect backyard through the large over-the-sink window. This window is worth every dollar my dad spent enlarging it and clearing away any obstacles or plants.

Taking a deep breath, I slowly exhale. I was fighting my overactive flight instincts, which were shouting at me to run. But I can't run. Not this time. Not before facing my parents, Alec, and possibly my past.

I won't run. God help me, but it's time to reveal those long-guarded destructive secrets.

Facing the fact that a battle was imminent, the dizziness and sudden nausea I was experiencing couldn't be ignored. I seem to be having trouble with my lungs functioning properly. The panic attack I've been fighting off is threatening to surface just from the thought of exposing my secrets.

Closing my eyes, I run through the mental checklist I've relied on heavily this past week. I'm not sure how long I stood there, staring out my mom's favorite window, lost in my own internal battles, before Alec appeared in the doorway.

"Hey," he softly asks. "Are you okay?"

Turning to face him, I tell him the one truth I know at that moment, "I will be."

With a look of approval or concern, Alec says, "Your mom wanted me to let you know that brunch is about to be served."

Feeling rattled by the cycle of unpleasant thoughts drifting through my mind, I force myself to look away from the view and respond, "Okay, yes. I'm coming."

Instead of heading back to the dining room, Alec comes over to me, a look of concern etched on his handsome face. Alec seems worried about me or our situation, but he's definitely nervous. He doesn't need to be. I'm not even mad anymore. If I had to describe how I feel, I'm more confused than angry.

Alec doesn't stop his forward approach until he is well within my personal space bubble. His closeness is confusing. His presence at my parents' house is confusing. Wanting to know what he thinks of me and what he learned about me is confusing. I was confused.

My traitorous body wasn't acting confused; I had to fight the overwhelming urge to lean into him, to wrap myself around him, and to let go of the shield I put in place where he is concerned.

I wanted to ask Alec what was happening. What exactly did he want? Like, did he still want me?

But my lungs still struggled to function. I couldn't come up with a single thing to say to Alec. I had no clue how to ask him any of the confusing questions.

Alec wasn't saying anything either. He was just all up in my space, watching and studying me. Stepping even closer, Alec places a finger under my jaw to lift my face an inch from his. His scrutiny is unnerving.

Alec was hesitant, careful, guarded, but he wasn't speaking. Just as I was about to say a word or two, he made his move. Alec grabs my face with both of his large yet gentle hands, then says, "Fuck it!"

That was the only warning I got before Alec claimed my mouth with his. Still cradling my head, Alec tilts my face so our lips can move perfectly in sync as he deepens the most incredible kiss I've ever experienced.

And in that moment, with embarrassingly little resistance and no fight left in me, *I let him.* I let his tongue erase the doubt from my mouth and then from my mind. I let his lips erase the fear inside me.

I gave up trying to stick to my resolve of never putting my heart on the line again and surrendered everything.

From the tips of my toes to the top of my head, the spark of ecstasy and awareness threatens to consume me. When I open my eyes, I see Alec watching me, assessing my reaction. My own desire reflected in his dark chocolate eyes.

Alec must come to his senses; he takes a small step back just as I'm about to climb him like a tree. The low groan that escapes him tells me he would've welcomed it if we were anywhere else.

Before I can say a word, we hear my dad's voice outside the kitchen door, telling my mom he'll find us. Perfect timing.

Quickly, without any verbal agreement, we step farther away from each other just as the door swings open. We were acting like guilty teenagers getting busted for kissing. I wonder what my dad would think if he knew I wanted to do much more than kiss in their kitchen.

Dad was smiling at us as if he knew what we were up to. It shouldn't matter either way; we were both adults. But since this was my childhood home, it felt almost forbidden.

The three of us head toward the dining room table just outside my mother's over-the-top butler's pantry. Looking up, I see Alec glancing my way. I can't read his expression, but I meet his gaze with a reassuring smile, hoping to convey that I'm not upset about him kissing me. I'm actually excited about the possibility that he still wants me.

Surprisingly, brunch wasn't awkward; it was enjoyable. My parents seem to really like Alec, and I could tell Destiny was already wrapping her grandpa around her little paw. No telling how much he was sneaking to her under the table.

Mom seemed happier than I had seen her in a long time. Apparently, her new Accounts Manager role at one of my dad's companies was a great decision for her.

Dad brought up the talk we needed to have. But to my relief, he asked to schedule it for Wednesday. He also requested that, with my permission, Alec be allowed to join the meeting. Dad quickly told Alec that he was not under any contractual obligation to do so.

As I was grabbing my doggie bag, literally, because Dad wanted to send some food home for Destiny and me, I asked Alec, "I didn't see your Yukon. How did you get here?"

"It's in the shop. I took an Uber," he mumbles.

Then I hear dad yell from the den, "Oh yeah, I told him he still had to come and that you'd give him a ride home."

Alec looked a little sheepish at my dad's proclamation, but I was fine with it. "Sure, Dad, I'll take him home."

Alec leans in and whispers, "Are you planning to take me home with you?"

Smiling without confirming or denying my intentions, I walk to the sitting room to give mom and dad hugs goodbye. "I love you both. Dad, I'll talk to you on Wednesday."

"Alright, sweetheart. I'll see you then," Dad says reassuringly.

While Mom was busy giving Destiny a thorough rub-down, Alec exchanged a few words with my dad before turning to give my mom a warm hug. They seem closer than I expected for an employee-employer relationship.

Extricating Destiny away from my mom, we head toward the front door. Good old Mr. Whitaker is already holding the door open for us. For a man his age, he moves around surprisingly quietly. We don't see or hear him until he's needed. Then he's just magically there.

Before we get to my car, Alec, being the kind of guy he is, holds out his palm and says, "I'll drive."

"It's okay, I got it," I say, knowing full well he will not go for this.

"Em, give me the keys… please." The please part seemed to hurt him a bit. I wonder what he would have done if I had resisted.

I laugh at his expression and the mental image of him giving in to let me drive. I couldn't help but laugh. His words, along with the pitiful look he gave me, were funny.

Alec raised an eyebrow, clearly not amused.

It was a running joke, or more like a rule. Alec and Dex both agreed that unless they had two broken arms and a broken leg, they would not willingly let any of us girls drive.

It had something to do with Roxy always doing curb checks, me hitting a couple of mailboxes years ago, and Sarah driving like a grandma.

I hand over my keys; that was my plan all along, but it was amusing to see his brief moment of panic.

After getting Destiny settled on the blanket across my back seat, I happily sit in the passenger seat.

Having learned the hard way more than once, Alec used the seat controls to move the seat all the way back before knocking his head on the door jam. Thank goodness he remembered; otherwise, I would have started laughing uncontrollably all over again. It's a curse.

As it was, I was struggling with the mental image that he had forgotten and had concussed himself.

Shifting my thoughts since Alec wasn't talking, I reflected on that kitchen kiss. Alec probably didn't realize how much that one act of kissing me passionately gave me hope and convinced me I had to fight for us.

Chapter Forty-Two
THE WATER BOTTLE
Alec

Leaving Em's parents, our moods shifted. The moment the car doors closed, everything changed. We could almost hear our synchronized inhales and exhales; it was eerily quiet. An electric tension pulsed back and forth inside the car. Whether it was lust or anger, I wasn't sure. Whatever it was, it was wild, like someone flipped a power switch.

Love and hate are essentially the same powerful emotion. The only difference is that they typically reside on opposite sides of the heart. No idea which side Em's emotions lean toward.

Yes, I kissed Em. And yes, she kissed me back. But I can't shake the nagging feeling that I still don't know if Em has forgiven me. She didn't slap me, at least there's that. That was promising. Then again, she hasn't said a word to me since we left her parents.

The thought that her kindness and smiles were just fake, especially because we were with her parents, keeps running through my mind.

Deciding to accept the Wilsons' invitation to brunch was difficult. I wasn't sure how Em would react if she saw me there. Since she dislikes surprises, it could have sparked a fight or led her to ignore me completely. Fortunately, neither happened;

instead, Em was friendly and caring toward her parents and warm to me.

Kissing Em was an impulsive decision on my part. Seeing Em there and missing her, I couldn't help myself. I went for it and was lucky I didn't get slapped.

Brunch was relaxed and fun. I enjoyed watching Mr. Wilson feed Destiny under the table while Em pretended not to see. Mrs. Wilson kept a steady flow of conversation on different topics. Mr. Wilson and Em listened to her mother speak softly with indulgent smiles.

No one acknowledged the elephant in the room or the negative parts of the past. AKA, Trace Roberts Junior. How they ignored that fucker was anyone's guess. But I definitely wasn't going to bring him up. For once, I wasn't leading an operation.

I was relieved that Mr. Wilson postponed the heavy, uncomfortable conversation until Wednesday. He made the invitation to join them sound like I had a choice, which I definitely did not, but he was trying to be diplomatic. I really appreciated that.

Kissing Em was an impulsive, risky, and bold move on my part. And yes, it was stupid too. Afterwards, Em acted like nothing had happened, and by all accounts, she behaved as if we were just friendly neighbors the whole time. I would have preferred her to get upset, ask me to leave, slap me, kick me in the junk, anything except pretend that the incredible kiss didn't happen. That hit hard.

I know it's crazy for a grown-ass man to get his feelings hurt over being slighted, but it happened. Honestly, I was upset and confused. She kissed me back, dammit!

When Em agreed to give me a ride home, I was surprised and pleased. That was until I realized that, of course, she'd willingly take a *"friend"* home. How could she explain it to her parents if she refused?

So many thoughts and doubts compete for my attention. I was so distracted by my thoughts that I didn't realize we had already returned to the condos. Not until we entered the garage. The scariest part was that I was the one driving, and I couldn't remember our trip.

Taking me out of my thoughts, Em's voice breaks the silence, "I'm going to take Destiny to the park before heading up."

"You want company," I hedge, completely unsure of how she will respond.

"Um, sure, if you want to. You don't have to, though," Em says, looking hesitant. I really hate how awkward we both were. But that's on me.

Re-hooking Destiny's leash before helping her out of Em's backseat, I share, "I want to." I don't know what I would have done if she had said no. The unsettled, doubt-filled man in me needs to know where we stand with each other. The patient man, who understands I did this to her and us, knows I have to let Em take all the time she needs.

Now I had to either find the courage to bring up the subject or hope that Em would mention it herself. Ignoring everything that happened isn't an option. Tiptoeing around eggshells won't help us either. The problem is that patience isn't one of my strengths.

Reaching the park trail, we walk along the water's edge. The ducks fall silent as we approach, providing a peaceful break from their quacking. Destiny never once tugged on her leash to chase after them. It's hard to believe Em only adopted her a few days ago. She's genuinely well-behaved, and I'm glad Em got her.

Feeling content to be with Em, I let her set the pace of the walk and the conversation, or the lack of one, which is currently the case.

Apologies, questions, and concerns all swirl inside my mind, each vying to be voiced. Remaining silent is torture, yet I know it's the one act of restraint Em needs most from me.

"Wanna sit for a while?" Em asks, already heading off the trail toward a cluster of large shade trees. The massive branches provide plenty of shade over the grass below. It offers excellent protection from the sun but does nothing to combat Houston's humidity.

"Sure," I reply, and we stop nearly at the same spot where I found Em and Destiny sitting days ago.

Facing the water, I feel content to be here with her. How can I possibly feel at peace when a war rages in my mind? It doesn't make sense, but having her close and knowing she's safe comforts me in a way I don't deserve.

Since Em arrived at her parents', a current of energy has existed between us. Our bodies seem to instinctively recognize each other, recalling how good it felt when we were together. The intense, passionate, intimate moments we shared stay vivid in our memories. Despite the confusion and hurt we've felt, our bodies remain drawn to one another.

Beyond a thin layer of comfort, I have a troubled conscience. I fucked up. By rushing into a relationship with Em before being fully honest with her, I took away her right to choose. Em deserved to know the real person she was committing to. I robbed her of the chance to accept me for who I truly am.

I only have myself to blame for whatever happens now. I bought this. My only choice now is to listen, to let Em drive the conversation or the ass chewing. Either way, she has the right to have a safe space where she can freely express her anger and disappointment. I'm here for it, even knowing how painful it will be to hear how much I hurt her.

Glancing over, Em's chest rises and falls with deep, audible breaths. Slowly, very slowly, her next exhale is long and slow, like a pinhole in a balloon. Instinctively, I knew that the next words out of Em's mouth would not be favorable ones.

Without conscious thought, my body braces for the impact. My heart clenches, knowing I have to let Em say whatever she needs to say. I owe her that much and so much more.

Em's first words, though expected, hit hard. And they're completely justified. No amount of preparation could soften the powerful, well-deserved blow.

"You did me wrong, Alec. You knew all along who I was. What could have happened to me? You knew because it was your job to know. Because you were investigating me and my life."

"Em, I…." I croak out, only to be cut off.

"No, Alec. No, you don't get to control how this unfolds. Please listen to what I am about to tell you. Really listen. Your deceit is worse than my parents'. You befriended me. You integrated yourself into my life, my home, and the lives of Roxy and Sarah. Alec, I considered you one of my closest friends. I let you in."

Hearing Em's voice crack as she fights back her emotions guts me. I did this. Everything she said is the sad fucking truth, and Em wasn't even done slaying me with her words.

"You gotta know, what I shared with you, I never shared with another soul. I told you about my past, the past you already knew. You of all people, had to understand that sharing the details of my attack wasn't easy for me. It hurt. It reopened old wounds. But what hurts me the most is that you knew me, but I never knew you."

"Em, I couldn't tell you…I…"

"Stop, Alec. I already know about your contractual obligations. Your excuses don't change the fact that you slept with me, for Christ's sake! How can you justify maintaining a contract with my parents while ignoring that breaking your word to me is just as serious? You made me believe I could trust you; isn't that just as important?" Em states firmly.

"Em, Baby, you are the most important thing to me. You can trust me. Please believe me." Pleading with Em is just the first step in doing whatever it takes to make her believe in me again.

"Was becoming my friend and sleeping with me part of your contract? Was I part of your payment?" Em asks with accusation.

"God, no! Come on, Em. Of course not. I'm sorry. I should never have let us be more than friends until my contract was finished. I've felt so much guilt. I regret taking your choice to be with me away from you. It was selfish of me," I admit, disappointed in myself.

"Be honest, Alec, were you ever planning to tell me?" It was the earnest, defeated look on Em's beautiful face that kept me from lying.

"No, I already told you. My original plan was for you never to find out the truth. I never wanted you to know that I entered into a contract with your parents or the real reason I came into your life," I admit reluctantly.

Confessing this was just as difficult as admitting to Em who I truly am. My mistakes are piling up quickly.

"Oh, Alec, how could you?" The tears brimming in Em's eyes are my fault. Her pain is my doing. I caused this. Her disappointment in me is entirely my fault. Maybe sharing the details of how we first met will give her a little comfort.

"I might have known who you were, but I never intentionally set out to hurt you. Originally, I planned to watch from a distance and never be intrusive in your life. Do you remember the first time we met? I don't think we even exchanged names that day. I was coming back from the gym when I heard you before I saw you. You were cussing like a sailor."

"Oh yeah, my favorite water bottle still has the dents to justify why I got so pissed off," Em says. I can hear a reluctant smile in her voice.

"Right away, I understood your dilemma. You were wearing a short, tight navy skirt and a white blouse. Your heels were at least 3 inches high. Watching, I noticed you could barely crouch down to see where the bottle had rolled under your car. There was no way you could crawl and get it. Not without destroying your outfit," I recall.

"I remember, not my finest moment. I was debating whether to take the risk of moving my car to pick it up. Knowing my luck, I would run over the damn thing, and it'd cause some serious damage to my car," Em confides. I can definitely hear the smile in her voice now.

"It didn't take much convincing for you to accept my offer. All I had to do was point out that I was already sweaty and needed a shower. I quickly retrieved your bottle, and just as quickly, you thanked me and left," I reminisce, remembering how flustered Em had been that day.

"I was running late for our monthly board meeting. All the staff would be there, and I can't stand walking into a meeting that's already started. I'm glad I took the time to thank you at least," Em shares, her face appearing more relaxed than I've seen it in days.

"You were appropriately grateful. Then a few days passed, and we crossed paths again. You, Dex, and Roxy were coming off the elevators when you noticed me. You looked cute. When you went to introduce us, you realized then that you didn't know my name," I share, chuckling.

"I was worried that it was more about me forgetting your name than realizing I never knew it to begin with," Em says, looking chagrined.

"Still, you didn't miss a beat. The invite to join you guys for dinner was unexpected. I couldn't bring myself to decline your sincere offer. Then Roxy and Dex chimed in for me to come. You guys were so welcoming. My acceptance wasn't about the job, but rather a genuine interest in making new friends," I confess, knowing that what I just said makes me sound pathetic.

"Part of me believes you, but knowing what I know now, there's also a part of me that feels taken advantage of. It won't be easy for me to move past the feeling that you deceived not only me but my friends as well," Em confesses.

"That was never my intent. I genuinely care about Dex and the girls, and you know how I feel about you. You guys accepted me. For the first time in my long career, I was accused of mission creep because of the gradual and incremental way I became involved in each of your lives. I slowly became part of your circle."

"Why? Why now? I guess I don't understand what makes our situation different from any of your other clients," Em inquires, truly unaware of the pull she has and how magnetic she is.

"It was a kind of development," I oversimplify, trying to come up with a proper response and hoping it will help Em understand that it was not premeditated.

"A development... hummm. Interesting, let's hear it," Em challenges. Shit, I'd better come up with something damn spectacular and quick.

Chapter Forty-Three
THE DEVELOPMENT
Alec

Em was listening; she was present and not running away. That alone is a victory. The time she spends with me is my chance to explain why this feels different between us, why I did what I did.

"From our very first encounter in the garage, I knew you were different. You were special. It was during that first year that my feelings for you started to blur the boundaries of my job. I realized I no longer found my work fulfilling. Instead, I felt it was a noose around my neck, holding me back from what I wanted most, choking out my will to live a better life and stifling my desires," I boldly admit, laying my heart wide open.

"Basically, it was a two-year contract of pure hell for me. I had to fight so hard to keep my caveman instincts in check. I had to suppress my own wants and desires," I admit, feeling incredibly vulnerable sharing so much, especially since Em hasn't shown me any signs that she's leaning toward forgiving me.

"Because you were protecting me, right? It was your job," Em states, still not hearing me, let alone believing me.

"Babe, it was because I wanted you for myself. Hearing you girls talk openly about other men, or dates, or hell, even discussing in detail what you girls thought of a dude's body on TV. That shit almost did me in."

"You wanted me. So that's why you were always stoic and distant. And sometimes borderline rude. Because you wanted me?" Em asks, with accusation written all over her face.

"Yes. Em, I wanted you. I wanted to remain in your life and in your inner circle. I'm not trying to convince you that I was in love back then. It takes two to build a relationship. But I wanted the freedom to explore more with you. The option to pursue a relationship with you. The contractual chains restrained me, but when the two years were over, I was done waiting. Done fighting against myself. I loosened the hold I had on my restraint and allowed myself to jump the gun."

"What I want to know is, if you were done with the contract with my parents or close to it, why couldn't you tell me who you are? You felt close enough to have sex with me, but not to talk openly with me?" Em accuses.

"Em, please. You know it was more than just sex between us. We have a connection, a driving force that unites us. But I won't lie to you. When I told you that I never wanted to tell you for fear of losing you as a friend, that was my intent," I admit.

When Em doesn't comment, I continue my admission, "In hindsight, I realize that was where I really fucked up. My thinking was whacked. Wrong. For that, I'm truly sorry. I was foolish to believe our relationship could succeed with secrets hanging over us. Not just my secrets, but yours as well."

"Babe, meeting you and becoming friends with all of you made me happy. For the first time in my life, I wanted to be selfish and live life for myself. That first year, I bought my condo and started my own business here in Houston. Em, I was ready to settle down, and I'd be lying if I didn't admit it was with you in mind." My words came out quickly, knowing that at any moment, Em could run, and by extension, she could shut me out.

Em didn't respond to my honest explanation or anything I just shared. She focused her attention on the splashing and honking ducks. Watching her rhythmically pet Destiny, I knew she heard every word I said. She was listening. I decide to take this as a win and use it as my cue to continue.

"After I truly got to know you, my feelings started to change and deepen. They were no longer just about friendship. Over time, my feelings grew stronger and harder to control. Seeing you with Josh... well, it broke my restraint. I felt jealous. I knew I didn't have a right to, but I felt it anyway. Watching you smile at him... it drove me crazy. Then, I shouldn't have kissed you that first night at my apartment. Tasting you was my final undoing. I wanted all of you. And Em, I can't bring myself to regret it," I confess.

"Let me get this straight. You see me with a guy, and suddenly, I'm up for grabs. Both figuratively and physically?" Em snaps.

"Em, that wasn't a conscious decision on my part. I can't deny I felt a sense of urgency, but you have to understand: my feelings for you aren't new ones, born of jealousy. Waiting until my contract was up has been the biggest challenge I've faced since my years in service. And technically, I completed my original 2-year contract last month," I hedge, still pleading my case.

"Then, I really don't understand why you didn't just tell me," Em says, sounding frustrated and genuinely confused.

"Em, time was not on my side. Extending my contract was the only way I could legally continue investigating what my team had already confirmed as an oversight by your former security company. When our initial research was done, I wanted out. But Mr. Townsend, your dad's attorney, warned me that without legal grounds, anything I found would be useless. Proof or no proof, it wouldn't stand up in court," I state, hoping she can understand the legality and timing of it all.

"Alec, we were friends. You could have told me all of this. You could have even asked me not to say anything to anyone. You could have trusted me just a little. I confided in you, sharing things no one else knows, not even Roxy or Sarah," Em says. Hearing the hurt in her voice is painful.

"You're right. I fucked up. The biggest mistake in my life was not telling you everything before letting our relationship progress." Denying it was pointless. I only have myself to blame. If Em never wants to see me again, I'll have to accept that reality.

"You did fuck up. And honestly, I don't know if I can forgive you or even want to. Now that I think about it, you probably already knew there was more to my story, that I was a victim. Not cool. You deceived me in so many ways, and you broke my heart," Em loudly sobs on the last sentence. Her body, which was relaxed just moments ago, is now tense. With her arms wrapped tightly around her bent knees and her head tucked low, Em draws inward, trying in vain to hold in her emotions.

"No, I didn't," I whisper, feeling so regretful.

The choking sounds coming from Em break my heart in two. She's been pretending to be strong, maintaining her fragile composure until she couldn't anymore.

The tears, the most powerful, emotionally charged little bastards. They are the worst. They gut me. Not being able to wrap her in my arms and make everything better feels like a well-earned punishment.

"Baby, you have to believe me when I say that I never meant to hurt you. Please try to believe that. Sorry isn't a powerful enough word to express my sincere remorse. I handled this all wrong. Please don't cry," I beg for forgiveness, knowing I don't deserve to receive it.

From the bottom of my guilty soul, I meant every plea to Em. The churning in my stomach. The sick sinking feeling in my gut. Reinforces my fatal mistake. I have destroyed any hope that Em will ever trust me again. It's horrible to realize that, after all my successful missions, I underestimated my own personal situation. How poorly I judged the repercussions of my own fucking actions.

"Alec, I believe you didn't mean to hurt me, and I'm not even mad anymore. I'm not so unreasonable that I can't see why my dad did what he did. I can even understand why he hired you. You were in my life for a reason. I get that more than you know. What I'm struggling with, even as I try to forgive, is the feeling of being violated all over again." Em confesses, and it hits me hard. I did this. Me. I only have myself to blame.

"Oh Em. No. I'm sorry…. I was selfish and careless," I share, feeling the gut-wrenching remorse all the way down to my toes.

"Yeah, you were. Now, I'm also dealing with the feelings that come with losing a friend and the hope of a future with you. You invaded my privacy and disrupted my life. My friends, too, by extension, have all been hurt by this intrusion. I can no longer trust my instincts. Twice, I have misunderstood someone else's intentions. Now I have to accept that you were only in my life because my parents paid you to be." Seeing Em's constant flow of unchecked tears is worse than a week of eating MREs. And I hated that shit.

"Em, you're hurt and you're mad. You have a right to be. But don't cheapen what we had or make it sound vulgar. I'm sorry for how my actions made you feel. I'll apologize as long as I live. I know I fucked up badly. I hate that I'm the reason for your pain and tears. But you have to know, I've never lied outright to you."

"Umm… not telling me… You don't think that's the same as lying?" Em retorts. She might be crying, but she's not backing down.

"Okay. Yeah. You're right. I lied by omission, and I have to live with that," I admit. It is the truth. How in hell did I rationalize to myself that this wouldn't blow up in my face? I'm a lying, delusional idiot.

Alec, don't oversimplify what you did. Everything was a lie! It's about more than just hiding information. You intentionally concealed your true identity, blending my life with yours and involving my friends. It was like a day at the office for you to get involved in my activities and invite yourself into my life. Friday and Saturday nights as the chauffeur, Sunday football, all under the pretense of being my friend. In reality, it made your babysitting job easier for you," Em fires back.

"Em, you know that's not true. You're not being completely fair," I hedge, realizing too late how that sounded.

"Fair! Am I not being fair to you? Are you serious right now? And how would I know you weren't who you claimed to be? My truth is my reality. You know who knew the truth? You and my parents," Em seethes. Anger replaces the sad tears.

"I shouldn't have said that. But you know me," I say, feeling my confidence fade.

"Do I? I thought I did. Not so much now," Em challenges.

"Em, shit, the me you know hasn't changed. I was your friend. I am still your friend. But I was also your bodyguard, watching over you without controlling your every move. I was there for your safety," I say, wanting her to understand my role in her life.

"I guess Roxy's cockblocking theory wasn't far from the truth. You were there to guard me. To keep anyone from getting too close to me. OMG! Does Dex work for you?" Em's face shows a horrified expression.

"No! No, Dex does not work with me. He has never worked with me in any capacity. I swear," I say, hoping she believes me.

"But you said he told you…." Em recalls.

"Em, I promise, Dex only found out about me the day you girls went to Galveston. That day, when I couldn't get a hold of you, I reached out to Dex to see if he'd spoken to any of you. When he hadn't, I didn't handle the news well. It wasn't just about my job duties. I told you, my feelings for you ran deep. Beyond friendship," I share, hoping like hell I say the right things so she believes me.

Em was listening and processing my words and hasn't told me to shut the fuck up yet, so I continue, "I had this irrational fear clouding my common sense. A fear that was foreign and all-consuming. I felt like a caged tiger, pacing the floor, on alert, and pissed off. Dex must have picked up on my mood when I called him. It wasn't even ten minutes later that Dex was at my door, presumably to check on me. Soon after his arrival, Dex witnessed me losing my collective shit!" I confess, hoping that Em understands just how much she means to me.

"Not to piss you off, but it sounds like you overreacted. What did you think happened? Regardless, it doesn't explain why you told Dex who you really are," Em accuses, calling me out while showing me that she has heard every word I've said and plans to hold me accountable. I can't tell her, but I'm proud of her take-no-shit mentality. She hasn't always shown that level of strength.

"My explanation isn't simple. Hear me out. Maybe I overreacted. But in my defense, in the two years we've known each other, you've never once completely shut down communication. And it was Sunday. We haven't missed a Sunday dinner together, as a group, in months. Then there's the fact that I let my growing feelings for you and my concerns for your safety cloud my judgment," I confess, hoping she hears the sincerity.

"But, Alec, you told him before you told me? Does that mean Dex also knows I was raped?" The hurt I see in Em's eyes cuts deep, like a knife to the heart. I can't help but wince at her flat, resigned tone and delivery. She sounds so defeated and sad. The knife hits home; I feel heartbroken for her.

"No. Not specifically. But I did tell Dex about Trace and the other women," I admit, staying true to my promise not to lie to her, no matter how tough it is to share the uncomfortable truth.

At that proclamation, Em's spine becomes ramrod straight. Coiled so tight I fear it could break if pushed. "You told him?"

"I only told him what that fucker was accused of, and that he was an acquaintance of yours back in college. I did not tell him you were also a victim," I reiterate, realizing how weak my response sounds.

"Semantics. Another copout by omission scenario. He knows. And, you know, he knows. Don't pretend otherwise." Em's response is both surprising and accurate. Unfortunately.

"Yes, Dex assumed, but I did too. You only provided half-truths; the rest of the story was just fill-in-the-blank. And I'm still missing answers," I say, hoping she considers that I could only share the minimal information she gave.

"None of what you are saying explains why you went to Dex. He can't fill in the blanks for you or tell you the other half of the true story," Em pushes, barely holding back her right to be angry. I understand her perspective and how going to Dex might seem to her.

"The only explanation is that I needed someone who knew me and who knew you. Someone who wouldn't be afraid to tell me I was thinking crazy or acting irrationally. I needed a friend. Dex is someone I can trust, and so can you," I share, realizing how true this all is for me. Dex has become that kind of friend, the one who knows the good, the bad, and where the bodies are hidden.

Chapter Forty-Four
JEALOUSY AND JAIL TIME
Alec

"That's the truth, babe. I talked with Dex because I needed a friend's advice. Everything I felt for you, the worry that you girls were in a ditch somewhere, wreaked havoc on my self-control. I didn't even recognize myself." I share this to help her realize that nothing was premeditated or planned.

My building emotions were like a giant Jenga tower. When I managed to pull out an unwanted emotion, it quickly added itself to the top of my growing pile of uncontrolled feelings. I knew I was about to collapse, but I couldn't stop it. I've never felt more vulnerable or powerless than I did that day.

"Okaayy, you needed a friend. For advice. About me. Why now? What changed? You say you've been into me for the last two years, but I didn't see it. I had no clue. I don't know, Alec. What am I missing?" Em asks, looking more confused than ever. There's determination there, too. I can clearly see she isn't satisfied with my responses. It all needs to come out anyway. Truth.

"It all started with that fucking dress!! Then, when I saw you with Josh, happy and familiar, my resolve to stay away from you crumbled and fell apart. That's why," I relent, deciding to tell it like it is.

How do I explain to Em the series of events that caused my control to explode? I've never felt the intense blaze of jealousy consume me before. Jealousy was the catalyst for my poor judgment and subsequent actions afterward. How can I share this with Em without sounding like a completely barbaric asshole?

"So, it's about jealousy, that's what changed? You can hear how this sounds, right?" Her little, indignant huff would cause a smile if this were a different situation. Now is not the time for me not to take her concerns seriously.

"Not just jealousy. I can't deny that I hated you with Josh, and...," I start, only to be cut off.

"Seriously, Alec? Seeing me happy made you swoop in and claim me as your property? Like Roxy said, I was the tree, and you were pissing all over your territory. The sad part is that when you marked me as Alec, my hot neighbor, that was kind of hot. But as my security detail or bodyguard, not so much." Em sassily responds; she's not giving me a break at all. Shit, but I'm so proud of her.

"Em, shit. My actions weren't well-thought-out decisions. I definitely wasn't acting as a bodyguard. My thoughts were irrational and instinctive. Reactive. I see that now. We've already established that I fucked up. I mishandled the situation between us. I'm not proud of that, and an apology feels like a weak attempt to get forgiveness."

"Thank you for telling me about... well, everything. I heard you, and I believe you. I'm not mad like I was before. Of course, the hurt will take longer to heal, but it will. And Alec, you know I've always considered you a friend. A close friend. And I want to forgive you. That's half the battle, I think," Em says. Her words fill me with hope. Something I didn't think was possible just moments ago. There's hope that we can get past this.

"I'll be whatever you need or want me to be for you, Em. Just please don't shut me out of your life." I want to say more, but something in her expression makes me hesitate. I realize now isn't the time to push. Just hearing her say she wants to forgive me has to be enough for now.

"Alec, they say time heals all wounds. So, I'm asking you to give me that time. There's a lot for me to think about and process. And I need to do that on my own time," Em requests.

"Okay, babe. I understand. Please remember that I am sorry for putting you in this situation and for handling everything so poorly. I regret that my lapse in judgment has hurt you and damaged our friendship. You might not be ready to hear this, but I love you. Hurting you is the last thing I'd ever want to do."

"You're right, Alec. I'm not ready to accept that. What I know is... You don't do what you did to people you love," Em states, not holding back her thoughts or backing down.

"Can you accept that I will do everything in my power to fix this?" I ask, as if she has no choice in the matter. I plan to do whatever it takes to earn her forgiveness, and hopefully, someday, I'll win her heart.

Em's barely perceptible nod is probably the best I'll get. She has doubts about me. I caused them. Which means I have a lot of work to do. She'll see, I'm ready for the challenge.

The ducks, seemingly upset by the calm, take off. Their loud squawks and honks demand attention. It's interesting how those sounds signal that they need to move. Every duck nearby, whether flying or floating, is now heading to the other side of the lake. It's captivating to watch.

As the noisy ducks reach the other side, I hear something from Em that I wasn't expecting. Not now. Maybe not ever.

"I decided to testify. Hearing from you that Trace never served a day in jail because of who his father is makes me feel beyond disgusted. And I don't think I can live with myself knowing that he's free to do what he did to me to another woman," Em confidently states.

"Em, you do realize that you'll have to testify and share what happened? It might even go to court, where you could have to face Trace. Em, sweetheart, I need you to understand everything the trial might ask of you." I felt sick and a little apprehensive on Em's behalf.

"I'm not making this decision lightly. I know it will probably be the hardest thing I'll ever have to do," Em responds, leaning forward to rest her face on Destiny's fur as she hugs her.

"I'll be with you every step of the way. I won't leave your side. You don't have to face this alone. Your parents, the girls, and Dex will be there for you too," I promise. I'm in awe of

Em's strength and bravery. The look on her face shows conviction and determination. I'm even more proud of her.

"I'll take all the support I can get. I'm not dumb enough to try to face my demons alone. Do you know what the next steps will be?" Em asks.

"Right now, what you can do is write down all the details about Trace and the attack. Include any dates if possible. No detail is irrelevant. If it pops into your mind, write it down," I state. Not sugar coating the task ahead. I know without her saying anything that this task will be difficult. It's never easy to rehash old painful memories.

"Okay." Em's expression looks bleak and worried. I can tell she's getting more anxious.

"Em, you can do this. I have no doubts. Tomorrow, I'll contact the authorities to discuss the steps they want us to take. They will probably want you to come in to give a formal statement as soon as we report the crime. You'll be better prepared if you jot down the notes beforehand," I explain, observing her.

"Alec, you mentioned there are other girls. Will they... umm, have they agreed to testify?" This answer is crucial to Em, I can tell. I'm sure Em doesn't want to face that monster alone.

"This is something I'll have my team work on first thing tomorrow. The girl from last year did testify on record. We can assume she'll testify again now. There is strength in numbers. My team has already started reaching out to other potential victims. I hope that once the other victims realize they are not alone, they will be willing to testify to strengthen the case."

"Okay." Em's voice sounds small and hesitant. Part of me is relieved she recognizes the challenge ahead. The other part wants to wrap my arms around her and shield her from all of this.

"We need to meet with your dad. Sorry, Em, but I need to know. Have you shared what happened to you with your parents?" There's a very slight shake of Em's head, confirming what I had already assumed.

"Do you want me there with you when you tell them? Because you have to tell them sooner rather than later," I caution.

"I know I do. I can't figure out how to bring up the subject right now," Em confesses, looking dejected and scared.

"Whatever you need from me, just ask. I'll even tell your dad for you if you'd like. You don't have to face any of this alone."

Instead of accepting my offer, Em reaches for Destiny's leash as she gets up. Turning to face me directly, I hear her say with finality, "I'll get my written statement done."

Before I can stand with her or comment, Em walks away without looking back, not even once.

Chapter Forty-Five
REVENGE, THE MENTAL MOTIVATOR
Emily

It felt like a haunted presence was looming over me, taunting and daring me. A shiver of dread clung to me all the way home, its weight heavy and oppressive.

Each step toward my unit deepened the fear, confronting the monumental task of reliving a past I've fought hard to keep buried. Part of me wanted to second-guess my decision to testify, to back out. But I won't. No matter how tough it gets.

The ghost of my past followed me inside, hovering as I fed Destiny. It lingered, slowing me down, turning the simple act of changing clothes into a sluggish ritual. My mind's way of stalling, of protecting itself from what was coming, digging into the darkest parts of my personal hell.

"Okay, Em, you can do this. You *will* do this." My little pep talk fell flat. "Come on, girl. You Got This!" Better, louder, but still weak. Destiny's ears twitched, her head tilting as if to ask, *You talking to me?* Nope, I was talking to myself, trying to muster a mental rah-rah cheer loud enough to drown out the fear swirling in my head.

Finally, I crossed to the small desk nestled between the kitchen and the laundry closet, grabbing my laptop. My destination is my comfy gray microfiber couch. It wasn't a new couch when I purchased it, but it's my favorite piece of furniture in my apartment. Soft, squishy pillows and a turquoise and blue throw from Belk make it my comfort zone, the perfect place to face what I'd been avoiding.

Most of my leisure time is spent here on my couch. It's perfect for snuggling in and feeling content. As silly as it may seem, I was optimistic that by sitting here, instead of my desk or the bed, I would be able to pour my guts out.

Opening my fully charged laptop, a wave of sweaty panic hits. The gloom that followed me home solidifies into a weight on my chest, daring me to dig up what I've buried, old fears, barricaded memories, details I've repressed and watered down to survive. Just thinking about exhuming them sends a paralyzing fear skittering through me.

The tightness in my chest comes on suddenly. My breathing turns shallow and rapid, a warning that I needed to pull up my big-girl panties and get my shit together. I draw a deep breath and let sheer determination take over where my weak mind falters. Out loud, I remind myself, "You can, and you will do this."

Everything comes down to one objective. I want my fears and shame to help put Trace away. To stop him from doing to others what he did to me. Revenge is a formidable ally and a powerful motivator.

The hovering dread begins to shift, giving way to an overwhelming sense of urgency. I just need to start. Dump it all out. No dwelling. No second-guessing. Just get it out of my head.

With determination, this quote comes to mind. *"Let paper remember so you can forget,"* the motivational mantra rings loud and clear. Permitting myself, I approach my daunting task clinically, not focusing on the emotions or the vivid details unless they spring to my typing fingertips. If the authorities need more, I'll address that hurdle then.

I'm not sure how long I had been at it, but I managed to do it, ten typed pages. Once I started, the story came out surprisingly easily. I was telling a story, that's all it was. Not an experience. By distancing myself, I was able to separate from the details, a mental coping mechanism.

After saving the document, the emotions I avoided while typing have resurfaced in my mind. All that remains is a feeling of emotional exhaustion and sadness. Still, all that pain is briefly overshadowed by the considerable accomplishment of completing what I set out to do.

Putting the events in order was both healing and brutal. For years, I blamed myself, convincing myself I'd had too much to drink, sent Trace green light signals, kissed him, flirted, and made myself vulnerable. After the attack, I twisted and distorted the truth until I believed it was my fault.

Learning from Alec that I was a target, that I'd been drugged, lifted some of that terrible weight. Yes, I was foolish in places; I ignored signs and let a popular senior's attention feel flattering. But my only crime was being a naive young girl who happened to be boy-crazy. Not unlike all the other college girls.

I'm done wasting time, done crying over the loss of my younger self and her innocence. I had let Trace steal my future hope and crush the belief that my little girl fairytales could ever come true.

A renewed sense of determination blankets me. I'm wrapped up with purpose and strength. I will do everything within my power to lock that sick, perverse fucker away. While Trace is behind bars, maybe he'll get what he deserves. I've heard enough prison stories to hope that Trace becomes someone's little bitch, no pass-out drugs for him.

Feeling stiff and emotionally drained, yet also feeling accomplished, is an odd combination. Before standing, I make sure the document of truth and power is saved before the battery dies. Before shutting down my laptop, I also saved the statement to a USB drive to give to Alec.

I did it. I overcame my self-preservation hurdle. I deliberately thought about and recounted the events of that dark, life-changing night. After years of suppressing and avoiding all memories, I let my mind revisit the most difficult experience of my life.

I should have taken the time years ago to confront the details. Listing the events of that night and the days leading up to it was revealing and eye-opening. It allowed me to see the entire experience from a new perspective. Realizing that, even without knowing it, I hadn't done anything wrong.

Not telling anyone or seeking therapy was my choice. In hindsight, keeping what happened a secret was a mistake. Maybe if I had shared my story earlier or gotten help to deal with the aftermath, I might have prevented him from victimizing another woman. I have to live with that and move on.

First, I need to forgive myself for being weak. For accepting the blame too easily for Trace's actions. For shutting my family out and letting my life become just a shell of what it could have been. I will work on that.

But right now, I need to take Destiny out for her nighttime potty break.

Uncertain about when I'd see Alec again, I decided to slip the USB drive under his door while I was out. I looked for an envelope but realized the box was empty. Then I remembered the unopened note from Alec. Perfect. I could reuse his envelope.

Locating the forgotten note, I tear it open with care, trying not to damage it. One glance at the handwriting, and I know it's Alec's. But it takes me a moment to process what I'm actually seeing.

It's a letter from Alec Miller Santos to Mr. and Mrs. Wilson, dated over a year and a half ago.

My heart stumbles, then stutters, as the meaning of the words sinks in. It's a resignation letter, Alec's way of telling my parents that earlier that day, he met the most beautiful, thoughtful, vibrant woman. He wrote that he heard her before he saw her, that her colorful words caught his attention, but it was the woman herself who captured his heart. He knew right then she was the one for him.

The letter went on to say he wanted out of his contract, that there was no need to pay him for doing what he would already be doing for the rest of his life.

Wow.

For a man who is usually in control and stoic, those words revealed a softer, deeply romantic side of Alec I never expected to see. He told me he never lied to me, and now I believe him. Every word about love, about wanting a future with me… it was all true. He loves me, and apparently, he has for longer than I ever could have imagined.

Wow, okay. I'm going to need time to process this. But first, Destiny needs to go out. And anyway, my mind has already processed enough for one day.

"Wanna go outside?" Seeing her little tail thump is a sign she's starting to understand what that means.

"Let's go!" Destiny gets up, spins once, and barks in response. She happily allows me to put the harness on her. As I slip on my flip-flops, we head toward the elevators.

In the hallway, the lights are all rimmed with rings, like the halos you get from swimming too long. My head is threatening a headache, the by-product of hours at a computer. But I did it. I need to celebrate that.

Taking the elevator down to the ground floor, my appearance isn't suitable for human interaction, but I can't bring myself to care too much. Hopefully, we can reach the pet-friendly area without anyone noticing.

Destiny did her business after just a few sniffs. Picking up her poo still makes me cringe. I find the task super gross, but it's totally worth it to have her in my life. I'm already hopelessly in love with her.

Hearing the grumbling, growling noises from my belly reminded me I hadn't eaten since brunch. Sweet peppers and hummus will have to do; it's already too late in the day for a complete meal.

Plus, the thought of making a meal, even a small one, seemed impossible. Exhaustion seeped into my bones, fogged my mind, and weighed down every limb. I could feel myself collapsing inward, like a balloon slowly leaking air and losing its bravado.

I take my snacks and water to my bedroom. I climb into bed. Sadly, I don't even bother changing into PJs, and I'm doubting my ability to get back up to brush my teeth after I eat. While surfing Netflix, I settle into a semi-vegetative state, searching for the best distraction.

Destiny's warm presence eases my loneliness and quiets the leftover chatter in my head. I can see clearly how much Trace has changed my life. How little I allow myself because of my false sense of responsibility.

We all only have one life to live, and half of mine was taken from me. Learning about the date rape drug is empowering.

Ironically, it's not unlike a fresh start. I feel like, for the first time, I'm ready to confront what happened. I'm ready to heal.

After my attack, instead of seeking professional help, I read several books on trauma and grief. The books all conveyed the same concept: take back control of your life one step at a time.

The physical damage, both inside and out, was its own torment. It took nearly three months for my body to heal, and skipping medical care only made it worse.

But the visible scars were nothing compared to the mental ones. Those wounds ran deeper, unseen, and far more brutal. I carried them for years, and they still appear uninvited, knocking on the door of my subconscious, creeping into my nightmares.

I can only hope that learning I was a victim of a date rape drug will prevent further mental attacks, both consciously and subconsciously.

I'm proud of what I accomplished today. Not only did I share my deepest, darkest secrets, but I also came to terms with my involvement in the attack.

I don't expect to suddenly get over what happened to me or to move forward as if the past 6 years of blaming myself never occurred. However, I refuse to see myself as a broken and emotionally crippled victim any longer. I won't live with the persistent fear of him coming back for more.

I had been a coward inside my apartment for days after that night. When I finally came out, I was terrified. The following three years were spent constantly looking over my shoulder, never trusting anyone, and always staying on alert.

Sarah and Roxy became the exceptions, saving me from my paranoid, self-destructive tendencies. Unknowingly, they became my lifelines. They gave me reasons to smile, laugh, and make the most of what I thought was left of my shattered life.

Their friendship and acceptance of me held together the fragmented pieces of who I am. It's comforting to know without doubt that they will be here for me now, even after learning about me. They will help piece all the jagged pieces of me and my life together again, making me whole. Not perfect or pristine, but no longer damaged. Side perk. They will happily help me lock that bastard away.

Chapter Forty-Six
POOR CHOICES
Emily

Noticing the dancing starburst dots on the otherwise black TV screen is a clear sign that I had finally fallen asleep while watching a series called Dance Moms.

Now it will be a pain in the ass to figure out where I actually left off instead of where it stopped playing. With an audible groan, I mutter, "At least it does stop at some point rather than running through the whole series."

This series, which I just came across last night, is a ruthless, competitive reality TV train wreck. But I'm already hooked.

After finishing my brain dump exercise and thinking about Alec's letter, my thoughts wouldn't quiet down enough for me to fall asleep. I was so exhausted, yet emotionally charged like I'd had an espresso shot that lasted well into the early morning hours.

The only way to mute my thoughts was to watch the Dance Moms stab each other in the back while the coach berated their girls. Don't forget the blatant favoritism. The combination was a great distraction from my troubles. Still, I was surprised that I eventually fell asleep despite the shouting.

Turning off the TV, I give Destiny some belly rubs while grabbing my cell phone. I'm unable to return to work right now.

Deciding to take the easy route, I text my boss. He expected this and probably wouldn't mind the non-verbal way of communicating.

Before I forget, I also sent Roxy a message.

Em: *You're on your own today*

Roxy: *Figured – you okay?*

Em: *Yes – we'll talk soon*

Roxy: *Holding you to it, slacker*

Roxy: *Love and hugs*

Em: *Love ya more*

Roxy will talk to Sarah and maybe even the guys.

Giving Destiny a few more belly rubs, I get up to pee. There is always a sense of urgency in the mornings. I know my bladder demands attention. I bet Destiny's bladder does too, and she needs to hold hers down 16 flights and a short walk to the pet-friendly area. I rush to finish for her. We girls have to look out for one another.

By some miracle, we managed to avoid seeing anyone. The odds were against us since people were heading to work. For once, luck was on my side.

My neighbors were lucky, too. No one should have to endure the visual disaster I was putting out. I was a hot mess in last night's clothes, with hair in disarray and bad breath from my unbrushed teeth. I wasn't fit for human interaction, let alone talking. But for Destiny, I'd risk the humiliation.

Remembering the advice I received from the pet shelter, establishing a routine for Destiny is crucial, especially when I return to work full-time. She needs to understand and anticipate the potty, meal, and potty schedules before I leave, and then again when I get home.

There haven't been any accidents, but I haven't been away from Destiny for more than a few hours. I'm not worried; she consistently exceeds my expectations.

Leaving Destiny happily munching on her expensive, human-grade dog food, I head to my bathroom to heat the water for a much-needed shower.

Standing under the nearly scalding spray, my mind races through the past few days' events. It only shows brief snippets of the vast number of thoughts that have been swirling around in my head, without settling on any one topic. Just flashes of trepidation. The feeling of apprehension battles against my resolute determination.

Today, my parents and Alec, and God too, will hear the details of what Trace did to me, what he took from me. They will understand how demented and vile he used my body. They will see how my poor choices, at the very least, helped him in his effort to get me alone.

Today, I will bare my soul. I will share my deepest, darkest regrets and shame. They will see how Trace stole my innocence and ultimately destroyed my fairytale dreams, and how his attack changed the course of my life.

Feeling the water cool, I realize I've stayed in the shower long enough. I was only putting off the inevitable, letting my mind create all sorts of fears and doubts: humiliation and shame. I wasn't going to let my mind second-guess my decision to finally reveal the secret I've kept securely locked away for years.

Drying off with my big, fluffy pink towel, an uninvited thought crosses my mind. Yesterday, Alec said he wanted me to forgive him, that he wanted me in his life. The letter backs his claim. But will he still feel the same once he learns how Trace used my body? How dirty and broken I am because of Trace?

My statement will likely shock Alec. My dad will blame himself for not doing enough to protect me. My mom will feel pity for me. Everyone else will see me differently. I won't just be Em to them anymore. I'll always be a victim of rape, a pawn in a twisted game of revenge.

I already feel sorry enough for myself. Having everyone I love and care for feeling sorry for me is a new kind of humiliation. I won't be able to control what happens after my story is out or how others will see me.

Without professional guidance, I handled my attack on my own. I didn't curl up in the fetal position. Well, not for longer than a week anyway. I got up and took the necessary steps to move forward in my life by using avoidance and repression, pushing the bad memories to the back of my mind. It was the best I could do.

The semester after the attack, during my sophomore year, I took an Introduction to Counseling and Psychotherapy class. We learned the steps to cope with the physical, emotional, social, and cognitive responses caused by a significant life-changing event. I self-medicated, for lack of a better word. I learned techniques specifically for sexual assault victims. I learned about the different stages of survival. I read articles from other women who successfully regained the parts of themselves they thought they had lost.

I clearly remember feeling ashamed and embarrassed to seek professional help or even research anything related to rape until that class.

Writing my statement, I remembered a time during the attack when Trace told me I was just a dumb freshman and that if I told anyone, nobody would believe me. I'm sure that was also a reason I never shared it with anyone. Fear of the unknown and rejection are powerful deterrents.

To survive, I built walls around my heart and kept it guarded from potential entanglements. I protected my heart from getting hurt by limiting my interactions and hoarding all my secrets. I hid everything from my family and those I considered my friends.

I'm realizing now that it wasn't a conscious decision on my part. It was a survival tactic, my body's way of coping. Momma bear is protecting my more vulnerable younger self.

Chapter Forty-Seven
ALEC GIVETH AND TAKETH AWAY
Emily

There's no doubt that the clarity I'm experiencing now, thanks to what I learned from Alec, is reassuring. I'll never forget what happened to me, but I'm done letting the memory of Trace control my life. I want to live, move past the repressed memories, and overcome my self-imposed limitations.

Being with Alec as a couple, even for a short time, gave me a taste of what I've been missing. Whether consciously or unconsciously, I never allowed myself to be in any romantic situation that required trusting a man or being open to having an emotional and physical relationship with one. The freedom to choose intimacy.

Being with Alec gave me renewed hope. With him, over time, it wouldn't be hard to open myself up to love and to be loved. It might not follow the fairytale script from my youth, but nothing is saying we can't write our own fairytales.

Thinking about what my new fairytale could look like, I see the possibility of a life partner, a lover, and a friend, a happy, fulfilled life. A life that is free from the constraints of my past. Even after his deception and lies, my mind can only see Alec filling those roles.

I hate myself for only being able to picture Alec in my new fairytale. What does this say about me? My heart still wants him even after he hurt me so badly. By his own admission, his deception was a calculated risk he took, with no plans to ever tell me the whole truth. Does Alec think that giving me the letter will magically erase all the pain he caused?

Alec's reasoning for keeping it from me made sense. As fucked up as that is, I understand. He said he waited until his contract was over and was waiting to start a life with me, free from his contractual obligations and free to live life for himself. I guess that would mean my parents refused his resignation.

Knowing all of that and knowing myself, I accept that the only way Alec can stay in my life and have a chance to build a relationship with me is if I can forgive him. And that's easier said than done.

One thing is sure: I couldn't bring myself to regret, even for a minute, being with Alec, letting him into my heart, and revealing the soft underbelly of my vulnerabilities.

Honestly, my life would have remained stuck without his involvement: no progress, no growth, and no opportunities for more. I wouldn't have realized what opening up and allowing someone to see the parts of me I usually hold back can bring.

For a blissful few days, I felt loved and cherished by a man I never thought could be mine. Oh, I dreamed of him, but the dreams I had of Alec were centered on other, more carnal, stuff.

If nothing else comes from our brief relationship, if I can't find my way to forgiveness, I believe Alec when he says he'll still be my friend. And I'll make a conscious effort to be his friend, too, and not hold a long-term grudge.

Being deceived by Alec and my parents might have set back my trust in opening up to others, but understanding their motives helps. It slows my impulse to withdraw into my old, guarded patterns. An added benefit is that I feel more resilient and determined than ever.

I'm going to be okay. Alec will help me navigate the legal system to file a case, just as a friend would. Well, as an employee or former employee of my parents, he'll be there to support me through the process.

Thinking of my parents, I've delayed calling them long enough to confirm a time. Mom answers on the second ring. Skipping the usual 'hello,' she asks right away if I'm okay. I can't lie, that question makes my heartbeat spike with anxiety for a moment. Mom is just being mom. I know she means well.

Taking a deep breath, I say, "Hi, Mom, what time should I come over today?" I sound very calm despite the butterflies fluttering in my stomach.

"Your dad said he'd be back home for lunch. You can come anytime, though. I'll have Chef prepare us something." My poor mom, she sounds concerned and hesitant. I did this to us. I'll fix it and get our relationship back to one of ease and affection.

"Sounds good, Mom. I'll be there. Is 1:00 okay?"

"Of course, darling, will it just be you? Or are you bringing my fur grandbaby? Or Alec?" Mom knows this visit will be tough for all of us. I thought about asking her not to sit in during the retelling, but she deserves to hear it from me.

"I'm not sure about Alec, Mom. I'll bring Destiny. She loves getting extra treats from dad."

Mom asks, "Did your father sneak her food under the table?"

"Yes, shamelessly so. Dad's probably trying to make sure he's her favorite," I tease.

"We'll see about that," Mom huffs indignantly, but the smile in her voice is comforting and reminds me of our old, carefree banter.

Chapter Forty-Eight
MAKING PLANS
Emily

After hanging up with my mom, I chicken out on calling Alec. Instead, I decide that a text will do. It's to give him an update on my statement's progress, not to beg him to go with me to my parents.

Em: *Statement is complete- I'm going to my parents at 1 pm today to talk to them*

Not waiting for a reply, I finish getting ready. It's silly, but I want to look good today. When you look good, you feel good. When I'm put together, I feel more confident. And I need all the positive vibes I can get.

I'm not naive enough to pretend I don't know how tough today will be. The dancing butterflies in my stomach are into hip hop, and boy, do they have some dance moves.

I'm feeling nervous and anxious, along with a bit of fear. My stomach fluttering and jitters are just part of what my body is going through right now. Dread is creeping in, trying to throw me off with doubt. I worry about how my parents will react and fear that sharing the story might trigger another panic attack.

There is unease knowing Alec will likely be there because my dad asked him to come. Alec will hear the details as facts, rather than suspicions. He'll learn the shameful truth about what

Trace did to me. And when he does, those words in his letter, his love, his promises, will be put to the test.

At the same time, I know I need Alec there. If for no other reason than that, I can't tell my story twice. I'll get there. But I know I'm not there yet. Sharing my story is going to be a shit show of epic proportions. It's not easy to even begin to describe how my sharing what happened to me will be received.

How does someone begin to share with her overprotective dad, her helicopter mom, and her fantasy man turned lover about how she was brutally raped? Especially considering how many years I've suppressed that shit. My walls were not just to keep people from getting close enough to hurt me; they also held everything in. My own fortress of pain, fears, and shame. My regrets and humiliation guarded the doors.

My life, the one I have left to live, has been tightly locked away. It hasn't improved, but it hasn't gotten worse either. It was protected and stored, the only way I knew how, by barricading the events of that dark time at the back of my mind.

But now, the people I care about most will learn the truth, every terrible detail I've kept silent about all these years. It's overwhelming.

Destiny's warm nose on my leg is a comforting distraction from my train of thought. Her paw draped over my thigh reminds me that I am safe, present, and in control.

"Come on, Destiny, let's get this finished."

Heading down to the parking garage with Destiny leading the way, a backpack of her food and treats over my shoulder, I stumble and nearly trip upon seeing a man right outside the garage elevator doors. This man, I knew all too well, even when naked. Apparently, he was waiting for me. Destiny, the little minx, had her whole booty going side to side in her excitement to see Alec.

As Destiny wiggles with pure joy, I foolishly stand there, unmoving and unresponsive. Hearing Alec's gruff voice say, "Hi, let me take that," oddly becomes the magic words that finally get me unstuck.

"Are you waiting on me?" It felt like we had planned to meet and go together. Without hesitation, after seeing his nod, I handed him the backpack before walking to the passenger side of his truck. Secretly relieved.

A warmth spreads through my belly. A gentle, comforting sensation that reminds me I don't have to face my past alone anymore.

Alec being here, supporting me in whatever way I need, feels good. It feels right. I carried the burden of my past alone for way too long. However, the thought of actually verbalizing what happened is scary as hell.

Alec must sense my inner turmoil. With his warm palm against my lower back, he nudges me into his truck, giving me the words I didn't know I needed to hear. "We got this, don't stress. I'll be with you every step of the way."

Apparently, I didn't climb in quickly enough, so Alec lifts me and gently places me fully onto the passenger seat. Destiny, being a showoff, notices Alec opening the back door and jumps right in. As if she's done this a hundred times before, she rests her paws on the center console and sticks her head between the seats to press her cold nose against my arm.

"You girls ready?" No. No, I wasn't ready, but I managed a nod. The question from Alec and the reality of what I was about to do both slam into my solar plexus. I can't respond verbally. He'll have to accept my weak nod for what it is, reluctant fear.

Chapter Forty-Nine
FIGHT DIRTY
Alec

I hadn't planned to attend last Sunday's brunch, but both Mr. and Mrs. Wilson *"felt it was advantageous for me to do so."* Their wording, not mine. They weren't wrong. They probably coordinated the timing between my arrival and Em's.

Seeing Em there, talking with her, and watching her interact with her parents was all wonderful. But that kiss, it was something else. It was hope.

Her agreeing to give me a ride home was an opportunity, an opening. But our conversation at the park was a turning point. The talk was heartfelt and inspiring. And I'm so proud of her strength and resilience.

Even with all her bravado, I wanted to be there for her when she told her parents, to offer her any support she might need or might not.

Getting the text message earlier from Em about her planned time at her parents' and that she completed her statement was a relief. Part of me wasn't sure she'd want me to go with her.

But she obviously did; she didn't hesitate to get in my truck. That showed me she felt she needed my support more than she needed time apart to think. Or at least, she wanted a buffer between her and her parents. Regardless of why I received my invitation, I was glad that Em felt safe enough with me to include me.

Knowing the details of the case and her involvement doesn't change how I feel about Em. Now that I no longer officially work for her parents protecting Em, I'm free to fight for the woman I love. Sometimes, that means fighting dirty.

Not having Em in my life isn't an option. I lied when I told her I could settle for just her friendship. That was total bullshit. I'm not sure who I was trying to convince with that load of crap, myself or her.

Thinking back to where it all began, I was inexplicably drawn to Em through nothing more than her parents' photos. The photos, along with loving stories about Em, pulled me in.

Through the pictures, I caught a glimpse of the woman she was and the woman she was destined to become. Those glimpses had a magnetic pull on me. The photos drove me to uncover the mystery behind her circumstances. Then, after meeting her, I was inspired by the woman herself to pursue success.

I tried for several months to stay unattached and unobtrusive, but Em and her circle of friends wouldn't let me observe from a distance. They pulled me into their group, and that's when my feelings for Em really started to grow.

At first, I justified my involvement in their lives as a way to gain access. It gave me an excuse to watch over Em in different settings. I was even happy to be the one providing transportation, making sure she was safe when going out and coming back.

More importantly, being part of the group gave me insight into her schedule. This was much more information than I would have been able to gather had I stayed uninvolved.

As time went on, it was no longer about having insider information or the chance to be part of her plans. My reasons changed. They became more emotional instead of the covert operation it had initially been.

The truth is, I lost sight of the purpose of my operation. After earning Em and her friends' trust, the line between work and personal life started to blur. I wanted to be there, more for my own reasons than just for the job.

I appreciated the chance to spend time with her and her friends. They all genuinely became my friends as well. But this is where I fucked up. I kept hiding my true self from people I considered close friends. And my undercover operation was, in many ways, mostly ignored.

It was challenging to follow my initial contractual agreement with the Wilsons, and even more difficult to wait until after my two-year contract was over before starting a romantic relationship with Em.

I failed to expect the unexpected, to foresee a potential derailment. I really fucked up by not considering, "the what's next" if Em ended up being a victim.

In hindsight, I oversimplified my assignment. I only looked at the end of the 2-year contract and not beyond. I never considered what would need to happen if Em were a victim.

To make matters worse, I failed to adjust my position after learning that Em spent time with Trace. Never once did I consider that it was during the same period when Em went through a transformation in her first year of college. It also didn't click immediately when Em mentioned she had a bad experience her freshman year.

At that moment, none of it registered in my mind. My Special Operations skills were dulled and diluted by my own desires.

Learning about Em's past forced me to change my stance. Protecting Em was no longer enough. I had to focus on helping her face her history and fight for justice. That required removing every layer of pretense and finally revealing the truth about who I am and why I had initially entered her life. It also meant admitting that our relationship started under the shadow of my deception and lies of omission.

I felt deep down that a relationship is less likely to last when built on lies. But I'm committed. I'm prepared to fight for the woman I love and admire.

Now that I've come clean, no more lies are holding us back. There are no remaining obstacles of deception to overcome, and there's nothing stopping us from making this work.

Em knows who I am and why her parents brought me into her life. She understands how I feel about her, and she recognizes that my intentions were never malicious. Admittedly, my actions were not well thought out or executed, but I can't bring myself to regret them. Those actions led me to Em.

All that's left for me is to grovel and beg, to let Em know, without any doubt, that I will fight for her. I will fight for us, the us I know we can be and the us we both deserve to have, regardless of how we ended up in each other's lives.

Neither Em nor I said much as I drove to her parents' house. My mind was busy planning how to keep Em in my life while also wondering how this lunch would go and how I would react to hearing about Em's attack. How will her parents handle it? And most importantly, how will Em cope with sharing it?

Chapter Fifty
LUNCH AND LIES BY OMISSION
Emily

Well, it went exactly as I expected. Telling my parents was a major, sold-out tickets, front row seat to my life's shit show. An emotional episode of epic proportions. It was horrible and not worth the price of admission.

God bless my dad. He started our talk by laying out everything he already knew, not sparing any of the gory, depraved details. I was surprised to notice that Mom must have heard this before. Her reaction wasn't one of hysterics but more in the vein of withdrawn remorse.

Alec teamed up with Dad to share what he knew about Trace and the other cases, outlining the grim trail of destruction left by Trace Junior.

My poor mom grew paler with each statement Alec shared. The devil is in the details.

Then it was my turn. I had listened to my dad and Alec share the details from a spectator's perspective. My mind didn't connect with the story. At least not until three sets of eyes were watching me expectantly, waiting with apprehensive curiosity.

Starting slowly, I filled in the blanks that Dad and Alec hadn't already shared. That was somewhat easy, in a detached way, until it wasn't. Until my own story of the actual attack was left unexplained. I had skirted over those details, delaying the inevitable shame of when what happened to me had to be revealed.

Once the story turned personal, it felt less like a terrible plot twist and more like an episode of Law & Order: Special Victims Unit, where I was the star, and tears welled up.

The more I shared about the attack, the more tears came, so many tears. There was no way I could hold them back or choke them down. I'm pretty sure some snot was involved, too.

The tears weren't all mine. Both my mom and dad shed more than a few, and even Alec had watery eyes.

As expected, my dad felt responsible and kept apologizing. My mom couldn't stop crying and wouldn't leave my side.

It was my mom's, "Oh, honey, no," along with her look of sheer pain, that broke down my resolve to stay strong and independent.

I welcomed her embrace. Mom held me so tight and kept telling me how proud she was of me, especially for my determination to take action now.

The fact that neither my mom nor dad was mad at me for not telling them or shutting them out was guilt-inducing. I robbed them of their chance to support me, and here they were accepting the blame and praising me for my cowardly efforts, which took me nearly 7 years to share.

Their support now doesn't erase the hurt caused by their deception. It doesn't remove the feelings surrounding the distrustful events that brought us all together.

The truth is, I didn't trust them with what happened to me, and they didn't trust me to explain why I needed an Alec. So many lies. It doesn't change anything in my mind that they were lies by omission. A lie is a lie, no matter the reason or intent.

There will be a lot of healing needed for my parents and me. Forgiveness is given. Empathy is something that should be shared and understood. Moving forward.

My parents felt like they had failed me, especially after hearing me call that time my darkest days. They felt sad and responsible for not being there for me. And I hated to hear them both say that. But you can't help what you don't know.

Along with the sorrow, there was an air of tension laced with anger. That was all, Alec. You could see the barely contained emotions play across his face.

If I had to describe the emotion, I'd say he was radiating waves of murderous thoughts. Alec was in control right now, but only by a thread. With every pertinent question, the rage bubbling under the surface of his ever-present control was threatening to make an appearance.

Instinctively, I knew Alec wasn't directing his anger at me. But there was no denying that Alec was furious, and I sensed he was fighting an internal battle for self-control amid his murderous thoughts.

I wasn't afraid of that potential explosion. No. My biggest fear was that Alec and my parents wouldn't see me the same way or that they would treat me like a delicate, broken person, someone who could shatter at the slightest provocation.

Then there was the real possibility that Alec wouldn't want me anymore. Now that he knew what had happened to me, wouldn't it be a turn-off for him? A reason to pull away from pursuing a relationship with me. Maybe when this was over, he wouldn't even want to be friends with me.

Even with all these fears and doubts swirling in my mind, I felt lighter. Like a huge secret had been lifted. A burden shared and released. Revealing my sordid past was freeing in some ways, but also felt restrictive in others. Now that my story is out, I no longer have to carry that burden alone.

With the support of these three people, my resolve has grown stronger. I regret not trusting them, or myself, enough to share what happened sooner. I often wonder how different my life might have been, but I know that hindsight is a foolish thing.

I'm ready to move forward with my life. I believe that helping to lock Trace away while confronting my demons will allow me to heal and release my past. It will enable me to lower the walls of my fortress of necessity and live the life I was always meant to live.

Time will reveal what happens between me and Alec. For now, I feel relieved to have him on my side. In my corner. Regardless of how his involvement came to be.

For all their blustering and apologies, I know my parents will support me. They want the best for me, and I realize that more than ever. Their willingness to do whatever it takes to keep me safe goes far beyond words or money. They took keeping me safe to a whole new level of stalkerish behavior.

Chef Ray brought lunch, and I was surprised to see it was almost 3 o'clock. I guess time flies when you're spilling your guts.

None of us ate much of the delicious chicken salad sandwiches on toasted croissants that he prepared. I only picked at a few pieces of chopped fruit, which are now sitting heavily in my stomach.

Because Chef Ray is my favorite among my parents' cooks, I ask him to pack ours and Alec's to go, promising him that we'll eat ours later.

Taking our plates, he winks at me but doesn't say a word. I'm sure our puffy eyes and somber moods tell him all he needs to know about why we all picked at our food. The wink shows me he holds no hard feelings.

Clipping Destiny's leash and repacking her bag of dog toys, I handed them to Alec before turning to face my parents. Confronting them, I felt some apprehension, though it was unnecessary; both of my parents were right there with warm, longer-than-usual hugs and reassurances. No judgment.

I've never said this before, but I knew what they needed from me at that moment, and I felt I had to get it off my chest too. "Mom, Dad, I'm sorry. I'm sorry I shut you both out, and I'm sorry I didn't come to either of you for help. I never meant to hurt you. I love you both very much." Those traitorous tears kept springing to life. I hate crying. But hearing my sincere remorse spoken aloud is both healing and painful. I can clearly see how shutting my parents out of my life hurt them and me.

"Emily, sweetheart, I'm sorry I didn't push harder. I should have insisted more. We sensed something was wrong, that you were struggling. I regret not fighting harder to find out what my instincts were telling me wasn't right. I feel like I let you down, and I have to live with that. Know this: no matter what you're going through, I want to hear about it. I want to help. I love you. You're my precious daughter." Hearing my dad's voice crack brings on a fresh batch of tears.

Hugging my dad more tightly, I admit. "I know you've done everything you could to keep me safe and protected. Now, you'll help to fix the wrongs done to me. I'll never take your love for granted again. Thank you, Dad."

His nod told me he heard me. The shine in his eyes told me he couldn't speak at that moment.

Mom was there by my side with open arms. Turning into her embrace, I gave her an extra-tight hug. "I'm sorry, Mom. You tried to talk to me, to give your unconditional support no matter my reluctance, and I didn't give you an inch," I confess, feeling truly remorseful.

"It's okay, sweetheart. You told us now, and we will help you in any way you need. I love you very much. Nothing will change that," Mom shares, giving me a warm, reassuring smile.

I was feeling more than remorse; I felt guilty and ashamed, too. I had so many emotions that I couldn't focus on just one. My mind felt like it had been blended on high speed for five minutes. It was all scrambled and mixed up.

I basically had just one day to sort that shit out. We planned to meet the next day with my dad's team of lawyers. Dad said I didn't have to attend. My thinking is that, at least if I showed up, I would be facing friendly fire with my story instead of inevitably facing Trace's legal team.

Alec was meeting with his team today after our lunch. My dad had his marching orders. The more data and details they could gather on Trace Junior and his father, the better prepared Dad's lawyers will be.

I was feeling emotionally drained and vulnerable. It felt as if my insides had been turned inside out for everyone to see, laid bare and raw. I know I might be a little dramatic, but I genuinely felt exposed. Letting go of those dark secrets took a heavy toll on me today.

I was ready to head home. I needed time to prepare myself mentally for the next steps. Time to process. Time to power up for the meeting with my dad's lawyers. Time to unscramble my thoughts.

Of course, Mom wanted me to stay with her. I declined. I didn't want to hurt her feelings, but how could I explain that what I needed most was time and space to reflect on everything that was revealed today, from all of us?

It's a lot to absorb. I need time to understand how the people I love acted and reacted to the details of my rape. What I don't need is to be smothered, watched, or hovered over for signs that I might fall apart. I've already done that, and I've already had to glue the shattered pieces of myself back together.

Pointing that out seems harsh. Today has already been a whirlwind of emotions, with a presentation of distrustful actions that we each learned had serious consequences. All four of us cautiously wielded our metaphorical swords to defend our causes and motives. Each of us felt justified in our actions and in how we managed our perceived fears.

Reflecting on everything we shared, we all feared losing something. Whether it was life, privacy, or relationships, it doesn't matter in the grand scheme of things. None of us trusted each other enough to share the details behind our fears.

That has to change.

Chapter Fifty-One
TIME, DISTRUST, AND FEAR
Alec

This morning, I thought I was ready for today's meeting with the Wilsons and Em. I was mistaken. I can't quite put it into words, but hearing her bravely recount the details of the rape and attack to her parents made my heart ache. It made my blood boil. It brought the harsh reality of the situation into sharp focus.

I've never wanted to kill anyone outside the line of duty to keep our country safe, until now. It was difficult to sit and listen to Em tell us what had happened, every bit of the suffering and pain she went through. All at the hands of a Trace Fucking Roberts Junior.

I want him dead. His dad dead, and maybe even his mom. Shit, maybe even the grandparents. Being that fucked up had to start somewhere. Probably some inbred bullshit.

It's taken me the entire drive home from her parents' to get my intense thoughts and emotions under control. I was literally afraid to open my mouth. Unsure if I could speak to Em without scaring the shit out of her or making her fear me. I hardly recognize myself. The deep-seated hate for this motherfucker is a new feeling for me.

I'm not sure how I'll handle seeing this dickwad in court. On the street, forget about it. Filled with uncontrolled anger, I honestly question my ability to face this sick coward and stay out of prison.

Pulling up in front of the DalRock, I realize neither of us said a word during the 30-minute drive home. Wish I knew what Em was thinking. There's no way I'd dare ask her. I'm barely holding back my need to blow. Punch something. Shoot something or someone.

These dark thoughts are not a part of myself I would ever want Em to see. It's not something I am proud of. I will get this inner demon under control for Em. She'll need me, not this internal monster, by her side as she faces the challenges ahead.

I'm so fucking proud of her willingness to testify, to relive through her testimony the horrors she endured. She's being strong. I'll make damn sure that I am strong enough to support her and strong enough to do whatever legal actions are available against Trace Roberts Junior and Senior. They will pay for their crimes.

"Do you want me to take your sandwich up and refrigerate it with mine?" Em asks, breaking the silence in the cab of my truck.

"Sure. If it's alright with you and it's not too late, I'd like to stop by after my meeting." A part of me is tempted to plead with her. I want to show how much I wish I could check on her and spend time together, but I hold back. If she wants me to come by, she'll let me know. I can't force myself into Em's life; she has to want me there.

Catching Em making a move to get out, I quickly get out and meet her at the passenger door to help her down. Opening the back passenger door, I scoop Destiny out as well.

Handing the leash to Em, I notice her face is filled with concern and apprehension. Cautious hesitation. I instantly dislike her uncertainty. She should feel safest with me. I will always protect her. I'd tell her, but I doubt she would believe me right now.

"Em, you, okay? Need anything before I go?" I hedge.

"I'm good. You can come by any time. I'll be up." Those words from Em are such a relief. I was about to beg later if necessary. I hated that I had to leave her now.

"I'll text you before I head over to make sure you're awake and still want company," I tell her. The truth is, I already know I'll be there. I can't stay away. I need to see that she's okay, that the weight of old wounds isn't crushing her when she's alone. Leaving her to face those memories alone feels wrong.

Em might be one of the strongest people I know, but she's delicate. She's precious. And she's mine. Mine to protect and cherish.

That knowledge and reminder made leaving her at the condos bearable. Knowledge is power. It's the driving force behind change and justice within the legal system. In all areas of life, actually.

Gathering knowledge is the best way I can help Em right now. My team has taken on that role with fierce dedication, a commitment that I can never fully repay.

The only gratitude they seek is to see Junior and Senior rotting in prison. All of us joined the CIA driven by a duty to protect and serve our country, as well as to protect and serve others who can't always defend themselves.

That protective instinct doesn't fade when someone changes careers. It grows and adjusts to fit their new surroundings. No matter the job, the need for justice and safety stays the same.

Janet is a wiz with a keyboard and the internet. She uncovered a lot of dirt on those two fuckers. We can't use hardly any of the hacked data, but it shows us where to look for physical proof. Who to investigate. It reveals what kind of sick, demented motherfuckers we are dealing with.

Juan and Stewart are tracking those disgusting leads through their dark underground sources. I don't want to know those details. My only request was for them to find something we can legally use as proof in court.

Rudy is also using unconventional methods to gather data. He's a technological genius and can access most locations without being detected. He has mastered skills in audio and visual surveillance. Twice, he told me not to ask questions I don't want the answers to. However, he assured me that he knows what I'll need and will make sure I get it.

Felix and Mike are focusing on our other clients, ensuring business runs smoothly. Both offered to assist with my case in any way I needed.

The thing is, I didn't even need to tell my team what I needed. I didn't have to ask them to jeopardize themselves, use any resources, or cover their tracks. They want to help. They want justice. They want to do the right thing because it's in their genetic makeup. That's who they are on the inside.

We are a team. Then and now.

Their efficiency generated a substantial amount of data to discuss, which led me to stay at the office longer than I initially planned. On one hand, I was gaining valuable information. On the other hand, I felt pressed to get back to Em.

Before heading back home, I sent a text to Em. I decided not to ask but to tell her I would be there in 15 minutes. If she truly didn't want me there, I was confident she'd reply with an excuse. Instead, she responded with a thumbs-up emoji. Thank fuck.

The drive home gave me a few minutes to process and decompress from all the crazy shit I learned. There was a lot of crap to take in, but the data was still riddled with holes.

Since nothing is certain, I will only provide Em with a high-level update if she requests it. And I really hope she didn't ask me tonight. That would be the equivalent of layering poop on top of more poop on top of even more.

What I needed to do was fully commit to listening and supporting Em, giving her an outlet to share what might have been triggered by bringing all that up to her parents. Not overwhelming her with more to think about, especially since we have very little concrete information.

Em needs to understand that no matter what, I will be there for her. Nothing has changed for me regarding Em. She'll realize that eventually. I intend to stick. To stand by her through all her past and future challenges.

I'm really hoping Em will let me be part of her life after this. I'm ready to build a future with her, to love her.

For now, supporting her through all of this has to be enough.

Chapter Fifty-Two
WHAT I WANT
Emily

Hearing the ping on my phone was both expected and painfully anticipated. Part of me knew if Alec said he'd text me, he would. Yet, another part was pleasantly surprised and thrilled that he actually followed through.

I can't explain it, but even though Alec hurt me deeply with his deception, I understand it. I see how he believed he had no other choice, how he felt honor-bound to my parents and wanted to start fresh, a civilian life, supposedly with me.

Understanding his motives makes his deception easier to accept. I'm realizing that his good qualities surpass his flaws. And how Alec didn't abandon this clusterfuck that is my life when it would have been easier for him to do so. All of this makes it possible to forgive him.

Alec has promised to ride this roller coaster from hell with me. His support isn't just words, but actions. I trust him when he says he will continue to help. He'll be there through the whole process. I can count on him. I know this is true.

Alec cares for me outside of his job and beyond his contractual obligations. I tried to convince myself that he was only with me because it was easier for him to do his job, that his wanting me wasn't real. But my heart knows that he does. And if I don't forgive him and let him back into my heart, I know without a doubt that he will settle for just being my friend. He will honor my wishes.

But I can't settle for anything less than having everything. I did that for far too long, and I deserve to live a happy, fulfilling life.

Just this week, I found an article about healing after tragedy. I realized that healing from being a victim of rape isn't just about the physical, but also the mental. Healing involves closing the deep wounds that fester and seep into every part of your life after the attack.

Healing involves moving beyond what happened to you and forgiving yourself. True healing lies in permitting yourself to let go of the past. It means moving past mistakes and embracing a better future. It's about finding peace and forgiveness within your mind, body, and soul.

Without that healing, every part of my life will struggle. My growth, trust, and happiness will all become stagnant and stale.

I understand now. I can see clearly what I couldn't grasp before. If I don't push myself to heal, I'll never have enough to offer Alec or anyone else I bring into my life in the future. And, if I can stay on the path of forgiving myself and move past the attack, living a normal, happy life is possible.

I would be lying if I said all this talk about healing and living a fulfilled life wasn't centered around Alec. With him, I feel strong and capable. I feel ready, as if I've jumped over the barricaded wall I've built around my heart and myself. It's more of a leap of faith than a testament to my own strength. Still, this realization is something I can take pride in.

Just then, there's a quick, firm knock on my unit door. Instantly, eagerness to see Alec fills me with giddiness. There's trepidation, too. I really want to know if he still wants me like he said he did. If he still desires me after learning how my body was used and discarded. After learning how damaged I am. How I concealed and absorbed the ugliness I endured.

As I open the door, I'm immediately surrounded by a warm, demanding hug. Alec is holding me tightly, squeezing the shit out of me. When he pulls back but keeps holding me, Alec says, "Hi. You, okay? I hated leaving you so abruptly this afternoon."

"Yeah. I'm okay," I say, stepping back from his hold but grabbing his hand to pull him further into my apartment. "You hungry? We still have our lunch sandwiches, or I can make us something else."

"No, babe, I'm good. They had pizza delivered to the office. You eat if you haven't already. But I'll take a beer if you have one," Alec says, holding my hand a little longer before squeezing it and then letting go.

Turning toward the kitchen, I hear a plop on my couch. I've done it myself enough to recognize the sound. As I head to the kitchen for his beer and a bottle of sparkling water for myself, I return to find Alec sprawled on one end of my couch. Legs wide apart, arms crossed over his muscular chest, eyes locked on mine. Watching, waiting, assessing.

My steps only hesitate briefly before my renewed determination drives me forward. Sitting with Alec on the couch, neither of us taking our eyes off each other, I decide to ask the one question that's been bothering me.

"Alec, after everything you've learned about what happened, do you still want me? As more than just a friend?" I boldly ask, watching him closely.

"Babe. I absofuckinglutely still want you. I told you, I love you; nothing you can say or do will ever change that fact. And Em, none of what happened to you was your fault. No one, including me, has the right to judge you on how you handled the attack. Nothing I heard could ever make me love you any less. I'm fucking proud of you." Alec's statement blows me away. I was sure he wouldn't want the damaged pieces left of me.

None of the other questions that had been swirling around my mind just moments ago seem as necessary now. Of course, I want answers about what he learned today, about my case. What will the next steps be? But none of that feels as crucial as letting Alec know how I feel about him, how I forgive him, and how much I want him in my life.

But the words wouldn't come. They felt lodged in my throat, stuck and unyielding. So many emotions are clogging my ability to speak. My only option was to scoot closer to Alec and give a soft, sweet kiss on his warm, waiting lips.

What started as sweet and gentle didn't stay that way for long as Alec took charge of the kiss. It heated up and became intensely passionate. Effortlessly, Alec pulled me over his lap, not breaking contact but deepening our kiss. His large hands held my head exactly how he wanted. The kiss was completely under his control.

But as quickly as the fire started, Alec extinguished it. Pushing back, Alec adjusted my position, so I was partly on him and partly on the couch. My legs now draped over his thigh, and my butt rested on the cushion. It felt like time froze as we looked into each other's eyes. Our breaths were quick and ragged as they blended together.

Okayyy, that was nice until it wasn't. Why did he suddenly stop kissing me? Why do I feel like a barrier just snapped into place? A barrier that isn't mine.

"Alec? What's wrong?" I hedge, uncertain if I want to hear the answer. His words and his actions are at odds with each other.

"Em, babe, nothing is wrong," Alec says, but he's already creating distance between us. In more ways than one.

"Okay, then what is it?" The shift in him is unmistakable now. His focus sharpens, and his manner is all business. A heaviness settles in my stomach as I realize he has a purpose tonight, and nothing, not even me, will distract him. For the first time, I get a glimpse of the man he must have been with the CIA. And I like it.

"My team and your dad's team have uncovered a lot of damaging information on both Trace Junior and Senior. The fucked-up part of that is we've only managed to review a small portion of all the data we've already gathered. Em, we're going to get this motherfucker, his daddy, and anyone else connected to them who is involved," Alec says with conviction.

"What did you guys find so far?" I ask hesitantly, unsure if I want to hear his answers.

"Babe, I need you to trust me on this. I don't want to share anything more until we get clearer information. You've been through enough and understand the basics of what we're uncovering," Alec pleads. And he's right, I don't need to know more than I already do.

"Okay," I relent, realizing that Alec is still taking steps to protect me, not just physically but also mentally.

"Em, I'm not going anywhere. I will be here with you every step of the way until that bastard is locked away," Alec promises.

I heard Alec's words and believed them. Wholeheartedly. But my mind is focused on the *"until"* part of his statement. Then what? Before I can stop my mouth, those words come out.

"Then what?" I ask.

"Are you asking what will happen to Trace after he's convicted?" Alec asks, looking confused by my question.

"No, um, you said you'd be with me *'until'* then. So where will you be?" I boldly ask.

Alec was staring at me as if he were trying to decode something. "Em, have you not heard a single word I've said about how I feel about you?"

"I'm listening. And I'm glad you are helping me and my dad with getting justice," I state.

"Em, fuck! The case is only a small part of what I'm trying to tell you. Although it's important, it's not more important than you. I'm here for you. I'm asking you to trust me to do what's best for you, and I told you I love you. I'm not going anywhere," Alec confirms.

"You love me, love me? And when this is over, you still want to see me?" I question.

"Yeah. But Em, you gotta know. I don't want to date you," Alec states.

"You don't? But you said…"

"Babe, I'm too old for pussy footing around. I don't want to date you; I'm not trying to see if you're a good fit for me or to learn if we have chemistry. This isn't a test run between us. What I want is a partner, a friend, a wife, and a family. I want it all. And I want it all with you. I know this is a lot to throw at you, especially after what must have been hell for you to share. But I want you to know where my head is at," Alec states this as if he hadn't just rocked my world. As if he hadn't just said the one thing I've wanted to hear most, because it's also what I want.

"Em, I want to give you some time to think about it, about us, and our future together," Alec states, watching me intently before continuing. "What do the short-term and long-term plans look like in your mind? In other words, do you want to live here at the DalRock in one of our units, or would you prefer to buy a house in the suburbs? As the maintenance man here, I have the inside scoop and know that the mega unit on the ground floor will be up for sale next month. It's four times the size of this unit, with three additional bedrooms and a den. The kitchen is huge, with all-white shaker cabinets on top and espresso-colored cabinets on the bottom. Oh, and there's a garden tub in the master. It's really nice. Plus, being on the first floor, there's a small, gated yard and patio that will be perfect for Destiny," Alec says while rubbing Destiny on her head. He is unaware of how much his thoughts about Destiny and our future mean to me.

"The maintenance man rouse huh? Are you still faking it?" I tease, trying to avoid the avalanche of feelings stirred up by everything he was sharing.

"Officially, I'm still employed until the end of this month to train Kenny as my replacement. Truth be told, he's more than qualified for the role and has been handling it alone for months. I plan to give him a huge bonus, equal to my salary from last year, when I resign," Alec confirms.

"That sounds fair and makes a lot of sense. Otherwise, how would you have time to babysit me and start a new company? And go out at night with us? Isn't a maintenance man on call 24 hours a day?" I ask, trying very hard to keep the sharp edge of hurt from reappearing.

"It's been difficult to hide my different roles behind false pretenses while forming genuine friendships. But I would do it again, knowing I get to have you in my life. I can't bring myself to hate the job that brought you to me. I do hate that my deceptions, whether intentional or not, hurt you. I am sorry for that," Alec shares.

"I know you're sorry. I believe you, and I've thought about it. I can understand why you did what you did and how you handled it. I can't sit here and say that even if you had confessed it all to me from the beginning, we would be where we are now. I can't predict how I would have reacted, but I do know that I forgive you." I wanted, no, I needed Alec to know that. I did forgive him.

"Thank you, I won't let you regret that for even a minute. You're stuck with me now," Alec adds, sealing the promise with a warm, gentle kiss. It was both welcoming and reassuring.

My arms instinctively wrap around his neck to pull him closer, giving me better access to deepen the kiss. Just as I was about to crawl back onto Alec's lap, he pulled away, far enough that my arms dislodged.

Seeing the surprise and confusion on my face, Alec leaned in to give me a gentle, sweet kiss, a kiss full of apologies and promises of more to come, before pulling away again.

"Not too much of that," Alec says, subtly adjusting himself so I only catch a quick glimpse. I suddenly feel deprived.

"Babe, don't look at me like I just took the last donut. I told you I wanted to give you time to think about everything I said. For me, this is about more than just the physical connection; I want it all, your bad moods, your little feisty attitude, and everything that makes you who you are. I can and will wait as long as needed. First, we need nothing left hanging over our heads," Alec shares. I clearly see the conviction there, the promise of more to come.

"Okay, Alec." Agreeing with everything he said is my only choice right now. He's right; there's a lot to consider and take in.

"Okay?" Alec presses, searching for any sign of confusion on my part. Nodding my head in confirmation is all I can manage right now.

"Are you ready for me to explain the next steps in the case with you?" Alec asks, still watching me closely.

"Sure," I readily agree. I'd be a lying fool if I didn't admit to myself that my mind was still focused on everything else Alec shared. Barely able to do the brain shift to the topic I needed to understand, but didn't want to know more about.

It felt so wrong to bring Trace into this space, especially after learning that Alec still wants me. Still plans to stick by my side after everything he knows. But knowledge is power and all that shit.

Chapter Fifty-Three
THE CASE
Alec

Hearing Em say *"sure"* should be a red flag. It indicates that Em is lost in her thoughts and does not fully understand the topic shift. The problem is, I need her to have a heads-up on the process and understand the commitment she's making by agreeing to testify. She needs to be mentally prepared to face the obstacles and challenges this case will bring.

Selfishly, I wish all Em had to think about was where we would live together after this case was finally closed. I was no longer professionally obligated to report anything to her parents. But first things first.

"Our focus has been on gathering data. My team has been using both traditional and unconventional methods to find anything that can be used against Trace Junior and Senior. Your dad has his own team with their own strategies. We are consolidating and cross-checking daily reports from both teams. Your dad's legal team believes the evidence we've already collected is enough to arrest Trace. However, we want to secure a strong conviction, one that prevents dismissal or parole because of a weak case."

"Is there anything else you need from me?" Em asks.

"Your witness statement is all the evidence we need from you right now. But babe, you've got to be mentally prepared.

Stay strong," I hedge, needing her to understand the gravity of the situation without freaking her out in the process.

"Okay, Alec. I've decided to start seeing a therapist. It's time, and I figure it can't hurt," Em states, looking confident in her decision.

"I'm proud of you, babe. You've taken some big steps. Your courage in coming forward, no matter how much time has passed, strengthens the case," Alec says with a reassuring smile.

"Law enforcement might contact you directly for more information. We've already provided the video footage and an eyewitness account showing you were with Trace that night. That, along with your statement, isn't enough yet to bring him in. But every piece matters. Investigators will look for physical evidence, DNA, digital trails, texts, and social media posts. They'll interview witnesses, victims… and maybe even Trace himself. It's a process of building timelines, following leads, and connecting dots," Alec says, watching me closely.

"Both my team and your dad understand how serious this is. Sexual assault cases require accuracy, patience, and integrity. A conviction only stands when the evidence supports it. That's why we must be meticulous. And that's why you need to be prepared, Em. What's coming won't be easy, but you're not facing it alone," Alec shares reassuringly.

"I think I am ready. But I couldn't have done all of this without your help and support. I wouldn't even be here; I've spent the last six years repressing any thoughts or memories from that night. Refusing to face it, let alone share it with others.

So, thank you for sticking around even after I told you to leave me alone," Em shares with gratitude and conviction.

"I wouldn't want to be anywhere else. I want to be here for you, even after the case is closed. I'm not going anywhere." I tell her the truth that I feel deep down in my soul, hoping like hell she believes me. Counts on it. Depends on it.

"Will I have to testify in person and see Trace? Because I'm acting all brave and shit now, but I'm not sure how I'll handle seeing him face to face," Em asks with so much vulnerability that I won't sugarcoat the truth. She needs the facts.

"If the case goes to Criminal Court, victims often have to testify, and sometimes the defendant does too. I won't lie; that part can be overwhelming and intimidating. The defense will cross-examine you, trying to twist your words or even make you feel like you're to blame. The prosecution will guide you through direct questioning, asking for details that can be hard to relive. But, babe, if that feels like too much, you have another option. You can submit a victim's impact statement instead. It allows you to tell your story, in your own words, about how this crime has impacted your life. It carries weight, even if you choose not to testify. Whatever you decide, I'll back you. Every step of the way."

"I'm assuming the written statement isn't as effective as being on the stand," Em states, more as a question.

"No, babe, it won't have the same impact, but it's within your rights to choose that route," I hedge. I won't lie to her, and I won't force her to choose one over the other. She has to make that decision on her own. She'll have to live with her choices as well.

"Okay, I'll think about it. Currently, I plan to be there to confront that creep. At least until my bravado takes a nosedive," Em states, but her commitment to still go to trial is admirable.

"Good, babe. Let me know if your bravery begins to waver. After the trial, the judge will set a date and time to announce the sentencing. If you can't make it to the trial, you can still appear at the sentencing hearing, something to consider," I share, trying not to influence her decision in any way.

"Thanks for taking the time to explain it. It does help to know that I have options. I'm not so sure my dad would have been so forthcoming with the information," Em confesses, looking more at ease than I would have thought possible a few days ago.

"I'm going to bounce. I'm exhausted, and I have a team meeting at 0700 tomorrow to discuss our other jobs. I need to make sure everything is covered," I say. Immediately noticing the wince on Em's face after my announcement.

"What's wrong?" I ask, not willing to ignore her reaction. We've come too far to start holding back now.

"It's nothing. I'm just being silly," Em says as she starts to get up.

Grabbing her arm gently, I pull her back down. "Babe, where did your mind just go? You know you can tell me anything. I want you to be open and honest with me. We both need to prioritize that," I plead, hoping she hears the sincerity of my words.

"It's stupid," Em confesses.

"If it's on your mind, then I want to know," I prompt.

"Well, it bothered me hearing you say, *'other jobs,'* even knowing the purpose behind it. I'm mostly over it. I forgive you and my parents. I need to accept the reasons and stop getting butt hurt over it," Em confides. She shares a lot in that one statement. I am so proud of how far she has come.

"Babe, you can always tell me what you're thinking or what's bothering you. That was poor wording on my part, but I've told you, I can't hate the job assignment since it brought me to you." I tell her the truth just before placing a soft kiss on the corner of her mouth.

"Okay, Alec. Do you really need to leave? I mean, you could stay," Em almost shyly suggests.

"Yeah, babe, I gotta go. We both need rest, but more importantly, I really want you to take some time for yourself. Time to think about the future and what you want," I say, hoping like hell she includes me in those plans.

"Okay, Alec. I guess you're right," Em agrees.

"Of course, I am," I reply.

Em scolds, "Conceited jerk."

"Ouch, you wound me," I tease, dramatically clutching my chest.

"You'll be fine," Em says with a smirk, tossing it back.

I ask, "I'll be better if you agree to have dinner with me tomorrow."

"Dinner? That sounds an awful lot like a date," Em shoots back.

"Not a date. Dinner. We no longer have to hide our relationship, and we both need to eat. So, will you have dinner with me?" I ask.

"Sure, that sounds nice," Em readily agrees. I'd mistakenly thought she'd have some reservations, but I'm pleasantly surprised she doesn't.

"Great. Now kiss me," I demand. Getting to my feet, I bring Em up to stand in front of me.

Stepping onto her tippy toes, Em presses her warm, soft lips against mine. The kiss is brief but packs a punch. Watching Em closely, I see desire in her eyes that I'm sure mirrors my own.

Giving her space will probably test my self-control more than ever. I remember how her body feels beneath mine and the sounds she makes when she reaches her climax. Her moans and whimpers play in my mind at the worst times. These vivid memories of Em will likely challenge my resolve to give her all the time and space she needs. But I owe her this. I selfishly took away her choice to be with me. She entered a relationship with me without knowing who I truly was. That shits on me.

"I'll call you tomorrow to let you know what time to be ready. Are you back to working?" I ask, belatedly remembering she's been off work.

"Yes, tomorrow will be my first day back. However, I plan to work half days to help Destiny get used to being alone, which will give me more time to establish a routine for her when I return to full-time work. I'm working from home after lunch, so just let me know whenever you want to go," Em says, following me to her front door.

"Good to know. Get some rest, babe. Is Destiny good for the night, or do you want me to take her out?" I ask, disliking the idea of Em walking around at night, whether on gated property or not.

Em supplies, "She's good. Thanks for the offer, though."

"Night, babe, lock up, and I'll talk to you tomorrow," I say, forcing myself to leave her apartment, even though I really want to stay the night and pick up where our relationship left off before I was forced to tell her the whole truth. But I can't and won't. Not yet.

Chapter Fifty-Four
FRUSTRATION ON STEROIDS
Emily

It was over a week before more helpful information about the case against Trace Junior became available. Alec shared a little here and there. But every day and nearly every night, he was busy. If he came over, he was quick to tell me he couldn't stay long.

During the week, we had one outside *"dinner"*, not a date, at a fantastic Italian restaurant in downtown. The atmosphere was lively and romantic. It felt surreal being on Alec's arm, with the prospect of being more than just friends.

The other four days this week, Alec only managed to stop by. We either ordered food in or I cooked. However, he never stayed long or overnight.

Our kisses were the best and worst parts of the evening. Each kiss was like fuel to a fire. They burned so hot. But before we could act on our primal urges, Alec would extinguish the spark that had ignited between us. He was a complete wet blanket.

I was frustrated beyond telling. Nothing I did or said could break Alec's ever-present control. For some fucked up reason,

Alec thought he needed to give me time, time to make sure I've thought about what I want for the future.

All week, I shamelessly tried in vain to get us back to where we had once been. To break Alec's restraints. Hell, to get him to my bedroom. Or even naked on my couch. He was a master at evasive maneuvers and letting me down without calling me out on my feeble attempts at seduction.

I was really outside my comfort zone here. But there was no hiding the fact that Alec was just as turned on as I was. I kept noticing him adjusting himself more than once.

I resorted to outright telling Alec that I wanted him, that I wanted an *"us."* A future with him. But nothing seemed to break his ironclad control.

After he left last night, I had a realization. Something was stopping him from taking what I know he wants, what we both want.

I've noticed him being tempted over the past week. His hands would briefly wander over my body, but never where I wanted them. Alec was being a tease. And I had the female equivalent of blue balls as a result. He must now be sporting something closer to midnight blue balls.

Last night, I was very frustrated and annoyed with him. I practically begged him to stay the night, but his control was firmly in place, and he left soon after, promising to come for dinner the next night.

Lying alone in my bed, I understood what was happening. This beautiful, honorable man was punishing himself. I remember him telling me that his biggest regret was that he took the choice to be with him away from me. He felt bad that I entered into our relationship without knowing everything about him. In his twisted mind, he wouldn't allow himself to have me, be intimate with me, or bring us back to where we once were, back to the time before the truth was reluctantly revealed.

He was punishing himself for his deception, and I'm almost sure that's what I'm dealing with. What he hasn't realized yet is that I am D.O.N.E. with his noble bullshit.

Since Alec is coming over for dinner tomorrow, I've decided it's time to break down his control and shatter his resolve to keep his distance. I plan to escalate my approach. I've already told him that I forgive him, that I understand why he did what he did, and that I want there to be an *"us."* However, since none of those words has broken through his resolve to stay distant, I'm going to raise the stakes.

Tomorrow, on my way home, I'll stop at Sara's Secrets. They have a wide variety of skippy outfits to choose from. I'll show Alec just how sure I am that I want him. And I see some fuzzy pink handcuffs in our future.

For the first time this week, I went to bed with a smile on my face and something to look forward to. Alec's ever-present control was going down.

The next afternoon, on my way home from the Sara's Secrets trip, where I bought a nightie and some other *'I'm going to break Alec's control"* items, I heard my phone ding with a text message. At the next traffic light, I took a peek.

Alec: *Hey, babe – it's going to be a long night. I'll call you later with an update; do dinner without me.*

That wasn't disappointment I was feeling. Okay, maybe it was. I know Alec wouldn't cancel unless it was for a good reason. Before I can sort out my hurt feelings, another text message comes in.

Alec: *I wouldn't cancel if I didn't have to – we're onto something in the case. I'll tell you more as soon as I have more details.*

Em: *Okay, Alec*

I wanted to tell him that he could still come over tonight, no matter how late, or that I would wait up as long as he needed me to. But I chickened out. A simple *"okay"* is all I got.

Arriving home, I am stopped by our doorman carrying a large frosted blue vase filled with peach, red, and yellow roses. The roses are surrounded by greenery and baby's breath. It looks gorgeous.

"Hello, Miss Emily, these came for you. I'd be happy to carry them up for you," Mr. Carter offered.

"Thank you. That would be great," I tell him, genuinely smiling at the older man. He reminds me of my mom's dad, who passed away a few years ago. His eyes shine brightly with kindness and joy. He's always so happy.

Riding in the elevator, my eyes kept drifting toward the flowers. They are beautiful, and the fragrant aroma fills the elevator cabin. The plastic stick in the middle holding a small card is what really catches my attention. I really want to grab the card to see who the flowers are from. But I wouldn't want Mr. Carter to think I've never received flowers before, even though I haven't.

I can wait. But my mind is filtering through a short list of potential givers. Anticipation, curiosity, and excitement all war within my mind.

Arriving at my unit and unlocking the door, Mr. Carter follows me into the entryway. Destiny barks at first, but then her whole body shakes with excitement. She knows Mr. Carter. She remembers his little dish of dog treats. Her little doggie booty was going all the way left, then right.

Before Mr. Carter can leave my unit after placing the flowers on my entry table, Destiny jumps up and down on me for her love and rubs. She's entirely focused on me, and I love it. Even hearing Mr. Carter say, "Have a good evening, you two," didn't distract her from focusing on me.

That damn card was calling my name. My curiosity clashes with my need to be a good dog mom. Grabbing her collar and leash, I quickly get her harnessed for her first walk of the evening.

At the designated doggie area, Destiny doesn't immediately squat and pee, which reassures me that she wasn't doing the pee-pee dance before I got home. Stopping at Sara's Secrets took longer than expected. There are so many fun items to consider. It's actually an educational experience.

Returning to my unit, I deliberately avoid the beckoning card to give Destiny fresh water and feed her. It's essential to maintain her routine. I can wait. I'm showing myself that I have some self-control. But the control was short-lived. As soon as the food bowl hits the floor, I make a beeline straight for the small pink envelope.

As I read the small card, I feel a strange emotion I can't quite identify. The lump in my throat makes swallowing hard.

*"**Em,** sorry for canceling dinner at the last minute. Just know that I'm here wishing I was there with you, **Alec.**"*

Wow, that was really sweet and thoughtful. That man is turning my dream man into a reality.

I decide to eat some hummus and carrots instead of leftovers. Something light appeals to me more than leftover spaghetti.

Before Destiny and I get too comfortable, I leash her up for the promised evening walk around the block. She sniffs everything she can easily reach without pulling on her leash. She's the perfect dog. Sweet, smart, gentle, and so loving. I can't imagine my life without her in it.

Giving Destiny all the time she wants, we gradually make our way back to the entrance. Even though we aren't huffing it, the Houston humidity still makes us both sweat. It's a sticky kind of sweat, clammy dampness for me and a musty odor for Destiny. Then there are the pesky mutant mosquitoes. Those little bastards are relentless in their quest for my blood.

As I went back upstairs to my unit, the floral scents greeted me warmly. The sweet aroma of roses filled my space, and instead of being overpowering, it brought a smile to my face, reminding me I hadn't thanked Alec yet. To avoid bothering him, I decided to send him a quick text instead.

Em: *Thank you for the flowers – they're beautiful.*

Alec: *Glad you like them.*

Alec's reply came instantly. I waited a few minutes, but no other messages came through. Alec said he was busy, so I shouldn't get butt-hurt over him not texting more or calling like he promised.

What I should do is take a shower and give Destiny one, too. She's showered with me before, standing still and patient while I wash her. Afterward, I towel her off, leaving a couple of beach towels on the floor so she can finish the job herself. It's adorable watching her scoot across them on her back legs, twisting her head and body side to side. It's not just cute, it's effective.

Leaving her to it, I decide to take my time, finally giving myself some overdue self-care. I work a deep conditioner through my hair while shaving nearly everything.

Stepping out, I smooth lotion all over my body before wrapping myself in my soft, plush robe. The simple ritual leaves me feeling clean and relaxed, something I haven't felt in weeks, maybe even longer.

I gather the damp towels and clothes for the laundry, grab a bottle of water, and turn off the lights on my way back to my room. It's still early for bed, but curling up with a good book feels like the perfect substitute for missing dinner with Alec.

Yeah, right. Not even close.

Looking at my phone on the bedside table where I left it earlier, I see that Alec hasn't texted me again, but Roxy and Sarah have. They are demanding an update. I quickly reply to the girls' group message, promising to give them all the details over drinks this weekend. Both of their responses come quickly.

Roxy: *Your time's up, girl - Saturday works*

Sarah: *Yeah, what she said...kissing emoji*

A few of my favorite authors have recently released books, but I decided to be really lazy and watch TV instead. As I scroll through channels, I land on the Grand Tour series. I can watch these episodes repeatedly. I swear I catch a new comment each time. This series is better than the shouting on Dance Moms.

With Destiny's warm body curled beside me, I soon felt my eyes grow heavy. I could sense myself drifting into twilight sleep, the stage where you're still aware of your surroundings but otherwise gone. Before passing out, I manage to turn off the TV before I fall asleep.

The warm body wrapping around me was both strange and familiar. This dream felt so real that I was sure I could even smell Alec's distinct, masculine scent.

Awareness dawns on me as the body behind mine pulls and draws me closer, wrapping a large, warm arm protectively around my stomach. "Alec?" I sleepily mumble.

"Yeah, Babe, go back to sleep," Alec whispers in my ear. So close, I not only hear him, but I also feel his breath ruffle my hair. Having him here with me does the opposite of what his words ask. Instead, I'm awake and aware that Alec is in my bed, big spooning me. "Alec, what are you doing?"

"Go back to sleep, Em. I'm wiped," Alec pleads, and I can hear the exhaustion in his voice.

"Okay," I say, then drift back to sleep.

It was the persistent beeping that woke me up next. I found myself torn between wanting the noise to stop and not wanting to leave the cocoon of warmth I was so comfortably wrapped in.

The decision was taken from me when I felt my body being moved just before the beeping stopped. Reality hit me hard then: Alec was here with me, in my bed.

In a rough, sleep-deprived voice, he asked, "Morning, babe, what time is it?"

"It's 5:00 am," I say, feeling like there was something important I was missing. Then it hit me. Alec was in my bed.

"Hey, Alec, how'd you get in here?" I ask, wondering how I hadn't heard him and why Destiny hadn't barked.

"Used a key, babe. Do you need to be somewhere this early?" Alec's raspy voice asks.

"I get up early for Destiny. I walk her to the pet area when we first wake up, then I feed her. After getting ready for work, I walk her again. I'm trying to get her on a schedule. The pet worker said routines are important to maintain. What key?" I ask, not ready to let this detail go.

"I see. You want me to walk the baby girl for you now?" Alec asks. He looked more alert than he had a few seconds earlier.

Looking at Destiny still curled up at the end of the bed on what is usually my side, I say, "She's not showing any signs that she's ready to get up. I'm still working on the timing thing. How did you get a key to my unit?" I ask again, still not letting this shit go.

"Babe, it's the maintenance master key. Is there a problem?" Alec asks, acting like it's no big deal. And I guess it's not a big deal, but still.

"Guess not," I mutter, sounding like a petulant child to my own ears.

"Good. Now kiss me," Alec demands.

"You're being awfully bossy for someone who broke into my unit and crawled into bed with me," I snap. Secretly, I'm totally okay with it.

"Yeah. Now. Kiss me," Alec demands again, not wavering from what he wants.

"Gees. Fine." Turning to face him fully, I lift my lips to meet his in a gentle, chaste kiss, just a peck.

"A real fucking kiss, Em," Alec states, still demanding and relentless in his request.

"That was a real kiss," I sass back.

"Not even close to what I have in mind. Let me show you what I'm talking about," Alec challenges. He spins me around completely, capturing my face in his large, warm hands. I see his intent just before his lips claim mine. Without much prompting, my lips part on their own, morning breath be damned. Alec kisses the hell out of me. Tongues dueling and all.

The moment his hands find me, heat rushes through me. I've missed him more than I want to admit. Pushing against his shoulders, he willingly drops to his back, allowing me to straddle him.

I had fallen asleep last night wrapped only in my robe, which suddenly feels like fate. My naked nether regions are pressed perfectly against his already hardened bulge, which I just now notice is cased in black boxer briefs.

Alec is so hard. When his hands slip under my robe to cup my ass cheeks, a satisfying groan escapes him. "You've been naked all night, and I'm just now realizing it? Fuuuck!" Alec growls.

Shamelessly, I apply pressure where I need it most. Leaning forward, I kiss Alec while my hands are on a determined path to bare skin. Tugging at the hem of his undershirt, my only focus now is to get Alec naked. Finally.

Before I can reach my goal, I can almost feel Alec's control snapping back into place. "Babe, sorry, I need to get home and take a shower. There are a few things I need to finish today, and I need an early start."

Wow, am I feeling disappointment? Yep, I am. Sadly, I'm all too used to that feeling. "Oh, okay, Alec," I say, holding back the urge to sound pitifully sad and maybe a little angry.

Alec skillfully extricates himself from underneath me, gently placing me back on my side of the bed while placing a sweet kiss on my still-tingling lips. Before the spark has a chance to reignite, Alec leaves the bed.

All I can do is watch him get dressed, caught between the urge to ask questions and the need to hide my frustration. The feeling of rejection hovered just above my desire for answers. With so many mixed messages and conflicting emotions, I struggled to find clarity. But my pride wouldn't let me ask him why he was leaving or why it seemed so easy for him to do so night after night.

Before I can stop myself, I ask, "Will you be able to come tonight for dinner?"

"Can I call you later today to confirm? I'm not sure what my day will look like until I meet with my team," Alec supplies.

"Of course. Just let me know," I say, feeling dejected and confused the entire time.

Hearing the snick of my unit door closing is a louder-than-normal indicator of the walls that separate us. Alec is withdrawing and putting up walls. But why?

If distance is what he wants and division is what he seeks, then fine. I'll see if Roxy and Sarah can switch to drinks tonight. Even if they can't, I've decided not to make myself available to Alec.

Happy time doesn't have to take hours; he could find time for us to reconnect intimately if he wanted to. Busy or not, if he desires me, he will make time for me.

Words are meaningless without action. I'm finished with Alec's kind of lip service. My frustration level requires some self-preservation.

Tonight, I'm going out. To hell with Alec's self-control. It seems that my emotions have settled on anger. So be it.

Chapter Fifty-Five
TRUTH SERUM
Emily

Luckily, the girls were available for drinks tonight. I sent a text as soon as I arrived at work this morning. Without giving details, they understood me well enough to realize something was going on. I rarely initiate a night out.

Roxy, Em, and I planned to meet at the DalRock after work and then go to The Rusty Nail. It was our comfort spot, free from unwanted attention or trouble. Sarah's boss, Ricky, made sure it stayed that way for each of us.

Ricky was a great boss and an all-around good guy. He was in his late forties, with salt-and-pepper hair. He was also a bit thick around the middle, but otherwise still quite handsome. And, very married.

It was during our second round of drinks that I felt my phone vibrate in my back pocket. I saw on my Apple Watch that the iMessage was from Alec. I barely managed to resist reading the message.

Both Sarah and Roxy agreed that I should create some space between myself and Alec, so I'm not always at his beck and call.

By the third drink, I confessed Sara's Secret plan, all the while ignoring the vibration against my butt cheek. They encouraged me to stick with that plan, agreeing that Alec's self-control needs to be challenged.

During our fourth round of drinks accompanied by shots of tequila, Ricky came over to confiscate the keys, promising to get us home safely.

By 11:00 pm, we were all pretty drunk, the small amount of appetizers we had eaten wasn't helping much, and we knew we would regret it the next day.

However, it was a successful night. Not only did they help me develop my plan, but we also talked about Sarah's relationship with Michael and Roxy's non-relationship with Dex.

We all agreed that it had been way too long since the three of us girls went out together without any distractions from the cock blockers' peanut gallery. So, we decided to schedule a girls' night out at least once a month.

It was just after midnight when Ricky led us into the lobby of DalRock. We assured him that we could find our way to our units on our own. However, Mr. Carter noticed the situation and kindly offered to escort us to our respective floors.

We dropped Roxy off first, and I was second. Fishing my keys out of my pocket, I fumble at first but finally get my door unlocked. Waving at Mr. Carter and Sarah, I enter my unit. Destiny was there to greet me, jumping up and down and wagging her tail.

Damn, I hadn't thought much about coming home and then having to take her out while drunk. Maybe I can persuade Mr. Carter to come back and do it.

Before I can devise that plan, a light turns on in my living room. I stand frozen with fear and confusion until I hear Alec's voice. "I already walked her this evening. She's good for the night."

"Oh. Okay. Um, thanks." I stammer out, sobering a little from the jolt of fear that just coursed through my body.

As I watch Alec standing in my living room, I realize two things. First, he's only wearing his black boxer briefs. No undershirt this time. And second, he doesn't look happy.

Before I can think better of it, I blurt out, "Did you break in again?"

"No, I used a key. Are you drunk?" Alec asks.

"Maybe a little," I snark back.

"Come here," Alec demands.

"No, you come here," I sass, feeling 10 feet tall and bulletproof. Alcohol has that effect on me.

"Where have you been? Did you drive home?" Alec questions.

"No, Ricky drove me home," I reply, not missing the glaring look Alec is giving me. And it's none of his business where I was.

"Ricky? Ricky who?" Alec asks, seeming calmer than his expression and tone suggest.

"Sarah's boss. Why are you here?" I snap back with a question of my own.

Alec accuses, "I told you I would call you. But you didn't answer. And you didn't respond to my text messages."

Still feeling 10 feet tall, I remark, "I didn't feel like waiting around on you."

"I see," Alec says, watching me through the faint glow of the living room light with those assessing eyes that reveal nothing. His control is still firmly in place.

I walk past Alec, trying to move with dignity and grace to my bedroom. I need to pee and then get into bed. If I trip or stumble, it will surely ruin my parting shot.

Once I close myself in the bathroom, I take care of my business, brush my teeth, and strip down before grabbing my fluffy robe. I've slept in it before without enticing Alec, and this time probably won't be any different. I'm too drunk and exhausted to dig into my Sara's Secret stash anyway. Not that I'm in the mood.

Exiting the bathroom, I'm not surprised to find Alec in my bed with the covers low over his waist and my dog curled up next to him.

The nerve of this guy. I want to feel irritated and annoyed with him, but I'm unable to summon those feelings. I don't care if he wants to sleep here. I actually prefer it. No way, I'll tell him that though.

Approaching the bed, Alec lifts the covers for me to crawl under. In my drunken state, his warm body is calling me. Scooting closer, I snuggle up to him, causing Destiny to shift to our feet with a tiny, annoyed huff.

Alec reaches over and turns off my bedside lamp, plunging us into darkness. The darkness gives me the confidence to rest my arm over his warm stomach and fold my knee over his thighs. With my head resting on his chest and shoulder, my eyes close on their own.

The room spins slightly before settling, due to the lack of movement. I feel myself drifting into sleep until I hear a rumble just above my ear, "Want to tell me what's going on?"

"No," I mumble back.

"Do it anyway, Em," Alec demands.

In my drunken state, my brain convinces me I should tell Alec everything. So, I do. I tell him how his self-imposed walls are irritating me and making me mad. I say I feel like he's being a tease; either that or he doesn't want me anymore. I tell him I'm done with his stupid self-control and that I plan to handcuff him to my bed to take advantage of him. I also say to him that he's being dumb for holding himself back from having sex with me.

Throughout my entire rant, Alec doesn't comment or interrupt. His body remains still and unresponsive. Until it suddenly wasn't. Before I can process his movement, Alec has me pinned beneath him.

In a strained voice, Alec says, "Damn it, Em, of course I want you. I've told you that. But you've been through hell, and I want to give you time to heal, especially after everything you've learned about me. I never want to take your choices away again. I thought waiting until the case was over would help, that it would give us a fresh start. However, I now realize that my good intentions only made things worse. My effort to give you control back has only added to your confusion, and I apologize for that. It's been harder than I can say to give you the space you need. I was just... trying to do the right thing."

I might be drunk, but all those reasons seem like good ones.

Stretching up, my lips meet Alec's in a kiss. It only takes a second for Alec to take control, his tongue slipping inside while his large hands position my head where he wants it. I'm all about his kind of control. Wrapping my leg over his calves, my body undulates beneath him, trying to create friction where I need it most. My body is ready. It's been too long since we last made love, and I want this. Now.

"Alec," I beg, knowing without a doubt that he knows what I'm asking for.

But before I can untie my robe, Alec has moved away from me and is standing by the side of the bed. Watching him press against his impressive bulge, I figure he's about to strip. But then his words hit me: "Not tonight, Em. You're drunk, and I would feel like I'm taking advantage of your trust in me again."

What the hell is wrong with this man? "Are you serious right now?" I snap, feeling mad all over again.

"Babe, let's get some sleep tonight, and we'll talk about everything tomorrow. I promise. I won't leave until we've had a chance to talk. Please, Em, let's go to sleep," Alec pleads.

The fuck of it is, I guess I can understand his reluctance, especially given my past and his concern about taking my choices away. "Fine," I snap. Not able to avoid feeling rejected and pissed.

With a huff, I roll over and pull the covers up to my chin. The copious amount of alcohol I drank sloshes in my belly. The room spins as Alec reenters the bed. As he sidles up to me, he says, "Night, babe." I think I reply as I throw one leg out of the covers, but I'm not sure because I immediately drift off to sleep.

The persistent beeping jolts me awake. Damn, my head is pounding. Before I can reach the nightstand, the beeping ceases.

Then I hear Alec's voice. "Morning, babe. Go back to sleep for a bit. I'll walk Destiny and feed her."

"Okay," I think I mumble. I don't have to be told twice. I feel like roadkill. The next second after that thought, I passed out.

The next time I woke up, it wasn't from the beeping. It was from gentle, tickling caresses from Alec's mouth and fingertips across my abdomen up to my breasts. The light touches continued from my stomach to my hipbones and thighs. My robe, which was tied securely around my waist when I went to bed, was now wide open, revealing all my naked glory.

Alec's hands and mouth, which began gently, transitioned to sucking, nipping, licking, and pinching. Not targeting any specific spot, but instead exploring everywhere. Each stroke or touch was warm and unyielding. Exploring. Sweet torture of pleasure and pain.

I was aroused but apprehensive. If Alec got me all worked up and then said he had to leave, I might physically hurt the man.

Feeling him trail kisses from my navel to my pubic bone almost sent me into a panic.

"Alec. Wait!" I blurt out, needing to know what he intended. Either that, or he'd need to stop now.

"Babe? You good?" Alec asks, leaning in to give me a warm, wet kiss.

"Umm. I'm not sure," I manage to say.

"I'd like to hear more about the pink fuzzy handcuffs," Alec says, smirking.

Closing my eyes, I groan. "I told you about my Sara's Secrets stash. Damn tequila, it's my truth serum."

"No, you didn't tell me there was a whole stash. I'd like to see that."

"Umm, are you about to leave?" I manage to ask between the kisses and caresses.

"No, babe, unless you'd rather I go. Just to say, I heard what you said last night, and you're right. I haven't thought about how my actions might affect you. It was never my intention to make you think I didn't want you. I really felt like I was doing what was best for you," Alec states, rolling onto his side next to me.

"Oh," is my stellar response.

"Tell me what you're thinking, babe. I want to know," Alec requests.

"Alec, it bothered me that you made walking away from me look so easy. Putting distance between us, resisting all my advances. Your words said one thing, but your actions contradicted them. Those mixed messages bothered me more than they probably should, but you seemed unaffected when you pulled back," I admit, I feel vulnerable sharing my insecurities.

"Babe, I wanted to call more. I wanted to come over every night, pick up where we left off before everything fell apart. I know how I feel and what I want you to feel, but I didn't want to rush you. Don't think for a second that just because I haven't stayed over or pushed for more, I'm not interested. I am. I haven't changed my mind about you or about us," Alec says, kissing my nose.

"Before you, I thought my life had been full, serving, protecting, living for Uncle Sam. But now I know better. I'll never be content in a life that doesn't have you in it," Alec says softly, his fingers tracing lazy patterns over my skin.

"Oh, okay." That's all I say, lying here naked and vulnerable, feeling exposed and defenseless against his honest explanations.

"Are we done talking?" Alec asks, kissing down my neck to the swell of my breasts.

"Ah ha," I mumble, my thoughts slipping away as Alec's lips trace gentle paths across my bare skin. The warmth of his touch silences everything else, leaving me craving more.

"Glad we got that settled, now give me a kiss," Alec demands, hovering over me with his lips ready.

Leaning in, my lips meet Alec's in a warm, though brief, kiss. That was before Alec took control, devouring my mouth with his. It was all tongues and teeth, nibbling and sucking, with no holding back. Alec is a man who doesn't care about morning breath.

It seems Alec is no longer waiting to reconnect, which is evident when he lifts my hips and shoves his bed pillow under my ass. Then, sitting back on his knees, his hungry gaze lingers intently on my core. I know I should feel self-conscious, but the look in his eyes tells me he likes what he sees.

Alec glides his hands up my legs, his fingers spanning to my hips. With his large hands, he's able to grasp the tops of my thighs while using his thumbs to spread my lower lips, completely exposing my sex. With my ass tilted upward, I'm sure Alec can see everything from my clit to what's between my ass cheeks.

Feeling embarrassed, the need to close my legs was overwhelming. But Alec's hands were firm, keeping me in place and completely exposed to his view.

"You're so beautiful, everything about you is perfect," Alec murmurs, his gaze deliberately sweeping over me before settling on my eyes.

What surprises me most isn't just his words, hearing him refer to me as *perfect*, but it's the calm I feel, even though I'm being pinned down. There's no panic, no urge to flee. I feel a solid and undeniable trust; it's right there in his eyes. I know I'm safe with Alec.

Still, his thorough perusal leaves me feeling confused. Why is he just staring at me? "Um, Alec," I start, but I'm interrupted.

"This view. Beautiful. Do you often sleep naked with only a robe on?" Alec bizarrely asks.

"Only when I'm lazy," I manage to reply, watching Alec lean forward. Just when I was about to ask him why he'd care, Alec's tongue firmly licks me from my entrance to my clit before sucking my clit hard.

My hips buck of their own accord. With Alec's hold on my hips, he tilts and lifts my pussy for more. He devours me. Licking, sucking, and tongue fucking like a starved man.

Alec is relentless with his pace until I am writhing and undulating my hips upward for more. It was too much and not enough at the same time.

As my climax builds and hovers, Alec pulls back before entering me with two fingers while avoiding my clit. My breaths are choppy and ragged. My need for an orgasm intensified while at the same time it waned.

It's like Alec knows I'm just one stroke against my clit away from exploding.

"Alec," I plead.

"I know what you need. I got you," Alec states, right before running his finger, wet with my juices, around my clit, but not touching it.

With my body wound so tight, on the verge of release, I was becoming increasingly frustrated.

Just when I was about to beg, Alec's mouth back on my clit, sends me into a climax that rivals all other climaxes. I felt it all the way from my head to my toes. The aftershocks were powerful mini orgasms that kept the pleasure coming and heightened.

Before I can fully come down from the most intense orgasm of my life, Alec grabs me by my hips and enters me in one quick thrust. I will never tell him, but as relaxed as my body was, I felt a pinch of pain before the pleasure.

"I've missed you, missed this," Alec says in a growl. Using the tight hold on my hips to bring my body to meet his. Pulling and pushing me at a steady rhythm, until he wasn't.

"Flip over, babe, hands and knees," Alec demands, removing my robe from my arms and tossing it to the floor.

I make moves to do as I'm told, but apparently not fast enough for Alec, who effortlessly lifts and turns me around.

"Cheek to the bed," Alec insists, pushing my upper body down toward the mattress.

"Babe, tilt your ass in the air," Alec instructs before slamming back in. He was being bossy and controlling, but it felt too good to care at the moment.

Alec moved with fierce intensity, chasing his own release. His forceful thrusts felt charged with need and something more profound, like surrender, possession, and promises. Each thrust backed his words.

My body was building toward another epic climax. The only sounds were our heavy breathing, my occasional whimpers, and the slapping of our bodies together.

"This ass. You have the greatest ass, babe," Alec rumbles. Pulling my hips back to meet his forward thrust. Alec sets a punishing rhythm. Then, without warning, I feel the pressure from one of his fingers against my ass.

Before I can tense up too much, Alec reaches around and strokes my clit. Applying just the right amount of pressure to both, the trifecta assault becomes overwhelming. I scream as an orgasm rips through me. My scream is immediately followed by a guttural groan as Alec releases warm cum into me.

It was official. I was a ragdoll, boneless, and utterly exhausted. I felt weightless and content. Before I could roll to the side, Alec managed to flip us, resting his back against the headboard before smoothly repositioning me on his dick again. A dick that, surprisingly, is still hard.

"Ride me, Em," Alec commands, lifting me up and down with his hands gripping my ribs. He manages to control the movements himself. Can't he tell that I'm a ragdoll, lacking stuffing, boneless, and floppy?

"I can't," I manage to say. I don't have the energy to take control.

With Alec controlling my movements, he instructs, "You can. Grab the headboard, don't let go."

Alec's control in the bedroom is the only time his bossiness is acceptable.

Apparently, my boneless ragdoll state was only temporary. With my knees pressed firmly against Alec's hips, I ride him.

The sloppy sounds from our previous orgasms mingled with our heavy breathing, creating the soundtrack to the best sex experience of my life. It wasn't even 8:30 am yet.

Evidently not moving fast enough, Alec takes control, lifting me and slamming me down. A frenzied, exhilarating ride to ecstasy. "Get yourself there, come on, baby," Alec encourages, "Touch yourself."

Without giving a second thought to his request, I do as I'm told. Watching me get myself off while riding him must satisfy Alec; he erupts in a roar, and I'm right there with him.

I collapse onto Alec's chest, feeling satisfied and content. Alec slides down onto the bed but doesn't lift me away from him. I can still feel the pulse of our connection. Alec's semi-hard state was an anomaly. With my head against his chest and our combined breathing the only sound in the room, I close my eyes. Relaxed and thoroughly fucked.

Experimentally, I tighten my inner muscles, and I'm not all that surprised to feel Alec's dick start to harden again.

"You're ready to go again?" Alec asks, sounding relaxed.

"No. No way, I think you did break me." Recalling a discussion we had the first time we were together.

"I'd never hurt my pussy. I'm quite fond of her," Alec teases. "Babe, go shower. I'll start the coffee, and I've already fed Destiny, so I'll take her for her second morning walk. Oh, and earlier I texted your boss, Scott. I informed him you had a situation to deal with this morning and would be late," Alec adds.

"A situation, huh?" I playfully ask. I realize then that a shower is just what I need to soothe my sore muscles. Parts of my body had a workout without any stretching first. Plus, I felt sticky and kinda gross.

Entering the shower, the hot water felt incredible against my overstimulated body. Alec was meticulous with his attentions; I had three orgasms as proof. The shower felt so amazing that I had to remind myself I needed my job to pay my bills. So, I forced myself to turn off the shower.

Alec is fully dressed, sitting on the edge of my now-made bed when I come out, wrapped in a fluffy towel. In his hand is a steaming cup of coffee. My fantasy man, in more ways than one.

"Here, babe. I gotta run. I have a Zoom call in 45 minutes and need to shower. I'll call you later. I'll try to let you know what time I'll be here. Might be really late. You good?" Alec asks, watching me intently.

"I'm good, Alec," I say, knowing it's the complete truth. "Just let yourself in," I say, smiling.

"Come give me a kiss," Bossy Alec commands.

Without thinking about how much control he has over me, I do what I'm told. Again. Approaching the bed, I give him the kiss he asks for.

"Gotta run, babe," Alec says, smacking my towel-covered ass before leaving the room. A second later, I hear the front door click and the lock engage.

Chapter Fifty-Six
I CHOOSE YOU
Alec

"This fucking sucks!" I say to the entire room. Every team member is either sitting around the conference table or leaning against the windowsills. No one is happy with the news we received today about Trace fucking Roberts.

This morning, we learned that he was being charged with four counts of aggravated sexual assault. At first, this seemed like good news, but then we found out he would be appearing in court today. It's unusual for the justice system to act this quickly, especially without some form of corruption or influence involved.

I wanted to attend his arraignment, and I had only 30 minutes to reach the courthouse downtown. I arrived just in time to witness Trace's dramatics; his performance definitely didn't disappoint. He put on quite the show.

The spineless, whiny manchild actually broke down crying at the arraignment hearing. The judge moved to skip ahead directly to sentencing on charges of aggravated sexual assault related to drug use, pushing for him to be tried as a serial rapist. His sentencing could then carry the maximum penalties. Trace might face consecutive sentences of 20 years to life.

But when the judge asked the dumbass defendant how he wanted to plead, the weasel admitted to the crimes right before his statement to plead not guilty by reason of insanity. That shocked the shit out of me, and I think it surprised the judge, too.

One thing we can't deny is that actions, whether purposeful or not, support his claim of being mentally ill. It's as if Trace Junior didn't understand or grasp how serious his statements were, much less the charges against him.

His defense lawyer must be a real tool to let Trace make that plea. It explains why this idiot came in crying and sniffling. They had planned to push for a plea of insanity.

Surprisingly, after all that, the Judge ruled that the defendant could be released on bail. Of course, the defense attorney had cash on hand to bond the fucker out.

"The only inconvenience Trace Junior will face right now is an electronic ankle monitor. He won't even spend a night in jail!" I seethe, feeling pissed all over again.

"Yeah, I don't get that. But there's another thing I can't figure out. With Trace's dad being a judge, why would he let his son plead like that? It seems crazy and reckless," Mike adds, genuinely looking confused.

"That's a good point. Also, with his Senior's international ties, how in the hell did they not consider him to be a flight risk?" I ask, not really expecting anyone to answer. They are all looking at me, probably gauging *my* mental stability.

"It's also interesting how he was brought in this morning and was able to get in front of the Judge the same day. I have to wonder if that Judge wasn't bought. It all just moved so quickly, yet the next hearing isn't scheduled until after Christmas," I grumble.

Leaning my head back to face the ceiling, I get my anger under control. Taking a deep breath, I breathe out slowly. I'm ranting, and I don't usually rant. Ever. But this bastard hurt Em. He should be suffering and rotting in a prison cell. That wasn't the case, and I need to accept that fact.

"Okay. Sorry, guys. That really pisses me off, but he'll get his time in prison. I'll make sure of it," I say, feeling confident in that promise.

"Damn right. The hearing in December will give us more time to gather dirt on him and his father. We'll collect so much evidence that no judge can deny the maximum sentence. Not without looking like they either forgot the law or they were bought off," Juan says with complete conviction.

"Boss, I've gathered a lot of information. Now, I need a few of you to help me review the data. We should focus on finding proof that his attacks were premeditated. I've already given Rudy several names of people who might be involved or could serve as witnesses," Janet shares. She is the best and most thorough hacker I've ever worked with.

"I've already got ears on two of the individuals. Trying to track down and make contact with another one this week," Rudy proudly shares. He's a technology genius. His ability to obtain live, long-range information feeds is remarkable.

"Are we going to be able to use any of this information, and can we get access to his health records, such as his psychological evaluation?" I ask, well aware that we all know our actions aren't always legal or admissible in court.

"That's the goal. Have faith, man. We all want to nail this bastard to the wall just like he deserves. Also, this is the most action any of us has seen since our retirement. It's kinda fun," Rudy shares, smiling like a crazy man.

"He's not wrong. This is fun. Metaphorically killing bad guys just like the old days," Felix says.

My team understands my need for justice and recognizes that this is personal to me. Coming clean about my deception and subsequent relationship with Em was a hard truth to share.

I had been their commanding officer for several years, ultimately responsible for their safety and survival. Following procedures and rules was essential. I had to admit that I not only broke protocol but was also deeply involved in it. And if that wasn't enough, I've dragged them into my pursuit of justice by any means necessary.

It was a big ol' piece of humble pie I ate. Still, I can't bring myself to regret my decisions. Having Em as my reward is priceless and something I will never take for granted.

My team and partners have assured me multiple times that they are fully committed to assisting in any way they can. They understand the potential consequences but remain determined to achieve their ultimate goal: justice.

As everyone disperses to do what they do best, I send a quick text to Em.

Alec: Hey, babe. I should wrap up around 8 – I can bring dinner

Em: Hi. I'll make dinner – how's your day going so far?

Alec: *Not the best, but not the worst. I'll update you this evening*

Em: *Okay, Alec*

I'm not sure what I did in a past life to deserve her. She is the light of my life. There are no other memories in my 30-plus years that shine as brightly. I will protect her at all costs.

It was after my 3:00 pm. client meeting that I received the call I had been waiting for. Mr. Wilson called to inform me about Trace's arraignment. He took the news about as well as I did, which was not good at all.

He shared that his legal team would challenge a Privacy Impact Assessment (PIA), which will include claims of insufficient risk evaluation. This oversight will grant them legal rights to access previously closed and hidden cases involving Trace Junior.

His legal team has already contacted the other identified victims. They have prepared their statements and a list of willing witnesses who are ready to testify if we proceed to trial.

"Alec, I know you can gather more information. Get me whatever you can, anything you find, and my legal team will work to make it admissible in court," Mr. Wilson states. No hesitation.

"I hear you. My team is also working hard to gather usable information. Our methods might be in a gray area, but we're using them to identify who or what to target. We will also review any documents to try to counter the insanity plea," I reply, hoping to ease Mr. Wilson's conscience a bit. His bringing that up tells me he's worried we won't have enough evidence for a conviction.

"Okay, Alec. I trust you," Mr. Wilson supplies. Instantly, I feel relief. Releasing a long exhale, I say, "Thank you."

"So, the wife wanted me to ask if you'll be joining Em for Sunday brunch," Mr. Wilson asks with a smile in his voice. He knows Em's mother is still trying to play matchmaker.

"I'll talk to Em tonight. Please tell Mrs. Wilson thanks for including me." I know Mr. Wilson will catch the hint that I'm seeing Em later, and he'll tell his wife. With any luck, she'll take the message and realize her matchmaking services are no longer needed.

My last meeting didn't last as long as I expected, and it ended with some good news. One of our first clients wants to renew their contract and expand coverage to their four other locations.

It's a big, lucrative contract, and it comes with the realization that we will need to hire more team members. Juan assured me that he has already started reaching out to some of our former military units, promising not to recruit active military personnel. We all understand that we don't need another issue to irritate Commander Nelson.

This day has been a roller coaster with its ups and downs. The lowest point was the news about Trace, who was released on bail. That news almost completely took the happiness away from my morning with Em.

I'm hopeful I'll end my day just like I started it: in Em's bed, in her arms, between her thighs.

Alec: *Leaving early. Need anything?*

Em: *Just you*

Arriving at the condos, I decide to make a quick stop at my unit. I need to shower away the day and pick up a few things for the night.

I quickly finish my shower and change into lounge pants and a short-sleeve Henley. As I stuff a change of clothes into my duffle, I grab a bottle of Em's favorite wine before heading out.

Suddenly, I can't wait to see Em and even Destiny. There's a sense of rightness in it all. My girl wants me; her parents approve and trust me, and I feel confident in myself, ready to do whatever it takes to make Em feel safe.

I don't hesitate to let myself into Em's unit. She needs to get used to the idea of me coming home to her every day.

Destiny greets me enthusiastically and kisses my chin when I reach down to pet her. I never thought about getting a dog of my own. We worked with a few military dogs, and I enjoyed spending time with them during their downtime. But Destiny is an incredible, cool as fuck dog. She's converted me into a dog lover before I even realized it was happening.

"Babe. Something smells great," I say as I walk into her galley kitchen to put the wine away.

"Hey," Em says from behind me. Turning, I see her in a cami and sleep shorts. The tiny pink roses and lace edging look incredibly sexy. Part of me was hoping for the robe without anything underneath, but this little outfit might be my new favorite.

"Like the outfit, babe. Now come kiss me," I demand, stepping toward her as she steps toward me. The kiss was warm and inviting, a promise of more to come.

"I'm starving. Are you hungry?" Em asks.

"You don't have to wait on me, ever. My hours are irregular, and you need to eat," I say, a bit annoyed that she went hungry waiting for me. She still hasn't regained all the weight she couldn't afford to lose. But even I know not to bring up a woman's weight.

"I'm fine. I had a smoothie an hour ago. Plus, I nibble as I cook," Em reassures.

Now all I can think about is Em nibbling on me. "Do you want me to take Destiny out while you plate our food?" I ask, needing a minute to let my little head simmer down. I don't want her to feel this is all about sex for me.

"Sure, that'd be great. I was planning to ask you. Destiny already ate and is probably ready to go out," Em supplies, already turning toward the stove.

Not even 15 minutes later, we're back upstairs. Destiny did her business and headed home. It seems Em has conditioned her to be quick at night.

Em greets us at the door with a treat for Destiny, telling her what a good girl she is. It's cute to watch. They both eat that shit up.

I notice the bar is already set with our plates and drinks, and I can't help but love the cozy, domestic feel of it. "Babe, this roast is incredible, so tender," I say, savoring another bite. It's perfectly seasoned, moist, and bursting with flavor.

Em supplies, "I cooked it in a pressure cooker. It cooks in half the time, and the end result is better than a slow cooker."

"It's excellent. Thanks for cooking. I have some news to share about the case. Do you want to talk now or later?" I ask, knowing she has the right to know the details if she wants them.

"I'd like to know what is happening," Em responds. She looks more assured than I've seen from her in a while.

"They held the pre-trial court arraignment this morning. Trace did not deny the charges brought against him for the four counts of aggravated sexual assault, but he did plead not guilty by reason of insanity," I share, watching Em's reactions closely.

"Okay. What does that mean?" Em cautiously asks.

"His defense team is going to try to argue that he lacked the mental capacity at the time of the crimes and therefore should receive treatment for his mental illness," I share, knowing this information sucks. Still, I need her to grasp the situation.

"Oh," Em mumbles.

"Because he made that plea, it becomes his and his defense team's responsibility to prove at trial that he was disturbed and lacked the mental capacity at the time the crimes were committed," I share.

"What happens if he is found to be insane? Will he still serve time for what he did?" Em questions, looking somber and hesitant.

Understanding the need to offer some reassurance, I say, "If they can prove Trace was insane, he won't go free. He'll be transferred to a mental hospital; he could stay there for many years, sometimes as long or longer than a prison sentence. But, babe, pleas of insanity are rarely successful. Also, I'm not sure how they can argue he snapped and wasn't in control during four separate attacks. My team and your dad's team are working hard to find proof to the contrary. Let's not worry about that possible outcome right now. If I have my way, he'll be rotting in a prison cell for years and years."

"Okay. So where will Trace be until then?" Em asks, posing the one question I really don't want to answer.

"The Judge ordered Trace to submit to a mental examination in exchange for granting him bail. His attorneys came prepared with the mental evaluation and the necessary funds to pay the court; they bonded him out immediately. He didn't even serve one night in jail," I admit, I'm getting pissed all over again.

"I don't understand that. You said Trace didn't deny committing the crimes. How did he get bail?" Em inquires, showing some of her own anger.

"Bail isn't uncommon in similar cases, but the speed of the pre-trial and his release is unusual, especially with his next hearing not until after Christmas. Being out on bail doesn't mean he's free, though. He'll have travel restrictions and an ankle monitor," I explain, hating every word. I wanted to tell her he was behind bars for good. But that day will come, soon.

"Does my dad know?" Em questions.

"Yes, your dad knows. His team of lawyers is working closely with my team to strengthen the case against Trace. That way, when we go to trial or present the evidence against him, there will be no way for him to go free. Not even his dad will be able to dispute the charges and the proof that will be brought against his son," I say.

"That's good. All I really care about is that Trace can't hurt anyone else. Part of me hopes he gets assigned to a Nurse Ratched; he deserves to spend the rest of his life around mentally insane people with a nurse hell bent on making her newest patient suffer," Em shares, smiling at the thought.

"The movie One Flew Over the Cuckoo's Nest is a great consolation prize. It makes that potential outcome bearable. Shit, I'm willing to throw some cash at a nurse to give him a little extra care. I'm sure your dad would match my contributions. He wasn't happy about the outcome today at all," I share, hoping to make her smile again.

The outcome is currently beyond our control; all we can do is prepare, just like in any military operation. You must do your research. Reconnaissance is the most critical part of any mission. You need to understand your target and be able to predict their next move.

"Dad called me today but didn't mention the case. He asked if I needed anything and said he just wanted to check on me. He was sincere, but I found it somewhat unusual. Usually, Mom calls me," Em confides.

"Speaking of your dad, he had a message from your mom for me, asking if I would be joining you for Sunday brunch. She's still trying to match us up. Let's congratulate her on a job well done," I say, laughing.

"We can't. If we do, we'll never hear the end of it. Mom will take credit until the day we die, and she'll remind us of this whenever she wants something. It's too much power to hand over to that woman. She needs to figure it out on her own. Trust me," Em states. Smiling with a genuine smile, not a small one either. I'm so relieved that Em mentioned there being a future us.

"Noted. So, what other plans do we have for the weekend? Dex mentioned restarting our Sunday football watch parties and something about going two-stepping at the Red River Saloon. But that's all you guys," I add with a laugh. She already knows the truth. I'm not a fan of dancing, especially country and western.

"Ooh. Two-stepping is my favorite. You wouldn't take me dancing if I wanted to go?" The little minx taunts. I think she knows there is very little I would deny her.

"If the group wants to go, I'll go. I might or might not dance, though. Let me know what the girls decide. Do they know we're together together?" I ask, wanting to know if Em has shared our current status with them.

"Yes and no. Roxy and Sarah know there's something between us again, but they also know I was frustrated by your noble stupidity. I haven't dissuaded them of that notion yet," Em supplies.

"I wasn't being noble or stupid. I really thought you would need time. If it makes you feel any better, it hurt me more than it frustrated you. Being close to you, holding you, and kissing you, only to leave you, that shit was really hard for me," I share. I wanted her to understand that it wasn't easy for me.

"And Em, I choose you. I will always choose you. What I didn't do was give you a fair chance to make your choice. You entered into a relationship with only part of the pieces to a bigger

452

puzzle. I don't want to rush you. But what I want most of all is for you to choose me. The real me. This me. Forever," I say, gauging her reaction.

"Oh, Alec, I do choose you. I told you I forgave you. How can I hold your deception against you when it was the catalyst that gave me back my life?" I say, taking a deep breath before admitting, "I held myself back from relationships, intimacy, and emotional connections. I gave up on fairy-tale dreams and happily ever afters. Now, with you, I want more for myself again. I want you," Em says, moving the stand between my parted legs. With her hands draped over my shoulders, eyes on mine, she leans forward with a sweet kiss to reinforce her statement of truth. My brave Em has spoken.

"Sweets, I will give you everything you want, even if I have to beg, steal, or borrow to do it. I will make you happy. I'm very much in love with you," I say confidently.

"I know it's quick, but I love you too. You're already giving me so much more than I ever could have imagined for myself. Getting justice is only a small part. With you, I feel like I have everything within my reach," Em says, placing kisses on my jaw and lips.

"You do, babe. You have me, and together we'll make our best life happen. I don't want to rush you, but I'm ready to move forward with you. I'd love for us to get the first-floor unit and start bringing all your fairy tales to life. Bonus, if we're living together, think of all the baby-making practice we can get," I say, knowing from Em's smile that at least part of what I just said is on board with her.

"You don't think it's too soon? That everyone will think it's weird or worse, doomed?" Em asks, showing genuine concern.

"For me, it's not too soon. I know what I want and who I want to be with. I know you. I have no reservations, no doubt when it comes to you. I choose you now. But I'll also choose you in a month or a year from now. And I don't care what anyone else thinks. This is about you, me, and Destiny," I reaffirm what I know to be true. The conviction I feel about Em has not wavered one bit. I'm all in.

Chapter Fifty-Seven
I WIN
Emily

My work was only semi-productive today. My mind kept replaying clips from last night on a loop. On one hand, it was frustrating and very inconvenient at work. On the other hand, it was validating and reassuring.

Alec spent the evening making love to me. He was still in control, taking, yet giving with equal generosity, but this time it was more. It was reverence. It was tenderness. With every touch, he showed me how completely he chose me.

I felt loved and wanted. The damaged pieces inside me responded as if Alec were the superglue for my soul, fusing me back together, restoring the broken parts, and healing what I thought could never be repaired.

I don't know what the future holds for us, but I want what Alec is offering. I want to believe that with him, all my hopes and dreams can come true. I'm eager to see what our future holds.

I was excited to meet Sarah and Roxy for lunch at the courtyard cafe. The idea of some much-needed girl time and catching up made me smile. I couldn't wait to tell them about my progress with Alec.

"Over here, Em!" Roxy calls out to me. "We snagged the primo table!"

After quick hugs all around, the questioning started before I could even sit down. With my new work schedule and Alec's dinner visits, we haven't spent much time together, aside from the other night.

"Em, was the Sara's Secret run a success?" Sarah asks eagerly.

"Did you have to use the handcuffs to get his cooperation?" Roxy asks with a smirk.

"I never got to use any of it. Alec had a lot of explaining to do, and he did. His explanation boils down to him wanting to give me some time," I say, trying to take a little of the heat off Alec.

"Time? To do what?" Sarah inquires.

"Time to think about us, to get over his deception. Mainly, it's time to adjust to sharing the details of my attack verbally. Guys, it was so hard telling my dad and Alec what happened. No dad or lover wants to hear what I shared. My mom looked stricken, completely overwhelmed by pain and remorse," I say, feeling the pain of humiliation hit my chest. The shame from sharing what happened slithered down my spine, settling like a rock in my stomach.

"Oh, Em, I'm sorry, babe. That couldn't have been easy for you," Sarah says, giving my hand a squeeze on the table.

"It was embarrassing and painful to share. Dad wanted as much detail as I could remember. Mom looked on with horrified remorse. Honestly, I don't think I could have gotten through it without Alec. When I faltered, he filled in the parts he already knew, shaping the story so I didn't have to relive every moment out loud. He provided the details, allowing me to fill in the blanks instead of forcing me to share it all."

"Damn, Em. Shit. I'm sorry about the attack, and also about the need to rehash it. So, Alec thought you might not want a sexual relationship with him after having to relive those horrors?" Roxy asks, still wanting to understand his change of heart regarding the sexy time department.

"Not exactly. I believe Alec was punishing himself for being intimate with me while not being honest about his true self. He kept expressing that he felt guilty for taking that choice away from me. He mentioned that he was giving me time to process the deception, to forgive him, and to start considering a future together." I share, gaining a better understanding of his perspective through the retelling.

"I see. A future with him, huh?" Sarah questions, a knowing smile on her face.

"Can you believe he says he loves me and doesn't want to wait any longer to start our lives together?" I say, my voice bubbling with cautious excitement. "He even texted earlier; he's trying to schedule a viewing tonight for that Mega unit on the first floor. He says he wants to make my fairytales come true."

"That unit is the shit. I watched Mrs. Townsend's cat last Thanksgiving for her, and I fell in love with it. The place was like a mix of Shabby Chic and Metropolitan Couture. It was stunning. I thought their moving was just a rumor. They just had ten or more closets redesigned last month with California Closets," Roxy shares. She knows more about those neighbors than I do.

"You don't think this is all too soon? Too crazy?" I ask, wanting them to tell me what they really think.

"Listen, only you two can be sure of that. But you know each other, this isn't a man you just met a month or two ago. This is Alec, your friend and now your boyfriend," Sarah supplies, sincerely meaning it.

"You do you, boo. That's my motto. If it feels right, go for it. Alec wouldn't say those things if he didn't believe they were true," Roxy shares. Touching on the point I keep coming back to, Alec is not a man to say things he doesn't mean. He doesn't play.

"I agree with Roxy. Alec isn't going to say those things or schedule viewings for a place clearly meant for both of you if he's not in it for the long haul. I think you know this deep down. If you want my approval, you have it. You both deserve to be happy, and it would make me happy if you could be happy together."

"I'm happy for you, too, but I'm really excited about the prospect of the mega unit. I hope you guys get it. It could be our new hangout spot," Roxy says, smiling.

"Honestly, I feel excited too. Sharing my tragedy has been healing and eye-opening. I allowed that monster to keep taking from me long after the physical attack. I see that now clearly. I gave Trace the power to control my happiness. Joke's on him. I win," I say, feeling whole for the first time in a very long time.

"I love that for you," Sarah says.

I love it for me too. It was my attack that brought Alec into my life, turning my pain into a new beginning. The evil villain may have scarred my soul and shattered my heart, but Alec helped set me free from that dark place. With him, I have found healing, and together, I believe we will build a life full of love and happiness.

"What do your parents think?" Roxy asks.

"And how is Destiny adjusting?" Sarah interjects.

"My parents approve of Alec. Destiny is in love with him, and Alec seems smitten with her too. He mentioned that the mega unit has its own small, fenced yard for Destiny," I state, my confidence growing with everything I'm sharing.

"I hope you get the unit. It'll be a fresh start for both of you. But Em, this opportunity is also because of you. You're taking the necessary steps to reclaim your life and happiness. That's no easy feat," Sarah says.

She's right. It's been difficult to rise out of the sludge leftover from the dirtiness I went through and later shared. But I'm getting there.

The conversation shifted to Michael and Sarah. Sarah looks happier than I've ever seen her. She admits things between them are moving faster than they should. Of course, I have no room to talk.

Roxy denies everything. Her only mention of Dex is that they've agreed to quit while they're ahead, valuing their friendship above all else.

It's not that simple at all. Roxy is full of emotions when it comes to Dex, something we rarely see from her. But it's her story to share and her circumstances to work through. I hope they don't give up on the book but instead find a way to get on the same page.

I love the idea of them together, but I'll keep that to myself for now.

Both Sarah and Roxy want to go dancing tonight instead of Saturday. Something about the quality of the clientele: after a quick text with Alec, we confirm tonight's plans. We will meet at Sarah's around 7:30 pm, and Alec will drive us there.

Alec's message also confirmed he'd be home early and that he scheduled the Mega unit viewing for 6:00 pm. That will give me just enough time to get home, feed, and walk Destiny before the viewing and before we head over to Sarah's.

Although we are well past the time when Alec made me feel insecure about the dress situation, I wasn't planning to repeat that potential fiasco. It's going to be a jeans and boots night for me.

The mega unit was impressive. A little ostentatious. but stunning in its abundance. It has everything I could ever want in a home and much more. I suspected the price tag was representative of this. When I asked about it, Alec ignored my question. Since the unit wasn't officially listed on the MLS system, I couldn't determine the price. Even Mr. and Mrs. Townsend acted like they didn't hear my inquiry.

There'd be time later to discuss the financial aspects of our relationship. I have some money in the bank, but I also have a trust fund that I've never touched. I'm not familiar with Alec's financial portfolio, but I'm sure his line of work is lucrative. His parents come from old money, and he's briefly mentioned as having received an inheritance from his grandfather.

After walking through, I was already half in love with the unit. Alec told the Townsends he'd let them know by Monday our decision. That he'd conduct the transaction without an agent if they would be willing to wait until after we confirm our interest in the unit. I was wondering if Alec was interested or not. His ever-present control was firmly in place; he gave nothing away. When I looked at him expectantly, his only response was, "Later."

Alec and I share a quick kiss as we part ways in the elevator. He drops me off at my floor before heading to his unit, promising to be back before 7:00 pm to walk Destiny one more time before we head out.

After giving Destiny some extra loving and her dinner, I take a few minutes to change and freshen up. Realizing, this will be our debut outing as a couple. Instead of being nervous, I felt excited. And relieved.

Chapter Fifty-Eight
OUR DEBUT NIGHT
Emily

Going out with the group felt just like any other time. Nothing had changed. The guys were still deterrents, blocking any sensible man from approaching, and still determined to get our drinks.

No one seemed surprised that Alec and I were together. Alec made it very clear we were a couple as well. His hands and lips were never far from me. He had no problem with PDA, and I loved it.

Our group grew when Michael arrived with Eric. Josh was back in Dallas. Then two of Roxy's friends from yoga class showed up. Clara and Dena are both beautiful single women. I hope they weren't planning to hook up tonight. It won't happen with all the testosterone hanging around us.

The testosterone increased when Sam, a neighbor from our building, joined the group. Sam is a nice guy, handsome in that nerdy way. A little socially awkward, but Dex mentioned once that he's a tech genius. In my experience, most IT guys are geeks.

The guys kept us supplied with a steady flow of drinks. My eyes couldn't help but drift to Roxy and Dex, then Eric, looking for any sign of tension but finding none. There was no lingering hostility from Roxy's flirting tantrum a few weeks back among any of them. We were just a group of friends at a country and western bar.

We had fun dancing. With so many of us, Alec only felt compelled to hit the floor once. Getting him out that one time only happened because I coerced him. I made a little *"this for that"* bargain. I'm satisfied with the exchange of my bargaining chip; it will be a win-win for both of us when we get home.

It was nearly 1:00 am. when we finally returned to the condos. I was a little drunk and exhausted, but the evening had been a blast.

Alec was coming home with me. He said he would take Destiny out so we could sleep in the next day. Once he left, I decided to take a quick shower. I didn't just dance my ass off; I sweated it off, too.

Grabbing my undies and an oversized T-shirt, I see the Sara's Secrets bag lying conspiratorially next to my dresser. Instantly, my sleepiness took a back seat to my desire to put handcuffs on Alec. To be the one in control.

In the bathroom, I quickly open the packages, discard the evidence in the wastebasket, and then place the items under my pillow. I also decided to replace the T-shirt option with the sexy red nightie I bought.

For my plan to succeed, I needed him to be distracted. The red lingerie should do the trick. Hopping into the shower, I quickly wash and rinse. Luckily, my body hair hadn't grown back fast, and I shaved this morning.

Slipping into the outfit, I instantly felt sexy and turned on by my own prowess. Just as I put on my robe, I hear Alec and Destiny returning.

Before I can finish brushing my teeth, Alec doesn't knock as he enters the bathroom. "Babe, I'm going to rinse off. I brought us some water and aspirin if you want them." Good thing I wasn't on the toilet doing something he wouldn't want to see.

"Thanks," I say, resigned to the fact that closed doors mean nothing to him. Alec does whatever he wants.

By the time Alec emerges naked, I am already unrobed and under the covers. I had the bedside light on, but I wasn't ready for him to see me yet. Timing was everything when you planned to cuff your CIA Special Operations man to the bed.

It's like Alec knew I was up to something because he came right over to my side of the bed. Before I could react, he yanked off my covers, exposing me and my little red outfit. "What do we have here?"

"How did you know I had anything?" I ask, genuinely amazed.

"Babe, I do investigative work for a living. And you left the tags and the packaging in plain sight," Alec supplies, smirking with his little *you can't get anything by me* smile.

"Okay, well. Let me show you something else I got," I say, just before quickly reaching under my pillow to grab the pink handcuffs.

As Alec was saying, "Let me see," I snapped one end of the cuffs onto his wrist. Of course, he was faster, so attaching the other cuff to my bedpost proved impossible.

Before I knew what was happening, Alec had managed to put the other cuff around my wrist, essentially locking us together. His right hand is now cuffed to my left hand, with him leaning over me.

"Hey, that's not what I planned! No fair," I whine, feeling annoyed that my attempt at seduction was foiled.

"What did you have planned, sweets?" Alec asks, smiling down at me.

"I want to be in control. And maybe I want to be on top," I pout, unsure why I should really care either way. Before I can say, never mind, Alec effortlessly flips us over, wrists still linked.

"Straddle me, babe, and give me those lips," Alec demands, gripping my ass firmly with his left hand. Following his command, I lean in and kiss him.

Sparks ignite, and heat builds between us. I start to regret my decision to restrain him when Alec unexpectedly unlocks his cuff and clips it onto my right wrist.

"Wait, how did you unlock yours?" I demand, narrowing my eyes.

Alec's mouth quirks into a smile. "Used the key, babe," Alec says, with complete arrogance in his tone.

"But where did you get a key?" I ask, confused. I deliberately left the key in my bathroom drawer, not in plain sight.

Alec was laughing now, a rich baritone with a warm cadence. Hearing him and feeling his vibrating body beneath mine made me realize that Alec doesn't laugh often enough. It's nice to hear.

"You think you're so funny. Where did the key come from?" I ask, laughing as well.

"From the drawer. I told you, babe, I saw the package and knew you were up to something. It was luck to run across the key, though. I was looking for toothpaste," Alec shares, while both hands roam over my ass before grabbing my cheeks, shifting us up for him to lean against the headboard.

"I like this outfit," Alec says, his tone low and teasing. "And the handcuffs, definitely working for me." He shifts me slightly, drawing me close until I can feel the heat between us.

"This is not what I had in mind," I reply, trying for stern but failing miserably. "They were supposed to restrain *you*, to stop you from leaving me hot and bothered."

A knowing smile spreads across his lips. "Well, it's working," he murmurs. "Because there's no way I'm leaving you now." His touch remains, gentle, purposeful, and filled with promise, until Alec's index finger pulls at the G-string and makes it snap, then trails down my ass cheek toward my core, briefly dipping inside.

"Alec," I whimper, feeling my body ignite like a live wire. There's something about being restrained and at my partner's mercy that draws me in. Alec has barely touched me, and yet, I'm incredibly turned on.

Before I can tell him what I need, Alec flips us over, positioning himself above me. Both of my hands are bound above my head, with his knees between mine. His forearms prevent him from crushing me. His knowing smile reassures me that he is ready to fulfill my every need while enjoying himself in the process.

"Grab the headboard slats, babe. Don't let go. If you do, I'll be forced to cuff you to it," Alec demands, with no smile in sight. Still, I know he won't hurt me.

Doing as I'm told, I grab two adjacent slats. Alec leans back on his haunches and stares at my body from head to toe and back again.

"You are so beautiful, Em. I'm a lucky bastard that you have allowed me to be in your life. I will never take that for granted. You trust me?" Alec asks, not hiding the predatory look in his eyes.

"I trust you," I say to him, knowing it's the truth.

"Good. If you ever feel uncomfortable, say the word. Okay?" Alec bizarrely says.

"Umm, okay?" I reply, still unsure why he felt the need to clarify this at that moment. Maybe I was feeling a little apprehensive, too.

Leaning forward, Alec kissed me with a sense of possession, passion, and dominance. As his tongue entered my mouth, a duel of wills began between us. Both of us wanted more.

Abandoning my mouth, Alec trails open-mouthed kisses down my neck and then lower to latch onto a nipple over my nightie. My body arches off the bed. His roaming hands compete with my nightie, which covers every aching spot. Alec must be feeling the same frustration because, in that moment, he rips the G-string apart and pulls the bodice down to settle under the swell of my breasts.

His mouth and his hands make good use of the exposed access. Alec pinches my nipples while alternately sucking. They feel so hard and erect. I feel painfully close to orgasming just from that. The need to hold him in place is almost too much to ignore. But I know the threat to cuff me to the bed is not an idle one, and for some reason, I'm not ready for that.

My legs shift for something more, and I swear Alec knows this and is teasing me. When I try to wrap my legs around his waist for more friction, Alec pins me down with his weight.

When I'm about to beg, Alec gets up off the bed. With his eyes on mine, he strips, and his gorgeous cock stands at attention. Pink and swollen, it must be feeling the same frustration I am.

As Alec advances, his gaze sweeps over every inch of my exposed skin. Then, with gentle hands, Alec removes the shredded bottoms. He then tugs the top bodice down my hips and legs, tossing them to the floor.

"Bend your knees and spread your legs for me," Alec demands. Standing near the foot of the bed, looking at me, staring, devouring.

It's awkward and a little embarrassing, but I do as he requested. I can only imagine the view he has, everything he can see.

"You're being a good girl, Em," Alec says, still not approaching the bed.

"What the hell, Alec? Stop playing around," I snap, finally reaching the point where he's starting to piss me off. I'm tossing these handcuffs in the trash at the first opportunity.

What does he do? This motherfucker laughs. That beautiful, rare laugh from moments ago is now grating on my last nerve.

"It's not funny. I want you to remove the cuffs. Nothing about this is what I planned!" I semi-yell, frustrated.

"No," was Alec's maddening reply. But he moves to the bed. With both hands on my inner thighs, he pushes my legs farther apart. I'm flexible, so it wasn't uncomfortable exactly, but it was very exposing. Something I'm realizing Alec enjoys.

Without conscious effort, I attempted to close my legs only to be met with resistance. Right then, I forgot why I wanted them closed. Alec was there. Right there. His tongue and lips are kissing me, devouring me, consuming me.

When Alec added one finger, then two, I exploded. The orgasm was like an internal bomb in its intensity. The fact that my hands were bound and I couldn't touch him made the experience even more intense.

Still, I wanted more. And apparently, Alec wanted to give me more. With his hands pressing my knees apart and wide, Alec enters me in one forceful thrust.

With Alec on his knees, his hands spreading me wide, he was in complete control of my body. With no use of my hands or legs, all I could do was hold onto the slats and enjoy the ride.

Abruptly, Alec withdraws and gets off the bed. Before I can protest, he yanks me to the edge, dislodging my hands from the slats.

With Alec standing next to the bed, he maneuvers my legs to drape over his forearms before thrusting in deep. This was a new position for us, and I liked it.

Just when I thought it couldn't get any better, Alec repositioned my legs over his shoulders without slowing down at all. This position increases the tension between us, creating just the right amount of friction.

"Talk to me, Em. You good? What do you need?" Alec solicits.

"Yeah. Good," I barely manage to say, on the verge of another orgasm, really close. But just then, Alec pulls free and flips me onto my knees. With my hands still bound, he presses my upper body down to the mattress, with my ass in the air.

With a tug further to the edge of the bed, Alec enters me from behind. His thrusts are powerful. The sound of our bodies slapping together and our combined breathing creates a soundtrack of Alec dominating me. There was no discomfort. No complaints. Never once did I feel unsafe with him.

Leaning forward, Alec reaches around to my clit, and that immediately sends me over the edge, followed by his roar of release.

As Alec pulls away from my body, I feel his warm lips kiss my ass cheek. "Lay flat, baby. I'll get you cleaned up," Alec requests before heading to the bathroom.

Between the alcohol and Alec's attentions, I couldn't have moved even if I wanted to. I felt sated and content. I must have dozed off because the next thing I knew, Alec was removing the handcuffs. Then, I felt a warm, wet rag gliding along my sensitive seam.

I felt the bed dip as Alec pulled my now limp body against his chest, giving a warm, gentle kiss on my shoulder. My last conscious memory was Alec whispering, "Love you, baby."

"Babe, wake up, sleeping beauty. Someone has been texting you for the last ten minutes," Alec says hoarsely, trying to penetrate my foggy brain.

"Who? Just answer it," I mumble, still too groggy to care.

"What's your code?" he asks, sounding more awake now.

"It's 3323," I manage to say before burrowing back under the covers.

"Babe, both Sarah and Roxy want an update on the success of the Sara's Secrets stash. Your mom wants to confirm that we're coming on Sunday. And Dex, well, he's wondering where the hell you are. His last text says he's heading out without you for his run and that you owe him ten miles next week," Alec reports calmly, though the humor threading his voice gives him away. Maybe giving him access to my phone wasn't the brightest idea.

I sit up and reach for it, only to be met with resistance. "Give me a kiss first," Alec says, grinning, completely unfazed about morning breath.

Leaning in, I give him the kiss he's been asking for, only to realize too late that he's still flipping through my messages. "Wow, Em, you were really mad at me, huh? I'm sorry, babe. I can see now that I was misguided in my attempt to do the right thing for you," Alec says, holding my phone just out of reach.

"Alec! Don't be rude. Stop trolling through my messages. If you read something that disturbs you, it serves you right. I share everything with my girls," I snap, feeling truly annoyed with him.

"Relax, babe, you're right. Sorry. I saw my name on the message before this morning's and read it. Not cool on my part. But sometimes I'd do anything to know what's in that head of yours. My code is 1212, and you are free to go through my phone. No limitations," Alec confesses, appearing sincere on both counts.

"It's all good, Alec. I also don't have anything to hide. But when I say we share everything, I mean it. Everything from periods to poops. It could scar you for life," I share, laughing.

"Point taken, babe. Why don't you shower while I take Destiny out and feed her?" Alec offers, already getting up to pull on his discarded jeans from the floor.

"Thank you. I appreciate you taking care of her. A shower does sound good. I feel a little rough this morning. Next up, coffee," I say, with a grateful smile.

Alec offers, "I'll make you a cup when I get back."

"What else do we have planned today?" I ask, already getting up to head to the bathroom completely naked. And I wasn't even self-conscious about it either. That's another win for me.

"Your dad said he has some information to share with me. If we're going there for tomorrow's Sunday brunch, I can talk to him then. Other than that, I have some paperwork to do and need to meet up with a few of my team members," Alec says, slipping his shirt back on. What a pity to cover that body.

"Yeah, we're going. Mom asked us to arrive around 11:30 am. I already confirmed for both of us. It was easier that way. If you couldn't go, I'd wait to tell her when I arrived alone," I admit, heading to the sink to brush my teeth.

"Sounds good to me. We'll be back," Alec states, already walking toward the living room to harness Destiny, who is just lying there, waiting, watching, and trusting Alec to take care of her. I know the feeling.

Chapter Fifty-Nine
MEMORABLE SUNDAY
Emily

Sunday brunch turned out to be a day to remember. Dad informed us that his attorneys had uncovered shocking news: Trace's father plans to turn state's evidence against his own son, insisting he had no prior knowledge of his son's actions or his dealings with his constituents.

Dad's voice carried that sharp edge he gets when he's eager to share some news. "It was implied that if Roberts Senior cooperated, my legal team would hold off digging into his involvement," he said, almost too casually. "He didn't deny exchanging emails with his son, emails that listed potential victims, but he claimed he never condoned or approved any of the actions."

I could tell by the glint in Dad's eyes that he wasn't done. He leaned back, a hint of satisfaction crossing his face. "What Roberts Senior doesn't know," he continued, "is that my team had already shared our findings with the federal authorities. Their investigation also includes his connection to suspected terrorist activities."

"This is good news, right?" I hedge.

Dad's reassuring smile eased some of the tension in my body, but his following words brought a different kind of satisfaction. "Roberts Senior admitted, on record, to receiving emails from his son that listed the possible victims," Dad said evenly. "Legally, when a third party becomes aware of another party's intent to cause harm, they have a duty to act, to warn or protect potential victims. Failing to do so can open the door to a lawsuit for emotional distress and loss of enjoyment of life."

Dad went on to explain that, based on this new evidence, his attorney had already started the paperwork to file a third-party civil lawsuit for emotional distress against the Roberts family. This lawsuit would also include the other victims and their families.

The recommendation was clear: seek the maximum amount in monetary restitution. Strike them where it counts. Each victim had lost years of their lives, and some were still fighting to reclaim what was taken. How do you even begin to assign a dollar amount to a life interrupted? To the simple act of feeling safe in your own skin again?

The Roberts family could afford it. Their net worth was well beyond what most would call excessive wealth, which somehow made the idea of compensation feel both justified and hollow at the same time.

For me, it wasn't about the money. I didn't even want it, tainted as it was by everything that family had done. What mattered was the act of standing up, of holding them accountable. For the first time in years, I felt a sense of peace about moving forward. I was ready to leave this all behind and move on with my life. But before I can fully do that, I want justice to be served.

Yesterday, when I confirmed with mom that we'd be there for Sunday brunch, I couldn't shake the worry that things might be awkward now that all the secrets were out. Part of me feared my parents would ambush me and push for another conversation about the events that changed my life. But to my surprise, they didn't. It turns out they're ready to let it go, too. Ready, like me, to leave the painful details where they belong, in the past.

What made Sunday brunch unforgettable was when Alec asked my dad if he could marry me, right in front of me. He just went for it!

He addressed the room, not me, saying that if I preferred, we could have a long engagement. Although he hadn't formally asked me to marry him yet and there wasn't a ring on my finger, those details didn't seem to matter to Alec in his pursuit of permission.

Mom was visibly excited, with tears in her eyes and a big smile on her face. Dad didn't even ask if marrying Alec was something I wanted; he granted permission anyway.

My only response was silence. If Alec wanted it, wanted me, he'd have to earn it. I refused to be treated like a toy in a Happy Meal, handed out for free as part of the meal. I wasn't going to become his wife just because he wanted it that way. So yes, it was definitely a Sunday to remember.

Not long after Alec dropped the bombshell at my parents' house, staking his claim without even asking, we made our exit. Meanwhile, my parents were still floating on cloud nine, thrilled not only for me but also because their "grand dog" was spending the night with them.

Personally, I was feeling disgruntled. Of course, I would marry Alec. However, he can't just assume that. What a high-handed jerk. Okay, that's not nice.

The drive home was quiet. I stayed silent, and Alec did the same. He just drove, unaware of my inner tantrum.

After parking in the underground garage, Alec still hadn't spoken a word as he got out of the truck and helped me out. I managed to mumble a "thanks." But just barely.

"Babe, let's head over to the Mega unit. I want to take a closer look at some of the rooms," Alec suggested.

"Okay," I manage to say. We still haven't discussed the plans for purchasing it or the associated costs, but I'm relieved it's still a possibility.

As we enter the unit, Alec stops me from moving ahead by grabbing my hand. "Do you like this place?" he asks, watching me closely.

"Yes, it's gorgeous, and so spacious," I say, glancing around before turning to Alec. "How about you? Do you like it?"

"I do," he replies. But doesn't elaborate, and I don't push. Instead, we move together toward the kitchen. In the center of the island sits a tall glass vase overflowing with at least two dozen long-stemmed red roses, surrounded by soft greenery and delicate sprigs of baby's breath. It's breathtaking, classic, romantic, and the sweet fragrance wraps around us, filling the entire space.

Before I can find the right words, Alec stops me and gently turns me to face him. The look on his face catches me off guard; there's uncertainty. It's such an unfamiliar expression on a man like Alec that it instantly unsettles me.

"What's wrong?" I ask, confused by his behavior since we left my parents' house and by the hesitation I see in his eyes.

Without replying, he reaches into his pocket and pulls out a small set of keys. A pink ribbon is looped through them, and at the end of the ribbon, a ring glints softly in the light. Reflexively, I take the keys, my heart pounding in my chest.

"Alec?" I whisper, unsure how to interpret his silence. "What is this?" The question slips out unsteady, even though I already suspect the answer; I just can't understand his behavior.

He finally meets my gaze. "You know I love you, and that I want a life with you," he says, his confidence returning with every word. "What I just handed you is the beginning of our future. In your hand, you're holding the keys to this unit and your engagement ring."

There it is, that familiar spark of self-assuredness in his eyes. The uncertainty is gone, replaced by the Alec I know and love, bold, determined, and just a little smug.

"My engagement ring? Did I miss the part where you asked me to marry you? Because I'm pretty sure I would remember that," I sass, feeling a little taken aback by his assumptions but also secretly excited.

"It was implied, babe. We talked about this," Alec says, clearly believing that telling me is the same as asking me.

"You still have to ask, and I still have to answer. Even if you know my answer will be yes, people will want to know how you proposed. We need a story to tell our kids one day," I retort, frustrated by his assumption that I would marry him just because that's what he wants.

Additionally, I'm unsure how I feel about him buying the mega unit without talking to me first. That kind of behavior doesn't belong in our relationship. Marriage is a team sport, dammit!

"I can see that the formalities are important to you, but you gotta know that saying *No* is not an option. You're mine, and I'm yours. We don't have to rush into marriage; tell me when you're ready. I'll wait, but I really hope you don't make me wait long," Alec said with conviction.

"Are these roses for me?" I asked, needing a moment to process what Alec had just shared.

"Yes, everything is for you. Emily Sue Wilson, will you be my wife for life?" Alec asks, his eyes filled with pleading and sincerity.

"Yes, I thought you'd never ask," I reply softly, deciding to spare him the lecture about making decisions for *us* without actually consulting me. All those thoughts dissolve the moment

I see his smile. It's the kind of smile that could light up an entire room, steady, brilliant, and full of love. Like a lighthouse cutting through the fog, it guides safely in from the dark.

"Kiss me. Let's seal it with a kiss, my future wife," Alec playfully requested, lifting me to meet his lips. He took the keys he had given me from my hand, untied the tiny pink bow, and placed the ring on my finger.

"Oh, Alec. It's beautiful," I sniffle, looking down at the princess-cut diamond ring set in a platinum band. Its simplicity makes it stunning, perfect for me. Suddenly, a wave of emotion washes over me.

"Don't cry, baby. This is a happy time for us. It's you and me starting a new and better life together. We have so much to celebrate!" Alec says, trying to lighten the mood. "Speaking of celebrating, I've taken the initiative to keep two of the guest bedrooms furnished. We could go and take a closer look, maybe check out the mattresses to see if they're comfortable."

As he speaks, he brushes his knuckle over my hardening nipple through my T-shirt, playfully teasing me.

"It wouldn't hurt to check out the brand," I reply, with no more tears. Instead, I feel happy and content.

Two weeks later, our individual units were ready for sale, and we were excited to host Sunday Football in our new home. The spacious unit was perfect for entertaining guests. We decided to buy several pieces of existing furniture because the Townsends had excellent taste, and everything was in like-new condition.

The living room featured an oversized leather sectional that provided plenty of seating, along with four matching armchairs. Alec's only must-have request, aside from the furniture, was to keep the impressive 75-inch TV and sound system. My must-have was the frame-matted picture that included Alec's letter. It's proof, if only to me, that men can believe in fairy tales, too.

Next to the living room is a game room with a popcorn machine similar to those in movie theaters. It also features a pool table that we purchased, along with a built-in bar area equipped with a refrigerator, an ice machine, and a wine chiller.

Destiny already loves the small, fenced yard, which can be accessed through the kitchen's double doors. This outdoor space features a small table with four chairs and a flat-top grill, making it perfect for cooking hamburgers, buffalo wings, and stuffed jalapeños, our favorite foods for a football day.

We had the space, so we invited Sam and Michael. The yoga girls were also invited, but they didn't commit to coming. Eric was on the guest list, but he was traveling at the time.

Our lives are similar yet different. Living together turned out to be better than I expected. It wasn't awkward or invasive, and it never made me feel smothered.

It exceeded any dream I could have imagined. This fairytale might not have the Disney castles from my childhood, but I had my prince and my wet dream man, and they were both mine.

Honestly, I don't feel like I'm missing out on anything. I am happy and excited about our future, even though we haven't set a wedding date yet. Alec respects my pace and isn't rushing me.

My therapist reinforces my newfound belief that I deserve to be happy.

I still experience moments of weakness when the past tries to resurface and steal my joy. However, I am stronger now, and my biweekly therapy sessions give me the space to talk openly about the attack and the parts of myself that I'm still learning to forgive. Despite everything, I can honestly say that I'm a little dented but not damaged.

The cases involving Trace Junior and the civil lawsuit against his father are still pending and unresolved. However, I no longer care about either of them. I'm ready to move on from that chapter of my life.

I have a future I'm looking forward to, a life worth living.

The End.

The story continues in

Damaged Road

Book Two in the Damaged Series - Coming Soon.

The truth always surfaces…eventually.

Keep reading for a sneak peek.

SNEAK PEEK
from
DAMAGED ROAD

Book Two in the Damaged Series

By Lee Emery

One date changed everything.

Not a romantic date, but a date on the calendar. A specific date.

It marked the beginning of loss, loneliness, and the kind of grief that never truly heals. Even after thirteen years, it still has the power to knock me down, shock me, and evoke sadness, anger, guilt, and emptiness.

I was a carefree eighteen-year-old with dreams painted on a blank canvas. But that day shattered it all, leaving me scarred, cautious, and searching for something beyond the numbness. Beyond the denial.

This is what happens when one careless decision destroys the life you thought you'd have, and what it takes to rebuild from the ashes.

To discover what happens next, look for Damaged Road, coming soon from Lee Emery.

ACKNOWLEDGEMENTS

To Erica, my biggest fan, thank you for motivating me, encouraging me, and helping me navigate the overwhelming process of publishing and promoting my first book. Your support and *"let's get this done"* attitude kept me moving forward, even when doubt tried to take hold. I wouldn't have gotten this far without you.

To Dawn, my personal cheerleader, your enthusiasm for my characters, their chaos, and their hearts means more than you know. Your thoughtful feedback has helped shape my stories, and your support has fueled my confidence. And thank you for being my Facebook admin… even though I volunteered you without asking.

To Aunt Sandy, my first family member brave enough to read my book, and who inspired my phrase *"DON'T JUDGE THE SMUT."* Thank you for your honest review and advice. And, for taking one for the team.

To my family, who may not have fully understood why I was always "editing," but who supported me anyway, thank you for helping me through the chaos and believing in me, even though you didn't know if I could actually write more than my ABCs. Your quiet confidence made all the difference.

To Bette, thank you for your inspiration, positivity, and support. Your energy and encouragement continue to motivate me.

To Allison, thank you for your support with my promotional items and your excitement on my behalf. Your ideas inspired me to get creative.

To Bradley, I appreciate you turning my ideas into stunning promotional artwork and branding designs.

To my circle of supporters, my team, thank you for walking beside me on this journey as a debut author. This dream became real because of all of you.

ABOUT THE AUTHOR

Lee Emery is a contemporary romantic suspense author and proud mom to a teenage daughter who keeps life interesting. When she's not escaping into a love story, she's supported by her husband of twenty-five years and her loyal dog, Charlie, who's always by her side. Born and raised in the Dallas, Texas area, Lee is excited to share her debut series, The Damaged Series. She invites readers to follow along for book news, teasers, and a little fun in her online reader community.

"From broken pieces to forever love, every heart deserves its happy ending."

by Lee Emery

https://www.leeemeryauthor.com/

Follow me on Facebook for sneak peeks, upcoming releases, and a little love between the pages."

Lee Emery Author Page

https://www.facebook.com/profile.php?id=61578239725878

Facebook – Let's make it fun and informative.

Lee's Secret Smut Seekers Readers Group

www.facebook.com/groups/secretsmutseekers/

Don't Judge the Smut!

Lee_Emery_Author

https://www.instagram.com/lee_emery_author

www.ingramcontent.com/pod-product-compliance
Lightning Source LLC
Chambersburg PA
CBHW050609110726
47899CB00001B/41